THE SEVERED BONDS OF FRIENDSHIP

Athas, world of the dark sun. Ruled for thousands of years by power-mad sorcerer-kings, the cities of Athas have become vile centers of slavery and corruption. Only heroes of the greatest strength and bravest heart can stand against the might of these overlords. The Prism Pentad is a tale of such heroes. . . .

Tithian I—the power-hungry ruler of Tyr, determined to allow no one, either friend or foe, to prevent him from becoming an immortal sorcerer-king.

Agis of Asticles—the master of psionics and firebrand senator who must capture the king and bring him back to stand trial . . . on a charge of slave-taking.

Fylo—the half-breed giant who wants acceptance at any cost and finds that friendship, whether with giants or humans, can be both elusive and deadly.

PRISM PENTAD

Troy Denning

Book One
The Verdant Passage

The Obsidian Oracle

TROY DENNING

TSR Inc.

THE OBSIDIAN ORACLE

First Printing: June 1993.
Printed in the United States of America.
Library of Congress Catalog Card Number: 92-61089

9 8 7 6 5 4 3 2 1

ISBN: 1-56076-603-4

TSR, Inc.
P.O. Box 756
Lake Geneva, WI 53147
U.S.A.

TSR, Ltd.
120 Church End, Cherry Hinton
Cambridge CB1 3LB
United Kingdom

Dedication:

For Michael T. Griebling, never forgotten.

Acknowledgements:

Many people contributed to the writing of this book and the creation of the series. I would like to thank you all. Without the efforts of the following people, especially, Athas might never have seen the light of the crimson sun: Mary Kirchoff and Tim Brown, who shaped the world as much as anyone; Brom, who gave us the look and the feel; Jim Lowder, for his inspiration and patience; Lloyd Holden of the AKF Martial Arts Academy in Janesville, WI, for contributing his expertise to the fight scenes; Andria Hayday, for support and encouragement; and Jim Ward, for enthusiasm, support, and much more.

THE ESTUARY AND SURROUNDING LANDS

GREAT
IVORY
PLAIN

BODACH

ESTUARY

LOST PORT

OF

BALICAN
PENINSULA

THE

BALIC

SMUGGLER'S REST

N

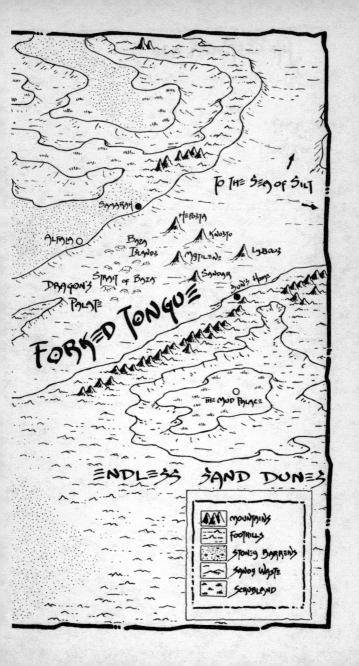

Out of the corner of her eye, Neeva glimpsed the crimson flash of a sun-spell. Despite the impending victory of her militia, she felt the cold hand of panic closing around her heart. The flare had come from the direction of the Sunbird Gate, which guarded all the hidden treasures of the village—most especially her young son, Rkard.

To her dismay, Neeva was in no position to rush to his aid. She stood atop the mountainous shell of a dead mekillot, using nothing more than a pair of short swords to fight three men armed with lances and daggers. In the narrow streets of Kled, her militia-men were mercilessly butchering the raiders who had come to take slaves from their village. The few invaders who escaped the dwarves' bloody axes were fleeing toward one of the many breaches in the town wall, opened at the start of the assault by the mighty reptile upon which Neeva now stood. Considering the speed with which the slavers had struck, the battle was going extremely well, but that did little to

1

cheer the worried mother.

"Enough of this!" Neeva growled, hurling one of her swords at the nearest attacker.

The steel blade split the man's sternum with a muted crack and sank deep into his chest. The militia commander did not wait to see him fall. Instead, she dropped to a knee and spun, extending her other leg to its full length. As the next slaver stepped forward to attack her back, Neeva's ankle smashed into his knee and swept him off his feet. She continued her spin, slicing the man's throat before he hit the ground. The third slaver's lance came darting for her breast. She batted the point aside with her free hand, then drove her sword deep into the man's stomach.

Neeva freed her swords from the bodies of the dying slavers, hardly hearing their groans of agony. Her eyes were already searching the streets for her husband, hoping Caelum had been the one who had cast the sun-spell at the Sunbird Gate. She found him on the opposite side of the village, too far away to have caused the flash.

Confident that her militia could finish routing the slavers without her direction, Neeva slid down the mekillot shell. She scrambled over the rubble of several crushed huts, then slipped into a narrow street and ran for the Sunbird Gate. Twice, she paused to kill panicked raiders who stumbled across her path, but, in her hurry to reach the gate, she allowed several more to escape.

Fifty yards from her destination, she glimpsed a trio of inixes scurrying down a parallel street, their serpentine tails whipping from side to side and smashing holes into the stone huts that lined the avenue. The lizards were about fifteen feet long, with ash-colored scales, stocky legs, and beaks of bone that could bite a woman in two. On the shoulders of each beast sat a lance-bearing driver, while cargo howdahs, huge boxes made of sunbleached bone, were strapped to their backs.

Neeva knew instantly that the slavers had not chosen her village by chance. Whoever had planned the attack knew of Kled's secret wealth and where to find it, for the howdahs of the first two inixes brimmed over with riches stolen from behind the Sunbird Gate: bronze armor, steel axes and swords, even the golden crowns of ancient kings. It crossed the commander's mind that the slave-taking had been nothing more than a diversion for the inix-mounted thieves, but she quickly rejected that idea. The raiders' losses were too severe to be a mere distraction.

When Neeva saw the contents of the third lizard's howdah, all thoughts of the slavers' motivations slipped from her mind. Instead of treasure, this beast carried two men. One was a burly human dressed in polished leather, holding a steel long sword that he had no doubt stolen from Kled's armories. The other, a hateful-looking half-elf with a short black beard and sharp features, wore a billowing robe and carried no weapon. Instead, he held the struggling form of a young boy. Although the child was only five years old, he already stood as tall as most dwarves, with a thick-boned body covered in sinew and muscle. Completely bald, he had a square jaw, angry red eyes, and pointed ears that lay close to his head.

"Rkard!" Neeva gasped, sprinting down the alley after her son's kidnappers.

She had no need to ask herself why the raiders had taken her son instead of filling the third howdah with more treasure. The boy was a mul, a human-dwarf crossbreed who would bring a small fortune in any city with a slave market. Blessed with the powerful frame of his dwarven father and Neeva's human agility, he would be sent to the gladiatorial pits and cultivated into an arena champion. Having spent her own childhood in the pits, Rkard's mother knew first-hand the horrors that would await him there.

Neeva reached the end of the alley and leaped the inix's whipping tail. She plunged a short sword through the scales on the beast's flank and used it to pull herself atop its rear quarters. The lizard roared in pain and tried to whip its head around to snap at her, but the driver thrust the tip of his lance toward the thing's lidless eye.

"Forward, Slas!" he cried, and the creature continued to scurry down the avenue.

Neeva yelled, "Rkard, be ready!"

The boy stopped struggling and raised one small hand toward the sky. At the same time, the armored raider leaned out of the howdah, slashing at Neeva's head with his steel sword. She blocked with her free sword, then circled the blade over the top of her attacker's weapon to disarm him. Unfortunately, the slaver was no stranger to a fight. He pulled his sword away before she could whip it from his hand.

"What's wrong with you, Frayne?" demanded the half-elf holding Rkard. "Kill the wench!"

"I'm no wench," Neeva growled, gaining her feet. "And that boy will be no one's slave!"

The angry mother pulled her first sword from the inix's flank and launched herself at the howdah. She attacked with a double chasing pattern, slashing at Frayne's longer weapon with first one blade, then moving forward to slice at his vulnerable face or throat with the one trailing. The astonished slaver had no choice but to give way, and Neeva leaped over the howdah's wall with her third series of thrusts.

Frayne stepped forward to take advantage of the temporary lapse in Neeva's attack, thrusting at her abdomen. She twisted her body in midair and snapped her front foot around to kick the slaver in the head. His blade slipped harmlessly past her midriff, and he fell against the far side of the howdah, barely raising his weapon in time to block a downstroke that would have split his skull.

With the grace of an elven rope-dancer, Neeva landed between Frayne and the half-elf holding Rkard. Her son's captor, she noted, had slipped one hand into the pocket of his robe, no doubt to retrieve the components of a magical spell. He was so concerned with Neeva that he did not notice her son's small hand glowing red with the power of the crimson sun.

Neeva pointed a sword at each of the men's throats. "Let my son go," she said. "He's of no value to dead men—and rest assured, you won't leave Kled alive."

"I'm afraid that isn't your choice," said the half-elf, withdrawing his hand from his pocket.

Rkard thrust his glowing hand toward his captor's face. Neeva looked away long enough to beat Frayne's guard down. A red light flashed behind her, then the half-elf screamed in surprise. She glanced back and saw the sorcerer's hands over his blinded eyes. Then she separated his head from his shoulders with a vicious slash.

By the time Neeva returned her attention to Frayne, the raider's sword was already slicing at her unprotected knees. She jumped the slash, bringing one of her blades around low and the other high to block the expected backstroke. To her surprise, the slaver did not follow up his first attack. Instead, he reached up and grabbed the side of the howdah wall, trying to pull himself to his feet again.

Neeva started to move forward, but the inix suddenly lurched to a halt. "Mother!" cried Rkard.

Neeva glanced over her shoulder and saw her son standing over the sorcerer's headless corpse. The boy was pointing at the driver, who had left his place on the beast's shoulders to climb toward the howdah. In the street beyond him, the other two inixes, whose drivers were paying no attention to the fight, were slipping out of Kled with their heavy cargoes of dwarven treasure.

Neeva tossed her second weapon to her son. "You know what to do, Rkard."

Not even waiting to see if the boy caught the weapon, Neeva stepped toward Frayne. The slaver had returned to his feet, a confident sneer on his lips. "A child against a lancer?" he scoffed. "That's as foolish as facing me with a single short blade."

"Perhaps," Neeva replied.

Although she did not allow it to show on her face, she felt more confident than ever. Frayne was an adept swordsman, but his comment suggested that like so many who learned to fight outside the arena, his attention was focused more on his foe's blade than on his foe. When fighting a gladiator, a person could make no greater mistake.

Neeva flipped her sword about in a block-and-attack pattern, moving forward behind the flashing blade as she knew Frayne expected her to. Determined to keep the advantage of his longer blade, the raider shuffled to the side, only to have his move blocked when she lunged forward and made a clumsy chop at his ribs. Taking the bait, Frayne whipped his sword at her head in a brutal backslash.

Neeva threw her legs from beneath herself and wrapped them around the slaver's waist, at the same time falling to her side. Frayne's blade sailed harmlessly over her head, then she hit the howdah floor and rolled. The sudden twist swept the raider off his feet. He landed flat on his back with her legs still wrapped around his waist. Neeva sat up, pinning his sword arm to the floor with one hand and driving the tip of her own blade deep into his gullet.

Neeva turned toward the front of the inix. She saw the tip of a lance coming straight at her head as the driver leaped into the howdah. Her son picked that moment to rise from his hiding place behind the wall, holding his sword in front of the slaver's belly. The raider's momentum carried him onto the blade. He screamed in agony and dropped his lance, burying Rkard beneath his bleeding torso.

Neeva reached out and finished him with a quick chop to the back of the neck, then rose to her knees and rolled the corpse off her son. The boy lay atop the sorcerer's headless body, covered in blood from head to foot.

"Rkard, are you hurt?" Neeva asked, going to his side.

The boy did not answer. His attention seemed fixed on the floor next to the sorcerer's body.

"Answer me!" Neeva said, pulling the mul into her arms.

"I'm fine, mother," he said, holding his hand up to her face. "Look what I found." Rkard held a square crystal of blood-smeared olivine.

Neeva took the gem from his hand and wiped it clean. "Where did you get this?"

She had to work hard to keep from sounding angry.

Twice before, when she had still been a citizen of Tyr, she had seen such crystals.

"It fell out of the sorcerer's pocket," Rkard explained. "Can I keep it?"

"I don't think so," she replied.

Neeva held the crystal out at arm's length, and the tiny image of a sharp-featured man appeared inside. He had a hawkish nose, beady brown eyes, and long auburn hair bound in place by a golden diadem. It was Tithian, the man who had once owned her.

"Neeva!" he gasped. "How did you come by my gem?"

"I killed your sorcerer," she growled. "You're next."

Tithian frowned doubtfully. "Come now," he replied in a smug voice. "I'm the king of Tyr. That would mean war."

"I doubt it," Neeva scoffed. "After Agis and his council hear you've been taking slaves, they'll want to cut your heart out themselves."

With that, she closed her fist around the gem, cutting off her magical contact with the figure inside.

The Giant

Agis of Asticles stopped his mount and wiped the grit from his stinging eyes, certain his vision had betrayed him. A steady wind rasped across the Balican Peninsula, its hot breath bearing long ribbons of loess from the Sea of Silt's southern estuary. To make matters worse, dusk had settled over the rocky barrens an hour before, leaving the road ahead swaddled in purple shadows and half-buried in drifts of plum-colored dust.

A short distance ahead, a craggy ridge formed a wall of black rock. It stretched for miles in both directions, rising so high that Agis had to crane his neck to see the stars glimmering above the summit. To his relief, the caravan trail did not climb the steep hillside, but entered a narrow canyon slicing directly through the heart of the bluff.

An immense boulder sat in the middle of the trail, blocking the entire gorge. Its shape resembled that of a seated man, save that it was larger than the gatehouse guarding the entrance to Agis's estate. Bats

9

wheeled high over the monolith's crown, silhouetting themselves against the haze-shrouded moons, and a flock of golden dustgulls roosted on one shoulder, their forms softened by distance and blowing silt. The nobleman could just make out two huge males pecking at each other with rapierlike beaks.

As Agis watched, the pecking contest erupted into a true battle. The angry birds rose into the air, slashing at each other with beaks and talons. The larger gull used his bulk to good advantage, relentlessly driving his foe back until the bird was trapped against the crag above their roost.

For the second time since Agis had spied it, the boulder shifted, and the noble knew that his eyes had not deceived him earlier. A massive hand rose from the dark silhouette to slap at the gulls. It caught both birds in its palm, smashing them against the shadowy crag. The blow landed with a resounding crack that made the ground tremble and sent runnels of sand cascading off the canyon walls. With a mad chorus of screeching and squawking, the rest of the flock launched itself into the air and fluttered about in anger, only to return to their roost as soon as the enormous hand crashed back to the ground.

The noble remained where he was, his kank's carapace quivering beneath him. The insect was twice the size of a man, with six canelike legs, a jacket of chitinous black armor, and a pair of bristly antennae on its blocky head. Although the drone's bulbous eyes were so weak it could hardly focus on the ground beneath its mandibles, Agis was not surprised by its alarm. The beast's drumlike ear membranes would be rumbling painfully from the thunderous slap that had killed the two gulls.

Agis urged the mount forward by tapping its antennae. "I don't care if that is a giant," he said, keeping his brown eyes fixed on the bulky form ahead. "We must get past him."

As the kank scurried forward, the details of the hulking silhouette became more clear. The giant's body was lumpy and stout, covered with gravelly skin and gnarled muscles that resembled nothing quite so much as the crags of a cliff. Long braids of greasy hair hung from his head, while scattered tufts of coarse bristle sprouted on his chest and back. The enormous face seemed a peculiar mix of human and rodent, with a sloped forehead, drooping ears, and a pointed nose ending in two cavernous nostrils. His eyes were set deep beneath his brow. Even under their closed lids, they bulged out of their sockets. A dozen jagged incisors protruded from beneath his upper lip, while a mosslike beard dangled from his recessed chin. All in all, Agis found the giant the ugliest individual he had ever set eyes upon.

Upon reaching the figure's side, the noble halted his drone and dismounted. The entire gorge stank of unwashed flesh, and each time the giant exhaled, the fetid draught of his breath made Agis gag. The titan sat squarely on the road, with a massive elbow resting against one wall of the canyon. His feet were pressed against the other.

Cupping his hands around his mouth, Agis yelled, "You're blocking the road!"

The giant's only response was a gusty wheeze that made the noble's long black hair wave.

Agis drew his sword, a magnificent cutlass as ancient as the city of Tyr, with a basket of etched brass and a long steel blade engraved with the weapon's history. He stepped forward and gently pushed the tip into the enormous thigh blocking his way.

A sonorous growl rolled from the giant's throat, then the behemoth lifted his hand. Agis barely had time to jump away before an enormous palm slammed into the leg he had pricked. The giant scratched his thigh, then his hand dropped back to the ground. He did not open his eyes.

Agis stepped over to the hand. The palm alone was the size of a large shield, while the fingers were almost as long as the sword in his hand. The noble took a deep breath and brought the flat of his blade down on the thumb joint, striking with all his strength.

A surprised bellow echoed off the canyon walls, then the hand shot high into the air. The giant's eyes opened. He sniffed at his thumb with his cavernous nostrils, then licked the joint with a carpet-sized tongue.

"Pardon me for disturbing you," Agis shouted, prepared to leap away if the giant attacked. "But you're blocking the road. I must get past."

The giant glared down at Agis. His enormous eyes looked like a pair of moons, white with deep craters of darkness at the center.

"Fylo sleep," he said in a booming voice. "Go 'round." The giant folded his hands across his stomach and closed his eyes.

"That just won't do," Agis called.

Fylo ignored him. Within moments, deep snores were rumbling at regular intervals from the giant's mouth, grating over the noble's eardrums and shaking the entire canyon. Realizing that courtesy would get him nowhere, the noble sheathed his sword and stepped to his kank's side.

Agis closed his eyes and focused his mind on his nexus, that space where the three energies of the

Way—spiritual, mental, and physical—converged inside his body. He visualized a tingling rope of fire sprouting from this nexus and running up into his throat, creating a pathway for the mystic power of his being.

When he felt his neck pulsing with energy, Agis opened his mouth and shouted, "Move!"

The word broke over Fylo's sleeping form with the force of a thunderclap, scattering the dustgulls on the giant's shoulder and reverberating down the canyon in a series of earsplitting barks. The titan sat bolt upright and peered into the murky canyon, his weak chin hanging slack in bewilderment and fear.

"Go 'way!" he yelled, addressing the receding echoes of Agis's voice. "Fylo strong as wind!"

"There's nobody in the canyon," called Agis, this time yelling in his normal voice. "I'm over here."

The giant looked toward Agis and breathed a sigh of relief, blasting the noble with a gust of foul breath. "Fylo say go 'round," he snarled. "Time for sleep."

Agis shook his head. "Not until you let me pass. I'll keep you awake all night if I must."

The giant frowned. "Fylo smash you like bear."

Agis raised his brow. "You mean like a . . . Never mind," he said. "It'd be much easier to let me pass. All you need do is raise your legs so I can lead my kank underneath."

The giant shook his head stubbornly.

Agis reached for his purse. "I'll pay double the normal toll."

"Toll?" Fylo echoed. He tugged at his beard, obviously puzzled by the term.

"To let me pass," Agis said, pulling a coin from his purse. "I'm sure a silver is enough." Holding the glimmering disk before him, he moved forward until he stood at the giant's side. "Here. Take it."

After Fylo lowered a massive hand, the noble tossed his coin into the center of the palm. The disk disappeared into the dark ravine of a massive lifeline, and Agis feared the giant would not see it. Fylo seemed accustomed to handling small objects, however. He licked a fingertip and pressed it onto the silver, then held the disk up to his eye.

"Fylo let you go—for this?"

Agis could not be sure of the giant's tone, but it almost seemed the bribe had insulted him. "If I've offended you, please forgive me," he said. "But in these circumstances, my assumption is only natural."

The giant considered this for a moment, then scowled. "What us-amp-gin, er, as-shump-ten, er, ass—" Unable to pronounce the word Agis had used, Fylo rephrased his question. "What d'you mean?"

Agis ran his hand through his long hair, stalling for time. If the dull-witted giant did not already realize that this was an ideal location to coerce money from travelers, the last thing the noble wanted to do was suggest it to him. "I mean you don't look very comfortable," Agis said. He pointed toward the open desert behind him. "Why don't you sleep over there—and let me pass?"

"Fylo not sleep," the giant said, an unexpected air of pride in his voice. He stuck the finger with Agis's coin into a satchel made from the untanned hides of a half-dozen sheep, then looked down at the noble. "Fylo guard road for friend."

"What friend?" Agis asked.

Instead of answering, the giant lowered his head to peer more closely at the noble and began whispering to himself. "Black hair, straight nose, square jaw . . ." As he listed each feature of Agis's face, he extended a finger as though he were counting. When his gaze fell on the noble's brow, he frowned. "What color eyes?"

"What does it matter to you?" the noble replied, hoping the moonlight was still pale enough so the giant could not see that they were brown. Someone had obviously taken pains to be sure Fylo would recognize him—and Agis suspected that he knew that person's identity. "Does your friend happen to be called Tithian?"

"No!" the giant replied, much too quickly. His eyes darted from side to side, and he pressed his jagged incisors over his lower lip. "Friend not called Tithian."

The obvious lie made Agis smile, not because the giant's ineptness amused him, but because it confirmed that he was on the right trail. Seven days ago, Neeva and a small party of dwarves had arrived at his estate, demanding that Tithian answer for sending slavers to raid their village. The noble had been unable to grant the request, for the king had mysteriously slipped out of the city a few days before the raid had taken place.

Neeva and the dwarves had declared that they would track the king down themselves, but Agis had insisted that only a Tyrian should bring the ruler to justice. Given Tithian's popularity in the city, any attempt by Kled to punish him could easily lead to war. After a contentious argument, they had come to a compromise. Neeva would wait at Agis's estate while the noble and a dozen other Tyrian agents fanned out to search for their errant king. If they did not bring the king back within two months, the dwarves were free to take matters into their own hands.

Fortunately, it appeared that Agis would return the king within the allotted time—provided he could get past the giant. He retreated to his mount, wasting no time pondering how his quarry had discovered that he was being followed. Tithian was a cautious man who had no doubt left a network of spies to watch his backtrail.

To Fylo, Agis said, "It doesn't matter who your friend is. You've taken my money, and now you must let me pass."

Fylo made no move to obey. "No," he said. "You Agis."

"What makes you say that?" the noble asked.

A cunning sneer crept across the giant's face. "You look like him."

"There must be a hundred men who look like Agis," the noble replied, tapping his kank's antenna. As the nervous beast shuffled forward, he added, "Now kindly lift your legs—or return my silver."

Fylo touched the satchel into which he had slipped Agis's coin, then frowned and scratched his head in indecision. Finally, he shrugged and raised his legs, bracing his feet against the canyon wall.

Agis guided his mount forward. His heart was pounding like a stonecutter's hammer, and a dusty taste had suddenly filled his mouth. Keeping his hand away from his waterskin only through a conscious exertion of will, the noble looked straight ahead and ducked under Fylo's knee.

No sooner had he passed beneath it than the giant's second leg dropped to the ground, blocking the way. "Let Fylo see eyes," the giant said, reaching for the noble.

Agis's hand strayed toward his sword hilt, but he quickly realized that his meager blade could do no more than slice the tip off an enormous finger. Instead, he allowed the giant's hand to clasp his body.

With surprising gentleness, Fylo lifted him into the air, leaving the noble's trembling kank corralled between legs as thick as tree boles.

Two dustgulls swooped down to see what the giant had plucked off the ground. They were hideous birds, with scaly red heads, hooked beaks filled with teeth as sharp as needles, and talons dripping filth and ichor. As the pair sailed past on their tattered wings, they watched Agis with red, rapacious eyes, clattering their beaks in gluttonous delight. "Go away," the noble whispered. "There'll be no scraps for you tonight."

After lifting Agis to the height of his own head, Fylo raised his captive into the pale light of Athas's two moons. The giant bent his head forward, squeezing a platter-sized eye into a squint, and tried to peer beneath the noble's shadowed brow. Agis closed his eyes and began to summon spiritual energy from his nexus.

The hand tightened, making it difficult for the noble to draw breath. "If Fylo squeeze, head pop off like lion's," the giant warned. "Open eyes."

Agis did not obey. Instead, he visualized his own face, though with blue eyes instead of brown, and with dun-colored hair instead of black.

"Let Fylo see!" the giant insisted.

"If that's what you want."

When Agis complied, he found himself looking into a huge pupil. Immediately, he tried to lock gazes with the giant, but the distance between Fylo's eyes was so large that he could not look into both of the great orbs at once. Instead, the noble focused on the closest one. At the same time, he concentrated upon the image inside his mind, using the Way to make the giant see the effigy instead of his true face.

Scowling in confusion, Fylo crossed his eyes, and Agis knew that his ruse was not working well. He had not penetrated the giant's intellect deeply, for that required more time, and by then Fylo would know the color of the noble's eyes. Instead, Agis was using his talents to contact only the part of the giant's mind that controlled his vision. Apparently, since he could look into only one eye at a time, the titan was seeing a different image in each one.

Fylo turned his face to the side, trying to look at his captive with just one orb. A moment later, he snapped his head around to study the noble with the other. When Agis smoothly shifted his attention from the first eye to the second, the giant whipped his head back and forth in an ineffectual attempt to glimpse his prisoner's face without locking gazes. At last, it became apparent that this would not work, and Fylo gave up, once again fixing both crossed eyes on his captive.

To Agis's surprise, a broad smile crossed Fylo's lips. "Fylo like seeing games," he said, tightening his grip on the noble. "Fylo guess little man have brown eyes."

With a sinking feeling, Agis turned his attention inward, replacing the mental effigy of himself with the image of a rapacious dustgull. A surge of energy rose from the core of his being to give the creature life, then the bird took on an existence of its own. It became his harbinger, a construct of his thoughts, yet it was detached and able to function outside his own head.

"Are you certain?" Agis asked, staring into the black depths of the giant's pupil. "You'd better look closer and be sure."

With that, the noble sent his harbinger to attack

Fylo's mind. The bird streaked from Agis's eyes into the giant's, disappearing into what lay beyond.

"What that?" Fylo demanded.

Agis did not answer, concentrating instead on the terrain he had discovered inside the giant's mind. The region was gray and hazy, with half-formed thoughts whirling past like the wild winds of a silt storm. Once, the noble glimpsed a giant's fist floating past, blood spurting from between the fingers. Another time he saw a pair of human legs protruding from a huge mouth, kicking madly as the victim was swallowed whole. As a master of the Way, Agis had no trouble understanding the significance of the images: the giant was considering ways to kill him. The noble had to take control quickly, before Fylo turned one of the ideas into a plan of action.

A craggy island drifted into view, with the crisp detail and solid aspect of a memory. Standing atop its sheer cliffs were six giants, all with humanlike faces. They were hurling boulders off the precipice, shouting, "Go live with dwarf, ugly!" and "Stay 'way. Fylo scare sheep!"

Agis turned his dustgull after the passing island. If he could seize command of the memory, he could use it for his own ends and quickly force the giant to release him.

Outside, a blast of hot, fetid air rushed over the noble's face. "Take bird back!" boomed the giant, squeezing so hard that Agis feared his ribs would snap.

Fylo's demand surprised the noble. As a seasoned practitioner of the Way, he was well-versed at slipping into the thoughts of others. That the giant even understood that his mind had been invaded suggested he had an innate talent, for there could be no

doubt that he was too dim-witted to have mastered
the art through the normal avenues—rigorous study
and discipline.

"Don't kill me, or the bird will stay in your head,"
Agis bluffed, barely able to gasp out the words.

Fylo's grip did not grow any tighter, but neither
did it slacken. "Stop, and Fylo not hurt you." The
giant's voice seemed at once determined and a little
anxious.

"Not until you let me go," Agis countered.

Even as he spoke, the noble continued to guide his
harbinger toward the island inside the giant's mind.
As soon as the dustgull's talons touched the rocky
summit, the six giants who had been hurling boulders over the cliff turned around. They launched a
barrage of rocks at the bird's featherless head, crying
"Go 'way, ugly bird!"

Agis summoned more spiritual energy, and visualized his dustgull changing into a mekillot. As the
boulders began their descent, the bird grew a hundred times larger, its feathered wings changing to a
bony carapace and its hooked beak into a blunt-
nosed snout full of sharp teeth. The rocks struck the
hulking lizard with a tremendous clatter, bouncing
harmlessly off its shell and disappearing over the
cliff.

At first, the noble feared that his foe had taken control of the memories, but he soon realized that they
were acting on their own. Behind the six giants, a
hairless rodent crawled over the rocky edge of the
cliff. The beast had squat legs ending in curled claws,
with loose folds of scaly hide and a ridge of bony
plates protecting its back. Only the head did not seem
particularly vicious, for beneath its squarish ears
were Fylo's bulging eyes and wispy beard.

The rodent construct rushed Agis's mekillot, but two giants seized its tail as it passed, bringing the beast to an instant halt. It struggled to continue forward, its curled claws clattering on the stony ground.

"Fylo not make good tembo," scoffed one of the giants, dragging the rodent backward. "His face too ugly!"

Taking advantage of the distraction, Agis moved forward, away from the cliff edge. The four giants who were not busy with Fylo charged. The noble stopped his harbinger, then waited until they reached him before lashing out. He snagged one in his bill-shaped mouth and, with a flick of the lizard's head, snapped the victim's back.

His attack did not even slow the other giants. The remaining three slammed into the mekillot's flank and shoved it toward the cliff edge, angrily shouting, "Go 'way, stupid lizard!"

The noble tried to counter, dropping the crippled giant in his construct's mouth and planting the beast's huge legs firmly on the rocky ground. He pushed back with all his unimaginable strength, but the effort was to no avail. Slowly, inexorably, the giants drove the behemoth toward the precipice.

On the other side of the rocky summit, Fylo was faring no better. The two giants that had grasped his tail were dragging him away, laughing cruelly and saying, "Fylo too stupid to be tembo—too weak!"

As his foes pushed him to within a few yards of the cliff edge, Agis visualized the top of the crag turning to a dustsink, leaving only a narrow rim of rock around the outer edge. A terrific swell of energy coursed through his body, then the stony ground of the summit dissolved into a powdery muck. The memory giants cried out in surprise, as did Fylo, and they all tried to leap for the solid ground ringing the pit. The agitation only caused the surface to become even less firm, and they sank to their waists almost immediately.

Although the mekillot's stubby legs disappeared into the muck as quickly as those of the giants, Agis was prepared for the surprise and began to change form instantly. His construct's shell, already half-submerged, was replaced by oily black scales. The bulk faded from his torso, until his body became slender and ribbonlike, with a wedge-shaped head at one end and a ridge of spiked fins running along the serpentine spine.

As Fylo and the giants continued to sink, Agis's eel slithered across the dust to the rocky rim, coiling up on the solid ground just in time to see the heads of his foes vanishing into the mire. The noble allowed himself a deep sigh, confident that he had won the battle. His efforts had tired him terribly, but he still had enough strength to take control of the island.

Outside the giant's mind, a horrible groan rumbled through the canyon, then Fylo's grip loosened, and Agis nearly slipped from his captor's grasp. The noble saved himself from a long fall only by throwing his arms over the giant's trembling finger.

"Release me," Agis said, looking into a bloodshot eye. "Now that I've captured one memory, it's only a matter of time before I control your whole mind. All I have to do is shape the island into your image, and—"

"No," Fylo hissed, his lips quivering with fatigue.

"You can't win," the noble said. "Losing a harbinger isn't so different from losing a limb—save that it's spiritual energy instead of blood gushing from the wound. You can't fight me any longer."

"Fylo not done!" the giant roared.

Inside Fylo's head, the dustsink began to churn and

froth. Agis slipped his eel over to the edge of the pond. Never before had he seen a foe create a new mental guardian after the first had been destroyed, but he feared Fylo was doing exactly that.

The noble summoned the energy to meet the attack, but it flowed slowly from his spiritual nexus, for the battle so far had been a tiring one. Before he was ready to change the pool back to stone, a pair of huge claws shot from the dust and locked onto his eel. Agis tried to writhe free, but the more he struggled, the more deeply the pincers' barbs impaled him. Finally, he stopped squirming and allowed himself to be lifted off the ground.

As Fylo's new construct crawled from the dustsink, Agis saw that it faintly resembled a mammoth dune-crab. Instead of four eyestalks, however, only Fylo's head protruded from the top of its biscuit-shaped shell.

"Agis lose," proclaimed the crab, his pincers tightening on the noble's eel.

"Then we both lose!"

Agis whipped his head around and clasped his mouth on his captor's neck. As the barbed pincers sliced through his body, his eel's teeth tore into the throat of Fylo's construct. His mouth filled with the taste of blood, then his body exploded with pain. The sound of his own screaming filled his ears and everything went white.

It took Agis several moments to realize that he had not died. Even then, he felt disoriented and sick, unsure of whether he had returned to consciousness inside Fylo's mind or outside it. His entire body ached with a fierce, stinging pain, and his stomach ached with a queasy emptiness, as if part of it had been removed.

Slowly, as Agis regained his senses, he realized that he was lying in Fylo's open palm. The nobleman rose to his knees, intending to run for his kank—until he realized that the beast was far below. The giant's hand rested upon his mountainous knee, high above the ground. Agis turned toward Fylo's face and found the giant's haggard eyes watching him.

"Fylo hurt," the giant commented.

"Agis, too," the noble admitted. "And we're going to keep hurting. It'll take days to recover from our losses."

Fylo groaned at the unwelcome news. "Then why Agis attack?" he asked.

"Because I must catch your friend Tithian."

"Not Tith—"

Agis raised his hand to stop the giant. "There's no use pretending," he said. "You know I'm Agis of Asticles, and I know who hired you to kill me."

The giant considered this point for a moment, then lifted Agis closer to his face. "Okay. But Tithian not say kill Agis," he said. "Only stop."

"You can't expect me to believe that," Agis scoffed, using the giant's thumb to steady himself as he rose unsteadily to his feet. "The king's not the type to balk at murder."

"Fylo tell truth," said the giant. "Tithian say 'stop friend Agis, but don't hurt. Protect.'"

"Protect me from what?" Agis asked.

Fylo's demeanor suggested that he was being honest about his instructions, which only puzzled the noble. Once before, when Agis had become involved in the rebellion against Tyr's previous ruler, Tithian had used his influence to protect his old friend. But that had been many years ago, before the noble had assumed leadership of the Council of Advisors and become the king's most effective political enemy.

After considering Agis's question for a moment, the giant shrugged. "Fylo forget why Tithian want you protected."

"Fylo never knew, because Tithian didn't say," Agis said. "He's not protecting me. He's trying to keep me from catching him."

"Only 'cause Tithian go dangerous place," Fylo insisted.

Agis raised his brow at this comment. "What dangerous place?"

"Balic," answered the giant. "Now you stay with Fylo till he come back?"

"Tithian isn't coming back," said Agis.

"Tithian promise," Fylo growled. The giant closed his fingers and grasped his captive tightly. "And Fylo promise to keep Agis here."

"It's right to want to keep your promise, but don't think Tithian will do the same," said Agis. "Whatever he offered you—"

"Fylo not for sale!" the giant boomed, squeezing Agis so hard that the air rushed from his lungs. "Tithian friend!"

The heated response gave the noble pause. From the cruel comments floating around in Fylo's memory, it seemed likely that the ugly fellow had led a lonely life. Tithian, as adept at exploiting emotions as anyone Agis knew, had no doubt sensed this and cynically extended his friendship to the lonesome giant.

"Once, I thought Tithian was my friend," Agis said, laboring against Fylo's tight grip to draw breath. "But it's not true. Tithian has no friends."

"Me!" bellowed the giant. "Fylo Tithian's friend."

Agis shook his head. "No—Fylo is Tithian's pawn,"

the noble said. "And after you've done his will, he'll never trouble himself over you again."

"Liar!" Fylo screamed. "Tithian come back soon!"

"Poor Fylo. Your loneliness has blinded you," Agis said. The noble gasped as his captor's fist tightened, then he added, "I can prove what I say."

Fylo relaxed his grip. "How?"

"I've known Tithian since we were boys," Agis said. "I'll let you send your harbinger into my mind, and you can see what he's like for yourself."

"No," the giant replied. "This trap to hurt Fylo."

"We're both too tired for another thought-fight," Agis said, shaking his head. "Besides, by letting you inside my mind, I'm taking the greater risk. If you think it's a trap, all you have to do is withdraw."

As he spoke, Agis pictured a vast, deserted plaza inside his mind, trying to create an open terrain where the giant would not be concerned about ambushes.

Fylo studied Agis for a moment, then the giant's harbinger appeared inside the noble's mind. It had a flat, disk-shaped body that undulated like a cloth in the wind, with a long tail that ended in a sharp point. The thing's mouth was on the underside of its body, while there were a dozen eyes spread along the rim of the top side.

Waving its flexible body like a pair of wings, Fylo's construct began to fly over the vast plaza inside Agis's mind. "Where Tithian?" the harbinger demanded.

Agis summoned his memory of the king. A foul, brown liquid seeped up from between several cobblestones. The stain formed itself into the shape of a man, then Tithian's gaunt visage appeared on the head. The face was not so different from that of the eel Agis had created earlier, with bony cheeks, a slender hooked nose, and a small puckered mouth. The eyes were beady and brown, at once wary and probing.

As the giant's strange harbinger glided down toward the memory, Tithian's image solidified into the full form of a man's thin body, then stood. Fylo stopped his descent just out of arm's reach and slowly circled the figure.

"That look like Tithian," the giant said, pointing his harbinger's slender tail at the memory. "But maybe you make him lie to Fylo."

"No," the noble said. "I'll release him. You can take control of the memory. That way, you can examine him as carefully as you want, and you'll know that I'm not interfering." When Fylo continued to circle without responding, Agis pressed, "If you're afraid of what you'll discover, Tithian can't truly be your friend."

"Fylo not afraid. Let go."

Agis created a small falcon from one of the figure's hands. After transferring his own consciousness into it, he fluttered off and landed a short distance away.

Fylo descended on Tithian's figure, completely engulfing it. The harbinger began to pulsate as he examined the memory, apparently confirming that Agis had truly yielded control of it. Several moments later, the giant finally seemed satisfied. He unfurled his harbinger and let it dissolve, transferring his consciousness into Tithian's form.

As Agis watched, Tithian became a young boy of no more than six or seven, with short-cropped auburn hair. His squarish ears stuck out from the sides of his head like half-opened hinges, and his hawkish nose seemed much too large for his small head. He had one hand raised as if an adult were holding it.

"This is Agis," said a man's voice, which the noble dimly recognized as that of Tithian's father. "You and he are going to be friends."

Young Tithian ran his eyes up and down, as if inspecting a doll, then he scowled. "Father, if you can't afford the best, I don't want a friend."

The image aged a decade. Now, Tithian was a young man, with a somber brow that always seemed furrowed in anger, wearing his hair in a long braided tail. He was dressed in the gray robe that he and Agis had worn as novices when they had studied the Way at the same academy. His eyes were glazed with exhaustion and pain from a particularly rigorous lesson with their master.

"I don't know what happened, Agis," said Tithian. "When the agony became more than I could bear, I thought of how well you were doing. Then my pain just vanished. Honestly, I didn't know I was transferring it to you!"

Again the image aged, this time only a couple of years. Tithian was wearing the red robe of a midlevel student. In his hand was a spiny faro branch, a symbol of passage to denote that he had succeeded at an important test of his abilities. "You're my best friend, Agis. Of course I shifted some of my pain to you," he said. "Besides, it's not really cheating. After all, we didn't get caught."

The image continued to age, showing a constant stream of the king's earlier years. Tithian appeared in the black cassock of a king's templar, denying that he had been responsible for the murder of his own brother. Later, wearing the gilded robes of a high templar, he came to Agis's estate under the pretext of friendship—only to confiscate the noble's strongest field slaves. Another time, Tithian admitted, without any trace of shame, that he had been using Agis's most trusted servant to spy upon the noble.

After this last scene, Fylo separated from the figure of Tithian, forming a new construct that resembled his own body. "No!" he bellowed, swinging a huge fist at the object of his anger. "Tithian liar!"

The blow knocked the king's image to the ground. Fylo began to kick and trample it, apparently determined to destroy the memory altogether.

"Wait!" Agis cried, through his construct's beak. "I need that!"

Still in the form of a falcon, Agis quickly returned to the king's figure and merged with it. He allowed Tithian to melt into the cracks between the cobblestones, then raised another construct shaped like himself.

"Do you believe me now, Fylo?"

The giant did not answer. Instead, his harbinger turned away and began to walk across the deserted plaza. With each step, he grew more translucent, and vanished completely after a dozen paces.

Agis barely had time to turn his attention outward before he felt himself being plunked onto his kank's back. "Go!" boomed the giant, raising his legs to let the noble pass. "Leave Fylo alone."

Agis urged his mount forward. Once he was safely out of reach, he stopped and looked back. "Fylo, don't be so glum," he called. "Tithian's fellowship was false, but you have a good heart. Someday you'll find a true friend."

"No," the giant replied. He gestured at his homely face. "Fylo half-breed. Too ugly for father's tribe, too dumb for mother's tribe."

"You may not be handsome, but I'd say you're far

from dumb," said Agis. "You recognized your mistake with Tithian. That's pretty smart."

This seemed to cheer the giant. A thoughtful look came over his face, then he fixed his eyes on the noble. "Maybe Fylo and Agis could be friends?"

"Perhaps, when we have more time to spend together," the noble allowed. "But right now, I must catch Tithian—before he hurts someone else."

Fylo smiled, then reached down and laid an open palm in front of the noble's kank. "Let Fylo carry you," he said. "Catch Tithian together."

TWO

Chamber of Patricians

Tithian stood in the anteroom of the White Palace, peering through a casement, counting the number of ships in Balic's harbor. The port lay at the edge of the city, where a haze of silvery dust lingered over the bay, drifting as far inland as the inns surrounding the dock area. Still, the Tyrian king found the task an easy one, for the masts rose out of the murk like the charred boles of a burned forest.

"What's your interest in King Andropinis's armada?" inquired Tithian's escort, a young man wrapped in the cream-colored toga of a Balican templar. He had a haughty chin, an upturned nose, and short hair as white as his robe. "Surely, at Tyr's distance from the Silt Sea, you've no reason to worry about our navy."

"I've no particular interest in the fleet," lied Tithian, continuing with his silent count. "But I had not imagined your port would be so crowded. How many craft does your king have?"

"That's not something we discuss with strangers,"

31

replied the templar, taking Tithian by the arm. "Nor do we allow them to count our sails."

Tithian jerked his arm free of the young man's grasp. "In my city, you'd be flogged for such impudence!"

The templar showed no sign of concern. "We are not in your city, and you are not a king in Balic," he replied. "Now, step away from the window."

"I will—when King Andropinis is ready to receive me," said Tithian, struggling to keep his temper under control. "If you touch me again, I'll kill you—and I assure you, Andropinis will do nothing about it." He slipped his hand into the satchel hanging from his shoulder.

The templar's guards, a pair of flabby half-giants standing almost as high as the ceiling, leveled their wooden spears at the Tyrian's chest. Dressed in leather corselets with white capes pinned over their stooped shoulders, the hairy brutes had slack-jawed expressions that did little to belie their slow wits. Tithian gave them a contemptuous sneer, then returned his attention to his escort.

"Give this to your master," said Tithian. He withdrew a small medallion of copper that had been molded into an eight-pointed star. It was the crest of Kalak, the sorcerer-king from whom Tithian had usurped the throne of Tyr. "Tell him I have grown tired of waiting."

The templar remained unimpressed. "I'll relay your message—and you shall wish I hadn't."

With that, the man spun on his heel and left, leaving his charge in the custody of the half-giants.

"You made a big mistake, Tyr-king," said one of the brutes. "That was Maurus, Chamberlain to His Majesty."

Tithian gave the guard a wry smile. "I think Maurus is the one who made the mistake."

The king returned his attention to the masts. From what he could tell through the haze, the harbor seemed unusually full, with no empty dock space available and dozens of craft moored offshore. To fulfill his needs, he would require only a small portion of the armada gathered in the bay.

Now that he felt certain he'd be able to procure enough troops and ships, Tithian allowed his gaze to wander over the rest of Balic. The city shimmered with a pearly light, for its blocky buildings were faced in blond marble and its avenues paved with pale limestone. Encircling the White Palace's fortified bluff were the pillared emporiums of the Merchants' Quarter, as striking in their size as in the clean lines of their architecture. Beyond this district lay the dingy warrens of the Elven Market, the stadium, the workshops of the artisans, and the chamberhouses where most of the city's population lived. All in all, Balic seemed a prosperous and pleasant metropolis, one which Tithian would have been glad to call his own.

One day, he chuckled silently, *I might.*

When Maurus did not return for several more minutes, the king allowed his thoughts to wander to the man who had been stalking him in the desert. Tithian had first learned of his pursuer when his spy, an elven desert runner hired to watch his backtrail, reported that a Tyrian noble of Agis's description had been asking about him at an oasis. Despite the reasonable fee the elf had quoted for murdering the noble, the king's heart had sunk. Of all the men who might have come after him, Agis was the only one he could not bring himself to kill.

It was a flaw in his character Tithian did not understand. He made many excuses for his weakness, telling himself it would be foolish to assassinate such a valuable statesman. When that did not seem enough, the king reminded himself of Agis's superior knowledge of agriculture, which made Tyr's farms more productive than those of any other Athasian city. Other times, he thought of the riots that would be caused by the noble's death, or of any of a dozen other equally valid reasons for leaving Agis alone.

Still, Tithian knew he was lying to himself. Agis had incited the Council of Advisors to defy the king in a hundred matters, from letting paupers drink free at city wells to converting royal lands into charity farms. Such insolence would have cost anyone else his life, but Tithian had always stopped short of murdering his old friend.

Even now, when Agis's meddling endangered the most important endeavor Tithian had ever undertaken, the king could not bring himself to kill the noble. Instead of telling Fylo, whom Tithian had found seeking employment as a caravan cargo bearer, to kill Agis, the king had merely asked the oaf to detain the noble.

Tithian hoped he would not regret the decision. Agis had demonstrated many times that he could be as resourceful as he was determined, and even a giant might not hold the noble for long.

Given that possibility, the king thought it might not be such a bad thing if Fylo ignored his instructions and killed Agis. Then, at least his friend's blood would not be on Tithian's hands.

He banished the hope from his mind as quickly as it came. Such an accident hardly seemed a fitting end for a king's only friend. Agis had not always been a political enemy, and there had been times that the noble had stood by Tithian when nobody else would. If the time came when his friend had to die, Tithian decided, it would be by the king's own hand.

Agis deserved that much.

The chamberlain's officious footsteps echoed down the hall, putting the king's concerns about his friend out of his mind. When he turned away from the window, Tithian found a smug grin on Maurus's narrow lips.

"King Andropinis normally addresses the Chamber of Patricians at this time," the chamberlain said, a malicious glint flashing in his eyes. "He asks that you meet him there."

Maurus and the guards led Tithian down a corridor lined by the lifelike statues of ancient statesmen, then across a broad courtyard to the White Palace's marble-faced assembly hall. The building was perfectly square, with a colonnade of fluted pillars supporting an ornate entablature. Without awaiting an invitation, Tithian marched up the stairs, but before he could enter the building, the chamberlain scrambled past and blocked his way.

"Allow me to hold that for you," said Maurus. Being careful not to touch his guest, he motioned at the satchel on Tithian's shoulder.

Tithian opened the sack and displayed its interior. "As you can see, it's empty," he replied. "No reason for concern."

Maurus did not move. "Nevertheless, I must insist," he replied. "Things are not always what they seem, are they?"

"They seldom are," Tithian allowed.

He reluctantly took the bag off his shoulder. Maurus's suspicions were well-founded, for it was a magical satchel that could hold an unlimited number of items and still appear empty. Before leaving Tyr, the king had placed inside an ample supply of food, water, coins, and many other items he expected to need on his journey. Of course, the supplies also included a broad selection of weapons, but that was not why Tithian wanted to keep the sack in his own hands. He had something else inside that would convince the Balican ruler to give him what he wanted, and he had wanted to keep the bag so he could time the appearance of the items for maximum effect.

Tithian handed the satchel to the chamberlain, silently cursing the man's caution and efficiency. "Now may I go inside?"

Maurus slipped the satchel over his shoulder, then waved his guest through the doorway. Tithian passed into a small anteroom, where a half-giant sentry stood in front of a pair of massive doors. After raising his hand to salute the chamberlain, the guard pulled a door open and stepped aside.

Tithian entered the next chamber. The air felt hot and moist against his skin, and it reeked of perfumed flesh. Save for the soft scrape of his own sandals on the floor, the place remained so quiet that the Tyrian wondered if he had entered an empty room.

As his eyes adjusted to the stifling murkiness, Tithian saw that was not the case. A gallery of marble benches ran down both sides of the huge chamber, partially concealed by two lines of marble pillars that supported the ceiling. Several hundred men and women waited patiently in the tiers, all dressed in white togas hemmed with silver and gold. They were of many races: human, mul, dwarf, half-elf, and even tarek. They all remained absolutely silent, sitting so motionless that not even the rustle of their silken robes disturbed the eerie quiet.

At the far end of the chamber stood an empty throne, constructed of translucent alabaster and stationed upon a pedestal of pink jade. Inlays of blue-tinted moonstone decorated the back of the magnificent seat, while the arms had been shaped from solid blocks of chalcedony and the legs from limpid crystals of citrine. All of the light passing through the room's narrow windows seemed to flow directly into the chair, which cast the radiance back into the chamber as a muted white glow.

Tithian walked forward, stopping near a graying patrician of about his own age. She had the pointed ears and peaked eyebrows of a half-elf, but her shape was somewhat plump and matronly for a woman of her race. Next to her, six gold coins rested in a shallow basket woven from the fronds of a soap tree. The woman did not turn to face the Tyrian.

"Is it not customary in Balic to greet strangers?" Tithian asked. His voice echoed through the still chamber as though he had struck a gong.

"Lady Canace cannot hear you," said Maurus, walking toward him. "Neither can she see you."

The Tyrian stepped around to face the woman. Ugly red burn marks scarred her sunken eyelids, leaving Tithian with the impression that she had no eyeballs.

Maurus stopped at the Tyrian's side, then placed a finger on the woman's lower lip. She jumped as though startled, then allowed her mouth to be pulled open wide. In place of a tongue, she had only a mangled stump.

"King Andropinis values the advice of his patricians," the templar said flatly. "But he also wishes to be certain that anything occurring here is never discussed outside the White Palace."

"A wise precaution," Tithian observed, stepping away from the woman. "It's unfortunate he is not so prudent with his chamberlain."

Maurus closed Lady Canace's mouth and whirled around to reply, but an acid comment from the throne cut him off. "Do not anger my chamberlain," said the voice. "It is the same as angering me."

Tithian looked toward the throne and saw a huge man before the pedestal. He stood taller than an elf and was as heavily muscled as a mul. On his head, a fringe of chalk-colored hair hung from beneath a jagged crown of silver. He had a slender face, a nose so long it could almost be called a snout, and dark nostrils shaped like eggs. His cracked lips were pulled back to reveal a mouthful of teeth filed as sharp as those of a gladiator. Unlike the patricians, he did not dress in a toga. Instead, he wore a sleeveless tunic of white silk, a breechcloth of silver fabric, and soft leather boots.

"King Andropinis," Tithian said. He did not bow, and his voice betrayed no sign of awe or reverence.

Andropinis did not answer, instead turning away to take his throne. As the Balican climbed the stairs, it became apparent that he was not entirely human. Beneath his tunic, a line of sharp bulges ran down the length of his spine, while small, pointed scales covered the back sides of his arms.

Andropinis took his seat in the throne, then glared around the chamber. *We are in chamber, my advisors*, he said, using the Way to broadcast his thoughts directly into the minds of everyone present.

The patricians rose from their seats, each holding a shallow soap tree basket in his or her hands. Tithian waited for the room to grow quiet again, then nodded to the chamberlain. "Announce me."

Maurus motioned him forward. "I suggest you announce yourself," he replied. "This audience is your doing, not mine."

Tithian walked forward until he stood before the throne. Andropinis's white eyes glared at him, as cold and stinging as hail, and the Balican said nothing. Compared to Kalak's pitiful form, this sorcerer-king seemed a brute. He looked as though he could bite a man in two or rip a half-giant's head off with his bare hands. Yet Tithian knew appearances could be deceiving. He had seen Kalak, as frail and decrepit as a hundred-year-old woman, kill slaves with no more than a glance and snap muls' necks with a twist of his wrist.

The one who stands before you is Tithian the First, King of Tyr.

Andropinis was off his throne and towering over Tithian before the king realized he had moved.

"Your identity is no concern of my patricians," the Balican said quietly, clenching the smaller king's shoulders. His fingers dug into Tithian's flesh like talons, and his breath smelled as though he had been eating burnt cork. "Be kind enough to speak with your tongue."

"If you wish," Tithian replied. Moving with deliberate steadiness, he reached up and gently pushed Andropinis's hand away from his shoulder. "And please remember that you address the king of Tyr."

"You may have killed Kalak, but you are no king," replied Andropinis. He circled Tithian slowly, looking him up and down. "You know nothing of being a king."

"I know enough to have won a war with Hamanu of Urik," the Tyrian answered. Strictly speaking, it had been Rikus who had won that war, but Tithian had been claiming credit for the victory so long that he had forgotten the distinction. "And I have won the favor of Borys of Ebe—the Dragon of Athas."

Andropinis stopped at Tithian's side. "You should not banter the Dragon's ancient name about," he warned, hissing into his guest's ear.

"I did not come to banter, as you shall see if we may discuss the reason for my visit," Tithian replied.

Andropinis nodded, then stepped toward the gallery where his nobles stood. "We will discuss it while I accept gifts from the patricians."

Tithian went into the tiers at Andropinis's side. Maurus fetched a large wooden basin from behind the throne, then followed a step behind the two kings. The trio stopped at the side of the first patrician, a wizened old man whose basket contained several glistening rubies.

Andropinis selected the largest gem and held it up to the light. "What do you want in Balic, usurper?" he asked, addressing his guest without looking at him.

Tithian's answer was direct and to the point. "I need two thousand soldiers and the craft to carry them over the Sea of Silt."

Andropinis raised a brow, then took all the rubies from the old man's basket and dumped them into the basin in the chamberlain's hands. "What makes you believe I would give them to you?"

Tithian gestured at the satchel on Maurus's shoulder. "If I may?"

Andropinis considered the request for a moment, then nodded. "But if you draw a weapon—"

"I'm not that foolish," Tithian said. He took the satchel from Maurus's shoulder, then slipped a hand inside. He closed his eyes for a moment, picturing one of the sacks of gold he had placed in the satchel before leaving his own palace in Tyr. When he had a clear image of it in his mind, he opened his hand. An instant later, he felt a wad of coarse cloth in his palm. Groaning with effort, he withdrew a heavy bag, bulging with coins and nearly as large as the satchel itself. He placed it in Maurus's basin, opening the top to reveal the yellow sheen of gold.

Andropinis stared coldly at the coins. "Do you think to buy my favor with that?"

"Not your favor," Tithian replied. "Your men and your ships." When the Balican's face remained stony, he added, "I'll pay the other half when I return, along with compensation for any losses we incur."

"And what of the losses I have already suffered?" demanded Andropinis.

"What losses would those be?"

"Five years ago, Tyr did not pay its levy to the Dragon, and it fell to me to give him a thousand extra slaves," he said. "I couldn't finish the great wall I had been building to enclose my croplands. Perhaps you heard about what happened next?"

"The Peninsula Rampage?" Tithian asked, thinking of the short-lived war in which a small army of giants had overrun most of the Balican Peninsula.

"The rampage cost me half my army and destroyed a quarter of my fields," Andropinis said, turning away from Tithian. He went to the woman next in line and examined her basket, then nodded for Maurus to take the contents. "I doubt there's enough gold in your magic satchel to pay me back for that," he added, glancing at his guest.

"You can build another wall," Tithian retorted. "But I still need your fleet. I demand it on the Dragon's behalf."

"Do not think to bluff me by invoking his name. I

should kill you for that," hissed Andropinis. He clamped a hand around Tithian's throat. "Perhaps I will."

"I'm not lying," Tithian said. "You'll realize that when I show you my prisoners."

Tithian reached into his satchel and visualized a chain of black iron. When he felt it in his fingers, he pulled his hand free of the bag, bringing with it the chain, which was attached at either end to a square iron cage containing a disembodied head. As they were removed from the bag, the two prisoners glared briefly at Tithian, then focused their eyes on Andropinis.

"Kill him, Mighty King!" hissed the first head. He had a shriveled face and ashen skin, with sunken features and cracked, leathery lips. "Slit Tithian's throat and drop him close to me!"

"No, give me the throat!" growled the other. He was bloated and gross, with puffy cheeks, eyes swollen to dark slits, and a mouthful of gray broken teeth. Like the first head, he wore his coarse hair in a topknot, and the bottom of his neck had been stitched shut with wiry thread. He licked the bars of his cage with a pointed tongue, then continued, "And let the coward live. I want to see the fear in his eyes when I drink his life!"

Andropinis took the cages from Tithian, at the same time removing his hand from the Tyrian's throat. "Wyan, Sacha!" he said. "Borys told me that he had disposed of you two."

"Rajaat's magic is not countered so easily," spat the bloated head, Sacha. "Now open this imposter's veins, Albeorn. He hasn't fed us in weeks."

"Albeorn?" Tithian asked.

"Albeorn of Dunswich, Slayer of Elves, the Eighth

Champion of Rajaat," snarled Wyan. "Traitor to his master and the righteous cause of the Pristine Tower."

Tithian knew that Wyan referred to a genocidal war that an ancient sorcerer named Rajaat had started several millennia earlier. It had ended more than a thousand years ago, when all of Rajaat's handpicked champions—with the exceptions of Sacha and Wyan—had turned against him. After overthrowing their master, the rebels had used his most powerful magical artifact to transform one of their own number, Borys of Ebe, into the Dragon. The other champions had each claimed one of the cities of Athas to rule as an immortal sorcerer-king.

Still studying the caged heads, Andropinis asked, "These two are your proof of the Dragon's favor?"

Tithian nodded. "When he said he had disposed of them, he meant that he had entrusted them to me," said the Tyrian. "They're acting as my unwilling tutors, so I might learn to serve our master as a sorcerer-king."

This seemed to amuse the Balican. "Is that so?" he asked, raising his brow.

"Of course not," sneered Wyan. "He's lying."

"Kill him!" hissed Sacha.

Andropinis smashed the two cages into the stone tiers of the gallery. A tremendous clang reverberated through the hall, making Tithian's ears ring. The heads slammed against the bars of their prisons and bounced to the other sides, then dropped motionless and dazed to the bottoms of the cages. When the Balican handed the chain back to Tithian, the corners of each cage were folded in from the impact.

"For now, I'll accept these abominations as proof that the Dragon wouldn't want me to kill you," Andropinis said. "You may remove them from my sight—and tell me what you need with my fleet."

As Tithian stuffed his dazed tutors back into the satchel, he said, "That's the concern of myself and Borys alone."

"Then you may leave your gold and go. Our audience is at an end," Andropinis said, resuming his inspection of the baskets offered by his patricians. "The chamberlain's guards will show you to the city gates."

Maurus smirked and waved the Tyrian toward the exit.

Tithian ignored him, asking, "What of my ships?"

"You have none."

"My demand is made in the Dragon's name!" Tithian snapped.

"Which is the only reason I suffer you to live, usurper," Andropinis replied. He pulled a wad of fleece from a basket held by a dwarven patrician, then used the Way to ask, *What is the meaning of this, Lord Rolt?*

House Rolt pledges a hundred sheep to feed Your Majesty's legions, came the reply.

Andropinis scowled, then grabbed the dwarf's thick wrist and snapped it effortlessly. A garbled howl of pain rose from Lord Rolt's throat and his knees buckled. Had the king not been holding him up by his broken arm, he would have fallen to the floor.

Despite his pain, the dwarf managed to reply, *House Rolt pledges a thousand sheep, Mighty King.*

Smiling, Andropinis released the patrician and allowed him to collapse to the floor. He glanced down, leaving no doubt in Tithian's mind that the exhibition had been for his benefit, and moved on.

Ignoring the implied threat, Tithian continued to press his demand. "If you deny me, you are also denying Borys."

"Perhaps, but I will not send out my fleet—not for you, and certainly not now."

"When?" asked Tithian.

Andropinis shrugged. "Perhaps in a month, perhaps not for many years," he said. "When the war between the giant tribes is over."

"Which tribes are at war?" Tithian asked.

"Your question betrays your incompetence to command my ships," scoffed the sorcerer-king.

"I'm sure we can circumvent their lines and keep your ships safe," Tithian replied.

"I'm not concerned about my ships!" Andropinis spat. "It's my city I want to protect. The first giants to spy a fleet in the estuary will assume I've taken sides with their enemies. They'll storm Balic, and I'll be drawn into a war that's none of my concern."

"I had not thought a few motley giants would frighten a sorcerer-king," Tithian countered.

"Only a fool is not wary of giants," Andropinis replied. He stopped at the side of Lady Canace, the plump half-elf to whom Tithian had tried to speak earlier. The Balican clucked his tongue at the contents of her basket, then slapped her face with the back of his hand. She fell to the floor, spilling the six gold coins she had brought as an offering.

Andropinis continued down the gallery, leaving Maurus to collect the coins. "Even if Borys were here to demand it himself, I would not entrust my ships to such an oaf," said the king.

"I'm no oaf." Tithian's voice remained calm.

"You are if you believe the Dragon can make a sorcerer-king of you," said Andropinis. He lifted a long necklace of diamonds from the basket held by the stumpy hands of a dwarven patrician.

"I think he is more than capable of bestowing the necessary powers on me—once I supply him with the Dark Lens," Tithian replied.

The Dark Lens was the ancient artifact which Rajaat's rebellious champions had used to imprison their master, and to transform Borys of Ebe into the Dragon. Shortly afterward, a pair of dwarves had stolen the lens from the Pristine Tower, and it had been missing ever since.

Andropinis dropped the necklace in his hand back into the basket from which it had come, then narrowed his eyes at Tithian. "So, I am to assume that you have discovered the location of the lens, and the Dragon has sent you to find it for him?" he asked.

"Yes," Tithian replied. He had hoped to avoid revealing so much to Andropinis, but it had become clear that the sorcerer-king would risk trouble with the giants for nothing but the most important of reasons. "Borys said you would cooperate by giving me the ships and men I need."

The Balican studied his guest for a moment, then said, "If you are truly attempting to recover the lens on the Dragon's behalf, then tell me where it is—so we'll know where to look if you fail."

Tithian gave Andropinis a wry smile. "Do you really want me to do that?"

The Dragon had warned him never to reveal the Dark Lens's location, for the artifact's ancient thieves had placed a powerful enchantment on it to prevent Borys and his sorcerer-kings from discovering its location.

Andropinis returned his guest's smile, revealing a long row of sharp teeth. "Perhaps the Dragon did send you," he said. "It took him many centuries to understand the magic protecting the lens. Certainly, without his help, you would not have learned its nature in a single lifetime."

"Borys warned me of the enchantment," Tithian confirmed. "From what I understand, it accompanies the knowledge as a stomachworm accompanies a slave. You cannot own one without owning the other."

Andropinis nodded. "Before we understood how powerful it was, I watched the brains of a hundred agents run out their ears when they tried to tell me what they had learned."

Tithian swallowed, glad that he had followed his instructions carefully. Borys had warned him that describing the location of the lens would be fatal, but had not elaborated on the gruesome details. Suppressing a shudder, he turned his thoughts back to the purpose of this meeting.

"So, you'll give me the fleet?"

"I'll give you the men and ships you seek," Andropinis said. "But don't return to Balic, or you'll wish that I had killed you today. My city won't be the one that suffers when Borys destroys the lens."

"Agreed."

Andropinis glanced at his chamberlain and nodded.

Maurus stepped to the Tyrian's side. "A guard will escort you to a guesthouse. I'll have a messenger contact you as soon as the necessary arrangements have been made." When Tithian made no move to leave, the chamberlain waved a hand toward the exit. "This way out," he said.

Tithian ignored him and kept his attention focused on Andropinis.

"Yes?" asked the Balican. "Is there something else?"

Tithian sneered at the chamberlain, then said, "It would be best if what passed between us could not be repeated, King Andropinis. My task will be difficult enough without the Veiled Alliance interfering."

"Maurus is trustworthy," replied the sorcerer-king.

"To you, perhaps," said Tithian. "But he has shown me no respect, and I'm the one who's sailing into giant territory—where it would be an easy matter to arrange an ambush. In Borys's name, I must insist that your chamberlain's tongue be silenced."

Andropinis shook his head at Tithian's boldness, then said, "Perhaps you will become a sorcerer-king after all, Tithian." He motioned for the chamberlain to step toward him.

Maurus dropped the wooden treasure basin he had been holding and turned to flee. "Please, my king!"

Andropinis slipped past Tithian to clamp a huge hand over the templar's shoulder. Long claws sprouted from the sorcerer-king's fingertips, then he used the Way to address the entire Chamber of Patricians.

Young Maurus, my chamberlain, is to be congratulated, he said. *I am bestowing the title of Patrician upon him.*

The applause was so thunderous that it shook the building.

THREE

Nymos

Agis stood at the quay's end, squinting out at the harbor. There, a ghostly thicket of white sails was just fading from sight, shrouded by the distance and a murky pall of dust that cleaved to the bay's surface like a ground fog. The sun had barely risen, shooting tendrils of blood-colored light across the emerald haze of the morning sky, and already the flotilla had reached the far side of the cove. On one of those ships, the noble felt certain, sailed the fugitive king of Tyr.

Agis had entered Balic the previous night, leaving Fylo several miles outside the city. He had begun searching for Tithian immediately. Bribing dozens of street paupers to answer his questions, he had traced his quarry first to the sorcerer-king's citadel, then to the harbor district. The trail had ended there, and the noble had spent more than an hour trying to find it again. Finally he had learned that, for the first time in a year, a Balican military fleet had sortied earlier that night. Given that Tithian had been seen traveling from the White Palace to the harbor, the departure had seemed more than a coincidence. Agis had concluded that the king of Tyr was sailing with the flotilla.

The noble started back down the quay. Pearl-colored loess lay heaped against the western side of the pier in great mounds, spilling over the stone walkway and making it difficult to tell the wharf from the silty depths it traversed. At the end of the dock, a chest-high hedge of yellow ratany ran along the edge of the harbor, its spindly boughs serving as a crude dust-break.

As Agis approached the end of the pier, he came upon a group of rugged men seated on crates. They were talking quietly among themselves, twining rope and repairing sailing tackle. They had tied scarves around their mouths and noses to keep out blowing dust, and their eyes seemed pinched into permanent squints.

"Hail, stranger," said one, speaking the trade tongue with the thick Balican accent. Although he looked at Agis as he spoke, his thick fingers continued to dance, twisting three yarns of black cord into a rope. "Are you looking to hire a craft?"

"Perhaps," Agis said.

"Before you hire Salust, take a look at his boat," said another, with broad red cheeks peeking over the top of his dusty face-mask. "My own bark is two craft down. She's as dust-worthy a vessel as you'll find in this harbor."

The man gestured to the left side of the pier. There, dozens of boats lay scattered along the edge of the bay, sails furled and centerboards raised so the hulls could rest flat in the dust. All were half-buried, with mountainous heaps of silt piled against their high-sided gunnels. In many cases, the loess had spilled over the tops, completely filling the passenger compartments and giving the craft the distinct impression of derelicts.

"I'm not sure I want to hire any of those boats," Agis commented.

"If you're going to steal one, take Marda's," commented Salust, staring at the red-cheeked man. "You'd be doing us all a favor, especially his family. That way, they won't lose their father when he drops his dingy into a sinkhole."

This elicited a round of laughter from the other men, who encouraged Salust and Marda as they continued to trade insults. Agis paid them little attention, for his thoughts were on more important matters.

"Can any of your boats catch the fleet that left this morning?" he interrupted.

This silenced the small crowd. "Why would you want to?" asked Marda.

"A criminal from my city sailed on one of those ships," explained Agis. "I must take him back to Tyr to answer for his crimes."

"Let him go," said Salust. "I promise you, he'll find punishment enough with the fleet."

"What do you mean?" Agis asked.

"The giants—"

Before Marda could explain further, a pair of Balican templars stepped onto the quay, leaving an escort of six half-giants behind at the ratany hedge. The sailors fell immediately silent, each man fixing his eyes on his work.

When the templars reached the group, one of them pointed at Agis. "You. How long have you been in Balic?" She was a hard-eyed woman with sour, harsh-looking features.

"Let me think," the noble replied. "How long has it been now?" He rubbed his chin, stalling for time as he prepared to use the Way. The energy flowed from his nexus slowly, for he still felt weak from the loss he had suffered in his thought-battle against Fylo.

"If you've been here longer than you can remember, then certainly you can tell us where you're staying," suggested the second templar, a blue-eyed man with curly yellow hair.

Agis pointed in the general direction of the harbor's entrance, where he had seen a single large inn stretching along an entire block. He did not speak, however, knowing that the name he gave for the building would probably be incorrect. As in most cities of Athas, Balic's sorcerer-king forbade common citizens the right to read. Consequently, the city's trade signs depicted pictures or symbols suggesting the establishment's name without actually providing it. So, while Agis remembered that the carving of a lion lying on its back hung on the inn's wall, he had no way of knowing whether the name was the Dead Lion, the Sleeping Cat, or something entirely different.

When Agis did not volunteer the name, the female templar said, "There must be two dozen inns in that direction. Which one?"

"I'm thinking of the Lion," Agis said, hoping an abbreviated name would suffice.

The woman's eyes narrowed, but before she could press for more detail, Marda said, "He means the Lion's Back, ma'am."

"We didn't ask you," snapped the woman's companion.

Marda lowered his gaze. "I'm sorry," he said. "I was just trying to help. I've met milord there many a morning."

The posture of both templars grew less tense, and they shrugged at each other. To Marda the woman said, "I'll let your mistake pass this time, but let us know if you see any other strangers in the quarter. A Tyrian left his giant in the fields of House Balba, and the oaf refuses to leave. Lord Balba is offering five silvers to anyone who delivers the scoundrel to his mansion."

With that, the two templars returned to their escort. As soon as they left the quay, every sailor in the group spat into the bay.

"My thanks for protecting me," Agis said, secretly amused by the image of a Balican lord attempting to persuade the stubborn Fylo to leave his lands.

"We weren't protecting you," said Marda. "We were repaying the king for his ill treatment of us."

"Andropinis won't let more than five of us leave port in a day," added Salust. "And when we get back, his templars confiscate half our cargo." He nodded toward the shore, where the templars' heads and shoulders protruded above the ratany hedge as they moved down the street.

"Tariffs," growled another sailor. Again, they all spat into the bay.

Agis nodded in sympathy, then looked to Marda. "Could your bark catch the fleet carrying my criminal?"

The sailor shook his head. "Not mine, or the ship of any man here," he answered. "But rest assured, no one on that fleet, including the man you seek, will live to set foot on solid land again. The giants'll see to that."

"Perhaps, but that won't satisfy the people he's wronged," Agis said. "I must return him to stand before those whose laws he has broken."

"Then you'll have to hire a smuggler," said Salust. "That'll be no easy task for a stranger."

Agis reached into the purse beneath his cloak, withdrawing a silver coin. "Perhaps you could help me?"

"I might show you where to look," said Salust, reaching out to take the coin.

Marda slapped the hand down. "Don't waste your silver, stranger. You can't trust any smuggler who consorts with the likes of Salust." He pointed toward one of the many buildings on the close-packed harbor front. "If you want to find one who won't slit your throat for the coins in your purse, go to the Furled Sail tavern and ask for Nymos. He knows that side of the harbor better than most."

"Many thanks."

Agis started to hand the coin to Marda, but the sailor shook his head. "Save it for Nymos," he said, smirking at Salust. "You'll need it."

The noble slipped his silver back into his purse, then stepped off the quay into the crowded harborside lane. Despite the ratany silt-break, several inches of pearly loess covered the walkways, and so much dust clung to the building placards that Agis could barely make out the pictures engraved on their surfaces. Nevertheless, he could usually tell the nature of the business he passed by peering inside. In the tackle shops, ropes, sails, oars, pulleys, and a thousand similar articles hung suspended from the ceiling, so that the patrons had to stoop over or push merchandise aside as they moved about. The warehouses contained huge bundles of untwined giant hair, stacks of rough-cut lumber, mounds of freshly shorn wool, and almost any product that could be traded for a profit. Only the taverns did not seem busy, with closed doors and window shutters fastened tight against blowing dust.

Agis came to a sign bearing the image of a sail furled over a yardarm. Like the other taverns, this one appeared closed, but the noble heard chairs scraping against stone as someone cleaned the floor. He knocked on the door, then stepped back to wait.

A moment later, an unshaven man with a round stomach and red nose peered out the half-opened door. In one hand he held a broom, in the other a sword of sharpened bone. "What?"

"I was told to ask for Nymos," Agis replied.

"So?"

"I have something for him," the noble said, withdrawing a silver coin from his purse.

The innkeeper's face lit up. "Good," he said, snatching the coin from Agis's hand. "I'll put this toward his bill."

With that, the man pulled the door open and stepped aside, then waved the noble toward a ladder in the back of the inn. "I let him stay on the roof. Keeps the birds off."

Agis climbed the stairs and stepped onto the inn's roof. It was a relatively flat surface of baked clay, enclosed by a waist-high wall and littered with shattered broy mugs. In one corner, the sunbleached bones of hundreds of dustgulls lay heaped around the blackened scar of a small cooking fire, with a water jug and a few pieces of chipped crockery sitting nearby. A short distance away, a canopy of untanned hide hung over a nest of gray straw.

At the front wall stood a jozhal. The short, two-legged reptile had cocked his slender head to one side, and he held a three-fingered hand cupped to his earslit as though listening to something in the street below. He had an elongated snout full of needle-sharp teeth, a serpentine neck topped by a jagged crest of hide, and a long skinny tail. In contrast to his bony arms, he had huge, powerful legs, each ending in a three-clawed foot. His eyes were covered with the milky film of blindness, and his free hand rested atop a slender walking stick.

"The innkeeper said I'd find Nymos up here," Agis said, walking to the reptile's side.

The jozhal jumped as if someone had shouted into his ear, bringing his walking stick around to defend himself. Agis blocked the swing, then grabbed the cane to prevent the creature from making another attack. As the noble did so, he glimpsed the reptile slipping a small, spiral-shaped shell into a skin pouch on his belly.

The jozhal disengaged his walking stick from Agis's grasp. "I'm Nymos," he grumbled. "What do you want, Tyrian?"

The noble drew a second silver coin from his purse and placed it in Nymos's small hand. "Marda said you could use this," he said, guessing the jozhal had identified him by his accent. "I'm looking for a smuggler with a fast ship who can follow the fleet that left last night."

Nymos rubbed the coin between the three fingers of his hand. "It'll cost you more than a silver."

"I'll give you another when I find a captain I like," Agis countered, wondering how the blind reptile could tell that he held silver instead of gold or lead.

Nymos slipped the coin into his stomach pouch. "I'm more interested in magic," he said. "You wouldn't have anything enchanted, would you?"

"I have nothing like that," Agis replied. "I'm no sorcerer."

The jozhal sniffed Agis's satchel and belt purse, then shook his head in disgust. "Like trying to squeeze water from a stone," he snorted. "I'd expect someone of your reputation to have an enchanted dagger or something."

"My reputation?"

"Of course," Nymos said. "Even in Balic, the bards sing of the noble who fought to free the slaves of Tyr—Agis of Asticles."

The noble's jaw fell slack in surprise. "What makes you think that's me?"

The jozhal held out his bony hand. "Answers cost."

Scowling, Agis gave him another coin.

"The streets are full of templars looking for the Tyrian who left his giant in Lord Balba's field," said the jozhal.

"So I've heard, but that isn't the answer I paid for."

"Your giant is less discreet with names than he ought to be," replied Nymos. "Especially considering who you are."

"I'm Tyrian, but that doesn't mean I'm *that* one," he said. "There must be a hundred men from Tyr in this city. Any of them could be Agis of Asticles."

"True," replied the jozhal. "But I suspect Agis is the only one with reason to follow Tithian." At the mention of the king's name, Nymos extended his hand for another coin.

"For one who charges so much, you certainly live in squalor," observed Agis, handing over another silver.

"My information is not always of such value. Besides, I have a certain fondness for broy." Nymos slipped the coin into his pouch, then said, "I overheard the high templar of the Balican fleet, Navarch Saanakal, escorting a Tyrian onto his flagship. He addressed the man as King Tithian."

"You'll have to do better for that last coin. I knew Tithian was aboard the fleet before I came here," said Agis. "Did the king leave Balic so fast because he knew I was here?"

"You're asking me to speculate," Nymos said, raising his hand again. "That costs—"

"You haven't earned my last silver yet," Agis interrupted.

Nymos sighed. "I doubt he knew you were here," he said. "The fleet left dock long before you reached the harbor—perhaps even before you entered the city."

"That's welcome news," Agis said. "Now, what of the ship I need to hire?"

In reply, Nymos rubbed his mouth.

"With what I've paid you, you can buy your own broy," Agis snapped.

The jozhal repeated the gesture twice more, both times slowly and deliberately.

"I'm not among those who wear the veil," the noble said, finally recognizing the signal for what it was. "But I can tell you that in Tyr, the Veiled Alliance would not have charged three silvers for its help."

"We are not in Tyr," said Nymos. He sat down in the corner, using his cane to motion Agis to do the same. "But we hope someday to liberate Balic as you and Tithian did your city—which is why I've lived on this rooftop for the last decade. Nothing leaves or enters this port unless I hear about it."

"So you have proven," Agis said, still indignant about the fee Nymos had demanded of him. "Does that mean you'll guide me to a reliable captain?"

"Yes, if you tell me what's going on here," Nymos said. "Andropinis is not the type to lend his fleet, especially to the king of the Free City."

Agis shrugged. "I don't know. All I can tell you is this: Tithian has more in common with Andropinis than with the hero legends make him out to be. The reason I'm following him is that he sent a tribe of slavers to attack a small village—one of Tyr's allies."

"Because I am short and blind, do not mistake me for a fool!" Nymos hissed. "Even in Balic, we know of Tithian's deeds. He freed the slaves. He made a public marketplace of the gladiatorial stadium. He gave the king's fields to the poor. He—"

"Yes, he did all those things," interrupted Agis. "But in Tyr, the king's power is not final. The Council of Advisors forced him to issue every one of those edicts. Rest assured that if the choice were his, Tyr would be a tyrant's plaything."

Nymos was quiet for a long time. Finally, he asked, "Why should I believe you?"

"Because if you know of Tithian's reputation, you must also know mine. I wouldn't say these things unless they were true." When this didn't seem to convince Nymos, he added, "From what I've said, you must realize that we can't both be honest. To choose between us, ask yourself who's sailing with Andropinis's fleet."

"Maybe he has a good reason for his actions," the jozhal suggested, still reluctant to accept that the legendary king of Tyr was just as corrupt as any other ruler.

"You know that can't be. King Andropinis would not help him if his cause were a worthy one," said Agis. "Besides, there's no justification for taking slaves. By breaking Tyr's most sacred law, Tithian has become a fugitive from his own realm."

"Not a fugitive," Nymos said. "If your king were fleeing Tyr's justice, he would have stayed in Balic, under our king's protection. No, Tithian wants something with that fleet—and whatever it is, Andropinis wants him to have it."

Agis frowned. "What could it be?"

Nymos shrugged. "I don't know," he said. "But the giants are fighting among themselves. By sending out his fleet, Andropinis has risked drawing Balic into the war. Whatever Tithian is after, it must be something of great importance."

Agis rose to his feet. "Which is the all the more reason I must hurry."

Nymos also stood. "This concerns Balic as much as it does Tyr. I'm coming with you."

"That isn't necessary."

"Perhaps not," replied the jozhal. "But in ten years, this is the first good excuse I've had to get off this roof. You have no choice in the matter."

"The trip will be too dangerous," Agis objected.

"Don't assume that I can't take care of myself," hissed Nymos. "Nothing makes me angrier."

Agis sighed. "Very well. I wouldn't want to upset you."

"Then we have a bargain?"

"Yes," the noble said. "But that means we're partners. I'm not paying you another silver."

"That's just as well," said Nymos, taking the noble's arm. "You'll need what's left to hire the smuggler. There's only one ship that can follow where the fleet's going, and its captain drives a hard bargain."

"Then you know Tithian's destination?" Agis inquired.

"Of course, I heard him tell it to Navarch Saanakal," the reptile replied. "It's Lybdos, the Forbidden Isle."

As they approached the ladder, Agis heard a woman

speaking in the tavern below. "The Tyrian, where is he?" It was the voice of the sour-faced templar who had accosted him on the quay.

"Tyrian?" came the innkeeper's reply. "There's no Tyrian here. As you can see, we're closed."

"Don't lie," growled Salust's coarse voice. "Marda sent him to see your blind pet."

"Pet!" hissed Nymos, pulling Agis away from the opening. "I'll show them who's a pet!"

The reptile turned his hand toward the rooftop, preparing to cast a spell. The air beneath his palm began to quiver, then a surge of energy, barely visible to the naked eye, rose into his hand. Although it appeared Nymos was drawing his magic from the ground beneath the building, Agis knew that was not the case. Most sorcerers could tap Athas's life-force only through plant life. The power for the reptile's magic came not from the land, but from the ratany hedge along the edge of the bay. The ground, and the building which sat upon it, were only the medium through which the energy passed.

From the room below, Agis heard the sound of an open hand striking the innkeeper's face. "Where have you hidden the Tyrian?" demanded the templar.

"The roof," replied the innkeeper. "Nymos sleeps up there."

Nymos continued to draw the energy for his spell. Agis was surprised, for if the reptile took too much power, the ratany would wither and die. The ground holding the roots of the plants would become sterile, staying barren until the blood and sweat of hundreds of slaves restored the soil. Despite the length of time the jozhal spent drawing his power, however, Agis knew he would not destroy the hedge. The Veiled Alliance was dedicated to preventing such desecrations, and no member of the group would do such a thing lightly.

The top of the ladder jiggled as someone began to ascend. Nymos closed his hand, cutting the flow of magical energy into his body. He grabbed a pinch of silt and spit on it, then daubed the mixture onto the corner of the hole. At the same time, he uttered his incantation. The dab expanded into a sheet of orange clay and sealed the opening, drawing a muffled cry of surprise from below.

"That should hold them," said Nymos, motioning for Agis to follow him.

The sorcerer led him to the other side of the roof, where a bone ring had been set into the wall, with one end of a coiled rope tied into it. As Nymos threw the cord over the side, a series of dull thumps sounded from the clay sheet blocking the opening to the roof.

"Always knew I'd have to leave in a hurry," the jozhal said, tucking his cane under his arm. "We don't have much time before they hack through my stopper."

Agis grabbed Nymos's arm and did not let him climb onto the rope. "One moment," he whispered, peering into the cramped lane below.

The sorcerer's rope hardly seemed necessary, for the alley was half-clogged by drifts of silt that would serve to cushion any fall. A single, hard-packed path ran down the street, winding its way past dust heaps, rubbish piles, and the few back entrances that determined shopkeepers kept clear. In one direction, the trail led deeper into the harbor district, a maze of lanes similar to the one below.

The alley ran about fifty yards in the other direction before opening onto the harborside street, where the hulking figure of a half-giant blocked the exit. The brute towered almost as high as the roofs surrounding him, with a helmet of albino kank shell covering his head. For armor he wore a corselet of bleached leather, leaving his loins concealed by nothing more than a dingy gray skirt. He carried only one weapon, a bone club spiked with obsidian shards.

"Which way are we going?" Agis asked.

The sorcerer hesitated before answering. "I'm not really sure," he said. "It's been years since I've been off this roof."

"Then how are we going to find our ship?" Agis demanded, watching the half-giant lumber down the alley.

"I've heard that it's docked in front of the Red Mekillot."

"Which is where?"

"Just down the street from the Blue Cloud, which is around the corner from the Gray King, which is two blocks past the—"

"Just go—but not toward the harborside street," Agis said, releasing the jozhal's arm. "There's a guard coming from there."

Nymos nodded, then climbed onto the rope. Agis hazarded a glance back toward the center of the roof. The clay stopper remained in place, but the sound of the templars hacking at it had grown less muffled. He summoned the spiritual strength to use the Way. As before on the quay, the energy came to him slowly, and the noble began to worry that his pursuers would clear the plug before he was ready to attack.

The half-giant's voice drew Agis's attention back to the alley. "In the king's name, stop!"

The order boomed through the narrow lane like thunder, shaking the dust off the walls and causing a four-foot rubbish slug to slither out from beneath a pile of trash. The half-giant broke into a run, his massive legs spraying plumes of silvery dust into the air as he plowed through silt drifts.

Nymos's feet touched the ground, and the jozhal turned away, sprinting down the alley as fast as a kank, waving his cane back and forth to detect unexpected obstacles. Had Agis not known better, he would have sworn the reptile could see.

"Stop!" the half-giant boomed, smashing his spiked club into the back wall of a tackle shop. The blow knocked a melon-sized hole in the clay bricks.

Agis glanced back at the center of the roof and saw a lump of clay fly up from the plug, then he jumped into the alley. He landed in a pile of silt, sinking to his waist and sending a billow of dust boiling across the lane. The noble waded out of the drift, his legs burning with the effort and his lungs choking on the cloud of loess. Once he was free, he did not turn to follow Nymos, but faced the sorcerer's pursuer.

The half-giant shifted his dull eyes from the fleeing sorcerer to the Tyrian, then rushed forward with a renewed burst of speed. To Agis, he resembled nothing quite so much as a rampaging dust spirit. The massive guard was lost from the waist down in a roiling curtain of silt, with each step sending silvery columns of loess shooting up past his head.

Agis focused his attention on the dust still billowing around his own feet.

The half-giant stopped at Agis's side and reached down toward the noble. "Got you now," he growled, keeping his club ready in the other hand.

"No, I have you," Agis replied, dodging the clumsy lunge.

He used the Way to inject his spiritual energy into

the whirling cloud of dust at his feet, then dove away. The small whirlwind increased tenfold, swallowing the half-giant in gray whorls and filling the alley with the shrill whistle of a gale-force wind. The guard roared in anger as the storm swept him off his feet. He crashed into the back wall of the Furled Sail, spraying Agis with shards of brick and filling the air with more dust.

The noble sprinted down the alley after Nymos, coughing and choking. Behind him, the giant flailed about madly, smashing holes into walls and trying to dodge away from the suffocating whirlwind that had engulfed him. His efforts were in vain, for the maelstrom followed him wherever he went.

Agis glanced over his shoulder, worried that the templars would be coming after him. To his relief, he saw that their task would not be easy. His whirlwind had engulfed the entire tavern, rendering it as impossible for them to see him as it was for him to see the building.

The noble turned his attention to catching Nymos. As he had hoped, it was a simple matter to track the sorcerer. The morning was still young, and not many feet had trod the back alleys. Agis soon picked out the jozhal's three-clawed footprints, then followed them through the maze of crumbling shanties that constituted the harbor district.

It quickly became apparent that Nymos had no clear idea of where he was going. The jozhal's tracks often doubled back on themselves, or circled around three sides of a block before continuing down the same lane that he had been in originally. At times, the trail became so confused that Agis could not follow it, and he would give a coin to a dirt-smudged child or grimy-faced mother in return for telling him which way the reptile had gone. On several occasions, he even asked directions of someone who told him that Nymos had asked how to reach a particular inn or tavern.

Finally Agis emerged from the shanty warren at the edge of the harborside road. Across the street lay a long wharf, along which rested six sloops with towering masts and huge sails furled on their yardarms. Slaves were busily laboring at each ship, unloading building stone, timber, wool, and even a flock of erdlus—tall, flightless birds with sharp beaks and huge legs.

Near the end of the dock, a two-masted caravel hovered on the surface of the bay. Its square sails hung unfurled and flapping in the breeze, ready to be drawn tight. The figures of more than a dozen men crawled over the rigging, making the ship ready to sail. The helmsman was looking down the quay, as if awaiting some signal to set the craft in motion.

Nymos was nowhere in sight, his tracks lost in the hundreds of others crisscrossing the road.

"I'm given to know yer lookin' for a ship," said a gravelly voice at Agis's side.

The noble turned to face the speaker and found himself looking into the savage eyes of a tarek female, as powerfully built as a mul and with arms so long the knuckles dragged in the dust. The tarek had a square, big-boned head, with a sloping forehead and a massive brow ridge. Sharp fangs filled her domed muzzle, while her flat nose ended in a pair of red, flaring nostrils. From the lobes of her barbed ears hung three copper hoops, a substantial exhibition of wealth for this part of the city—and one that suggested the woman was the match for any cutthroat who might take it into his head to steal the prized metal. She wore a filthy silken breechcloth with a broad belt around her waist, and her four breasts were covered by nothing but a leather harness holding several bone daggers.

"At the moment, I'm looking for a blind jozhal," Agis replied cautiously.

The tarek nodded toward the caravel. "Nymos's aboard," she said, slipping a hand inside Agis's cloak and reaching for his purse.

The noble clamped a hand around the tarek's arm, but did not have the strength to prevent her from plucking the sack off his belt. "I don't lack the skills to protect my wealth," Agis warned.

"And I don't lack the strength to take it," sneered the tarek, pulling the purse out. "But that's not what I'm about. Before I take ye on, I'll have a look to make sure ye can afford me ship."

She opened the sack and peered inside, then raised an approving eyebrow. "Kester's my name." She plucked fifteen silver coins from the bag, then handed it back to Agis. "This covers the first week."

"That's rather expensive," Agis answered, not closing his purse. "In fact, it's outrageous."

"It is," Kester assured him, slipping the coins into the purse hanging on her belt. "But ye won't be hiring any other boat to follow the king's fleet to the isle of Lybdos."

"I suppose not," Agis replied, closing his purse. "I trust you're worth it."

"Some say I am—and some say I'm a pirate," she replied, leading the way across the street.

"Which is it?" Agis asked. "After what I've just paid you, I deserve to know."

The tarek shrugged. "I never know from one day to the next."

No sooner had they set foot on the dock than a streak of blinding light sizzled past the noble's shoulder, striking a nearby sloop. A deafening crack rolled over the quay, and the ship's mast collapsed in a rain of splinters. Agis and Kester hit the ground, surrounded by screaming slaves. Together, they rolled to their backs, facing the harborside street as they returned to their feet.

Across the way stood the female templar and her colleague. The traitorous sailor, Salust, was just stepping out of the alley from which Agis had come. A few yards behind him followed several half-giant guards.

"Seize that man!" yelled the female templar, pointing at Agis. "I command it in the name of King Andropinis!"

Kester looked at the noble and raised her heavy brow. "Nymos didn't say ye were wanted by the king."

Seeing that there were too many opponents to disable with the Way alone, the noble reached for his sword. The tarek lashed out with her gangling arm and caught the noble's hand before he could draw. "A wise man'd leave that sheathed."

Agis fixed his eyes on Kester's face, summoning the energy to use the Way. "I see you've chosen pirate today," the noble replied.

An indignant frown flashed across Kester's face, but the tarek kept her eyes turned toward the templars and made no response.

Salust slipped between the templars. "The bounty is mine," he said, pointing at Kester. "I'm not splitting it with that smuggler."

Kester snarled at the man, then motioned for the templars to come forward. "If there's a reward, I'll be wantin' my share."

"And you shall have it," said the male templar.

He and his companion started up the quay, accompanied by the bitterly complaining Salust. The trio's half-giant escorts started to follow, but the woman signaled them to wait on the street.

"We have things under control," said the sour-faced templar, picking her way past a heap of building stone. "You'll just be in the way."

Kester abruptly released Agis's hand, then pulled a dagger from her chest harness. "I'll take the woman!" she hissed.

With a flick of her wrist, the tarek sent the dagger sailing straight to the templar's throat. The woman clasped her hands around the wound and dropped, gurgling, to the ground.

Even as she fell, Agis reached for one of Kester's daggers. The noble had no delusions about being able to throw a dagger accurately over such a distance, but he had other means of delivering the blade. After pulling the weapon from the tarek's chest harness, the noble tossed the knife at the second templar, then used the Way to guide its path. The dagger took its victim in the same place the tarek's blade had taken the female.

Salust paled and started to back away. At the same time, the half-giants waiting on the street screamed in fury, then stepped onto the quay. They did not rush, however. The half-giants were too large to run without the risk of tripping over a slave or stack of cargo.

"Thanks for standing by me," Agis said.

"Ye paid me already," the tarek replied in a gruff voice. She pulled another dagger from her harness. "Next time, I won't be so fast to take yer silver."

With that, she threw her weapon at Salust. The

blade sank deep into the sailor's breast. He collapsed, clutching at the leg of a passing half-giant. The brute angrily shook the dying man off, then hurled his club at Kester. The tarek ducked easily, and the big cudgel bounced off the hull of a nearby ship.

Agis drew his sword, bracing himself to meet the half-giants.

Kester grabbed him by the arm, "No need to fight," she said. "Those oafs can't catch the likes of us."

"Then why'd you kill Salust?" Agis said, glancing over his shoulder. Slaves and dockmasters were cringing in terror as the half-giants stepped over them, shoving cargo off the pier and cursing in anger.

"Never trusted him," she said, pulling the noble down the quay at a sprint.

They dodged past a stack of baled wool, pushed their way through a screeching flock of erdlus, then they were running for Kester's caravel. As they came closer to the ship, the noble saw that it carried a dozen ballistae and catapults on each side.

As they passed beneath the stern, the noble gestured at the weaponry. "Why all the siege engines?"

"Giants," answered Kester. She grabbed a thick rope dangling from the stern and handed it to Agis, then took another for herself. "Make way, Perkin!" she called as she began to climb. "Set a course for Lybdos, and be quick about it."

"Not Lybdos," Agis corrected, almost losing his grip on the rope as the caravel lurched into motion. "First, we go up-estuary a few miles."

Kester scowled at him. "That's no good," she said. "After what we just did, I don't fancy sneaking back past Balic. And the fleet's already got a lead on us. Every hour's costly."

"It doesn't matter. Before we leave, I have a promise

to keep," Agis said, throwing an arm over the gunnel. "Besides, with a little luck, a friend of mine just might be able to stop the fleet cold."

"If that's what you want," Kester said, dangling from her rope with one hand and using the other to push the noble over the railing. "But it'll cost extra."

FOUR

The Strait of Baza

To Tithian, the dusky shape to the *Silt Lion*'s leeward side did not appear to be a boulder. For one thing, it seemed to be moving parallel to the ship, and for another its profile resembled that of a massive head sitting atop a pair of colossal shoulders. Still, though the distance separating them was less than fifty yards, the king could not be sure of what he saw. For the fifth day straight, a heavy wind was ripping across the sea, lofting so much dust into the air that it was difficult to see clearly from the stern of the schooner to the bow.

Tithian turned to the ship's mate, who was holding a large cone of solid glass to his eyes. "What's that over there?" the king asked, indicating the direction in which he had been looking.

"A giant," the mate reported. "But don't worry. We're in the Strait of Baza. As soon as we pass into deeper silt, he won't be able to follow." The catch in the young man's voice belied his anxiety.

"Let me have the king's eye," Tithian said, ripping

the cone of glass from the sailor's hands.

"But the ship's blind without it, King Tithian," the sailor objected. "The dust is shallow here!"

Ignoring the mate's complaint, Tithian pulled the dust-shields off his eyes, replacing the grimy lenses with the broad end of the cone. He pointed the tip at the shape he had been watching. Thanks to the magic Andropinis had instilled in the glass, the silt haze no longer obscured Tithian's vision.

The thing was definitely a giant, with long braids of greasy hair hanging from his head and tufts of coarse bristle sprouting on the gravelly skin of his shoulders. His face seemed a peculiar mix of human and rodent, with a sloped forehead, dangling ears, deepset eyes, and flat nose that ended in a pair of cavernous nostrils. A dozen jagged incisors protruded from beneath his upper lip, and a mosslike beard hung over his recessed chin.

"There can only be one giant that ugly," Tithian growled. "Fylo!" He turned to the ship's mate and ordered, "Stop the ship!"

Navarch Saanakal, high templar of the king's fleets, stepped to the Tyrian's side. Even for a half-elf, he was tall and slender, towering two full heads over Tithian. Beneath the grimy glass of his dust-shields, the commander's eyes were pale brown and as fiery as embers. He had lean, sharp cheeks and a bony nose, but a silk scarf hid the rest of his face, protecting his airway from the dust.

"The *Silt Lion* is no dingy, Your Highness," he said with forced courtesy. "We can't stop her at a moment's notice." He took the king's eye and returned it to the mate. "If you please, Sachet needs the eye to guide the ship."

"Then bring us around," Tithian ordered, pointing

into the haze on the leeward side of the schooner. "I must speak to that giant!"

Saanakal rolled his eyes. "In the Sea of Silt, you avoid giants, Your Highness," he said. "Failing that, you run for deep silt, or fight if you must—but you don't talk to them."

"This giant belongs to me," Tithian said, putting his dust-shields back in place. "I must find out what he's doing here. He's supposed to be taking care of an important matter outside Balic."

"Very well," Navarch Saanakal sighed. To the mate, he said, "Bring the *Silt Lion* around. Have the rest of the fleet form a semicircle with us at the center."

As the mate relayed the orders, Tithian looked over the gunnel. He could see nothing but a pearly miasma of dust, with no demarcation between the surface of the sea and the air. Even the sun seemed half lost, its position marked only by a faint halo of orange light.

Despite the poor visibility, the king continued to search the murk for Fylo. No matter how he looked at it, the giant's presence meant trouble. Either the oaf had killed Agis and somehow tracked Tithian to the Strait of Baza, or he had realized that his "friend" was not coming back and released the noble.

The king didn't know which to hope for. If Agis lived, he would still be following, no doubt determined to make Tythian answer for the raid on Kled. Sooner or later, the noble would catch up and, probably, they would fight.

The king did not want that. His memories of their youthful camaraderie remained too vivid. Tithian could still hear a teenaged Agis pleading with him not to sneak out of the academy for a night of debauchery, then trying to comfort him after the master ordered him to pack his robes and leave the grounds. Later, after Tithian had betrayed his birth class by joining Kalak's templars, the noble had been with several young lords when they happened upon him in the Elven Market. One insult had led to another until the meeting came to blows, but Agis had fought on the young templar's side, saving him a severe beating. Then there was the time after his brother's death. . . .

Tithian could not allow himself to think of that, not until he knew whether or not he would have to kill Agis. He squeezed his eyes shut and forced the memories from his head, then looked to the ship's mate.

"Can you see my giant?" he asked.

"No," came the reply. "We're too far past."

Tithian turned to berate Navarch Saanakal for allowing Fylo to disappear, but the high templar was ready with a response. "With twenty ships looking for him, we won't have any trouble finding your giant again." To the mate, the half-elf said, "Ready the catapult slaves, all ships to do the same."

"I don't want Fylo killed," Tithian objected. "Not yet, anyway."

"I have no intention of killing him, but he may be disinclined to talk," said the high templar. "Until we have persuaded him to behave, perhaps you should join Ictinis. The floater's pit is the safest place on the command deck."

The high templar pointed to a shallow cockpit in front of the helm, where a gray-haired man named Ictinis sat with his palms resting on a table-sized dome of polished obsidian. Although he had the haggard aspect of a pauper, the gold rings on his fingers betrayed his true status. Ictinis was a shipfloater, a mindbender especially trained to use the Way to keep the schooner from sinking into the dust. He kept the ship afloat by sending his spiritual energy through the dome and into the hull. The task was a difficult one, requiring both physical endurance and psychic strength.

Tithian slipped into the chaperon's seat, a small bench where the floater sat while training his apprentices. During the last five days, the king had passed much of his time in this seat, learning Ictinis's art. He was not so much interested in keeping the ship afloat as in understanding how the dome worked, for it resembled the obsidian balls sorcerer-kings used to tap into the life-force of their subjects when they cast their most powerful magical spells.

Having begun his study of sorcery only five years ago, Tithian did not yet know any enchantments so potent that he could not cast them through the conventional means. But the thought had occurred to him that he could increase the effectiveness of his limited abilities by using an orb. Besides, he suspected that the sooner he learned to control the flow of mystic energy through obsidian, the easier it would be for him when the time came to learn the most powerful spells.

Ictinis suddenly looked up from the dome, his red-rimmed eyes opened wide in alarm. At first, Tithian feared that the old man had fallen ill, but the ship-floater twisted his head toward Saanakal's station to relay a message that he had received through the dome.

"Captain Phaedras reports that as he began his turn, he saw a wall of giants blocking the exit to the strait, High One," said Ictinis.

"What type?" demanded Saanakal. "How many?"

Ictinis turned his gaze back to the dome. His eyes glazed over, then he called, "Perhaps fifty, all beast-head."

"Beasthead?" Tithian asked.

"The giants are divided into two tribes, the human-oid and the beasthead," explained the sailor at the helm, an anonymous young woman whose face remained hidden beneath her dust-shields and silt-scarf. Although her voice was calm, she clenched the wheel so tightly that the veins showed in her fore-arms.

Saanakal scowled and peered into the dusty haze ahead. "So many," he said, shaking his head. "They must have come from Lybdos."

Tithian climbed out of the cockpit. "What for?"

"To ambush us. We're only a couple of days from Lybdos, and the beastheads don't allow visitors to that island," the high templar explained. "Now I must ask you to return to the floater's pit."

Tithian shook his head. "I prefer to see what is hap-pening."

"Then stand aside," snapped Saanakal, gesturing toward the gunnel. "We've a battle to fight."

Tithian started to object to the rude treatment, then held his tongue and did as he was asked. There would always be time after the battle to chastise the high templar.

Saanakal looked to the ship's mate. "Terrain?"

"Seven low islands to port," he said, peering to the left side of the bow. He swept the king's eye to the right, then added, "Scattered boulders—no, make that giants—a half-mile to starboard. Another fifty, I would guess." He lowered the glass cone and looked at Saanakal. "They're closing on our flank."

"Chain the catapult slaves to their weapons," said Saanakal, his voice strangely calm and quiet. "Have the wizard brought up and tell him to prepare the Balican fire."

The ship's mate blanched and swallowed hard. "As you wish, High One."

While the mate relayed the order to the rest of the ship, Saanakal spoke to Ictinis. "Close the line. The *Lirr Song* is to lead a run for the islands, but no one's to break formation. All ships are to use Balican fire in their catapults."

"Yes, High One," replied Ictinis. He returned his attention to the black dome, and his eyes grew vacant.

Tithian went to the quarterdeck rail to watch the battle preparations, hoping the crew would keep the ship afloat long enough for him to find Fylo. The king did not know what part the big oaf had played in this ambush, but it could be no coincidence that the giant happened to be crossing the Strait of Baza at this moment.

On the main deck ahead, a half-dozen crews were laboring to ready their catapults. The skein cords creaked in eerie protest as powerful dwarven slaves pushed against long levers, struggling to wind the cup arms down and lock them into place. With each weapon stood a templar overseer, complicating the dwarves' task by popping his whip over their bald heads and yelling for them to work faster.

Behind each catapult rested a stone vat, half-filled with grainy powder, while the ship's wizard, an old man with a bushy head of gray hair, stood at the far end of the deck. With him were two assistants, one pushing a cart-mounted tub of black sludge and the other carrying a long ladle.

Under the sorcerer's direction, the first assistant stopped his cart, and the second poured a ladle of sludge into the vat of powder behind the first catapult. The wizard turned his palm toward the deck in preparation for casting a spell. The process took a little longer than usual, for few plants grew in the Sea of Silt, and most of the energy had to come from a distant island.

When the sorcerer finally had enough energy, he uttered his spell over the concoction. A fiery yellow flash shot into the air, licking the yardarms and setting the sails to smoking. A foul, mordant odor drifted back to the quarterdeck, and the mixture began to burn with an unnatural golden light.

As the wizard moved to the next vat, Tithian turned his attention to the sea near the ship. The giants were still screened by blowing dust, but he could see that the Balican fleet had already closed formation. Off the stern, the *Wyvern* had come up so close that a strong man could have leaped from its bowsprit onto the deck where Tithian stood. Its foredeck ballistae, with their tree-sized harpoons already nocked, were more clearly visible than those on the foredeck of his own ship.

The wizard kindled his fire in the last of the stone vats, then went to the foredeck to await battle among the ballistae. The catapult crews locked their firing arms into place and stood by with bone ladles in hand, ready to load their weapons as soon as the giants were visible. The rest of the sailors, except those needed to work the rigging, stood in the center of the main deck. Half carried long barbed lances, while the other half, serving as a fire corps, held sacks full of dust. The flapping sails and crackle of Balican fire were the only audible sounds.

"Captain Phaedras is firing his catapults." There was a short pause, then Ictinis completed his report. "The *Lirr Song* has gone down."

"So fast?" Tithian gasped.

Saanakal nodded, and the ship fell even more silent

than before word had come of the *Lirr Song*'s fate.
Tithian stepped over to the gunnel and peered into
the featureless haze. "Tell me, Saanakal, how many
giants will we take with us?"

"A handful," the high templar admitted, his voice
emotionless.

"And the fleet won't survive?" Tithian asked.

"Not realistically," Saanakal answered. "We have
shallow silt all around, so we can't maneuver away
from our attackers—and no one has ever survived a
battle with a hundred giants."

From the haze ahead came the muffled thumps of
several catapult arms striking their crossbeams. A
half-dozen streaks of yellow light arced through the
sky, bursting into fiery showers as they started to
descend. By the time the spray reached the surface of
the dust, it had coalesced into a single curtain of
golden flame. Across the distance rumbled muted
roars and bellows, more akin to the yowls of wild
beasts than the cries of manlike beings.

"The *Giant's Bane* is taking a charge."

The shipfloater had barely finished his report
before the mate called, "Boulders!"

Instantly, Saanakal yelled, "Catapults!"

Tithian spun around in time to see the silhouettes
of a dozen giants wading toward the *Silt Lion*. He saw
the heads of a dozen different beasts—birds, lions,
wyverns, kanks, and more—resting on the shoulders
of manlike giants, then a barrage of stones came flying out of the haze. Most dropped short of the ship,
sending silvery plumes of dust shooting into the sky.
Four of the boulders found their marks, sending a
series of thunderous crashes resounding through the
decks.

One stone shattered a foredeck ballista. As its

tightly wound skeins sprang loose, the cords knocked half the weapon's crew over the side. Two more boulders hit the main deck, opening kank-sized holes in the planking and dropping a handful of reinforcements into the hold below. The last smashed a vat of Balican fire. Five dwarven slaves screamed in pain as yellow flame splashed over their shoulders, and small puddles of burning, syrupy liquid formed on the deck.

The fire corps rushed forward, pouring their bags of silt over the flames to smother them. At the same time, the catapult crews pulled their release cords to return the giants' barrage. Even the dwarves who had been burned unleashed their missiles, still howling in agony.

The Balican fire streaked away from the ship with a loud sizzle, lighting the sky and filling the air with such a caustic stench that Tithian choked on the acrid fumes. As the fiery balls reached their zenith, the ship's wizard raised his gnarled finger and cried, "Shower!"

The globes exploded, spraying burning gobs over everything beneath them. For a moment, all was quiet, then a portion of the sea itself erupted into fire and greasy black smoke. A chorus of pained screeches rolled across the silt and broke against the hull. Then, as the flames slowly sank beneath the dust, the cries died away.

When the smoke cleared, the twelve giants that had attacked the *Silt Lion* were gone. The reinforcements stopped battling the fire long enough to give a rousing cheer. The dwarven crews simply began to pry their catapult arms down again, though the five who had been burned earlier lacked the strength to succeed—no matter how hard their templar overseer lashed their charred backs.

Tithian turned to Saanakal. "I thought you said we were doomed?"

"Our wizard's timing was remarkable—this time," the high templar said, pointing over the stern. "But when his good fortune runs out, so does ours."

When Tithian looked in the direction Saanakal had indicated, a cold hand closed around his heart. In the heat of the *Silt Lion*'s exchange, he had lost track of the rest of the battle. Now, he found himself looking on in horror as eight giants charged the *Wyvern*. Each carried a large battering ram in his hands.

The *Wyvern*'s foredeck ballistae fired. One tree-sized lance lodged in the breast of a goat-headed giant. Another harpoon pierced the scaly throat of a serpent-headed giant. Both attackers fell immediately, vanishing into the silt as if they had never been there. The remaining six hit the ship with their rams, opening great breaches in the hull and shaking the masts with the force of the impact.

Dust poured through the holes in rivers, but the shipfloater continued to hold the schooner aloft. Dozens of sailors rushed forward to thrust their lances at the giants, while the catapult crews used their ladles to fling Balican fire over the side.

Neither effort was to much avail, for the giants slapped the lances aside and easily dodged the clumsy attempts to pelt them with flame. They pushed upward on the rams with which they had punctured the hull. The schooner, still levitated by the shipfloater, tipped easily. Men, catapults, cargo, and everything else not firmly attached to the decks went tumbling into the silt. After the shipfloater and his dome fell away, the *Wyvern* itself settled into the dust.

When it was about three quarters buried, it touched bottom and stopped sinking. Survivors immediately swarmed to the portion of hull still showing above the dust, but it was clear they would not live much longer. As the *Silt Lion* sailed away from the wreck, the giants were using their rams like clubs to smash the hull into tiny bits.

Tithian turned to Saanakal. "Cancel the order to flee toward the islands," he said. "Tell each ship to engage the giants at close quarters. They're to move the vats of Balican fire to the gunnels and dump them over the side as the giants tip their ships."

The high templar stared at him as if he were mad. "That's suicide!" he gasped. "Without a ship—"

"The giants will sink our ships anyway. We may as well take as many of our enemies with us as we can," Tithian replied. He looked to the ship's mate and helmsman, then added, "Does anyone else prefer a fighting death to that of a coward?"

The helmsman was the first to reply. "I will follow your orders, High One," she said, speaking to Saanakal. "But I prefer a fighting death."

Several junior officers added their support, which only angered Saanakal. "Silence!" he ordered. He switched his gaze back to Tithian. "King Andropinis commanded me to follow your instructions, so I have yielded to your wishes up to now. But what you ask is madness. I won't do it."

"That would make you a mutineer," responded Tithian. He allowed his hand to drift toward his satchel, but did not put it inside.

"Refusing to squander my fleet is not mutiny," countered the high templar.

"Your fleet will sink anyway," Tithian said, stepping toward Saanakal. "What is there to be afraid of?

Dying an honorable death?"

"There is always the hope—"

"Truly?" Tithian scoffed. He looked to Ictinis and asked, "How many ships remain?"

"Eleven," answered the shipfloater. "No, now only ten."

"Your schooners are sinking like stones, Navarch. The only men who stand a chance of surviving are those who can cross the silt without a ship." Tithian glanced at the young officers crowding the quarterdeck, then asked, "Who would that be? Your sorcerers, your shipfloaters, and perhaps your captains?"

The high templar's face darkened to an angry crimson, while bitter whispers of speculation rustled through the gathering of officers.

"I'm sure you have a magic ring or talisman that will see you to a safe place," Tithian pressed. Although he did not know whether or not Saanakal actually possessed such an item, it seemed a logical assumption—and that was what would matter to the crew. "Perhaps that's why you don't want to fight at close quarters. When the ship sinks, you can escape. But your magic won't save you if a giant grabs you."

"One more word and I'll have you launched from a catapult!" the high templar hissed. "Now return to the floater's pit and let me command the fleet!"

"So your crew can die while you escape?" Tithian replied, shaking his head. "No."

"Take this passenger below," Saanakal commanded, motioning for his first mate to obey the order.

Before the man could step forward, Tithian stared him straight in the eye. "Andropinis himself loaned me this fleet," he said. "By refusing to obey me, Navarch Saanakal is defying your king. Do you wish to join him in that?"

When the mate remained where he stood, the high templar cursed and reached for his dagger. "Enough!"

"I don't think so," said the first mate, grabbing Saanakal's wrist. "If I'm going to die, then I will do it as I have lived—at King Andropinis's pleasure."

With that, he handed the king's eye to the helmsman, then picked up the templar and pitched him over the side. Screaming in fear, Saanakal thrust a hand into the pocket of his robe. The dust swallowed him before he could withdraw the object hidden inside.

"Prepare yourselves to die like soldiers," Tithian said, giving his crew an approving nod. "And take us into battle."

As the astonished officers obeyed, Tithian had his shipfloater relay his attack orders to the surviving ships. Next, he took the king's eye from the helmsman and began to scan the haze.

"What are you looking for?" she asked.

"My giant," Tithian replied.

It did not take the king long to find what he was after. Within a few minutes, he saw Fylo's ugly form leading an attack against another ship. The giants had already thrown their boulders and were plowing forward through the silt, their rams cradled under their arms.

As Tithian watched, the ship fired its catapults, but the wizard mistimed his command word and dropped the flames behind the giants. Nevertheless, the king could see that the battle was far from over. Vats of Balican fire were lined up all along the gunnel, ready to be dumped on the attackers, and the ballista crews were holding their fire until the giants came closer.

Tithian gave the king's eye to a junior officer. "Which ship is that?"

"The *King's Lady*," he replied.

"Good," he said, pointing at Fylo's ugly face. "Do you see that giant?"

"The one whose head looks sort of human?"

"Yes. Keep us pointed toward him," Tithian replied. Next, he turned to the shipfloater. "Tell the *King's Lady* to hold her attacks. We're coming alongside and may be able to save her from this bunch."

For the next few moments, Tithian watched in grim silence as the *Silt Lion* bore down on its targets. The giants were approaching the *King's Lady* cautiously, suspicious of the lack of resistance from the ship. Nevertheless, they were close enough to hoist their rams and charge at any moment.

"Captain Saba asks permission to defend his ship," reported the shipfloater.

"No!" Tithian spat.

"But we'll never get there in time," objected the helmsman. "If they don't resist—"

"The *King's Lady* is sunk anyway!" snapped Tithian. "And I don't want anyone killing my giant—not yet."

Several of the ship's officers exchanged skeptical glances, then one ventured to ask, "Why not?"

"He must be the one who set up this ambush, and I want to know why—before I deal a very special punishment out to him," the king answered. He looked back to Ictinis. "Tell Captain Saba this: when the giants hit his ship, he'll be protected by the king of Tyr's magic—but only if his counterattacks don't interfere."

The shipfloater sent the message.

A moment later, Tithian and his officers watched as Fylo and his giants crashed into the *King's Lady*.

Unhampered by any resistance from the ship, their charge hit with such force that it ripped the foredeck off the rest of the ship. The ballistae discharged harmlessly and the vats of Balican fire toppled, instantly creating an inferno on the decks. Trailing long tails of flame, sailors and dwarves leaped over the sides, their agonized screams falling silent as they disappeared into the dust.

A burly man stepped toward Tithian, his silt-scarf hanging loosely around his neck. His jaw was set, and his puffy cheeks were pale with the horror of what he had just witnessed. "You said you'd save them!" he gasped.

"Come now," Tithian replied. As he spoke, he turned his palm to the deck, using his body to shield it from view as he drew the energy for a spell. "You heard me say that the *King's Lady* was lost. You knew I was lying to Captain Saba when I said I would protect him."

"When I tossed Navarch Saanakal overboard, it seems I traded a coward for a liar," growled the first mate, stepping toward Tithian. "You said we were going to kill giants—not protect yours!"

"This fleet has already killed more giants under me than it would have under Saanakal!"

With that, he collected a pinch of dust from the gunnel and threw it into the air. He spoke his incantation, then the mate, officers, and the helmsman all dropped to the deck, their eyes closed tight behind their dust-shields. Without a steady hand on the helm, the ship veered toward the burning *King's Lady*.

As the bowsprit of Tithian's schooner touched the blazing wreck, the ship's wizard leaped off the bow. He flew a hundred yards in the direction of the island chain before a giant swatted him down.

The jib sail of the *Silt Lion* burst into flames, and smoke began to roll over the main deck. Sailors and catapult slaves alike cried out in alarm and looked up to see what was wrong, then the whole ship shuddered as the bow crashed into the side of the *King's Lady*.

"Time to go," Tithian said.

The king drew the energy for another spell and used his magic to levitate himself. Taking care to stay away from any giant that could bat him down, he drifted out over the stern. Behind him, the *Silt Lion's* vats of Balican fire began to ignite, sending column after column of golden flame shooting into the pearly sky. Within moments, the schooner's wreck could not be distinguished from that of the *King's Lady*.

Tithian quickly identified Fylo's distinctive form at the other end of the conflagration. The giant stood near the detached bow of the *King's Lady*, the one piece of the ship that was not in flames, laughing in childish delight as he used a yardarm to knock the last few survivors off the upended hull.

Tithian drifted forward through the smoke and haze. At the same time, the king took the precaution of withdrawing a small glass rod from his satchel, but he did not fully prepare the spell that would turn it into a lightning bolt. Until he learned how Fylo had come to be a part of this ambush, and what had happened to Agis, he had no intention of killing the giant.

Tithian stopped just out of Fylo's reach. "What are you doing here?" he demanded, yelling to make himself heard across the distance.

The giant stepped away from the wreck, raising his yardarm to swing at the king. "Traitor!"

Tithian dodged back. The huge club sank into the

silt with a muffled whump, raising a curtain of pearly dust.

"Why are you attacking your friend?" the king asked, resisting the urge to cast his spell.

Fylo narrowed his eyes, gauging the distance to his target, then shrugged and turned back to the bow of the *King's Lady*. "Tithian liar, not friend," he said, using his yardarm to push a dwarf into the silt. "Agis real friend."

"What does Agis have to do with this?" Tithian asked. He felt both relieved and angry, for the giant's comment implied that he had released the noble and not killed him. "You promised to guard him!"

"Make promise before Agis show real Tithian to Fylo," said the giant. "Then we go to Balic, and Agis tell Fylo about fleet going to Lybdos. He say 'Warn giants. Maybe they let Fylo live with them.'" The half-breed brought his pole down on a templar, crushing the man like a beetle. "Him right. Now Fylo can live on Lybdos—with beasthead friends."

Tithian could not contain himself. "What makes you think anyone could tolerate a hideous moron like you?"

His eyes bugging out in anger, Fylo threw his yardarm at Tithian. The king tried to dodge, but the pole glanced off his shoulder, sending a terrible ache shooting down his arm and knocking the glass rod from his hand. He plummeted toward the sea, barely regaining control of his body in time to prevent himself from plunging into the dust. Fylo was on him instantly, grasping Tithian tightly in his massive fingers and preventing the king from reaching into his satchel for another spell component.

"Agis like Fylo!" the giant snarled. "Beastheads like Fylo!"

Tithian shook his head sadly. "I'm sorry," he said. "But Agis is just using you. So are the beastheads. When all this is done, they'll send you away. Fylo will be alone, just like before."

"No!" Despite the retort, the giant looked crestfallen.

"Yes," Tithian insisted. "I'm the only one who could like you. Everyone else thinks you're ugly."

Fylo shook his head. "Tithian liar! Tithian do terrible things to his friends in Kled."

"Did Agis tell you that?" Tithian asked, continuing his ploy. "I guess it shouldn't surprise me. He's been jealous of me ever since I became king. But what really hurts, Fylo, is knowing you believe him."

The giant looked surprised. "It does?"

Tithian nodded. "More than you can know," he said. "One has so few friends when he's a king. I thought that you and I . . ." He let the sentence trail off, then lowered his eyes.

"Fylo think so, too—once," said the giant. He returned to the bow of the *King's Lady*, then plucked the last templar off the upturned hull and tossed the unfortunate fellow to the wind.

"What are you doing?" Tithian asked, alarmed.

"Agis warn Fylo you try another trick," the giant answered, squeezing the king so tightly that he could not draw breath. "Agis say leave you here."

"You can't betray me!"

"Fylo get even before he go to live on Lybdos," the giant chortled. "Goodbye, *friend*."

He flicked the king's head with his huge index finger, and Tithian felt himself settling into a gray haze.

FIVE

Old Friends

In the shallow trough between two dust swells lay the severed bow of a Balican schooner. It rested on its side, blanketed by a gray mantle of silt, its bowsprit rising into the air at a shallow angle. On the hull lay a man, fully exposed to the crimson sun and as still as the sea itself.

"There he is!" Agis cried.

The noble pointed toward the debris. Kester, standing with him and Nymos on the *Shadow Viper*'s quarterdeck, turned her heavy brow to the caravel's port side. Her eyes quickly fell on the wreckage, for the day was a calm one, almost barren of wind and more stifling than a kiln.

"Yer sure that's him?" the tarek asked.

Although the distance was too great to see the prone man's features clearly, Agis nodded. "I haven't seen any other survivors, and Fylo promised that he'd leave Tithian where I could find him." The caravel began to slide down the dust swell's slip face, and the noble added, "Bring us alongside."

The tarek shook her head. "He looks dead."

"Living or not, I'm taking him back to Tyr."

"Not on the *Shadow Viper*," said Kester. "Ye hired me to capture a live man, not a dead one. I'll not have his spirit plaguing me ship."

"Then I won't pay you for the trip home," the noble threatened.

"Ye *will* pay—or I'll set ye off over there!" She pointed at a scrub-covered island less than a mile away.

Agis shook his head. "Our agreement was that you'd help me capture Tithian—and it doesn't matter whether he's alive or dead."

Kester reached for a knife, but Nymos interposed himself between the tarek and the noble. "This is foolish," said the sorcerer, his blind eyes focused on neither of them. "Why don't we go and see what Tithian's condition is? If he's not drawing breath, then you can argue."

"A prudent suggestion," said Agis.

Kester scowled for a moment longer. Then she shrugged her shoulders. "I'll bring us about."

The tarek turned her attention to the main deck, where the ship's canvas hung furled to the yardarms. Twenty crewmen toiled along each gunnel, thrusting wooden poles, each as tall as a giant, into the silt alongside the ship. After the long rods touched the shallow strait's bottom, the haggard slaves marched sternward, pushing the caravel along at a mekillot's pace. To keep everyone in step, the first man in each line chanted a deep-throated dirge: "Push-ho, push-ho, push-ho or die."

As the two singers reached the quarterdeck, they changed the chant. "Stop ye, stop ye, time to rest, mate!"

Both lines of slaves halted and withdrew their poles from the dust. After everyone had stopped moving, the man at the front of each group cried, "Front now, front now, to work with ye!" This sent them all scurrying forward to plunge their poles into the dust and start over again.

When the *Shadow Viper*'s bow reached the bottom of the dust swell, Kester braced herself against the gunnel and yelled, "Hard to port, Perkin!"

The helmsman spun his wheel, and the slaves along the left gunnel withdrew their poles from the silt. The caravel pivoted so rapidly that Agis had to grab Nymos's arm to prevent the reptile from tumbling overboard. Despite the sharp turn, the noble could see that the bow would plow into the next dust swell before the ship completed the maneuver.

Growling in anger, Kester leaped past her ship-floater and took a long whip off the rail. She jumped down onto the main deck and savagely lashed at the men on the port side. Each time the scourge's tail popped, a slave howled in pain and a welt rose on his naked back.

"I said *hard to port!*" the tarek yelled.

The port-side slaves angled their poles forward and pushed, as though trying to move the ship backward. The *Shadow Viper*'s bow snapped around instantly, the bowsprit just missing the next dust swell. Kester continued to lash her crew members, cursing their slow response and making sure to open a cut on the back of every man in line.

Agis went down to Kester's side and laid a restraining hand on her whip. "Don't you think that's enough?" he asked. "It's bad enough to crew your ship with slaves, but they don't deserve such abuse."

Kester bared her fangs. "This is my ship," she

snarled. Her breath was rancid, for long journeys were difficult on the tarek's system. Instead of live lizards or snakes, she ate salted and dried meats—which were only slightly better for her than the moldering faro her human crew ate. Agis suspected that the tarek's diet fouled more than her digestive system, for Kester's temperament had been growing steadily worse since leaving Balic. "I'll run her as I like."

"Not while you're under my hire," Agis replied, taking the whip from the tarek's big hand.

"These men were convicts before they became slaves," said Nymos, speaking from the rail of the quarterdeck. His milky eyes were focused blankly in the air above Agis's head. "They deserve what Kester gives them—and they owe their lives to her."

"That's right," agreed Kester. "Every one of 'em would have had his heart cut out in the arena if not for my purse."

"Saving a man doesn't give you the right to brutalize him," countered the noble, returning to the quarterdeck with the whip. "I won't stand for it—not even from the captain of a ship."

Kester followed him. As he returned the whip to its peg, she pointed at the flotsam ahead and asked, "I suppose what ye've planned for your friend isn't brutal?"

The *Shadow Viper* was so close to the wreck that Agis could see Tithian lying on his face, his long braid of auburn hair coiled over one shoulder.

"I have nothing planned for Tithian, except to take him back to answer for his crimes," replied the noble.

"And to find out what he and Andropinis are doing," Nymos added. "Your aversion to brutality had better not keep you from loosening his tongue."

"There are other ways to make Tithian speak," replied Agis. "Besides, no amount of pain can make him tell the truth if he doesn't want to."

"Especially not if he's dead," added Kester. The tarek's eyes were fixed to the starboard of the *Shadow Viper's* bow, which was just passing alongside Tithian's motionless body. She allowed her ship to creep forward a few more yards, then barked, "Dead stop!"

The crewmen lifted their poles, then angled the long shafts forward and plunged them back into the dust. The caravel lurched to a stop, its quarterdeck just aft of the derelict. The starboard slaves peered down on the wreck in weary silence, studying Tithian's inert form.

Kester jumped off the quarterdeck and grabbed a long plank. She pushed it through a slot in the bottom of the gunnel, guiding it toward the wrecked bow. Motioning Agis to the plank, she said, "Ye be careful. Just because the silt's shallow and the hull rests on the bottom doesn't mean she won't shift. If ye fall in, there'll be nothing we can do to save ye."

"What about tying a rope around my waist?" Agis asked, climbing over the gunnel.

"I told ye once, I'll not have any corpses on me ship," Kester replied testily. "By the time we dragged ye back, yer lungs would be full of silt."

"Why don't you use the Way to fly or levitate?" suggested Nymos.

Agis shook his head, more to himself than to the blind sorcerer. "That's not one of the areas my meditations have led me to explore," he answered. "And the king's too heavy for me to move with other forms of the Way. If I want to take him back to Tyr, I'll have to walk over there and get him."

The noble turned his attention to the plank of

mekillot rib in front of him. It was about as wide as his shoulders and more than ten yards long, with a weathered surface the color of ivory. Below it lay a pearly layer of dust, so loosely packed that it looked more like an oasis mist than a silt bed.

The other end of the gangway rested near the mid-point of the derelict bow, which lay with a steep slant toward the aft end. Because of the angle, only one corner of Agis's plank rested firmly on the wreck. The other hung without support a few inches above the wooden hull.

Tithian lay on his belly in the center of the wreck, his satchel strapped across his chest and his face turned in the opposite direction. The king's auburn hair was matted with blood, and the golden diadem around his head had been badly dented by a blow.

Agis released his hold on the gunnel and shuffled forward, his heart pounding in fear each time the gangway wobbled. As he crossed the halfway point, the plank twisted under his weight and began to slip down the hull of the wreck. He dropped to his stomach to spread his weight out more evenly, then pulled himself the rest of the way across without rising. It seemed to take forever to reach the end, but when he finally did, he breathed a deep sigh of relief and crawled onto the bow.

A muffled groan rumbled up from the timbers. The aft end slowly tipped more steeply toward the sea. Tithian's motionless form slipped closer to the silt, and Agis nearly lost his balance. The noble scurried forward and caught the king by the shoulders, pulling him toward the bowsprit and stabilizing the wreck.

Agis shook Tithian's shoulder. "Wake up," he said. "You and I have places to go."

When there was no response, Agis rolled the king

onto his back. The body turned limply, with no hint of tension in the muscles. If not for the shallow rise and fall of his chest, Agis would have thought him dead. Tithian's eyes were sunken, and dried blood caked both cheeks. From between his cracked lips protruded a dun-colored tongue, hugely swollen with thirst and as dry as the Sea of Silt.

"Even from here, he looks as dead as a toppled giant," called Kester. "Push him into the silt and let's be gone. It's not wise to tarry in these parts."

"He's alive, more or less," Agis reported. He looking back to see Kester, Nymos, and half the crew standing along the gunnels. "It's just that I can't wake him."

"Wet his lips," suggested Nymos. "Thirst is a powerful incentive, even to an unconscious mind."

Since no waterskin lay in view, Agis opened the king's satchel and peered inside. Despite its bulky outward appearance, it was empty. The noble closed the bag, then looked back to the ship. "Throw me a waterskin."

Kester took a half-filled waterskin from a hook on the mainmast, then tossed it toward Agis. The heavy sack fell short of the noble's grasp and dropped on the king's chest with a dull thump. Tithian did not stir.

"If that didn't wake him, nothing will," said Kester. "Ye'll have to carry him. If we don't hurry, that wreck'll sink beneath ye."

Casting a wary eye toward the unsteady plank, Agis said, "Let me try Nymos's way first."

The noble sat down and cradled Tithian's head in his lap, then poured a small amount of water over the king's mouth. A few drops ran down Tithian's swollen tongue into his throat. He coughed violently, but did not open his eyes or show any other sign of waking.

Thirst and heat, Agis knew, could thicken a man's blood until he lost consciousness, but the noble did not think that was Tithian's problem. If that had been the case, the king's skin would have been flushed and clammy, instead of sun-blistered and peeling. It seemed more likely he had suffered a concussion from the blow that had bent his crown and split his scalp open.

Agis pulled a tangle of blood-matted hair away from the crown and gently tried to remove the diadem. The circlet moved only a fraction of an inch before the dented section snagged on the edge of the king's wound. A distressed groan escaped Tithian's lips, and he instinctively tried to pull his head away from the noble's grasp. Encouraged by this development, Agis slipped a finger under the bent diadem and began to pry it off.

A gaunt hand flashed up from the king's side, seizing the noble's wrist. "Don't touch my crown!" croaked Tithian, his broken fingernails digging into Agis's flesh. Although his eyes had opened, they remained glazed and unfocused.

Agis released the diadem. "I think you'd return from the dead to keep this paltry circlet on your head."

Tithian released the noble's arm, struggling to focus his eyes on Agis's face. "You!" he gasped weakly. "Traitor!"

Agis dumped a stream of water into Tithian's mouth. "I'm not the traitor here."

The king choked, then managed to swallow. "You cost me a fleet!" he sputtered, his thick-tongued voice barely more than a whisper.

As Tithian struggled to push himself upright, his eyes rolled back in their sockets, and he groaned in pain. He raised his fingers to his smashed diadem, then asked, "How *did* you make that fool Fylo betray me? I know you didn't use the Way, because I tried that myself."

"Fylo's wise enough to know the truth when he sees it," Agis replied, handing the waterskin to Tithian. "Now drink. It would be better if you're still alive when I return you to Tyr."

Tithian accepted the skin and raised it to his lips. After he had taken a half-dozen gulps, he said, "I've no wish to return to Tyr at the moment."

"That's not your choice," replied Agis, laying a hand on his sword's hilt. "I'm taking you back to the city."

At the same time, the noble opened the internal pathway to his spiritual energy, preparing to defend himself with the Way. His palace spies had been keeping him informed of Tithian's progress as both a mindbender and a sorcerer, and the noble knew the king would be a formidable opponent if it came to a fight.

Tithian shrugged. "I thought you'd be glad to be rid of me for a while," he said. "But if you insist on taking me back, so be it. I'll go."

Agis narrowed his eyes. "Don't think that your false promises will work on me," he warned.

Tithian shook his head wearily. "We know each other too well for that," he said. "I'm hurt and exhausted. I couldn't resist if I wanted to." He lifted the waterskin to his lips and drank deeply, then tied the mouth closed and handed it to the noble. "You'll have to carry this, my friend."

Agis slung the skin over his shoulder, then

cautiously crawled toward the plank, motioning for the king to follow. Although the noble half expected an attack, Tithian caused no trouble. He followed close behind, breathing in labored, shallow gasps. As they moved, the bow slowly rocked toward the aft, tipping more steeply the nearer they came to their goal.

When they finally reached the plank, Agis waved the king ahead. "I'll steady it," he said, grabbing the end of the gangway. "You go on."

"It's nice to see you're finally showing your king the proper respect," Tithian joked, crawling onto the gangway.

"Concentrate on what you're doing," the noble ordered, his voice sour. "I want you alive."

"How considerate," Tithian replied, slowly pulling himself onto the plank.

As the king passed, Agis noticed the shadow of a mocking smile upon his lips. "Don't even think of trying to betray me," said the noble, lifting his chin toward Kester. "I'm paying that tarek well, and there's not so much as a king's bit in your satchel."

Tithian paused to look back, an expression of feigned indignity on his face. "Am I really so predictable?"

"Be quiet and get on with yer crawling!" called Kester. "That derelict'll soon be under the silt."

Tithian finished crossing to the *Shadow Viper*, where Kester seized him and unceremoniously pulled him over the rail. Once the king stood safely on deck, the noble wasted no time crawling onto the gangway. He had gone no more than two yards when a deep rumble sounded from within the bow.

On the *Shadow Viper*'s deck, Tithian closed his eyes in concentration.

Agis had just enough time to curse the king before the gangway trembled violently. A terrible cacophony of creaks and groans sounded from the wreck, then the derelict's bowsprit rose skyward and its aft end sank, sending a great plume of dust into the sky. The plank slipped and fell free, then Agis felt himself following it into the gray sea. He tried to scream, but managed no more than a strangled gasp as the mordant taste of silt filled his mouth.

Agis snapped to a stop less than a yard above the gray sea, his legs dangling in silt and his nose burning with hot loess. It almost felt as though someone had caught him with a safety line, though he knew that could not be. Nymos and Kester began calling his name, then the noble felt himself slowly rising through the gray cloud. The only explanation he could think of was that the blind sorcerer had used a spell to catch him.

As Agis rose through the roiling cloud of dust, he prepared a mental attack, determined to prevent Tithian from launching another assault on him. By the time he finished, the *Shadow Viper*'s hull was visible through the haze. He could barely make out the forms of the tarek captain and the others standing at the edge of the deck. Tithian was staring at him with a look of intense concentration, while Kester was grasping the gunnel and peering at him through the dust. Nymos stood at the tarek's hip, his earslit cocked toward Agis.

"Stop him!" the noble croaked, pointing at Tithian. He could barely choke the words out through all the silt clogging his throat.

Neither the tarek nor the wizard moved toward the king, so Agis drew his sword. As soon as he came near enough to the ship, he reached for the gunnel and pulled himself onto the deck. Kester intercepted him at the rail, blocking his way and grabbing his sword arm.

"It was Tithian that saved ye, so ye won't be killin' him on my ship," said the tarek. "It'd bring an angry wind upon us."

Scowling, Agis pulled his arm free and stepped around the tarek to see that Tithian had sunk to his knees. He was gasping for breath, while a pair of slaves supported his arms to keep him from collapsing altogether. His face looked even more haggard than when Agis had found him.

The noble sheathed his sword and stepped to the king's side. "What's your plan?" he demanded. "Why did you save me?"

"You could have let me die on the wreck," Tithian whispered, peering up at Agis. "Now we're even."

The noble shook his head. "You're not the kind who repays his debts."

Tithian accepted the frank appraisal with an impassive face. "There are exceptions, you know."

"Not likely," Agis snapped. "You wouldn't have saved me unless it served your purposes. Are you going to tell me what they are?"

"I have," the king replied.

"As you wish, then," the noble said. He grabbed a piece of giant's hair rope off a stanchion cleat, then stepped behind Tithian and began tying his hands. "In the name of the Council of Advisors, I charge you with the high crime of slave-taking. You're to accompany me back to Tyr, where you'll answer for your misconduct before the Court of Free Citizens."

Tithian jerked his hands free and struggled to his feet. "What's this?" he demanded. He glanced at Kester and Nymos to make sure they were listening, then asked, "Has your jealousy grown so much that now you can appease it only by fabricating council charges against me?"

"Save your breath. Your act won't fool anyone here."

"Kled was an accident," Tithian said. "My raiders weren't supposed to attack it."

"Then why did they do it?" Agis asked.

Tithian stared at the noble for a long time, then asked, "You mean you haven't figured it out?"

"Tell me."

"Borys," replied the king. "They were collecting prisoners to fill the Dragon's levy. Why do you think he hasn't shown up since Sadira returned from the Pristine Tower?"

A knot formed in Agis's stomach. It might have been anger or pity, or even guilt—he didn't know which. "Thank you for being so frank," he said. "I'm sure the Court will want to know that you've been buying Tyr's peace with innocent lives."

Tithian broke into a fit of laughter. "I fear your wits have left you, my friend!" he chortled, shaking his head in disbelief. "Do you really think a Court of Free Citizens will condemn *me* for sparing them the wrath of the Dragon?"

"Yes," he answered. "You've broken Tyr's most sacred law."

Tithian grasped Agis's arm as if they were friends. "Then you're a fool," he laughed. "If you give a man the choice between his family's safety and someone else's pain, the stranger will die every time. Your court will declare me a hero, not a criminal."

"This is a matter of law," Agis replied confidently. "It's the foundation of the Free City, and I'll personally make sure that our court understands the gravity of your crime."

"And will you present a new plan to spare our citizens Borys's ravages?" Tithian inquired. "Perhaps you've found the Dark Lens? Are you ready to kill the Dragon?"

Agis bit his lip, angered more than he liked to admit by the king's mocking tone. Together with his friends Rikus and Sadira, he had spent much of the last five years searching for the lens. They still had no idea where it was.

"However we protect Tyr, it won't involve slave-taking," Agis replied.

Tithian sneered. "Then I'll be glad to stand before your Court of Fearful Citizens," he scoffed. "When they understand the alternative, I think they'll find your law a petty thing."

"I think they'll understand that a king who would do such a thing would also betray his own people," Agis said, moving once more to bind Tithian's hands. "Your subjects are not so foolish as you think."

"Nor are they so brave as you believe," the king replied. Again, he moved away to prevent himself from being tied. "But before we begin our journey home, perhaps you should know why I've come all this way."

"That would spare you a considerable amount of pain," interrupted Nymos. He stepped forward, his forked tongue flickering in suspense.

Agis pushed the little sorcerer away. "He won't tell the truth," said the noble. "He's just trying to turn me from my purpose."

"Not at all," said the king, meeting the noble's gaze. "In fact, I think you'll find what I have to say very interesting."

"I doubt that."

"Then you've lost interest in the Dark Lens?"

"Of course not," snapped Agis. "What does that have to do with anything?"

"I've found it," the king replied. "In fact, I'm on my way to recover it right now."

"What's the Dark Lens?" demanded Nymos.

"The Dark Lens is an ancient artifact, Nymos," Agis explained. "The sorcerer-kings used it more than a thousand years ago to create the Dragon—and without it, we can't destroy him now." The noble returned his gaze to Tithian. "But I think the king is lying about knowing where it is. My friends and I have been searching for it for years. If we couldn't find it, I see no reason to believe he did."

"You mustn't be jealous, Agis," Tithian said with a smirk. "Over these past years, I've developed talents that aren't available to you."

"Then where is it?" Agis demanded.

Tithian wagged his finger at the noble. "I won't say," he replied. "But I'll tell you *how* I found it. That will protect my secret and convince you that I'm telling the truth."

"I'm listening," Agis replied.

Although he maintained a calm outward appearance, the noble's heart was pounding fiercely. The Dark Lens was the key not only to safeguarding Tyr, but to revitalizing the rest of Athas as well. The lens would complement the two things that his friends already possessed: Rikus's magic sword, the Scourge of Rkard, and the powerful magic with which Sadira had been imbued in the Pristine Tower. With all three elements together, they would finally have the power to put an end to the Dragon's rampages.

After allowing Agis to remain in suspense for a moment, Tithian said, "I found the lens by not looking for it."

"What nonsense is that?" demanded Kester.

"The lens was stolen from the Pristine Tower by two dwarves—dwarves who had vowed to kill Borys," the king explained. "When they died without destroying him—"

"They violated their focus," interrupted Agis, referring to the peculiar aspect of the dwarven personality that compelled them to dedicate their lives to an all-consuming purpose.

Tithian nodded. "When they died without fulfilling their purpose, they became undead spirits," he said. "I used my magic to locate their banshees, and that's how I know where to find the Dark Lens."

"And you offered to share this Dark Lens with Andropinis. That's why he loaned his fleet to you," surmised Nymos. The sorcerer stepped to Agis's side and laid a hand on the noble's hip, then pointed in Tithian's direction. "I say we tie him to a boulder and dump him over the side."

"That won't be necessary, Nymos," said Tithian, regarding the reptile with a wary expression. "You're correct in all your assumptions except one. I have no intention of keeping my word to Andropinis. I want the lens so I can kill the Dragon—for the good of Tyr."

"Forgive me if I doubt your motivations," said Agis.

"Good," said Nymos. "Let's throw him overboard and go after the lens ourselves."

"We can't kill him," said Agis. "I need him alive when he stands before the Court of Free Citizens."

"You can't intend to take me back now!" Tithian exclaimed. "This is the Dark Lens! It'll make us as powerful as sorcerer-kings!"

"I'm not abandoning the lens," said Agis. "You know it's too important for me to do that."

"Good," said Tithian, a smug smile on his face. "Then we'll work together—for the good of Tyr."

Agis shook his head. "You'll be spending this journey in Kester's brig—and returning to Tyr in shackles."

"We'll do this thing together, or not at all," said Tithian. "Otherwise, I won't tell you where to find it."

"What happened to your concern for Tyr's welfare?" Agis asked.

"That's what I'm thinking of now," the king replied.

"You're lying," Agis replied. "Besides, I know where to look—the isle of Lybdos."

Tithian's eyes opened wide. "You fool!" he hissed. "You can't succeed without me!"

"We can and we will," Agis replied, smiling. "I'm sure you'll find the brig comfortable."

The noble grabbed Tithian by the shoulders and turned him toward the center of the deck, where Kester's slaves had gathered to watch the exchange. "I'll try not to make the rest of your journey too unpleasant," he said, looping his rope around the king's wrists.

"I'm sure you'll do your best," Tithian replied, his voice rather distant.

Agis looked up to see the slaves staring at the king in rapt fascination. At first, he did not realize what was happening, for the noble had never seen such expressions come over so many faces at once. "What are you doing?" he demanded, cinching the knot tight around Tithian's hands.

"Perhaps you should explain that to me," the king replied. "I thought you disapproved of slavery, my friend?"

"I do," Agis replied. "But this is Kester's ship—"

"Perhaps you and I should free these men," the

king replied, keeping his gaze fixed on the crowd. "After all, slavery is illegal in Tyr, and are we not Tyrians?"

"There'll be no freein' of slaves on my ship," Kester growled.

The crew ignored her and, in trancelike unison, cried, "Hurray for Tyr!"

"Yes, hurray for Tyr!" Tithian shouted. "Help me, and you'll all become heroes. You'll live in great palaces and eat the fruit of the faro instead of the needle!"

With a stuporous cheer, the slaves surged forward to free Tithian. Kester leaped to meet them, yelling, "Back to yer poles!" She grabbed the first man in the mob and snapped his neck with a quick twist of her wrists. "I'll snap the heads off all ye mutineers!"

As the tarek reached for her next victim, Agis drew his sword and cried, "Stop! It's not their fault!"

The noble brought the pommel of his weapon down on the back of Tithian's skull, adding another dent to the battered circlet. There was a resounding thud, then the king's knees buckled, and he slumped to the deck at Agis's feet.

SIX

Mytilene

To Agis, the shipfloater's apprentice looked only slightly more healthy than her dead master, who had succumbed to a fever just an hour earlier. Beads of cloudy sweat rolled down her brow in rivulets, a murky yellow film clouded the whites of her eyes, and red, cracked skin surrounded her nostrils and mouth. Even the freckles dotting her keen-boned cheeks had turned from pink to gray, while her breath came in labored wheezes.

Agis snapped his fingers in front of the young woman's fine-boned face. Her puffy eyelids rose a sliver. She turned her listless eyes on his face, but she did not speak.

"Can you hold on alone, Damras?" he asked.

The apprentice nodded.

"Tithian is doing this to you," the noble said. "I'm going down to the brig to put an end to it."

"Hurry," she wheezed.

Agis climbed out of the chaperon's seat and started down toward the main deck. He had barely set foot on the ladder before Kester laid a restraining hand on his shoulder.

"What are ye doing out of the chaperon's seat?" she demanded. In her hand, the tarek held a king's eye, for the day was a breezy one, with a dust curtain hanging about half as high as the *Shadow Viper*'s main mast.

"Damras is dying—"

"She's just sick!" snapped Kester, cutting off Agis's explanation. Without even glancing in the direction of the floater's dome, she added, "Damras is young. She'll be fine."

"Denial won't keep us afloat," said Nymos, joining them. "If Damras dies, the *Shadow Viper* is doomed."

"I told ye, she'll be fine!" growled the tarek.

"No, she won't," Agis said. "Tithian is killing her."

"That's blather," growled Kester. "If he kills the floaters, he sinks with us. Why would he—"

A pained cry from Damras interrupted the tarek. Followed by Kester and Nymos, Agis rushed to the side of the floater's pit. Damras's condition had deteriorated. Her chin lay slumped on her chest, and her cloudy eyes stared into empty space. Her trembling hands had slipped to the edges of the dome and were in danger of dropping off the glassy surface altogether.

Agis climbed into the floater's seat, at the same time speaking over his shoulder to Kester. "You'd better head for that island."

The noble pointed to the ship's starboard, where a craggy, crescent-shaped island rose out of the dust haze. Although it was several miles distant, he could see the zigzagging line of a path traversing its precipitous slopes. The trail crested the ridge near a jumble of blocky white shapes that could only be buildings.

Kester shook her head. "That's Mytilene, a giant stronghold," she said. "Ye'll have to keep Damras awake until we can make a safer island."

Agis laid his hands on top of the floater's. Her knuckles felt as hot as sunbaked stones. "Damras will never make it to another island," he warned, moving the floater's hands back toward the center of the dome.

"Neither will we, if we land on this one," replied Kester. "Ye'd know that if ye had ever seen how giants treat strangers."

Damras focused her jaundiced eyes on the noble's face. *Can't last, but Kester is right about Mytilene,* she said, too weak to speak the words aloud. *Help me.*

I'll go after Tithian right now, Agis said.

The floater shook her head. *No. The* Shadow Viper *will be under dust by then. I need you here.*

Tell me how, the noble answered, swallowing in apprehension. To Kester and Nymos, he said, "Damras is going to teach me how to float the ship."

Kester and Nymos both winced, then the jozhal said, "We'll see to Tithian."

"No," said Agis. "The king has obviously recovered from his ordeal, and he'll attack you with the Way. Neither of you are powerful enough to resist him."

"I have my magic," the reptile insisted.

"And Tithian has his," the noble replied. "You can't open that brig until I'm there to counter his mental abilities. Otherwise, he'll take control of the crew again."

"The brig stays closed," said Kester. "I'll not have another mutiny on my ship." She stepped toward the helm, motioning for the jozhal to follow her.

Once they were gone, Damras placed her hands on

top of Agis's, leaving his palms in direct contact with the obsidian. An eerie chill spread from his fingers and into his wrists as icy tendrils of pain writhed up his arms. They spliced themselves into his bones, drawing the strength from his muscles and the heat from his blood.

Let the dome draw on your life-force. Damras's thought came to him distant and weak, and he felt her hands slip away. *See the ship's hull in your mind.*

Gritting his teeth against the numbing pain in his arms, the noble pictured the weathered planks of the *Shadow Viper*'s hull. At the same time, he opened a pathway to his nexus, allowing the dome free access to his spiritual energy. A warm stream of life-force rose from deep within himself, coursing through his body and down into his arms. The tendrils in his arms grew warmer as his energy flowed into them, then a golden glimmer flashed beneath his palms and sank into the depths of the dome. Suddenly, it seemed to Agis that the ship had become a part of him.

You must witness the sea as it was.

Inside Agis's mind, the dust curtain engulfing the ship suddenly lifted, replaced by a sparkling expanse of grayish blue. He heard the lapping of waves, then felt himself rocking back and forth to the gentle sway of the ship. The sky turned the color of sapphires, and a briny, wind-blown spray stung his cheeks. The noble licked a few droplets of the liquid off his lips and tasted water, salty as blood, but water nonetheless.

The sight took Agis's breath away. In all directions, stretching to every horizon, he saw nothing but water, as endless as the sky and as featureless as the salt flats of the Ivory Triangle. This sea was a stark contrast to the real one, alluring and majestic instead of foreboding and bleak.

When he had finally recovered from his shock, Agis asked, *What is this?*

The Sea of Silt, long before the sorcerer-kings, Damras explained.

That can't be, Agis replied. *The time before the sorcerer-kings was that of Rajaat. The world was green and covered with trees. I've read descriptions—*

Your descriptions were wrong, Damras interrupted. *But we have no time to argue. The world was covered with water. You must accept that.*

Very well.

As the noble spoke the words, a primeval attraction stirred deep within his spirit. He felt a restless longing as painful as it was powerful, and he almost did not notice as the crack of flapping sails sounded inside his mind. An instant later, a floater's cockpit materialized around him. Agis found himself seated in a chaperon's seat within his mind as well as that of the *Shadow Viper*.

Slowly, the rest of the ship began to appear inside Agis's mind. An unimaginable weight settled upon his spirit, so terrible that his heart, stomach, and all his organs ached as though they would burst. He cried out in alarm, but his pain prevented anything more than a strangled gurgle from escaping his lips.

You are the water, instructed Damras. *Your strength carries the* Shadow Viper.

As the floater spoke, the foul odor of rot rose from the craft inside Agis's mind, and his stomach churned in protest. The planks of the caravel's hull turned filthy dun, and a dark stain of adulteration began to spread outward from beneath the ship's keel, changing the color of the sea from sparkling blue to vile brown. The stench of decay grew stronger than ever, filling his nose with such fetor that he had to fight to keep from retching.

What's happening? Agis asked.

The fever, Damras replied. *It comes from the ship.*

You mean from Tithian, said Agis. *He's poisoning us through the ship's hull.*

Then he's very powerful. He's fighting against the dome's natural flow, replied Damras. *I'll help you resist as long as I can.*

You should rest, replied Agis. *You won't be any good to the ship if you die.*

You aren't ready to do this alone, she retorted.

They fell silent, and Agis concentrated on the task at hand. Although he tried to keep the *Shadow Viper* floating high in the water, the horrid stench of Tithian's attack and the dome's steady drain on his strength were difficult to endure. Soon, he found himself feeling light-headed and dizzy.

I think I'm about to fall unconscious, he reported.

That's not surprising, Damras replied. Despite the respite Agis had given her, she still sounded sick and weak. *It takes many days of practice before you can control the flow of your life energy into the dome. You rest and let me take over for a few minutes.*

Agis felt the ship lift off his spirit as she took its weight. The dark stain of Tithian's adulteration began to fade from the sea in his mind, and though he still felt tired, he began to feel less sick to his stomach.

The *Shadow Viper* sliced through the dust as usual, until Damras suddenly cried out in fear. A horrid death rattle escaped from her throat, then she pitched forward, and her hands slipped off the black dome. Before Agis could catch her, the floater slumped to the deck, her lifeless eyes staring into the sky.

The *Shadow Viper* lurched and slowed, then began sinking like a boulder. Agis caught it, visualizing the caravel riding upon the waves inside his mind. The ship's weight seemed even more crushing than before, and his stomach churned in protest as Tithian's foul stain of decay spread over the blue sea. It was all Agis could do to keep his thoughts focused on the lapping waters of the ancient sea, instead of the agony in his chest or the terrible nausea in his stomach.

Kester's domed muzzle appeared over the cockpit. "What's happening down there?" the tarek demanded.

Agis did not have to answer, for Damras's lifeless body made the trouble clear.

"From the way the ship lurched, I'd say we're about to sink," said Nymos, also appearing at the edge of the pit. "Perhaps we should consider landing on the island."

"If we were goin' to sink, we'd be choking on silt by now," growled the tarek. "Agis'll keep us afloat."

The noble shook his head. "I'm a mindbender, not a shipfloater," he said. "I'll be lucky to last long enough to reach the nearest shore."

Kester gnashed her fangs for a moment, then crumpled her heavy brow into a wrathful scowl. "All right, we'll chance the back side of the island," she snarled. "And when we get ashore, I'm going to snap Tithian's neck with me own hands."

As the tarek had her helmsman swing the ship around, the image of a kes'trekel appeared deep within the dome. The raptor's ragged wings flapped in great sweeps, lifting it out of the black depths and up toward the noble. At the elbows of its wings it had tiny, three-fingered hands, one clutching a many-stranded scourge and the other a curved scythe. On the bird's shoulders sat a human skull, a tail of long auburn hair dangling from beneath a battered circlet of gold. The bird continued to rise until its fleshless head filled the entire dome.

Agis! came Tithian's voice. *You can't float this ship for long, but I can. Let me take over.*

I'd sooner trust a scorpion, Agis replied.

This isn't about trust, replied the king. *It's about practicality. By working together, we're both more likely to recover the Dark Lens.*

So you can murder me and steal it for yourself? the noble asked. *I'd be mad to give you that opportunity.*

Consider the opportunity you're giving up, Tithian pressed. *Isn't the possibility of killing Borys worth the risk that I might recover the lens?*

Not if it's a risk I don't need to take, Agis replied. *Now leave me alone—before I slip and let us sink.*

The embers in Tithian's eye sockets flashed in anger. *You can't do this alone,* he said, diving back into the dome's black depths. *Before this is over, you will let me out.*

Kester appeared at the edge of the cockpit. "Look lively down there!" she barked. "We're taking silt over both sides!"

Agis put the king out of his thoughts and focused on the sea inside his mind. The water had grown slightly darker and more viscous. The difference was so imperceptible that the noble might not have noticed it on his own, but it was clearly affecting the ship.

Cursing Tithian for making his task more difficult, Agis visualized the sea as the floater had first shown it to him, sparkling and pure. He felt a brief surge in the stream of energy flowing from his nexus, then the water faded to a lighter shade of brown. The *Shadow Viper* in his mind rose a little higher, slipping through the waves as easily as it had when Damras had been there to help him.

"Better," commented Kester, nodding her approval. "Are ye sure ye can't do this for a dozen hours or so? We'd be wise to land almost any place but Mytilene."

Agis shook his head. "By then, I'll be as dead as Damras," he replied in a strained voice. "We have to land soon, so I can stop Tithian's interference and improve my control over the dome."

"If ye say so," sighed Kester. "But it'll be another ten minutes before we round the point, and who knows how long after that before we find a place to land."

"There must be someplace on this side of the island," objected Agis.

"There's one—where the giants wade ashore on the way up to their village," allowed Kester. "I'm sure ye don't want to land there."

"No!" snapped Nymos. "Our chances are much better on the back side. With the dust curtain hiding us, it could be days before they realize we've landed."

"I'm afraid not. Our masts will give us away," said Kester, gesturing at the great shafts that towered so high above the decks. "I'm just hopin' it will take 'em longer to catch us."

"What are you talking about?" asked Nymos, turning his slender head from side to side in an attempt to gain some sense of Kester's concern.

"The masts extend above the dust curtain," Agis explained. "I don't suppose you could hide them, could you Nymos?"

The jozhal thought for a moment, then said, "I can't hide the masts." He pulled a small wand from his stomach pouch. At the end of the stick was a tiny mask. "But I can disguise them as giants."

Kester rubbed her lumpy head in thought, then shrugged. "Go ahead and try," she said. "I don't see how ye can make matters any worse."

With that, the tarek returned to her usual station, and Nymos scurried off to work his magic on the masts. The *Shadow Viper* skirted Mytilene's shore slowly, steadily riding lower in the dust as Agis grew sicker and more fatigued. Soon, in addition to his nausea, the noble felt feverish and weak, and rivulets of bitter-smelling sweat ran down his brow. He began to think he would have to call for a chaperon to keep him alert, then Kester's voice boomed across the deck.

"Foredeck squads to their ballistae!" she ordered. "Crew one, raise the keel. All others, furl the sails!"

At the far end of the ship, a dozen sailors worked the ballistae windlasses, cranking back the arms on three separate engines. Within moments, the weapons were loaded with heavy harpoons, the ends tipped with barbed heads as thick as a dwarf's body.

On the main deck, a group of nervous slaves gathered around the capstan and leaned into the crossbars, winding a thick black rope around a massive wooden drum. As the line was gathered up, it pulled the keel—a mekillot's shoulder-blade—out of the deck's center slot. The bone had been laboriously carved into a finlike shape, and polished to a smooth sheen to keep silt from clinging to it.

While their comrades struggled to raise the keel, the rest of the slaves crawled up the masts and out onto the yardarms. Slowly, they pulled the heavy sails up to the wooden beams and secured them into place with quick-release knots. By the time they had finished, the *Shadow Viper*'s progress had slowed to a near standstill.

Agis heard Nymos utter a magical command word, then saw the jozhal standing amidships, gesturing at each mast with his tiny wand. A trio of giants appeared where the masts had been. They were all somewhat smaller and less hairy than Fylo, with lanky builds and rough, sun-bronzed hides. On the shoulders of the first sat a ram's head, on the second an eagle's, and on the third a serpent's.

"Man the plunging poles!" Kester ordered. The tarek was peering through her king's eye, her gaze fixed far ahead of the ship. "Ahead slow."

The crew took their positions and began to push. To Agis, this part of the journey seemed to take as long as the trip around the island. Once he almost retched, while another time he found himself gasping for breath as though he had been running. Still, the noble managed to hang on, and soon the craggy silhouette of a shoreline loomed just a few dozen yards off the bow.

"Ready the gangways," Kester called, still peering through the king's eye.

The slaves had barely moved to their positions when a lookout's voice echoed down from the crow's nest. "Giant to starboard!" There was a short pause, then he added, "Four more to port!"

"So much for disguises," Kester growled, lowering her king's eye. "How close?" she yelled, raising her gaze to the top of the main mast.

When the tarek saw three beasthead giants standing on her deck, her leathery skin went pale. At first, Agis thought it was Nymos's illusion that had flustered the tarek, but he quickly realized that was not the case.

"Not beastheads!" the tarek gasped.

In the same instant, a hulking silhouette came into

view off the port bow, six braids of hair sweeping back and forth like pendulums as he waded out to intercept the *Shadow Viper*. Although the dust curtain prevented the noble from getting a good look at the giant's face, he could see enough to tell that it was more or less human, with a blocky shape and a hooked nose as long as a battle-axe. As the noble watched, the colossus lifted his arms over his head, raising a huge boulder as high the *Shadow Viper*'s tallest mast.

"Go away, you filthy Saram!" he boomed.

As the giant cocked his arms to throw, Kester yelled, "Fire at will!"

Agis heard the sonorous throb of a skein releasing its tension. A tree-sized harpoon rasped off a ballista and sailed straight at the titan's chest. It struck with a loud crack, burying itself squarely in the target's sternum. The giant's breath left him in a pained gale. The boulder he had been holding slipped from his hands and plunged into the dust. Casting a slack-jawed look of surprise at the *Shadow Viper*'s bow, he lowered his hands and closed his fingers around the shaft, narrowly missing the ship's bowsprit as he pitched forward.

As the firing crew cranked the ballista arms back into the cocked position, Kester whooped in joy. "That'll teach ye to raise a stone to us!" she yelled.

"Should Nymos drop his spell?" Agis asked.

"Not now," came the reply. "Let 'em think it's beastheads killin' their friends, not the *Shadow Viper*."

She had hardly finished speaking before a second boulder sailed out of the dust haze and crashed through the rigging, tearing the crow's nest from the main mast and snapping ropes from the spreaders. Followed by the body of the screaming lookout, the rock bounced off the keel and plunged through the main deck.

"All back!" Kester yelled.

The slaves dipped their plunging poles into the silt and began to push the *Shadow Viper* away from the shore. Kester cursed them for being too slow, then peered into the floater's pit. "Keep us light an' lively, Agis, or we're lost!"

Two more giants came into view just beyond the bow, waist deep in silt and coming after the ship as fast as they could plow ahead. The leader held a huge boulder in front of himself, using it like a shield to protect himself and his companion from any more attacks.

"Tell the slaves to raise their poles," Agis said.

Kester furrowed her heavy brow. "Why?"

"Do you know what ice is?" the noble replied, turning his concentration inward. Without waiting for a reply, he opened his spiritual nexus wide, allowing his life-force to flow through the dome in a torrent. The sea in his mind lightened from a turbid brown to a pale yellow.

Agis heard Kester's voice yell, "Raise poles!"

The noble took a deep breath and visualized something he had seen only once in his life, on a bitter cold morning during a hunting trip into the high mountains: a frozen pond. In his mind, the yellow waters around the caravel turned the color of ivory and became as hard as a rock. The frost spread steadily outward, changing the sea into an endless white plain, as vast as the stony barrens and as smooth as obsidian.

The noble did not stop there. He visualized a pair of outriggers stretching down from the ship's gunnels. Where the floats should have been, there were obsidian runners, as sharp as swords and thick enough to bear the immense weight of the *Shadow Viper*. Agis imagined these outriggers growing longer and longer, lifting the caravel's hull out of the ice until it sat free, ready to shoot across the frozen sea at the slightest impetus.

A boulder crashed down on the deck of the bow, drawing the noble's attention away from his preparations. It smashed through a rack of spare harpoons and upended the foremast. As the great staff toppled over, a giant's angry voice jeered, "You other Saram will die, too!"

"Push off, Kester!" Agis yelled. "And tell everyone to brace themselves."

"Fast to stern!" yelled the tarek, not bothering with the warning Agis had suggested.

The slaves lowered their plunging poles and pushed. The *Shadow Viper* shot away from the giants like an arrow from a bow. The ballista crews, who had been holding their fire for the most opportune moment, triggered their weapons. The skeins throbbed and a pair of harpoons whooshed away. The first lance sank deep into a giant's stomach. He bellowed, clutched the shaft, and crumpled forward into a dead heap.

The second missile gashed across the last giant's elbow, spraying a cloud of red mist high into the air, then vanished into the dust haze. At first, Agis thought the titan had narrowly avoided death, but the fellow's eyes glazed over and he began to stagger about as though he were too intoxicated to stand. A moment later, his knees buckled and he fell into the dust, his muscles twitching madly.

"Poisoned harpoons. Now ye know why we call her the *Viper*," Kester chuckled, using the king's eye to watch the giant die. "That makes three of five.

What happened to the other two our lookout reported?"

Agis did not answer, for he had broken into a cold sweat and fallen to quivering. His temples throbbed with a fierce, maddening pain, and his intestines burned as though he had swallowed fire. He felt a terrible punishment rising from his gut, and the noble knew he had overreached the limits of his endurance. He found himself leaning over to void his stomach, still struggling to keep his hands on the floater's dome.

"What's wrong with ye, Agis?" demanded Kester. "If ye let us down now, we'll sink!"

"It's Tithian's fever!" Agis gasped, struggling to pull himself upright. "I can't—"

A tremendous boom sounded from the *Shadow Viper*'s stern, bringing the caravel to an abrupt halt. Agis flew out of his seat and rolled clear to the rear gunnel. He hit his head against a bone stanchion, then found himself lying in a tangled mess with Kester, the helmsman, and a half-dozen other sailors. A foul smell, almost as rank as the one he had left behind in the cockpit, filled his nostrils.

Agis looked up and found himself staring at two sets of immense blue eyes. Beneath each pair of orbs were a craggy nose and cavernous mouth filled with broken teeth as large as stalactites.

"They're too small to be Saram spies!" growled one giant.

The other scowled in confusion, then raised a sword-length finger to scratch between the mats of his hair. "We'd better take them to Mag'r," he said. "The sachem will know what they are."

SEVEN

Table of Chiefs

Bathed in the full fury of the crimson sun, Tithian and Agis stood on a slate-topped table more expansive than a Tyrian plaza. The heat shimmered off the black surface in torpid waves, blistering their feet and scorching their lips, leaving their parched throats bloated with thirst. Nymos lay half-conscious at the king's side, his reptilian body unable to cool his blood in the face of the scalding temperature. At the jozhal's side stood Kester, swaying and perilously close to collapsing herself.

The ship's crew cowered a short distance away. Despite the helmsman's efforts to keep them quiet, the terrified slaves murmured anxiously among themselves and cast nervous glances over their shoulders, where the end of the table overhung a sheer cliff that dropped a thousand feet into the Sea of Silt's pearly haze.

The walls of a mountain canyon flanked the table on both sides. A pair of stone benches, as tall and broad as Tyr's ramparts, had been carved into each of these rocky slopes. On these benches sat a dozen giants, all with blocky, humanlike heads marked by lumpy features and rough skin. Each wore the crude figure of his tribe's totem—a sheep, goat, erdlu, or similar domestic animal—tattooed on his sloped brow. Most wore their hair and beards in the long, snarled braids coveted as raw material by Balican ropemakers. Their angry shouts rumbled back and forth over the table like thunder, so loud that Tithian could understand only half of the words.

"We've been ignored long enough," Tithian growled.

The king started across the broken slate toward the head of the table, where a round-faced giant sat upon a throne of black basalt. Carved from the shoulder of a volcanic peak, the great chair was as large as the Golden Palace itself. On the titan's clean-shaven head rested a circlet of tree boughs woven into a brown-leaved garland of royalty, identifying the wearer, Tithian supposed, as the monarch. The giant's eyes were witless and dull, with puffy lids and brown irises that showed life only when they flashed in anger or malice. From his bloated cheeks sagged great jowls, hanging well over his fleshy neck and trembling like a loose sail whenever he bared his jagged teeth to sneer or laugh.

Tithian had taken only a half-dozen steps when Agis's fingers gouged into his arm. "What are you doing?" the noble demanded.

"Saving us," the king replied.

"Ye've done enough already," hissed Kester, her eyes narrowed in anger as she joined the pair. "We wouldn't be here if ye hadn't killed my floaters."

"I wouldn't have had to, if you hadn't locked me in the brig—but here we are," Tithian hissed. He looked back to Agis and locked gazes. "I warned you it would be impossible to recover the Dark Lens without me. Now I'll show you why."

The king pulled free and continued forward, stopping next to a clay tankard as high as his chest. The giant in the throne paid him no attention, but continued to bellow at a tribesman near the middle of the table, more than thirty paces away. Tithian casually turned his palm groundward and summoned the energy to cast a spell.

On the rocky hillsides above the giants' heads, grassy clumps of daggerblade and balls of yellow tumblethistle began to wilt as Tithian drained the life-force from their roots. Within an instant, every plant within the reach of a giant had turned to ash, leaving the canyon walls as black and lifeless as the surface of the slate table.

The giant's hand descended like a kes'trekel on a sun-bloated corpse. He grabbed his tankard and flipped it over, spilling five gallons of golden mead over Tithian's head, and placed the vessel over the king's shoulders.

"No magic!" he boomed.

Inside the mug, the muffled voice echoed painfully in Tithian's ears.

"Too late!" Tithian hissed.

The Tyrian brought his hands up and plucked a stray thread from the hem of his cassock, then wrapped this around the tip of his index finger. Pointing the digit at the giant, he uttered a spell and pulled the thread down past his first knuckle.

Again, the giant's voice reverberated through the tankard, this time screaming in surprise as his crown slipped down around his throat and began to constrict. Cries of alarm erupted all around, and the table began to shake as giants to both sides leaped to their feet. Tithian smiled to himself and twisted the ends of the thread, tightening the loop until his finger began to throb from having the blood cut off.

Tithian felt the tankard being lifted from his head. "Is this your idea of help?" Agis demanded, tossing the vessel aside. "You'll get us killed!"

"Do I strike you as someone with so little regard for his own life?" Tithian replied.

"You strike me as a maniac," sneered Nymos. The little jozhal teetered at the noble's side, holding himself upright by clinging to Agis's belt with a three-fingered hand. "Now cancel your magic, before—"

"Too late for that!" said Kester, pulling Nymos and Agis away by their arms. "Stand aside, unless ye want to get mashed with him!"

Tithian looked up to see several giants stretching their arms toward him, their palms stretched out to smash him flat.

"Stop!" Tithian yelled. "If I die, so does your chief!"

Tithian pointed toward the basalt throne. The ruler's crown had all but disappeared into the folds of his corpulent neck, and the giant's filthy nails were scratching great rifts into his flesh as he tried to work a fingertip beneath the constricting boughs.

"You're lying!" growled one of the giants, a lanky fellow with red beard and hair. "How can you kill our sachem if you're dead?"

"Magic," Tithian replied, raising the finger with the thread looped around it. "If I die, this string will tighten until it cuts the tip of my finger off. Your sachem's crown will do the same thing, except that it will cut off his head instead of his fingertip."

Several giants lowered their heads and eyed the digit raised toward them. Their breaths washed over

Tithian like a stale-smelling wind, but they made no move to attack.

The king smiled. "That's better," he said. "Now—"

He was interrupted by a rumbling voice from the far end of the table. "Let Sachem Mag'r go, or I'll sweep your friends off the Table of Chiefs."

Tithian glanced over his shoulder to see that a giant had laid his massive arm across the width of the table, and was ready to sweep Kester's cowering slave crew over the edge into the Sea of Silt.

"I don't care what you do with them," the king said, looking back to Mag'r. The sachem's face color had deepened from red to purple, and his eyes were bulging from his head. "They're no friends of mine."

"But they're me crew!" Kester growled, stepping toward the king. "I need 'em to sail the *Shadow Viper*."

"Crews can be replaced."

"Not out here," observed Nymos, standing several paces away. "If this is your idea of saving us, you're a fool."

"The crew is a liability," Tithian retorted. "If we let the giants think they're important to us, Mag'r will use them against us."

"I won't allow you to sacrifice them," Agis warned. "They're living beings, just like any citizen of Tyr."

The noble's hand dropped to his side, where his sword still hung in its scabbard. The giants, no more concerned with human-sized blades than a mul gladiator would have been with a child's wooden dagger, had not even bothered to take their weapons away.

"You've always placed too high a value on other people's lives, Agis," Tithian said, loosening the string on his finger. "But if that's what you want."

As the circlet loosened, Mag'r slipped a finger behind the boughs and ripped the crown off his neck.

He flung the broken garland into the mountainside, then grabbed his throat, wheezing and hacking. With each cough, he sprayed gusts of gale force wind down the canyon.

At the other end of the table, the giant withdrew the arm with which he had threatened to sweep Kester's crew away, drawing a relieved murmur from the slaves. Sparing them no more than a glance, Tithian drew a live firefly from his satchel and crushed it over the blade of his dagger, then quickly summoned the energy to cast another spell.

By the time he finished, Mag'r's face had returned to its normal color, and the giant had recovered his breath. The sachem looked down at Tithian. "I'll pluck your arms and legs off—one each day!" he growled, his eyes flashing yellow in his anger. "You'll wish you had died fast, like your friends!"

The giant reached out, and the king tossed his dagger into the air, at the same time uttering his incantation. The knife intercepted Mag'r's hand, burying itself in a finger and causing the sachem to jerk his hand back to his chest. A greenish yellow glow rushed outward from the wound, drawing a rumble of astonished comments from all along the Table of Chiefs.

Mag'r tried to pluck the dagger from his finger, but Tithian flicked his wrist and the blade withdrew itself. It hovered in the air a few feet from the sachem, ready to strike again.

"My dagger is like the sunwasp," Tithian lied. He kept his gaze fixed on Mag'r, who was staring at his glowing finger in stunned silence. "The first bite causes no true harm, but the second makes you sick for weeks." He paused to let Mag'r consider the words, then added, "And the third—well, let us hope it doesn't come to that."

Mag'r moved his finger to the side, holding it far away from his body. "Who are you?" he demanded. "Why do you come to Mytilene?"

Before Tithian could answer, the titan to Mag'r's left growled, "Them beasthead spies!" He was what passed for a venerated elder among the giants, with ribbons of gray hair tangled in his snarled braids, heavy folds of skin hanging over his milky eyes, and a few ivory-colored nubs where he'd once had teeth. On his head was an amorphous tattoo that might have been a lizard, an eagle, or even a snake. The giant swept his wrinkled hand over the captives. "Them come to Mytilene to spy on our army."

The giant to Mag'r's right peered down at the trio and said, "They're spies all right." He was much larger than the others at the table, with a hooked nose as big as a kank saddle and a black shawl draped over one eye. "What do we do with them, Chief Nuta?" he asked, looking back up. "Smash their arms and legs?"

Mag'r slammed his fist down on the table so hard that Agis and Kester were knocked off their feet. "No, Patch!" he thundered, his worried eyes fixed on Tithian's floating dagger. "We won't torture or kill them. I have a better idea."

The giants fell silent and looked to their sachem, waiting for him to explain. When Mag'r said nothing and began to appear uncomfortable, Chief Nuta narrowed his eyes and asked, "What idea?"

Deciding the time had come to do the giant a good turn, Tithian said, "As I'm sure Sachem Mag'r realizes, we are not beasthead spies."

Mag'r smiled and nodded. "That's right," he said, sneering at Nuta. "They're Balican spies."

An excited murmur rolled through the canyon, and Mag'r smiled triumphantly.

"So what now?" demanded Patch. "Do we skin the spies alive, then level Balic?"

"No!" boomed Nuta. He slammed his great hands down on the edge of the table, sending a terrific shock wave through Tithian's feet. He pushed himself to his feet and leaned over to press his face closer to Patch's. "Balic don't have our Oracle. It's the beast-heads who want to keep our Oracle from coming back to us." Nuta gestured at Tithian and his companions, then said, "We kill them spies, then we attack Lybdos."

Patch recoiled from the older giant's sudden anger, then recovered his wits and scowled at Nuta. Slamming his own hands down on the slate surface, he rose and also leaned over the table, pressing his face to Nuta's. For the first time since being placed on the table that morning, Tithian and his friends were shaded from the harsh rays of the crimson sun—though, judging by the angry expressions on the monumental faces overhead, they were in the shadow of a storm.

"The Balicans aren't supposed to take sides," growled Patch, his one good eye burning with anger. From his peevish tone, it seemed to Tithian that Patch was more interested in arguing with Nuta than presenting his own point of view. "We'll cut the feet and hands off these spies, then attack Balic." A wicked smile crossed his lips, and he looked down the table at the other chiefs gathered there. "We'll sack Balic and steal all the good stuff there," he said, drawing a chorus of agreement from the other giants.

"No!" Nuta snarled.

Tithian glimpsed an enormous fist rising from

Nuta's side. Only after crouching safely out of the way did he think to warn his companions, and by then he was too late. Chief Nuta's fist brushed past Agis and Kester, sending them sprawling, and caught Patch squarely under the jaw. The younger giant's teeth clapped together with the crack of a firing catapult, and his chin snapped back. He tottered on the brink of falling backward, then his head slumped forward. Boulder-sized teeth and bucketfuls of blood spilled from his mouth to shower down on the king and his companions.

"Look out!" Tithian yelled.

He grabbed Nymos by the arm and threw himself toward Mag'r's end of the table, glimpsing Agis and Kester as they rolled in the opposite direction. Patch's immense head slammed into the table with a deafening crash. Tithian and the jozhal were bounced several feet into the air, and when they came down the slate was still reverberating.

"You saved me!" Nymos gasped, his tone more surprised than thankful. "Why?"

"Because I had nothing to gain by letting you die," the king answered curtly. He returned to his feet, adding, "Besides, it serves my purposes to keep you alive. I can't reach Lybdos alone any more than Agis can."

Without further comment, Tithian turned around and saw Patch's unconscious form sprawled across the table. The shawl across his bad eye had shifted down to cover the good one, and the only thing visible beneath the giant's hairy brow was the scarred pit where his missing eye had once been. His cracked lips gaped open more than a foot, revealing a mouthful of broken teeth and allowing frothy blood to stream down the side of his mouth.

"Agis?" Tithian called. "Are you all right?"

Kester peered over the giant's back. "He isn't over there?"

Tithian studied the area on his side of the unconscious giant, looking for an arm or leg sticking out from beneath the immense torso. Already, the searing tabletop was heating Patch's blood, filling the air with a thick, coppery smell. In the red pond lay mice, varls, and other stunned vermin thrown off the titan's body by the impact of the fall. Nowhere did the king see a sign of his friend.

"I can hear someone groaning, over there," said Nymos. He was holding a small, spiral-shaped shell to his earslit and pointing in the direction of Patch's head.

Kester disappeared from sight, then the giant's head began to rock back and forth as she tried to raise it. From the strained sound of her grunts and groans, Tithian did not think she would ever lift it high enough, even with his help.

Looking up at Nuta, Tithian ordered, "Lift Patch's head so we can recover our friend."

Nuta sneered at him. "Nuta squish you," the giant scoffed, reaching out to make good on his threat.

Tithian dived away, somersaulting twice and coming up next to Patch's motionless forearm. He pulled a glass rod from his satchel, preparing to cast a spell, but was stopped by the feel of a human hand on his shoulder.

"That won't be necessary," said Agis's winded voice. "And I don't see how you're going to keep your promise to save us by angering the giants."

The king looked over his shoulder to see the noble standing in the crook of the giant's elbow. He was covered with blood, but other than that he was apparently none the worse for wear. "You're uninjured?"

"Thanks to Kester," the noble replied. "She raised Patch's head high enough for me to crawl free. Any longer, and I would've suffocated."

From the other side of the giant, Kester cried, "Watch yerselves!"

Agis drew his sword, and Tithian glanced upward to see Nuta's hand descending toward his head. The noble's weapon flashed up to intercept the attack, driving deep into the huge palm. The giant let out an earthshaking bellow and pulled away.

Agis's sword became lodged in the giant's thick sinews and would not slip free. Clinging to his weapon, the noble was lifted off his feet. Tithian grabbed him by the ankles, and even then they rose several feet into the air before the blade came free. They dropped back to the table, accompanied by Nuta's roaring curses and the even more thunderous guffaws of his fellow giants.

"You see?" Tithian asked, picking himself out of the blood pool into which he had fallen. "It takes both of us to handle these giants."

"I'd hardly say you're handling them," observed Nymos, his muzzle wrinkled in distaste as he waded through Patch's blood. "So far, you're barely staying alive."

Tithian started to make a sarcastic retort, but Nuta's thunderous voice interrupted him.

"Laugh, fools!" the chief yelled, glaring down the table at the giants who were snickering at him. "If we attack Balic instead of Lybdos, beastheads keep our Oracle locked on Lybdos forever!"

This quieted the crowd instantly, and the giant at the table's far end said, "Nuta's right. It's our turn to keep the Oracle, our turn to get smart, but those Saram beastheads want the Oracle to stay with them. They just want to make us Joorsh dumber and dumber— until even the dwarves are smarter than us!"

Agis's brow rose, and Tithian knew his friend also found the tribe names oddly familiar. Jo'orsh and Sa'ram were the dwarven knights who had stolen the Dark Lens from the Pristine Tower. The similarity between their names and those of the two tribes could hardly be coincidence, but the king did not have time to puzzle over the relationship.

Another giant pointed at Tithian and Agis. "What about them?" he asked. "We can't just kill Balic's spies. We must also punish the city for sending them."

Tithian turned to face the giant. "I can solve that problem for you," he said. "We aren't Balican spies— or even Saram spies. We came to help you."

This sent the giants into hysterics. The tempest of rumbling laughter did not sound so different from a massive rockslide.

"What do ye think yer doing?" Kester demanded, climbing over Patch's neck. "Getting them to spare us will be hard enough without fillin' their heads with such nonsense."

"It isn't nonsense," the king hissed. "And we stand a better chance with my strategy than by begging for our lives like terrified slaves."

"What do you know about bargaining with giants?" asked Nymos.

"More than you know about negotiating with monarchs," Tithian replied. "I doubt any of you could have talked King Andropinis into lending him a fleet." When no one rebutted his claim, he looked to Agis and added, "If you want to leave here alive, let me handle this."

The noble gave a reluctant nod, then followed close behind Tithian as the king moved toward Mag'r. The sachem raised a hand to silence his laughing tribesmen, then asked, "Do you have any more jokes to tell before I kill you?"

"Considering the circumstances, I would think the clans of the Joorsh would welcome help," Tithian countered.

"What can you do to help us?" chuckled the giant, waving a massive hand at Tithian's glowing dagger. "Drill a hole in the Saram castle with your flying needle?"

"Of course not," Tithian replied. "I have already done much more than that. Haven't you heard how my fleet lured the Saram into the Strait of Baza, where we slew many beastheads?"

A giant seated to Nuta's left called, "You lost many ships!" He raised all the fingers on both hands for his companions to see, then looked back to Tithian. "The Ewe Clan watched the whole battle. You didn't win."

The chief who had spoken was far from a powerful specimen of his race. He had limbs as skinny as the trunks of faro trees, and the sunken cheeks of one who seldom went to bed with a full belly. The tattoo on his brow depicted the scrawny figure of a sheep.

"Our goal was not to win," Tithian said. "It was merely to draw the beastheads into battle, so a stronger force could ambush them outside the protection of their castle. Apparently, we erred in thinking the Ewe Clan would be brave enough to take advantage of our plan."

The chief of the Ewe Clan scowled at the affront, then tore a boulder off the slope behind him. "The Ewes are as brave as any clan!" he thundered, raising his arm.

"Your insults will get us all killed!" Agis hissed.

The noble crouched with flexed legs, preparing to dive for cover, but Mag'r was on his feet instantly. "Orl!" the sachem bellowed. "Put that rock down!"

Tithian pulled Agis back to his full height. "You mustn't show fear," he said, smirking at the noble. "It makes us look weak."

With that, Tithian gave Orl an imperious stare. The giant looked away, then hurled the boulder down the length of the canyon and out over the Sea of Silt.

"Nobody told me to help the Balican ships," Orl grumbled, giving Mag'r a repentant glance. "But we would have. We're not afraid to fight."

Mag'r grunted his acceptance of the apology, then returned to his seat and fixed his gaze on Tithian. "King Andropinis promised to stay out of our war," he said. "Why did he attack the Saram?"

"He didn't," Tithian replied.

Mag'r frowned at this. "But you said—"

"That *my* fleet attacked the Saram," Tithian corrected. "And I'm not Balican."

"He's lying, Sachem," said Orl. "That was a Balican fleet, or I'm the chief of the Iguana Clan."

"They *were* Balican ships," Tithian admitted. "I hired them from King Andropinis. But it was a Tyrian fleet, since it was under my command, and I am King Tithian of Tyr."

"Them ships sailed from Balic," said Nuta. "So them ships Balican, no matter what you are."

"Maybe, and maybe not," said Mag'r, raising a hand for the chief to be quiet. "Let's say the fleet was Tyrian, King Tithian. What interest does Tyr have in attacking the Saram?"

"Yours is not the only tribe they have robbed," the king replied. "They have something as valuable to my city as the Oracle is to the Joorsh."

"What?" demanded Nuta.

Tithian smiled. "I'd be a fool to tell you that. You might decide you want it for yourself," he replied. "But from what I've heard here today, it seems clear the beastheads are hoarding people and artifacts that possess powerful magic. What for, I wonder? So they can rule the Sea of Silt?"

A hush fell over the canyon, then Mag'r leaned down to inspect the king and his companions more closely. "No one rules the Sea of Silt," he said.

"Not now, perhaps," replied the king. "But with what they stole from Tyr . . ." He let the sentence trail off. After a moment's pause, he added, "Let's just say it would be better for both your tribe and my city to work together to make sure they don't keep it."

The giant chiefs muttered quiet comments to each other, studying Tithian and shaking their heads suspiciously. Mag'r allowed the murmur to continue for a moment, then said, "Good story, but I have no reason to believe you."

"Perhaps you'd believe us if you knew the artifact had come from the Pristine Tower," said Agis.

Tithian cringed, for the noble was gambling that just because their tribes were named after the thieves who had stolen the Dark Lens from the Pristine Tower, the giants would know what the tower was. Agis's strategy seemed to work, however. A squall of concerned whispers rose from the entire gathering of giants, and Mag'r scowled at his captives suspiciously. "What do you know of the Pristine Tower?" he demanded.

"Very little, save that the legends claim my amulet came from there," Tithian lied. He cast an annoyed glance at Agis, then used the Way to send a message:

Your gamble was a bold one, but unnecessary. I have matters well under control.

I'll believe that when they let us go, the noble replied. Despite his acerbic comment, Agis did not voice any further doubts.

When Sachem Mag'r accepted Tithian's explanation without further inquiry, the king continued, "Andropinis loaned me a fleet because he believed what I said. If he was concerned enough to risk his ships, perhaps you should worry, too. The Saram must conquer you before they capture Balic."

"No one will conquer the Joorsh!" protested Orl.

Several other giants voiced their agreement, but Mag'r remained thoughtful and studied his chiefs for several moments. Finally, he raised his hand for silence and looked at Tithian with something other than spite in his eyes.

"If we let you live, how will you help us beat the Saram?" the sachem asked.

Tithian smiled. "That's for us to decide together," he said smoothly. "Perhaps your army can lure the Saram out to do battle while we sneak into their castle. We'll steal what we came for, as well as rescue the Oracle for you."

Mag'r shook his head. "We'll have to think of another plan," he said. "You're too small to carry the Oracle."

Tithian breathed a sigh of relief. "Don't worry about that. Together, Agis and I can lift even the largest giant here," he said, laying a hand on Agis's shoulder. "Isn't that right, my friend?"

"If we have to," the noble replied, stepping away from the king's grasp. *But that doesn't mean we're friends.*

EIGHT

The Bear

As the skiff crept around the craggy point, an unexpected wisp of dank air wafted over Agis's face. In the blackness of the night, it took him a moment to locate the source of the breeze: the gaping mouth of a grotto, less than a dozen yards away.

The cave opened into the base of a rugged peninsula, a stony bluff that rose straight out of the Sea of Silt. From Agis's perspective, its sheer cliffs appeared to stretch clear to the sky, but the noble knew better. Earlier that night, as Kester had poled the skiff across the dark bay, he had seen a ring of lofty ramparts crowning the summit. The walls stood twice as tall as a giant, with flying turrets at every bend and jagged crenelations capping the entire length.

Agis motioned toward the shadowy cavern. "This one looks small enough," he whispered. "Let's see where it goes."

Nymos raised his narrow snout and sniffed at the draft, then a shudder ran down the entire length of his serpentine neck. "That wouldn't be wise," he said.

140

"There's a dreadful odor inside."

"What's it comin' from?" demanded Kester, using her plunging pole to hold the skiff motionless.

"I'm not sure," replied the jozhal. "But it's foul and savage. There's no other way to describe it."

"Whatever it is, I doubt it's any more savage than her," said Tithian, looking up from his duties as floater.

The king pointed at a low isthmus curving out from the forested hills of Lybdos to connect with the rugged peninsula beneath which they hid. Directly behind the rocky neck, Ral's golden disk hovered low on the horizon, silhouetting a chameleon-headed Saram against its golden moonlight. She paced along the treacherous crest with great care, carefully studying the placement of each step before taking it.

"The less time we give her to spot us, the better," Tithian said. "Go into the cave."

"Let's try another," insisted Nymos. "Mag'r said the peninsula is honeycombed with grottoes."

"That may be, but it could take us all night to find the passage we need," countered Tithian. "We don't have time to look for a cave you think smells nice."

"I agree," said Agis.

"You see, we *can* work together," said Tithian.

"Agreeing is not trusting," warned the noble, his hand brushing a coil of giant-hair rope that hung from his belt. As soon as Tithian's freedom was no longer necessary to the company's safety, he would use that rope to bind the king—and this time, there would be a choke loop to tighten at the first sign of trouble.

Tithian smiled at the noble's gesture, then said, "But you must admit, it won't be easy to find another cavern like this. It's big enough to hide our skiff, yet small enough to keep giants away from it while we're gone."

"What does that matter?" objected Nymos. "This plan is ludicrous. It'll never work."

"Don't ye start with that again," growled Kester, pushing the skiff forward. "Sit down and spare us yer ranting."

They were all familiar with the jozhal's objections to the plan Tithian and Mag'r had worked out. Upon hearing that the Saram citadel sat upon a peninsula riddled with grottoes, and that caves opened both inside and outside the castle, the king had suggested they might sneak inside through a subterranean passage. Nymos had immediately pointed out that even giants were smart enough to seal off such a connection. Tithian had shrugged the reptile off, assuring him—and the others—that he could break any Saram seal and rescue the Oracle.

Mag'r had liked the idea, except that he wanted the companions to open the castle gates for his warriors so that they could rescue the Oracle. To make sure Tithian and the others kept their part of the bargain, the sachem had threatened to sink the *Shadow Viper* if the gates were not opened when he attacked at dawn.

As the skiff slipped into the grotto, it grew so dark that Agis could not see the bow of the craft, much less anything that lay beyond. Still, he did not kindle a torch, fearing that its flickering light would spill out of the cave mouth and draw the sentry's attention to them. Instead, the noble borrowed Nymos's cane and knelt on the forward deck. He swung the small rod slowly back and forth, searching for obstacles in front of the ship and softly tapping the walls to keep track of them.

They continued in this manner for many minutes

before a low rumble shook the cavern, stirring up a choking cloud of silt. So deep and muffled was the sound that Agis felt it in the pit of his stomach more than he heard it.

"Far enough!" hissed Nymos. His twitching tail thumped softly against the skiff's gunnels.

Kester stopped the boat, and Agis peered back toward the cavern exit. The noble saw nothing but deep, profound darkness. "Perhaps we're in far enough to light a torch," Agis suggested.

The others agreed. Nymos fumbled about in the bottom of the boat for a moment, then passed a rancid smelling torch forward.

"What about fire?" asked the noble.

"Allow me," said Tithian. The king rummaged around in his satchel, then said, "Kester, strike this stake over this plate."

The noble heard what sounded like a stick being drawn over a rock wall, then the acrid stench of brimstone filled his nose, and a white sparkle of light momentarily blinded him. When his vision returned to normal, he held a burning brand. In the bottom of the boat lay the greasy skin from which the torch oil had come, while Kester held a slate of white pumice and a blackened stick in her hands.

Nymos snatched the implements from the tarek's hands and sniffed them with his twitching nose. "Magic?" he asked, his tone covetous.

"Hardly," replied Tithian. "A simple bard's trick."

Kester retrieved her plunging pole from across the beam. "Magic or not, light is light," she said. "Now we can go on."

The tarek pushed on.

By the light of the torch in his hand, Agis saw that a stain of milky white calcium coated the ceiling of the grotto. Slender gray stalactites pierced the veneer in a hundred places. The tips of the pendant spears had snapped off at a height half again that of a man, leaving the ends sharp and jagged. The breakage puzzled the noble, but even after studying the formations carefully, he could not determine what had caused it.

As the company passed deeper into the gloom, the calcium stain began to cover the cavern sides as well as the ceiling, until the whole passage was coated in milky white. At regular intervals, the skiff passed limestone curtains flowing out of wall fissures, or shelf formations covered with knobby constellations of dripstone. Like the stalactites, many of these were scraped and broken, as if something just barely small enough to fit occasionally passed through the tunnel.

"The odor's getting stronger," Nymos warned. "Can't you smell it?"

Agis sniffed the breeze, but smelled only stale air and the acrid stench of burning torch oil.

"It's just a rotting animal," Kester said, her nostrils flaring. "Nothing to worry about."

In spite of the tarek's reassurances, the noble drew his sword. The passage meandered back and forth, growing larger and less cramped with each turn, until the noble could not have touched his blade to either wall. At the same time, the milky ceiling sloped gradually upward, and the stalactites were broken nearer and nearer to their tips. The skiff's hull scraped over several buried obstacles, and the caps of broken stalagmites started to jut from the dust bed.

Agis was beginning to fear that the skiff would go no farther when the cave intersected another passage, this one so large that his torch did not illuminate the ceiling or far wall. The floor, which sloped upward from their tunnel, was littered with broken stalagmites, weathered ship timbers, and graying skeletons—both beast and human.

"We'd better take a closer look at this," Agis said. He raised his hand, and Kester stopped the skiff just a couple of yards shy of the larger cavern's entrance. "Is the channel too deep for me to wade?"

The tarek eyed the length of plunging pole still showing above the silt. "It's possible," she said. "But I wouldn't fancy stepping into a hole."

Agis sat down on the bow, preparing to slip into the silt channel, and suddenly found himself gagging for breath. A thick, rancid odor filled the passage, so insufferable that it made his knees tremble with nausea.

The noble felt an eerie shiver at the base of his skull, and his entire body began to tingle with spiritual energy. The torch flame flared brilliant white, then abruptly turned black, plunging the companions into darkness. Had it not been for the soft hiss of burning oil, Agis would have assumed the fire had died away. But he could feel its heat against his skin, and, instead of tossing the stick back into the boat, he had to hold the useless thing in his hand.

"Light, Nymos!" said Kester, her alarmed voice echoing off the cavern walls. "Everything's gone dark."

Nymos's claws ticked nervously, and he uttered the incantation of a spell.

"What're ye waiting for?" growled Kester.

"Agis's sword isn't glowing?" the jozhal asked.

"No," reported Agis. "We're fighting the Way, not sorcery."

"I feel it, too," said Tithian. "And the skiff dome is crackling with energy."

A deafening growl rumbled out of the larger passage,

so sonorous and low that it made the skiff tremble beneath the noble's feet. A wicked presence, as black as the torch flame and just as scorching, tore into Agis's mind. The invader rampaged through his thoughts, attacking from behind its mask of darkness. In its wake, it left nothing except searing anguish and unnatural fear, a fear such as he could not remember feeling before.

Agis tried to form an image of the crimson sun, determined to expose his attacker. The red disk had barely formed when a huge black claw rose from the murk and swatted it away, plunging the noble's mind back into darkness.

Nymos shrieked in terror, as did Kester, and even Tithian let a groan escape his lips. Their reactions did not concern Agis so much as amaze him. He had never faced a mental onslaught of such raw power and could not imagine an attacker strong enough to press four such assaults at once.

A loud scrape sounded ahead as something huge forced its way into their small cavern. From the grating rasps that shuddered down both walls, it seemed to Agis the thing filled the passage from one side to the other. The noble tried to lift his sword and found that his arm would not obey his wishes.

"Push us back," Agis said. "I could use a little distance."

The skiff lurched into motion. It moved a few yards to the rear, then suddenly stopped.

"Kester?" Agis asked.

No answer came.

"I think the tarek is paralyzed with fear," Tithian said. "This thing must be powerful."

A loud snort whooshed through the cavern, sending a rancid wind washing over Agis's face. The scraping ahead grew louder and deeper, while the muffled clatter of claws on stone rose from beneath the dust.

Agis called, "Everyone, imagine my sword glowing inside your minds. We all have to fight, or this thing will beat us."

As the creature clawed its way toward him, the noble followed his own instructions. For a moment, the blackness in his mind seemed to grow thicker in response, and he could do no better than to visualize the faint gray outline of his blade. Then, as the others joined in, the beast was not strong enough to keep them all plunged into darkness. The noble's sword, both inside his mind and outside it, illuminated the grotto in glorious white light.

Still, Agis could not concentrate on the cavern around him. Now that the neatly ordered halls of his mind were illuminated, he saw the reason for his paralysis. On the bloody floor of a corridor lay his body—or at least he thought it was his body. The corpse had been terribly mauled, so that the noble could recognize it only by his long black hair and the Asticles sword clutched in one bloody fist, now glowing with Nymos's light spell.

From the gasps of his companions, the noble could tell that each had found a similar image inside his own mind.

"See yourselves standing," Agis said, still fighting to keep the sword lit in his mind. "We've tired the beast, and now we can defeat it—but we must work together!"

A throaty growl rumbled through the cavern. A heavy paw slapped at the skiff's bow, filling the passage with silt as it fell just a few feet short of its target. The foot sank into the dust with an ominous silence, then a loud scraping sound once again filled the passage as the beast dragged itself forward.

Agis focused his thoughts inside his mind, bracing his mutilated corpse to rise. The clawed foot of a beast materialized out of the ceiling and stamped down on his chest, pressing him back to the floor. He hacked at the leg with his glowing sword, showering himself with hot blood as he cut through ropy tendons and arteries.

Still, the foot did not move.

The noble stopped attacking and spread his arms out to his sides. He visualized his body changing into a spring-loaded legtrap, such as those used by slave trackers, lirr hunters, and others who preferred to catch their quarry without fighting it face-to-face. A surge of spiritual energy rose from within himself, then his arms became the jaws of the trap. They sprang up and clamped their sharp teeth into the massive leg that had pinned him to the ground.

The claw jerked back, but Agis's trap held fast. The paw twisted and pulled in every possible direction, tearing the flesh away until raw bone lay exposed on all sides. The thing continued to struggle for a few moments, until it became apparent the foot could not be freed.

The leg fell abruptly motionless, and the wounds on Agis's corpse began to heal. The terrible weight on his chest slowly eased, and the paw faded from his mind.

"I'm free!" Tithian reported.

"Me too," Agis replied.

As the noble spoke, the torch in his hand returned to its normal color, lighting the cavern in flickering yellow. Agis's sword, too, was glowing with the white light of the spell Nymos had cast on it earlier.

The noble shook his head clear, then raised his eyes to the creature that had so nearly used the Way to kill them. When he saw what had crawled into the passage after them, Agis almost wished that the passage had remained dark. He was staring at a fanged behemoth with a black nose the size of his own head and a squarish snout longer than the skiff's bow. The beast's enormous jaws hung parted in exhaustion, the tip of a scarlet tongue just showing from between its lips, streams of drool running off the flews of its mouth. At the other end of the muzzle were a pair of tiny, fatigued eyes, set into a round, thick-boned skull covered by brown fur. Atop the head sat a pair of perky round ears, eerily gentle in their juxtaposition to the rest of the fearsome mien.

The rest of the creature was even more horrifying than its head. Long tufts of brown fur rose from the joints of the articulated shell that covered its entire body. Its bulky shoulders touched the passage walls on both sides, its belly rested on the stalagmites in the dust bed, and the ridge of its spine pressed against the ceiling.

"Ral protect us!" gasped Kester. "A bear!"

Shaking the cavern with a great roar, the beast pulled itself forward and raised a massive paw out of the dust bed. Agis dropped his torch and leaped off the deck, bringing his glowing blade down in a wild slash. The bear's paw came down behind him, splintering the skiff with a single crunching blow.

With the terrified screams of his companions echoing in his ears, Agis sliced his blade across the black tip of the bear's snout. He saw a deep gash open in both nostrils, then felt his feet plunging into the dust. A gray cloud rose up to engulf him, and the beast roared again.

Agis's ankle scraped down the side of a submerged stalagmite, sending sharp pain up his leg as it turned against the joint. Fearful of sinking past his head, the noble grasped at the rocky column with his free arm. He tried to inhale, and it seemed that he took in as much dust as air. Coughing violently, he swung his sword at the bear's gullet. The blade clanged off the beast's throat armor without penetrating.

"Kester, help!" Agis croaked.

No answer came.

"Nymos?"

The bear opened its maw and lowered its dripping mouth toward Agis's head. He tried to fight it off with his sword, but the blade did no more than chip the thing's yellow fangs. Wheezing down what he feared might be his last breath, the noble pinched his eyes shut, let his knees fold, and dropped into the dust. He pushed himself blindly forward, grasping at a stalagmite's smooth stone with his free hand and kicking at the slippery floor with his feet.

With a ferocious snort, the bear thrust its huge maw after him. Agis felt a swell of displaced silt surge over his body, then a sharp tooth scraped along his ankle. He jerked the limb free, kicking madly with the other leg. His foot found purchase on the beast's snout and sent him forward. The muffled scrape of tooth on stone rumbled through the dust, followed by the muted crack of a stalagmite being snapped off at the root.

Agis pushed himself another step forward and rose. His nose barely cleared the dust before the crown of his head touched the bony armor covering the bear's underside. As soon as he opened his eyes, they were coated with silt and began to burn horribly, but he could still see well enough to make out what was happening around him. He turned around to find a pair of bleeding nostrils sniffing at the dust where he had been standing a moment earlier. Beyond the beast's muzzle lay a few shards of the shattered skiff that had gotten hung up on a stalagmite and failed to sink. The smashed bow had been ignited by the torch he had dropped earlier. By the light of its burning wood, he saw part of Nymos's striped tail curled around the top of a stalagmite. The noble did not see any sign of Kester or Tithian.

A knot of remorse formed in the noble's stomach. If the tarek had died, he would miss her. Even the thought of returning to Tyr without his prisoner sickened him. Assuming he managed to find the king's body, it would be a poor substitute for the public trial he had promised to Neeva and the dwarves.

Determined to accomplish at least that much, Agis shuffled forward as fast as he dared. He moved his feet cautiously along the floor, feeling his way around sinkholes and submerged stalagmites, trying not to draw the bear's attention back to himself. When he reached the shoulders, he took a deep breath and plunged the tip of his sword into the creature's armpit, pushing upward with all his strength.

The blade sank to the hilt, and hot blood poured down Agis's arm. The bear bellowed in fury and wrenched its head around, snapping at its attacker with slavering jaws. The noble ducked beneath the maw and, fearing the dying beast would collapse on top of him, dove forward. The bear's paw sliced through the silt after him.

It caught Agis just as he passed the base of a thick stalagmite. The stone pillar snapped with a muffled thud, then the noble's body erupted into pain, and his mouth opened to scream. He found himself choking as silt poured down his air passage. In the next instant, the bear's paw lifted Agis out of the dust, flinging both him and the broken stalagmite across the cavern.

Agis crashed into the wall, then dropped back into the dust and sank like a stone. Fighting back black waves of unconsciousness, the noble tried to push himself upright. His feet slipped into a sinkhole, and he lashed out with his arms, hoping to catch hold of another stalagmite.

Instead, he found a burly leg. A pair of powerful hands slipped under his arms, then he was pulled out of the dust and spun around in one quick motion. Agis found himself grasped securely in the burly arms of a tarek, his back to her brawny chest and two large fists clasped together over his abdomen.

"Kester!" The name did not escape his lips, for his lungs were burning from the lack of air, and his throat was clogged with silt.

The tarek pulled the heels of her hands into the pit of Agis's stomach, at the same time bearing down on his torso and sending bolts of agonizing pain through his battered ribs. The last few breaths of air in his chest rushed out of his mouth, carrying along the silt that had been obstructing his air passages. The noble coughed several times, wracking his body with more pain, then the breath returned to his lungs. With it came the terrible pain of the three deep gashes that the bear's claws had opened along the side of his body. Agis could only imagined what would have happened to him if the beast had not been forced to tear a stalagmite out by its roots to reach him.

Once Kester allowed Agis to return to his own feet, he realized that he had been knocked a short distance down the passage. By the dim glow of the burning bow, he saw the bear's huge silhouette a few yards away. The beast had collapsed on its stomach, its lifeless muzzle buried beneath the dust and its immense bulk blocking the exit to their small passage. So completely did the creature fill the grotto that only a few feet remained between its back and the ceiling.

"Sorry to let ye do all the fighting," Kester said. Beneath the silt, her hand was still on the noble's elbow. "But by the time I got myself out of the silt and cleared my lungs, ye were under the damned beast, and I didn't want to startle it."

"It was a remarkable battle," said Tithian, moving into the light of the burning bow. The king, shorter than either Agis or Kester, barely managed to hold his chin above the silt.

"Where were you hiding during the fight?" Agis demanded. He winced as a fresh bolt of pain flashed through his body. "A little magic might have been helpful."

"And interfere with such an artful display? Never," Tithian replied. "I saw Rikus kill a half-dozen bears during his time in the arena, and not one of those kills was as clean as yours."

Agis narrowed his eyes, but he saw no point in commenting on the king's cowardice. Instead, he said, "Let's get Nymos and go."

"We can go," said Tithian. "But there isn't much of Nymos to take along."

"What do you mean?" Agis asked.

Kester's eyes grew sad, and she shook her head. "The bear's first blow took us amidships, right where he was sitting."

"If you want to bring him along, you'll have to collect the pieces first," Tithian added. He moved past the noble and picked the jozhal's tail off the other side of a stalagmite, then offered it to Agis. "Personally, I don't think its worth the time."

"Let's hope the dwarves are as kind to you as the bear was to Nymos," Agis spat. The noble slapped Tithian's hand away and turned to see if he could climb over the bear's corpse.

It was then that he saw two huge eyes in the shadows between the bear's spine and the cavern ceiling. "I'm afraid we have company," the noble whispered. Of its own accord, his free hand dropped to his empty scabbard.

"So I see," said Tithian. He was already reaching for his enchanted satchel.

Kester grabbed the plunging pole and stepped forward. "Mind yer own business, beasty!" she growled, thrusting the tip into the gap.

The eyes vanished, then a mighty groan rumbled through the cavern, and the bear's carcass started to slide back into the larger passage, filling the air with billowing clouds of dust.

"Bad men!" growled a familiar voice. "Kill bear!"

The jaws of the three colleagues fell open, then Agis cried, "Fylo? Is that you?"

The bear stopped moving. "Me Fylo," came the muffled reply. "So?"

"Do you know who this is?" Agis called.

"Bear killers," the giant returned, again tugging on the bear. "Fylo take you and throw you into Bay of Woe."

"This is your friend, Agis."

The pink-gleaming eyes appeared in the gap beneath the ceiling. "Agis? What you doing here?"

"Don't answer that," Tithian whispered, pulling a glass rod from his satchel.

Fylo's eyes darted to the king's form, then they narrowed angrily. "Tithian!"

The eyes disappeared. An instant later, a long arm shot over the bear's back and tried to pluck Tithian from the dust channel. Kester quickly raised a dagger and jabbed it into a huge fingertip. Fylo's muffled voice uttered an angry curse, then he pulled his hand away.

"You and I are supposed to be friends, Fylo!" Agis yelled. "Is this how friends treat each other?"

"Good," Tithian murmured, fingering the glass rod in his hands. "Draw him out. All I need is one chance."

Agis pushed the king's hand down. "No."

"Tithian not friend," Fylo said, peering back over the bear. He had pulled the carcass far enough into the larger cavern so that he could push his entire head into the gap, albeit sideways. "And maybe Agis not friend, either. Why kill Fylo's bear?" The giant's cavernous nostrils twitched as he sniveled in remorse.

"If you're my friend, why did you let your bear attack me?" Agis countered.

Fylo furrowed his sloped brow, then said, "Fylo didn't know it was Agis."

"And we didn't know it was your bear," Agis replied. "We were just minding our own business when it attacked. We had no choice except to defend ourselves."

Fylo considered this for a moment, then said, "You invade bear's den. Him just defending home." The giant frowned and began to withdraw.

Before the giant's face disappeared entirely, Kester quickly asked, "What are ye doing living with a bear, anyway?"

Fylo pushed his head forward again. This time, there was a proud smile on his lips. "Fylo becoming

Saram—Bawan Nal's own clan," he explained. "But first, Fylo need new head—big one, since him full-grown. So Fylo make friends with bear, ask him to trade heads." As the giant came to this last part, a sad frown crept across his lips, then he groaned, "But now bear dead. Fylo not join Saram. Him have no-where to go—again."

The giant slumped down on the other side of the bear and fell silent.

Tithian came to Agis's side. "We don't have time for this," he whispered, holding his glass rod up. "Get that dimwit to show himself again. I'll take care of him so we can get on with our business."

"I know you'll find this hard to believe," said Agis, "but I don't betray my friends."

Tithian shook his head in disbelief. "Pardon me," he sneered. "I didn't realize your taste in friends had become so bad—though I suppose I should have, given your penchant for the company of ex-slaves and dwarves."

"I find it preferable to that of kings," the noble replied coldly.

Tithian's eyes flashed in anger. "That's your choice, I suppose," he said. "But if you're not going to kill this dimwit, at least get rid of him so we can get on with our business."

"I don't think that would be wise," said Agis. "In fact, I think it would be better if I talked with him for a while. Otherwise, he may decide that it's his duty to report us to the Saram."

"Which is why you should let me kill him!" whispered the king.

Ignoring the king, Agis waded forward and grabbed the bear's ear, then used it to help him climb onto its shoulders. The effort sent daggers of pain shooting through his ribs, and blood began to ooze from the dust-caked wounds on his torso.

"Fylo, I'm sorry about killing your bear," the noble said. In the flickering firelight spilling through the gap from the burning bow, the noble could barely make out the giant's bulging eyes. "Is there anything we can do to make up the loss to you?"

The giant glumly shook his head. "No."

"If you take the bear back to the castle later, maybe you can still trade heads with it," he suggested.

Fylo looked up. "Bear too heavy for Fylo to carry."

Tithian suddenly stepped over to the bear's head. "Maybe I can help," he said. "With my magic, I can lift it for you. It would be difficult, but I could do it—if you showed us the way through these caves and into the castle."

The giant looked at the king as though he were mad. "Fylo can't do that," he said, shaking his head. "Caves don't go into castle. They go down, under Bay of Woe."

"What?" demanded Kester. "We heard there were caves inside the castle!"

The giant nodded. "Yes. Magic caves," he said. "Very pretty, in different kinds of rock—not like these caves."

"That's it, then," the tarek groaned. "We'll never get my ship back."

Agis breathed a silent sigh of relief. The noble wanted to get inside the citadel as much as Kester and the king, but he would not use his friend to achieve that goal. If Fylo helped them get inside and the Saram found out about it, the giant would certainly meet an unpleasant end.

Tithian kept his eyes fixed on the giant, then said, "That's no trouble, Fylo. I don't need to take the bear through the caves."

"Don't, Tithian," Agis said. "I won't allow it."

The king smiled up at him. "Won't allow what, Agis?" he asked. "All I'm saying is that I can take Fylo's bear into the castle through the gate."

"Really?" the giant asked, a hopeful light in his eyes.

"Yes," the king replied.

The giant's expression changed from hopeful to sad. He shook his head sadly, then said, "Bawan Nal say bear must volunteer to trade heads. If bear dead, him can't volunteer."

"Are you saying Nal expects you to lead a live bear into his castle?" asked Tithian, climbing up the beast's snout to join Agis. He took a seat on the other shoulder blade. Kester remained below, shuffling through the silt in search of the valuable floater's dome.

Fylo nodded. "Yes. Him say bear must come by itself."

"And then what happens?" inquired the king.

"Magic. They cut bear's head off, then they cut my head off, and we change," said the giant. He lifted his chin proudly, then he added, "After that, Fylo beast-head."

"I see," said Tithian. "And you've seen this ceremony performed? You've actually seen a Saram let Nal chop his head off?"

Fylo frowned. "No."

"So you haven't seen him replace it with a beast's head, either?" the king asked.

The giant shook his head. "No, not yet."

"But of course you're going to," Tithian said. "I mean, before you let him chop your own head off."

Fylo looked concerned. "Why you ask?"

"Don't pay any attention to him, Fylo," said Agis, disgusted by Tithian's efficiency in planting such cruel doubts in the giant's head. "All you have to do is find another bear, and I'm sure everything will be all right with the Saram."

"Yes, I'm sure it will," said Tithian, nodding a bit too eagerly. He looked at Agis, then said, "You know me. Always ready to think the worst—but if I were going to change my head for that of a beast, I'd want to see the ceremony performed on someone else first.'

"You think Bawan Nal tricking Fylo?" the gian. roared.

"Don't listen to him, Fylo," Agis said, grabbing the king by the collar. "He's trying to take advantage of you—"

"Not at all," objected Tithian, patiently disengaging himself from the noble's grasp. "I'm just trying to protect our friend. If I were Nal, I'd want to convince everyone that Fylo, as big and brave as he is, isn't smart enough to be king. I'd make sure they knew it by playing a cruel joke—"

The word *joke* had hardly even left the king's mouth before Fylo rolled onto his knees and, bellowing in rage, gave the bear an angry shove. Agis and Tithian threw themselves flat, clutching at its bony armor to keep from being scraped off its back.

"Fylo!" yelled Agis. "Stop!"

"No!" thundered the giant. He rolled away from the carcass and started to crawl into the larger cavern. "Fylo mad! Been tricked enough. Go kill Nal!"

"You can't do that!" called Tithian. "He's inside his castle—and he has too many warriors!"

"Not stop Fylo!" he shouted over his shoulder. "Fylo too strong and brave. Him chase Nal out of castle."

As the giant disappeared into the darkness, the clatter of shifting rocks echoed through the huge cavern, punctuated by the occasional snap of one of the bones or timbers littering the floor of the chamber.

"See what you've done?" Agis growled, crawling toward the bear's rear quarters. "You should have let me handle this my way—without lying or playing off his fears."

"How was I to know he'd go mad?" countered the king. "Besides, can you be sure I'm wrong about Nal?"

The noble did not answer. Instead, he slid down the bear's backside and onto the floor of the larger cavern. The silt here was no more than waist-deep, though the sloping floor beneath seemed much more broken than had the one in the smaller passage.

"Fylo, wait!" Agis yelled, his voice echoing through the huge chamber. "How do you know Nal is tricking you?"

"Everybody always tease Fylo," came the reply, well ahead and to the noble's left.

"Not me," Agis called, wading after the giant. He stumbled on a submerged rock, but caught himself before he fell. "I've always been honest with you, haven't I?"

The echo of clattering stones fell silent, suggesting the giant had stopped crawling. "That true," said Fylo. "You never play joke on Fylo."

"Then maybe Nal isn't, either," said the noble. "If you attack him, you might be hurting someone who really is your friend. You won't know until you test him."

A timber cracked as the giant turned around. "Test?" he called. "How?"

"Perhaps Tithian and I can make the bear look like

it's still alive," Agis said. "We can take it into the castle."

"What for?" the giant asked.

"We'll see how Nal reacts to seeing you and the bear," Agis explained. "If he isn't surprised at your return and prepares the ceremony, we'll know he was telling the truth about changing heads."

"Nal get mad when him see bear is dead," Fylo objected.

"No," Agis replied. "I'll be very close to you. When I know Nal wasn't tricking you, I'll tell you a secret about the Joorsh that will make him happy with you—just like I did when I told you about the Balican fleet."

If he had to keep this promise, the noble would harbor no guilty feelings about betraying Mag'r's plan. Because he and his companions had agreed to go along with the sachem's plan only under the threat of the direst consequences, Agis did not feel honor-bound to do as the giant demanded.

"That good," said Fylo. "But even if you make him happy, Bawan Nal still kill you and your friends. Him not like little people on Lybdos."

"Thanks for worrying about our safety," Agis replied. "But after you tell Bawan Nal the secret, you aren't responsible for what he does. That's between him and us."

"If Agis want," Fylo agreed. "But what if Nal playing trick on Fylo—like Tithian say?"

"That will be even better," Agis said. "Then the joke will be on him."

NINE

Castle Feral

"Stop there," ordered a woman's hissing voice.

Fylo obeyed, halting at the edge of the rocky isthmus. It was not an easy task for him, since each of his feet was almost as wide as the narrow neck of land. He had to stand with one in front of the other, making it hard to retain his balance. "Who that?" he asked.

There was no answer. Fylo frowned and squinted ahead. The moons had risen high enough to cast a pale light over the broken ground before him, revealing a gravel apron strewn with boulders and drifts of silt. Farther ahead, at the mouth of a gulch coming down from the peninsula's summit, a pair of square towers flanked the castle gates. The woman who had spoken was not visible in the tower windows, or anywhere outside the gates.

"Where you at?"

As the giant peered into the dim light, his foot slipped off the isthmus. He nearly fell, saving himself only by hopping forward onto the apron. The bear quickly moved forward to stand at his side, and he laid a restraining hand on its shoulder.

Fylo found it difficult to think of the beast as dead. To him, it looked the same as it had a few hours earlier, before his friend Agis had killed it by mistake. It moved with the same powerful sway to its shoulders, voiced the same deep-throated rumble when he walked too fast, and even reeked with the same rank odor of half-digested flesh.

If the giant had not been the one who pulled the vital organs out of its torso, he might have forgotten that Agis and the others were inside. The noble was using the Way to make the bear walk, roar, and even twitch its ears. Tithian was using his magic to hide the death wound beneath the beast's leg, as well as the slit they had opened in its belly so Fylo could clean it.

"Fylo come back with bear," the giant announced. "Ready to change heads."

An indistinct shape stirred in front of gate, then stepped forward. The giant quickly recognized the form as that of a female Saram. Save for an ocher breechcloth, she was entirely naked, with a willowy build and pebbled skin that had changed color to camouflage her against the gate's veneer of yellowed bone. The sight of her lithe beauty stirred a primal desire in Fylo—though the sensation filled him with melancholy loneliness rather than excitement or hope. He knew better than to think such a woman might share her heart with an ugly half-breed like him.

The woman stopped less than a pace away from Fylo. She had the wedge-shaped head of a chameleon, entirely covered by small rough scales and with a broad flange of skin flaring out from the base of her jaw. Conical eyes bulged from the sides of her head, each moving independently and covered by a thick lid that left only a narrow peephole exposed at the tip. Ridges of serrated bone lined the inside of her crescent-shaped mouth, and from the tip of her snout sprouted a wicked-looking horn of gray bone.

"We weren't expecting you, Fylo." As she spoke, a club-shaped tongue flickered from between her lips.

"Why?" demanded Fylo, watching her for any sign that might suggest she was secretly laughing at him. "Brita think stupid Fylo can't find way back?"

Brita fixed both her peepholes on the giant. "No," she said. "But it's not often a convert brings his animal-brother to Castle Feral so quickly." The woman began to circle him, taking care not to step within paw's reach of the bear. "Especially not when it's a beast like this."

Fylo felt a cold lump forming in his stomach. Agis had taken great pains to explain that he would be killed if someone discovered three men hiding inside his bear, but the giant knew his friend was sorely mistaken—the beastheads, more brutal than the noble could imagine, would not settle for mere death. Despite the danger, the half-breed did not even consider abandoning Agis's plan. When the Saram had taken him in, a warm, secure feeling had come over him. For the first time in his life, others had looked at him as something other than an unwelcome outcast. The possibility that his acceptance by the Saram had been a cruel joke was his deepest fear. Now that Tithian had suggested the possibility, he could not ignore it, any more than he could have ignored a lirr gnawing on his ankle.

"Nothing wrong with bear," Fylo snorted, twisting his head to the side so he could look at her. "Brita just jealous."

This drew a scornful sneer from the lithe sentry. "You might want to be clumsy and rank," she mocked. "But I don't."

Fylo frowned. "What you mean?"

"When you cross Sa'ram's Bridge, you'll change more than your head," she said. "You'll take the spirit of your animal-brother into yourself. From that moment forward, his nature will be yours."

Brita stepped back and waved a hand down her body. Her skin color changed from pale yellow to dark blue, her long tresses darkened to obsidian black, and her beauty became dark and sultry rather than lithe.

"From my chameleon sister, I inherited the ability to change appearances," Brita said. She pointed at Fylo's bear, then snickered, "You, on the other hand, will be ungainly and smelly."

"Fylo be strong and fierce!"

Ignoring the outburst, Brita stepped over to the bear. "He doesn't look very fierce to me," she said. "In fact, he seems kind of languid."

"What languid?" Fylo asked, knitting his brow.

"Sleepy, like he was drugged," she said, focusing one of her conical eyes on the giant. "You didn't happen to slip the bud of damask cactus into his last meal, did you?"

"Bear not drugged," the giant growled. "Fylo not know about poisons."

"But he's so docile. Hardly what you expect from a ferocious bear." She leaned over to peer into the beast's eyes, and both her eyes darted to the dust-crusted slash on its nose. "What happened to his nose?" she asked, running her finger over the wound.

Fylo shifted his eyes away and ran a finger through his scraggly beard. When he could not immediately think of an explanation, he began to feel agitated and suspicious. "Why Brita ask questions?" he demanded.

"I'm the sentry. That's my job," she replied, keeping her attention fixed on the bear. "Why does that bother you?"

"Brita not want Fylo to be beasthead!" the half-breed exclaimed.

"Not if he doesn't deserve it," said Brita, her voice spiteful and domineering. "Which he won't, if he can't remember that we call ourselves Saram—not beastheads! Now, what happened to your animal-brother's nose?"

Her threat humbled Fylo. "Bear go to Knosto to eat Joorsh and their sheep," he lied, forcing himself to calm down. "Get full and fall asleep. Wake up with knife cutting nose."

Brita flapped the flange at the base of her neck. "You expect me to believe a story like that?" she spat.

Suddenly, the bear opened its mouth and roared as loudly as Fylo had ever heard it roar in life. It bared its mighty fangs and stepped toward Brita, taking the half-breed so by surprise that he did not move to stop the beast as it followed Brita to the gate.

"Don't let it attack!" Brita screamed, grabbing a long lance propped against the wall.

"Bear!" Fylo yelled. As he stomped after the beast, he could not keep from chuckling, for he was imagining how embarrassed the woman would be if she knew she was running from a dead bear. "Leave Brita alone!" he said, grabbing it by a plate of shoulder armor.

Brita leveled her spear at the beast's eyes. "You can't take that thing inside!" she hissed. "You can't control it!"

A hooting laugh, as loud as it was mocking, rolled

over the top of the gate. "If Fylo didn't have control over his bear, you'd be dead by now—isn't that so, Brita?" The voice sounded as deep as the Sea of Silt, but there was also a haunting, melodic tone to it. "Now stand aside and let our friends enter Castle Feral."

Brita folded her neck flange over her shoulders and turned her eyes toward the ground. "Yes, my bawan," she said, stepping aside and graciously waving the half-breed forward.

As the huge gates ground open, Fylo looked toward the top of the wall. The giant saw Nal's owlish head peering down at him. The bawan's face consisted of a circular mask of gray feathers, with a pair of huge golden eyes and a black, wickedly hooked beak at the center. His pointed ears resembled nothing quite so much as a pair of feathery horns, which he could turn at various angles according to what he wished to hear.

When the gates were at last fully spread, Nal waved Fylo inside. "Enter, my friend," he called. "Your return comes much before we expected it, but you are no less welcome."

The half-breed obeyed, stooping over to avoid banging his forehead on the gate's crossbeam. At the same time, he heard Nal's voice echoing inside his mind as the bawan used the Way to address the bear. *And will you grace us with your presence as well, my beastly friend?*

The question caused Fylo to stumble and fall, though his stomach was so knotted in alarm that he hardly noticed. The bear was just an animal, and, even when it had been alive, it had not understood giant language. The half-breed did not doubt that Nal realized this as well as he did, for the bawan was the smartest giant he had ever met. Why, then, had Nal addressed it in the Trade Tongue?

The bear came up behind the giant and sniffed at him with its nose, then tried to turn him over with its paw. Taking the gesture for a hint from Agis, the half-breed stood. He found himself in a small courtyard, flanked by a pair of lion-headed Saram armed with spiked clubs and dressed in loincloths of tanned hide. Behind the guards rose walls as high as the cliffs that ringed the rest of the peninsula. Fylo felt as though he were standing in the bottom of a deep pit. The only route out of the cul-de-sac was a path that traversed a granite cliff directly ahead. The trail ran through a deep trench that had been carved into the escarpment. At the top of the furrow rested a stone ball, as large as a Balican schooner, that could be rolled down the path to seal the gate tight.

High above, Bawan Nal's towering form lumbered across a wall to the top of the trench path. Like Brita and the gate guards, he wore nothing but a loincloth. A layer of downy gray feathers covered his stout body.

"Come, Fylo," he called. "Bring your brother to his new home."

The bawan's invitation helped soothe Fylo's mounting fears, and he obediently started up the path. The bear followed a few steps behind, grunting softly with each step. By the time they reached the midway point, the grunts had changed to a sort of labored wheeze, and the beast was stumbling more often than it should.

Fylo paused and laid a hand between the bear's massive shoulder blades. "Plan working good," he whispered, worried that the effort of animating the beast was tiring Agis more quickly than they had expected. "Not much farther."

The bear brushed past him and kept climbing. Then, three-quarters of the way up the slope, it tripped over a knob in the rocky trail and fell to its stomach. The giant waited for it to rise again, but the creature did not move, and from inside came muted voices. They were so soft that Fylo could barely hear them, but that did not diminish his concern.

"Get up, bear!" Fylo yelled, banging his fist on its mighty rib cage to alert Agis to his alarm.

"Fylo! Is that any way to treat a friend who's about to give up his head for you?" chastised Nal, waiting at the top of the path. The bawan's feathery ears were laid flat out to the sides, and his golden eyes were fixed on the bear's motionless form. "Perhaps your bear is ill. That would explain his fatigue."

The half-breed shook his head. "Bear strong—but clumsy."

This did not seem to satisfy Nal, who sent a query to the bear's mind, *What's wrong, my friend? Surely, you aren't afraid?*

Again, he addressed the beast as though it could understand his words, and once more Fylo's heart began to pound with fear. He looked toward the bawan, asking, "Bear can't understand. How come Nal talk to him like that?"

As the half-breed finished his question, the bear rose up on its hind legs and let out a long, furious growl that echoed off the ramparts.

"I think he understands, Fylo," chuckled Nal. "No bear likes being called a coward."

The bawan lifted his own head and issued a series of resonant hoots, every bit as loud as the bear's growl and just as savage. The lion-headed guards in the courtyard below answered with a pair of mighty roars, then a cacophony of wild yowls, bellows, caws, and other calls rolled off the clifftop. Even Brita screamed wildly, her hissing voice drifting to Fylo's ears over the top of the gate.

Nal turned to the ball at the top of the trench and banged his beak against the stone in encouragement, until the din grew so ferocious that the granite cliff itself trembled. Even the bear's body armor shook visibly.

Fylo laid a hand on the bear's shoulder and gently pushed it back down to all four feet, then led it the rest of the way up the path. When he finally stepped past the round stone at the top, Nal raised a hand to silence the maelstrom he had caused. The bawan walked slowly around Fylo's beast, then gave the half-breed an approving nod. "A handsome animal-brother," he said, taking Fylo's arm and leading him into the castle interior.

The place was nothing but an offal-littered plain of barren rock, with at least two hundred Saram giants roaming over the stark granite. Like all the beast-heads Fylo had ever seen, none wore anything more than a loincloth, and sometimes not even that. They were all going about their business in a state of chaotic disorganization—butchering sheep, sleeping, rolling around in vicious wrestling matches, even making love—with total disregard for what was happening a few feet away. In one place, an eagle-headed mother was trying to lull her newborn infant to sleep, while less than ten yards away, a dozen of her tribesmen danced in a circle, madly screeching, howling, and chirping at the twin moons.

In contrast to their parents, the children all had distinctly human heads, though their features were always marred by some gruesome blemish. Less than ten yards away, a seven-foot toddler was playing in a dust pit. She looked completely normal, save for the trunklike extension dangling off her nose. Near her, two brothers were playing catch with a full-grown ram. With their dark hair and patrician features, they did not look so different than the few Joorsh children that Fylo had seen, save that the oldest boy's ears dangled down to the ground, and the right eye of the youngest was so large that it covered the whole side of his face.

Beyond the two boys, huge walls of crystal stood scattered across the entire plain, each formed from a different mineral and each enclosing an irregular patch of ground. There were quartz enclosures, mica, tourmaline, and a dozen others. The compounds could not have been called buildings, for they lacked anything that looked like a roof, a door, or a window. Instead they resembled the cactus hedges that Fylo had seen around the estates of some Balican nobles when he went to steal sheep or grain.

The only thing standing higher than the crystal walls were the blocky fortifications that encircled the top of the stony bluff. The walls stood twice as high as a giant, with huge piles of stones heaped all along their foundations. These mounds were interrupted only occasionally, by rough-hewn staircases or murky doorways that led to the hanging turrets outside the castle. In many places, beastheads were passing boulders up the ramparts, where other giants loaded the stones into huge carts and transported them to strategic locations along the wall.

As Bawan Nal led Fylo toward the back of the citadel, he continued to hold the half-breed's arm. "You've done well to win the heart of such a magnificent creature, my friend," he said, twisting his owl-like head almost completely around to watch it. "Soon, you and he shall be the same."

"What you mean?" asked Fylo, worried that the bawan meant he would be dead—the same as the bear.

Nal smiled. "You shall see soon enough."

Without stopping, the bawan suddenly tipped his head back and sounded a series of deep hoots that set his feathers to waving. The cries were long and sonorous, more like the trumpeting of a horn than the call of a living creature.

A hush quickly spread over the yard. As Nal led Fylo and the bear toward a quartz enclosure in the far corner of the citadel, Saram giants began to fall in line behind them. The beastheads with the deepest voices sang an eerie lyric composed entirely of long, sad howls. Despite the lack of words, the strange song sent shivers down the half-breed's spine. When the procession reached the compound, the bawan raised a hand to halt the procession.

The bawan stepped into the entrance of the enclosure—an unadorned break in the wall of quartz—and addressed the tribe. "We will soon welcome a new warrior to the Saram," he said, his eyes gleaming yellow with reflected moonlight. "Fylo has already proven his worth to us by warning me of the Balican fleet, and he has proven himself worthy of our admiration by selecting as his animal-brother the mightiest of all Lybdos's beasts: a bear!"

The crowd broke into a chorus of wild growls. Fylo beamed at them in delight, then looked into the bear's eyes. He nodded, signaling Agis that now was a good time to reveal the secret that would keep Nal from being angry. The half-breed suspected that they did not have long before the bawan was ready to cut the bear's head off.

Nal continued, "As if he had not already done enough to earn our esteem, Fylo brought his animal-brother to us in a third the time that any convert has ever done it before!" The bawan gestured at the bear. "It only took him five days to convince this mighty beast to give up its head!"

Fylo did not miss the note of mockery in Nal's voice, but the wild shrieks and whistles that accompanied the crowd's cheer reassured him that all was well.

Nal gestured for Fylo to enter the enclosure. "Bring your bear inside, my friend."

The proud smile faded from Fylo's lips, and he could not tear his gaze away from the bear. He wondered why Agis was waiting so long to tell him the secret that would make Nal happy. The thought crossed his mind that his friend had betrayed him; maybe there was no secret.

"You give Fylo bear's head now?" he asked, already dreading the moment when the bawan found Agis and the others inside the beast.

"We should wait for dawn," Nal said. "But foolish Mag'r thinks he's sneaking up on us. The Joorsh army will arrive before dawn, so we'll have to do this tonight."

Fylo's jaw fell open in astonishment. "The Joorsh?" he gasped. "Here?"

Nal nodded. "It's taken a long time for them to get up the nerve to attack, but our losses to the Balican fleet finally gave them the courage," said the bawan. He fluffed the feathers beneath his beak, then eyed Fylo thoughtfully. "Strange how that worked, isn't it?"

The giant furrowed his brow. "How what work?"

"Sachem Mag'r and I had an agreement. If the Balicans interfered in our war, we were to suspend our fight and attack Balic." Nal reached behind the enclosure wall and grabbed an axe. It had an obsidian blade as large as a schooner's keel-board. "But instead of attacking Balic, the Joorsh are sneaking up on us!" the bawan yelled, obviously angry.

"Nasty Joorsh!" Fylo agreed, nodding vigorously.

The bawan laid the axe blade against Fylo's neck. "I think Sachem Mag'r doesn't need the Oracle as much as he claims. I think he's smart enough to send you here to warn me about the fleet, so we would attack it—and lose a quarter of our warriors!"

"Fylo no Joorsh!" Fylo gasped. "Sachem Mag'r filthy!"

Nal did not remove the blade. "And do you know what else I think?" he sneered. "I think *you're* not as dumb as you act. It's no coincidence that you returned on the eve of Mag'r's attack, is it?"

Fylo's recessed jaw began to quiver, and he shook his head. "Not Fylo's idea," he said.

Bawan Nal snorted. "What are you to do?" he demanded. "Wait until the battle starts, then use your bear to open the gate?"

Fylo shook his head. "No. Bawan think wrong."

"I think right," Nal replied, raising his axe.

The bear leaped forward, knocking Fylo aside and blocking the bawan's axe with an immense foreleg. The blow took the limb cleanly off. A trickle of cold blood spilled from the dead beast's wound, and it crashed face-first to the stony ground. Instantly, a dozen Saram warriors jumped on its back and began prying at its bony armor.

The half-breed stepped toward the bear, then abruptly stopped. He still did not know whether Nal had been lying about making him a Saram, so he couldn't decide whether he should try to correct the misunderstanding or attack Nal.

As Fylo contemplated his decision, the dead bear tried briefly to stand. The giants on its back weighed too much for even its great strength, and it collapsed back to the ground. The beastheads attacked with renewed fury, and a shoulder plate went sailing out of the fray. Soon, the half-breed knew, they would reach the bear's interior. They were so furious that he doubted they would even notice Agis's small body before they ripped it to pieces.

The thought of losing his first and only true friend made up Fylo's mind for him. He stepped over to the fray and grabbed a weasel-headed woman, throwing her off the bear.

"Get up, Agis!" he yelled.

Behind you, Fylo! came the reply. *Don't worry about us.*

The half-breed spun and saw Nal standing behind him. His axe was raised to strike again, but, astonished by the bear's mental message, he was staring at it in wide-eyed astonishment. Fylo gave the bawan a mighty shove, sending him crashing back into the quartz enclosure. Nal's head hit the wall with a resounding crack, and the axe slipped from his hands. His eyes grew glassy and unfocused, then he reached back to grasp a large crystal and brace himself.

Returning his attention to saving Agis, Fylo pulled another Saram off the pile, then a second and a third. As quickly as he flung one aside, another leaped into the missing warrior's place. Other beastheads began to attack him, clawing at his gravelly skin and raining thunderous blows down on his head. The half-breed could see that he would never free his friend in this manner, but be did not know what else he could do.

The bear's efforts were just as futile. Pinned as it was on its stomach, it could bring neither its three remaining legs or its muzzle to bear on them. It tried to roll over and crawl away, but met with no success. The immense weight bearing down on it probably would have been too great for a live bear, and Fylo knew that, as exhausted as Agis must be, he would not be able to infuse its muscles with even that much strength.

"Leave bear!" Fylo yelled, locking his arm around a lizard-headed Saram. "Bear not dangerous—Fylo is!"

The half-breed grabbed the warrior's chin and pulled, snapping the neck with a loud crackle. A death rattle gurgled from the beasthead's throat, then he dropped motionless to the ground. The other Saram hardly seemed to notice, save that some of those attacking him added their fangs to the battle.

Run, Fylo! Agis sent. *You'll do us more good if you escape.*

"But—"

Do it! Agis commanded. *Before Nal attacks you again.*

The half-breed grabbed a Saram attacker and spun around to see Nal leaping at him. The bawan held his fingers splayed like claws, while his hooked beak gaped wide open for the strike. Fylo hurled his captive at the owl-headed giant. Both Saram crashed to the ground with a tremendous rumble, Nal's fingers and beak slashing wildly at his tribesman.

Fylo stepped away, pumping his legs hard as he tried to sprint to safety. Three strides later, a handful of Saram hit him from the side. The half-breed slammed into the ground and heard himself groan as his breath was forced from his lungs. In the next instant, he found a beasthead warrior sitting on each of his limbs, with two more straddling his chest.

Gasping for breath, he arched his back and tried to roll. His efforts were to no avail. Like his bear, he could not battle the sheer crush of bodies holding him down. Fylo looked toward the beast and saw that the Saram had ripped most of its bony plates away. Now they were mercilessly gouging its dead flesh with their fangs and filthy fingernails. The half-breed summoned his remaining strength and made one last attempt to pull free of his captors, but could not liberate even a single limb.

Nal came over and stood at Fylo's side, holding his axe near the half-breed's head. "I accepted you into my tribe," he hissed angrily. "And you repay me with treachery!"

The bawan brought the axe handle down. A loud crack rang through Fylo's skull, and everything went black for a moment. His nose went numb, and blood began to stream back into his throat, filling his mouth with a coppery taste.

"Please," Fylo begged. "Don't let warriors hurt little people."

"Little people?" Nal asked.

The bawan struck again with his axe handle. This time, a terrible lancing pain shot through Fylo's eye. The lid puffed up instantly.

"In bear," Fylo said, using his chin to motion toward the beast. "They have secret for Bawan Nal."

Nal stopped hitting Fylo and twisted his fluffy head toward the bear. About that time, the half-breed saw a flash of blue, sizzling light glimmer over the beast's entire body. The Saram pinning it to the ground screamed in shock and clawed madly at each other in their panicked haste to leap free. With a great roar, the beast rose to its three remaining feet and galloped forward in an awkward hobble, heading straight for Fylo.

Nal stepped between the half-breed and his bear, hefting the axe and hooting an eerie war cry. The bear flung itself into the air, trying to leap over the blade and seize the bawan's head in its maw.

Nal ducked. At the same time, the bawan brought his blade around in a horizontal slice that severed the bear's remaining foreleg and ripped the bony armor off its chest. The animal's long snout plowed into the rocky ground and stopped, while the momentum of its charge carried it head over heels. Its immense rump crashed into the enclosure wall, and it came to rest flat on its back.

"Agis!" Fylo yelled, worried about his friend.

The bawan's axe flashed three more times, severing the bear's two remaining limbs and its head. Once the beast could cause no more harm, Nal positioned himself above its chest and swung his blade one more time. When it cleaved the bear's sternum, Fylo heard a trio of muffled screams sound from inside the beast's body.

Nal's ears pricked up. He pulled his axe free with a loud rasp, then reached into the wound with both hands to pull the sternum apart. The heavy bones separated with a sharp crack, and he opened it up like a walnut.

"What have we here?" the bawan asked. He glanced back at Fylo with an angry glimmer in his eye, then thrust a huge hand inside the bear's chest. "Lungworms?"

TEN

The Crystal Pit

An immense sheet of rock crystal covered the pit, its edges melting into the surrounding granite with no visible seam. So thin and pellucid was this lid that whenever one of the amorphous forms beneath slipped up to press against the veneer, Agis saw the ghostly features of a face. Usually the visage belonged to a child with a soft chin, fleshy cheeks, and hurt, questioning eyes.

"Why did you come to Lybdos?" demanded Nal.

The bawan stood on Sa'ram's Bridge, a stone trestle that arced over the pit. With one hand, he held Agis's ankles, dangling the noble far above the translucent slab. In his other hand, Nal clutched Tithian and Kester, his fingers wrapped so tightly around their chests that their faces had turned purple.

Tithian was the one who answered. "We've already told you!" the king declared. "Our ship wrecked on Mytilene. Sachem Mag'r promised to let us live if we helped him."

"The Joorsh are attacking at dawn," added Kester.

179

"That's when we're supposed to open yer gates."

"And what was Fylo's part in this plan?"

With the hand clutching Tithian and Kester, the bawan gestured across the pit, where four Saram warriors held the unconscious half-breed by his arms and legs. The rest of the enclosure was empty, for most Saram were busy preparing for the next day's battle.

"Fylo has no part in this," said Agis. "We tricked him into helping us."

"Don't lie to me," Nal hissed. "I'm wise enough to know that you are thieves, and that Fylo is a traitor to all giants." The bawan nodded to the tribesmen holding the giant. "Show our guests what awaits them."

The four warriors pitched Fylo's battered body onto the pit. The slab did not shatter or even crack, but merely sagged under the giant's great weight. The half-breed lay on his back, covering the silvery sheet almost completely, with his hands and feet hanging over the edges. Beneath him, the ghostly faces pressed their lips and noses against the sheet, their muffled voices crying out in the high-pitched tones of excited children. Many of the Saram backed away from the hole, covering whatever passed for ears on their beastly heads and turning away with fearful expressions on their faces.

After a moment, Fylo began to sink, slowly passing through the rock crystal. The faces began to swirl around him in blurry, saffron streaks. Then, as his shoulders and knees melted through the slab, the half-breed fell free and plunged into the hole. The ghostly countenances streaked into the darkness after him.

"The giant you just killed never intended you anything but good!" Agis yelled, glaring up at Nal.

"That is for me to decide," the bawan replied. "Besides, I doubt Fylo is dead—though he'll soon wish he were."

"What do you mean?" Agis demanded.

"This is where we keep our deformed heads after we become true Saram. We must give them playthings so they can amuse themselves, or they will fade away—and us with them," he said, his ears cocked at a cruel angle. "Be assured, the Castoffs will make Fylo pay for his treachery a thousand times over."

"I suggest you think carefully before sending us to join him," said Tithian. "If you release us, we can help you defeat the Joorsh. But if you try to punish us, nothing will stop us from helping them defeat your tribe."

Nal's eyes flashed angrily. "Your threats are as empty as your promises," he said. "What difference can three puny humans make in a battle between giants?"

"We may be small, but my magic is not," said Tithian. "It's for you decide whether I use it to aid you, or to oppose you."

Nal's hooked beak clattered in the bawan's equivalent of a chuckle. "I think you're overestimating the value of your magic," he said. The bawan leaned over and thrust the hand holding Tithian and Kester toward the pit, then opened his fingers and allowed the tarek to fall free. A short scream sounded from her lips before she slammed into the slab and lay motionless, the Castoffs swarming up to press their faces to the crystal beneath her body.

"If you are so powerful, save her," said Nal.

Tithian tried to pull his arms free. Nal continued to hold him tight, preventing the king from reaching for his spell components or making any mystical gestures.

"Loosen your grip," Tithian ordered. "I need my hands to use my magic."

"How unfortunate for your tarek friend," sneered the bawan, watching Kester's stunned form slowly rise to her knees. "I don't think I should trust you with free hands."

On the crystal lid, Kester rose to her knees and crawled toward the edge. She had traveled only a short distance before her arms and legs melted into the rock crystal. The tarek snarled in frustration and looked up at Agis. "I never should've taken your silver," she said, slipping the rest of the way through the lid.

After she vanished into the abyss, Nal turned Agis right side up, then lifted him and Tithian to the level of his golden eyes. "Now, tell me what you thieves want with the Oracle, or you will join her."

"We have no interest in the Oracle," Agis said. "It's the Joorsh—"

"Don't deny it!" snapped the bawan. "Sa'ram has told me that humans seek it."

"Sa'ram said that?" Tithian asked. "Why would he think we want your Oracle?"

Agis realized the answer to the question almost before the king had finished asking it: the Oracle had to be the same thing as the Dark Lens. It was the lens that the ancient dwarf and his partner had stolen from the Pristine Tower so many centuries ago, and only it would be so important to them that they were still keeping a watch over it a thousand years later. Probably, the noble reasoned, they had brought it here for safekeeping, and the artifact had eventually become a central focus of giant culture.

"Sa'ram does not explain his reasons to any giant—even me," Nal said, answering Tithian's question. "But to doubt him would be foolish."

"Of course, as it would be to doubt Jo'orsh," Tithian replied, nodding with exaggerated sincerity. "We know that even in Tyr. We also know that they're the dwarves who stole the Dark Lens—what you call the Oracle—from the Pristine Tower."

"How dare you say such a thing!" Nal roared, indignant. "Sa'ram and Jo'orsh were the first giants—not dwarves!"

Agis raised his brow, suspecting that both Tithian and Nal were correct. From the *Book of the Kemalok Kings*, he knew that Sa'ram and Jo'orsh had been the last dwarven knights. But, as the birthplace of the Dragon, the Pristine Tower had become a dangerous and magical place, where living beings were transformed from one kind of creature into something as different as it was hideous. Given that the two dwarves had penetrated to its very core, it seemed likely that they had come out as something else—in this case, giants.

"The race of Jo'orsh and Sa'ram is not important," Tithian said. "What matters is that they were thieves. We've come to reclaim what they stole for the rightful owner."

Agis frowned. "There's no need for lies," he said. "The truth will work better here."

Tithian fixed a murderous gaze on the noble. "I agree. That's why I *am* being honest, this time." He looked back to Nal. "I'm here on behalf of the true owner of the Dark Lens."

"How can that be?" scoffed the bawan. "Sa'ram has said that Rajaat fell more than a thousand years ago."

Tithian gave the giant a confident smile. "If you

know the history of Rajaat, then you also know who defeated him, and therefore who has the right to his property."

"You can't mean Borys!" Agis gasped. "Even you couldn't sink to such depths of corruption!"

"It's not corruption for a king to do what he must to save his city," Tithian replied.

"You care nothing for Tyr!" the noble accused, noting that Nal was silently watching the exchange with rapt interest. "By giving the lens to the Dragon, you would destroy everything the city stands for—as well as any hope we may have of saving the rest of Athas. What can be worth that?"

"That's not your concern," Tithian replied, pointedly turning his head away.

Knowing that he would learn no more by arguing, the noble fell silent and began to puzzle out the king's motivations for himself. Tithian was not the type to serve as an errand boy for someone else, especially not when the task involved dangers such as they faced at the moment. If the king had come here on the Dragon's behalf, there had to be a special reward in it for him—and Agis had to figure out what.

Tithian continued his discussion with Nal. "I suggest you give the Oracle to me now, Bawan," he said. "You'll save your tribe a terrible fight with the Joorsh."

Nal held the king out at arm's length and let Tithian's legs dangle free. "And what happens when I drop you instead?"

"You and your tribe will die, if not at Mag'r's hands, then at the Dragon's," Tithian replied. Had he been back in the Golden Palace addressing his personal valet, he could not have sounded any more calm and sure of himself.

"You're bluffing," Agis said.

The bawan nodded. "Your friend is right," he said, still holding the king over the pit. "I have nothing to fear from the Dragon. Sa'ram's magic prevents Borys and his minions from discovering the Oracle's location."

"Am I not Borys's servant? And did I not find the lens?" Tithian asked. "There are ways to bypass the spells hiding it—as my presence here proves."

Nal remained silent.

"Both Andropinis and Borys know I took a Balican fleet to search for the lens," the king continued, pressing his argument. "When not one ship out of twenty returns, how long will it take them to guess what happened? How many giant villages will the Dragon destroy before he lands on Lybdos?"

"Your audacity is astounding," Agis said. "No one else would dare threaten his captor in these circumstances—but I suppose I should expect no less. You've always been boldest when the prize was the greatest."

A cloud came over Tithian's face. "I warn you, don't interfere."

"Interfere with what?" demanded Nal.

"With the arrangements I've made to keep the Dragon from savaging Tyr," supplied Tithian, jumping in with an answer before Agis could respond. "Pay him no attention. Nothing he can say will change what I've told you."

Agis did not correct the statement, for if Nal was the kind of ruler who would allow himself to be intimidated, anything the noble could say would only make matters worse. Still, Agis perceived the lie behind the words, for he had long been suspicious of the purpose behind the king's preoccupation with sorcery and the Way. Now, it had become apparent that Tithian lacked only the Dark Lens to convert his dream into a nightmare for Tyr.

After considering Tithian's words for a moment, Nal said, "I wish to know what prize you expect to earn by giving our Oracle to the Dragon."

"All you need to know is that in the end, you'll give the lens to me, or the Dragon will take it from the ruins of your citadel," Tithian countered. "The choice is yours."

The bawan's neck feathers ruffled. "I've heard the truth in what you've said, Tithian," he said. "And before this is over, I'll also hear the truth in what you haven't said."

It disappointed Agis to see Nal restraining his anger, for it meant Tithian's threats had affected him. "I'm sure you'll find what the king hasn't said more interesting than what he did, Bawan," said Agis. "But first, it would serve you well to hear me out. I've also come to Lybdos seeking use of the Dark Lens, but my purpose is to kill the Dragon, not serve him. Only then can we return Athas to the paradise it once was."

"Kill the Dragon?" Nal muttered, incredulous.

"My friends have already gathered two of the things we need," Agis replied. "We have an enchanted sword forged by Rajaat himself, and our sorceress has been imbued with the magic of the Pristine Tower. All we need now is the Dark Lens."

"And what magic will keep the Castoffs in their cave after you take the Oracle away?" Nal demanded.

"The same magic that keeps them in the caves when it's the Joorsh's turn to keep the lens," Agis countered.

"Mytilene is only a wade of three days away from Lybdos, and even at that distance the magic is weakened. Many Castoffs escape and harm my Saram," he said. "If I allow you to take the Oracle farther away, my tribe will be destroyed as surely as if the Dragon took it from us."

"Perhaps we can find another way to keep them at bay," Agis insisted. "This is for the good of all Athas."

"What do I care about Athas?" Nal replied. "My concern is the Saram first, and all giants second."

"Killing Borys benefits giants, too!" Agis objected.

"Not as much as keeping the Oracle where it belongs," replied the bawan, lowering Agis toward the pit. "No matter how noble you believe your cause, I won't allow you to steal it from us."

With that, Nal dropped Agis onto the crystal lid.

The noble's knees buckled as soon as he hit, and he collapsed onto his side. The surface seemed curiously warm, and Agis could feel it buzzing with the flow of energy. Below his cheek, Castoffs began to press their faces against the translucent surface, and he could hear them crying in the lonely, frightened voices of young children.

Agis closed his eyes. Although he had not been able to use the Way to help Fylo or Kester, he hoped to save himself by buoying his body on its surface, much as Damras had shown him how to float a ship. He felt the familiar tingle of energy rising from deep within himself—then a brilliant flash exploded inside his mind, bringing with it the blaring clamor of a thousand trumpets. The noble's mind ruptured into unbelievable agony, and, though he could not hear it over the terrible din inside his head, a horrid scream rasped out of his throat. Every muscle in his body erupted into fiery pain, and a wicked, cramping torment filled his stomach. He tried to open his eyes, but found it impossible. From somewhere above him, he heard Bawan Nal laugh.

"That's but a small taste of the Oracle's power," the Saram said. "Do not call on the Way again—or the anguish you feel will be a hundred times worse."

The pain vanished as quickly as it had come, leaving Agis soaked in cold sweat and gasping for breath. A freezing chill ran through his body. He opened his eyes and found himself half-submerged in rock crystal. One side of his body had already passed through the translucent cover. It was visible only as a pinkish blur, and it was as numb as ice. The noble looked up and was surprised to see Tithian watching him with a remorseful expression, then he dropped into the abyss.

Agis plunged downward for what seemed like forever, his gaze fixed on the translucent cover above, his terrified screams breaking against huge quartz crystals growing out of the granite walls. The Castoffs streamed after him, their masklike faces strangely detached from any semblance of a head and glowing in the darkness like a hundred moons.

Agis crashed into something pulpy and warm, stopping with a terrifying abruptness that sent a fiery ache burning through his abdomen. His head smashed into a bony rib and his limbs slapped against hairy flesh, then a deep grunt echoed off the walls of the pit.

Agis found himself cradled in Fylo's midriff, more than a dozen yards below the pit's crystal cover. As he looked around, he glimpsed Kester's motionless form draped over the giant's shoulder, a dozen Castoffs teeming over her body. The giant's head was also being swarmed, with several glowing faces jostling for position as they each tried to slip over his visage.

The noble rolled onto his stomach, preparing to

stand, and found himself peering past Fylo's hip into the crystal-lined depths of a black shaft. It occurred to Agis that the half-breed had gotten lodged far above the abyss bottom, then the searing nettle of the Cast-offs' touch erupted all over his body.

* * * * *

Bawan Nal allowed Tithian a moment to contemplate Agis's fate, then pinched the king between a massive thumb and finger. "Tell me what reward you expected in return for stealing our Oracle," the Saram ordered. He pressed his fingertips toward each other, painfully compressing Tithian's chest. "Or must I squeeze the answer from you?"

"What does it matter to you?" the king asked. "You have no choice except to yield the Oracle."

The Saram's ears twitched several times, and he brought Tithian closer to his eye. "You're the one without choices."

As Nal's beak closed, the king heard the soft hiss of a deep breath. The bawan's eye suddenly grew cold and still, and Tithian found his attention riveted on the yellow orb. He tried to look away and could not.

Realizing that his mind was about to be attacked, Tithian visualized his defense: an unbreakable net of transparent energy, so fine that not even a gnat could slip through the mesh. At its edges, the strands were fused to the feet of a dozen huge bats, with red flame where their eyes should have been and mouths filled with venom-dripping fangs.

Tithian had barely managed to move his trap into position before a glimmering white lion with wings came roaring into his mind. The creature hit at a full charge, filling the dark grotto with sizzling echoes and flashing blue sparks. The beast stretched the net across half the cavern before Tithian's bats managed to catch up and close their web tightly enough to bind the immense wings to its sides.

The lion roared in rage, then plummeted straight for the deepest, darkest abyss in Tithian's mind. The king sent his bats up toward an exit. As they struggled to obey, Nal's construct changed from flesh to rock, growing heavier and heavier, dragging its captors deeper into the Tyrian's intellect.

Tithian summoned more energy to enlarge his bats. The effort wore on him, but he did not stop until each bat was the size of a kes'trekel. If he let the lion escape, he knew it would require so much energy to recapture it that he would be too weak to counterattack.

The lion's fall slowed for a moment, then the construct changed from rock to iron, doubling in weight all at once. The beast passed out of the main grotto, dragging Tithian's huge bats along into the black pit at the base of his mind.

The lion opened its mouth, but it was Nal's voice that came out. "Fool!" he chortled. "You cannot overpower me. I have the Oracle!"

The construct began to claw at its net, pulling the bats down toward its reach. Calling on the last of his strength, Tithian tried to dissolve the mesh and let Nal's construct fall free, but he was too late. The beast had the bats by their legs, and as it continued through the darkness, it clawed and gnawed at their stomachs. Within instants, it had devoured the Tyrian's ambushers and was plunging freely toward the center of the king's mind. It did not even bother to flap its wings and break the fall.

A short time later, there was a deafening reverberation as the lion's iron body struck the bottom of the pit. It gave a great roar, and golden beams began to shine from its eyes. "Let's see what you're hiding down here, shall we?"

The lion ran its glowing eyes over the pit walls, until it found a single, winding tunnel opening to one side. With a low growl of satisfaction, it bounded away. Venomous lizards leaped out of the shadows and clamped steel-toothed jaws around the beast's legs, while blood-drinking scorpions dropped onto its head to stab at its eyes with dripping barbs. The construct countered by crushing the reptiles underfoot and flinging the arachnids off with vigorous head shakes, but many attacks still found their marks.

The attackers' venom did not slow the lion down at all. Beads of syrupy fire dripped from the wounds on its legs, and tears of acid poured from the eyes. Both fluids neutralized the poison long before it could cause any damage to the beast.

The tunnel opened into a chamber supported by hundreds of ebony pillars. On each column hung a single torch, burning with a black flame that absorbed light instead of casting it. The only sound was of a man chuckling in a soft, maniacal voice.

The fur along the lion's spine stood fully erect. It dropped to its belly and slunk through the murk until it reached the front of the room. There, in a throne of human bones, sat King Tithian of Tyr. In one hand, he cradled the obsidian scepter of a sorcerer-king, in the other, the disembodied head of his only friend: Agis of Asticles.

"Now you know what Borys promised: my heart's desire," said Tithian's figure.

A purple light glimmered deep within his scepter's

pommel, then Agis's head spoke. "You may leave now. His Majesty prefers to be alone." To reinforce the command, Tithian pointed the scepter at the unwelcome intruder's head.

The lion opened its maw as if to roar, but the sound that filled the little room was a deep, booming laugh.

* * * * *

The Castoffs swarmed over Agis, pressing their ethereal mouths to his skin wherever it was exposed. Each touch sent a searing pain deep into his flesh, raising a ghastly red welt that continued to burn long after the agonizing kiss had ended. Although most of the lips pressing against him belonged to children, they were easily two or even three times the size of his own, and the blisters they left were enormous.

Agis rose. "Stop it!" he yelled, almost losing his balance as Fylo's stomach shifted beneath his feet. "Leave me alone!"

The Castoffs rushed away from him, staring in astonishment at his upright form. "How can he stand the pain?" gasped one.

"He must have a strong mind," said another.

"No, it's something else," replied the face of a button-nosed woman, one of the few visages that appeared to be an adult. "It might be wiser to leave this one alone."

As the faces voiced their opinions, Agis climbed toward Kester and had his first clear view of the pit. The shaft had an irregular, rectangular shape varying greatly in width. As he had noted earlier, the walls were covered with huge quartz crystals, and from the interior of each one shined a silvery light. By this pale glow, Agis saw more than a hundred yellowed giant skulls hanging on the walls, each carefully positioned on the tip of a crystal.

When Agis reached the tarek's side, the Castoffs descended on the noble again. They began to rub their cheeks against his skin, causing long streaks to turn brown and slimy. The putrid stains filled him with a dull anguish, and he felt instantly queasy and feverish.

Agis closed his eyes and focused his concentration on the core of his being, letting the sickening anguish of decay wash over him without fighting it. He focused all his thoughts only on the mystic truths of the Way, truths that allowed him to accept his pain and use it to transcend his mortal body.

Once he felt in control of his agony, the noble said, "Enough games. Leave us alone, or you shall regret it."

A few Castoffs stared at him in amazement, but most continued to assault both him and his friends. Agis closed his eyes and drew energy from his spiritual nexus. Soon, his tortured body buzzed with the power he needed. In his mind, the noble visualized more than a hundred open hands, then opened his eyes and projected one from inside his head to each spirit's cheek. The palms struck their targets with resounding slaps, melding into the face and leaving behind black impressions of themselves.

Once he had marked the Castoffs, the noble said, "That's to let you know I can carry out my threats. If I must defend us again, I won't be so lenient."

Crying out in alarm, the Castoffs rose into the air and hovered above his head.

Agis knelt down to examine Kester. Where the glowing faces had been rubbing against her back and shoulder, her thick hide had shriveled into a desiccated, wrinkled mass. The noble turned her over and found her front side in even worse condition. She had long since fallen unconscious, but her face remained racked with pain. The hide covering her neck and breasts was as grotesquely creased as that on her back, save that the outer layers of skin were falling away in a dusty powder.

Agis used a few strands of scraggly beard to secure her beneath Fylo's chin, then turned his attention to the giant. The half-breed's face had become as grossly misshaped as that of any Saram child. One of the eyes had nearly doubled in size and now bulged from its socket with all the precariousness of a ball at the edge of a shelf. The other had grown smaller, sinking so far beneath his brow that it was barely visible. His nose had somehow been rearranged so that it had a separate passage running down to each nostril, with a long cleft in between. Even his buck teeth had not escaped alteration, and now splayed out in opposite directions like the two branches of a forked stick.

Agis looked up at the faces hovering over his head. "Why have you done this?" he yelled.

The Castoffs descended toward him in a slow circle, their immaterial visages twisted into bizarre masks of regret or rancor, he could not quite tell which. Ghostly sobs poured from the lips of several children, while ethereal tears streamed down their cheeks and vanished into the black air.

"We're scared!" wailed a little girl.

"And lonely!" added a boy.

"Why did they put us down here?"

With each cry, a pang of anguish pierced Agis's breast, filling him with a deep sense of regret. Every complaint added to his sorrow, and his heart grew heavy and weak. Soon, he felt like a terrible weight was pressing down on his chest, and it hurt to breathe. Still, the Castoffs continued to pour grief into him, until he felt so gorged with misery that he feared he would burst.

"Stop it!" Agis yelled.

The noble summoned the energy to use the Way and closed his eyes again, this time seeing a hammer with white-feathered wings on its handle. Once he had it locked firmly in his mind, he looked toward the highest hanging skull and projected the image there. It appeared an instant later, its white wings keeping it aloft with slow, graceful arcs.

"This is your last warning!" the noble said.

When the Castoffs continued to wail, he drew the hammer back. Before he could strike, the face of the button-nosed woman who had spoken earlier descended in front of him. She looked more like a Joorsh than a Saram, with no obvious deformities and almond-shaped eyes that had a surprisingly gentle quality to them.

"Please, don't!" she said. "The grief you hear is genuine. They can't help themselves."

Agis held his blow, but pointed to his unconscious friends. "Could they help themselves when they did that?" he demanded.

"I know their behavior seems cruel to you, but you don't know the reason for it," she replied.

"Tell me," the noble said, still keeping the hammer poised to strike.

The woman shook her head. "I'll try, but how can you understand what you can't possibly feel?" she asked.

"You'd be surprised by what I understand," Agis countered.

"Not this. Your heart is too good."

Agis frowned, wondering if she were trying to flatter him. "What can you know of my heart?"

"I know that it's purer than those crystals," she replied, gesturing at the spikes of quartz growing from the walls. "Otherwise, you wouldn't have resisted the magic we draw through them."

Agis glanced at the silvery glow inside a nearby crystal. "Magic from the Oracle?" he asked, remembering what Nal had said about needing the lens to keep the Castoffs in the pit.

The woman nodded. "It's what sustains us—and it supplies the magic that runs through the crystal lid that keeps us locked in this prison."

"That's very interesting, but it doesn't explain the cruelty of your friends."

The woman cast a sorrowful look at the faces hovering above. "That is how children become when you lock them away," she said. "They'll take out their anger on whatever is weaker than themselves."

Agis allowed his hammer to fade away. "Then if we don't want them to be cruel, I suppose we'll have to free them, won't we?"

The spirit looked doubtful. "Don't raise their hopes," she said. "That isn't something you can do."

"I think it is," Agis replied, craning his neck upward to study the lid. "And you can help by reviving my friends. We'll need them."

As he spoke, Tithian's gaunt form landed on the crystal cover with a dull thump. A high-pitched hum reverberated through the lid, and the king's body began to pass through to the noble's side of the barrier.

The Castoffs started to rush up toward him. "We'll have none of that!" Agis yelled. To himself, he added, "Even if the serpent deserves it."

The faces stopped and looked to the button-nosed woman for instructions. "I suggest you do as he says if you ever want to return to your bodies," she said.

As the Castoffs reluctantly dispersed, Tithian passed the rest of the way through the cover. He plummeted onto Fylo's midriff, causing the giant's body to tremble violently. For a moment, Agis feared the half-breed would come dislodged, sending them all plunging into the dark abyss below, but the giant sank only a few feet. If anything, the impact seemed to lodge him into place even more securely.

Tithian groaned and tried to rise. Then, his eyes rolling back in his head, he fell motionless. Agis slipped down Fylo's chest and touched his finger to the king's throat. He felt a strong, regular pulse.

"It would probably be better for Athas if I killed you right now," Agis said, using a finger to lift one of the king's eyelids.

Tithian opened his eyes, then pushed Agis's hand away. "You don't have the nerve to murder me," he sneered. "But it makes no difference. Athas no longer has anything to fear from me."

"Why's that?" Agis asked, examining the king's head for signs of a serious blow. "Surely you don't expect me to believe you've decided not to go after the Oracle?"

"What you believe makes no difference!" Tithian yelled, grabbing Agis by the shoulders. He pulled the noble's face close to his and gasped, "That worm lied to me!"

"What worm?" Agis asked. "About what?"

"The Dragon!" Tithian cried. "Nal told me. Borys can't make anyone a sorcerer-king—not even with the Dark Lens!"

ELEVEN

The Cracked Cover

Fylo's knuckles landed on target, in a blackened corner of the translucent cover. A sharp crack rang off the pit walls, and the impact reverberated through the shimmering platform upon which he stood. The lid did not break. The giant drew back his fist to try again, then suddenly cried out in alarm as the temporary floor dissolved beneath his feet. He plunged, screaming, into the abyss.

Kester heard Agis call, "I've got him."

A black silhouette resembling the *Shadow Viper*'s foresail appeared just below the giant, stretched taut across the shaft and bound at each corner to a stout quartz crystal. Fylo plunged through the shadow without slowing, vanishing beneath its dark form.

Agis's curse rang off the cavern walls, then the ineffectual net dissolved. Kester saw the giant clawing and kicking at the jagged walls, ripping deep gouges into his palms and feet. One crystal broke off, sending a glittering spray of silver and crimson light shooting across the shaft.

Finally, Fylo passed through a narrow section of shaft and managed to bring himself to a stop. He hung motionless over the abyss, his ribs heaving and his limbs pressed against opposite sides of the pit. After regaining his composure, he looked up and fixed his gaze on Tithian. One of his eyes was still much larger than the other, but both orbs were slowly returning to normal—as were the other facial defects caused by the Castoffs.

"Tithian liar!" Fylo snarled, beginning the long climb back up. "Promise to hold Fylo!"

"It was a mistake," the king replied. He sat upon a large crystal twenty-five feet below the lid, at the height of the platform upon which Fylo had been standing. All around him hung discarded Saram skulls, each covered with the translucent, masklike visage of a Castoff. "What do I have to gain by dropping you?"

"If you can float a ship, you can give Fylo a place to stand," Agis growled, glaring down from his perch at the top of the shaft. "You let him fall on purpose."

"Yer letting yer temper think for ye," Kester snapped. She had positioned herself midway between the two, where it would be easy to intercede if their quarreling erupted into a full-blown fight. "Yer king wants out of here as much as we do. If he says it was an accident, it was."

"Tithian doesn't make those kinds of mistakes," Agis insisted. "He must have thought Fylo's blow cracked the lid. That's why he dropped the giant."

"Ye couldn't know what Tithian was thinking— unless ye were using the Way on him instead of doing yer own job," Kester said. She paused and pointed at the pit's crystalline cover, which was already tinged green with predawn light. "If the two of ye don't work together, we'll never get out of here before dawn—and if ye let Mag'r sink my ship because we don't have those gates open, ye won't have to kill each other. I'll do it for ye."

When the noble protested no further, Kester turned to Tithian. "Can ye give Fylo a steady place to stand or not?"

"He's heavier than I thought," Tithian replied.

Kester nodded. "I thought as much," she said. "We'll have to find another way out."

"Such as?" asked Tithian.

The tarek furrowed her heavy brow, absentmindedly rubbing her fingers over her leathery neck. The act loosened a small shower of dusty flakes, which fluttered into the darkness below. The tarek pulled her hand away from her throat, reminded that until she fully recovered from the injuries inflicted by the Castoffs, scratching what itched was a bad idea.

After a moment's thought, Kester started to descend the pit wall, swinging from one crystal to the next on her gangling arms. "If we can't go up, we'll try down," she said.

"No! You mustn't!" cried Sona, the button-nosed woman who served as the nominal leader of the Castoffs. She floated over to block Kester's descent. "The bones of the sacrificed animals rest down there. You can't disturb them."

Kester eyed Sona warily, remembering the anguish the spirits had inflicted on her after she had first fallen into the pit. "Out of my way," she ordered.

"No, Kester," said Agis. "We must respect Sona's wishes. I'm sure Fylo can smash this lid, if Tithian gives him a sturdy place to stand." He cast a bitter glance at the king.

Kester raised a brow at the noble. "And how many

jails have ye escaped from?"

"I've never seen the inside of a prison," the noble replied, taken aback. "Why?"

"'Cause I've escaped from dozens. Let me do the thinking," Kester replied. "We've got to take every chance we've got, and even then we might not find a way out."

"There's nothing down there to help you," Sona insisted. "You'll only disturb what should be left to rest."

"Thanks, but I'll look for myself," the tarek said.

"It's too dangerous!" Sona protested. "The animals—"

"Are a pile of old bones. They won't stop me from finding a way out of here," the tarek sneered. She reached for the next crystal.

Sona darted forward and closed her mouth around Kester's wrist. A sizzling pain shot up the tarek's thick arm, then her fingers closed against her will. Her fist banged into the crystal for which she had reached, and she narrowly saved herself from falling by grabbing another with her free hand. A foul smell rose to Kester's nostrils, and she looked down to see a putrid green stain spreading from beneath the spirit's lips.

"Get this thing off me!" she yelled, lifting her stinging arm toward Agis.

"You've made your point, Sona," said the noble. "I'm sure Kester has changed her plans."

"In a varl's eye!" the tarek hissed, clenching her teeth against the pain. "I'm not going to let anything keep me from lookin'. If we don't find a way out, we'll die anyway."

The noble shrugged. "Then I can't help you," he said. "This is Sona's home, and we must do as she asks."

"Ye faithless snake!" Kester yelled, climbing toward Agis. "By me ship's name, I'll rip yer arms off and beat ye dead with 'em!"

"You can't reason with him, Kester," said Tithian. "When it comes to questions of honor, he really is a stubborn boor." The king reached into his satchel. "However, I might be able to suggest a compromise."

Tithian pulled forth a pair of iron cages connected by a heavy chain. Inside the little prisons sat the disembodied heads of two men, their hair pulled into long topknots. One had sallow skin and sunken features, while the other was grotesquely bloated, with puffy eyes swollen to dark, narrow slits.

"Sacha! Wyan!" Agis gasped. He looked to Tithian, then demanded, "Where have you been hiding those two wretches?"

"That's none of your concern," Tithian replied. "But perhaps we should have them levitate down to the pit bottom. They could look for an escape route without disturbing any bones, then report back to us. That way, we'd know whether or not there's any point to this argument."

"We'd rather see you die here," said the bloated head, licking his chin with a long gray tongue. "At least we could make a decent meal of you."

"Sacha's right," agreed the other. "What makes you think we'd help you?"

Tithian fished a key from his satchel. Both heads fell instantly silent, fixing their eyes on the tiny piece of carved bone.

"I'm willing to set you free," said Tithian. "After all, we no longer have reason to remain enemies."

"Your personality is reason enough," sneered Sacha.

"His character can be overlooked, if he lets us out

of here," objected Wyan. "But what about Borys? As I recall, he told you never to let us out of these cages."

"I think you know about Borys," replied Tithian. "As do I, now. You could have saved me a lot of trouble by telling me he was lying."

A cruel smile creased Sacha's lips. "And ruin our fun?" he asked. "Watching you play at being a sorcerer-king was too amusing."

"Besides, would you have believed us?" asked Wyan. "You had to discover the truth for yourself."

"Then you'll help us?" demanded Kester, growing impatient with the searing pain in her arm.

"They will," answered Tithian, unlocking their cages. "If Sona agrees to my suggestion."

The spirit released Kester's arm and drifted away, leaving an ugly band of rotting flesh on the tarek where Sona's mouth had been. "As long as they're careful to touch none of the bones," she said. "Otherwise, everyone in this pit will have reason to regret our compromise."

The doors to their cages were barely open before the two heads floated out. They dropped into the depths of the abyss instantly, as if they feared Tithian would change his mind and return them to their cages.

"Are ye sure ye can trust those two?" Kester asked, scowling at the pair's quick escape.

"I don't trust them at all," Tithian replied, hanging the empty cages over a small crystal. "But if they don't come back, we'll know they found a way out."

This drew a frown from Sona. "If they don't come back, it'll be because they disturbed the bones," she said, returning to her perch. The spirit narrowed her eyes at Agis, then added, "Until then, I suggest you work on keeping your promise. You know how limited the patience of children is."

Agis looked down at Tithian. "If you fail again—"

"I won't," the king interrupted. He returned the noble's gaze with a hint of pain in his eyes. "Your treatment of me really is unwarranted," he said. "Especially considering what I intended to offer you, had my hopes of becoming a sorcerer-king not been dashed."

"I wouldn't have wanted it," the noble said.

"Really?" the king asked. "You wouldn't have been interested in an offer of life?"

"For that offer to have any value, you would have had to threaten me in the first place," the noble replied. "You could hardly expect me to be grateful for that."

Tithian smiled patiently. "Of course not," he replied. "But you misunderstand me. I had meant to offer you life in a different sense—in the sense of living forever."

Agis narrowed his eyes. "Now is no time for games," he said. "And you should know me better than to think you could buy me with such tactics."

A crooked smile creased Tithian's thin lips, and he clucked his tongue at Agis. "So suspicious," he said. "It's no wonder our friendship has always been strained."

"Our relationship has been strained because you're a liar and a thief," the noble countered.

"And a murderer, as well," Tithian added. "But I've never betrayed you."

"How about when you abandoned your duties to the citizens of Tyr?" Agis replied.

Tithian rolled his eyes. "You've always placed too much value in the banal tools of appearance," the king sneered. "I speak of life without end, and you are more concerned with a few promises we made to a bunch of ex-slaves and paupers."

"That's right," Agis said, without hesitation. "And with bringing you to justice."

"That'll be enough arguing," said Kester. She looked up at the green hues glimmering through the crystal ceiling. "Think about the job at hand. If we're going to open those gates before Mag'r sinks my ship, we'd better make this try a good one—or hope Sacha and Wyan find a tunnel down below." She glanced at Sona and pulled her muzzle back in a defiant snarl.

The trio waited in silence as Fylo completed his climb, then Kester directed the giant to wait near Tithian. Agis pressed a fingertip to the pit's translucent cover and closed his eyes, tracing a wide circle. A black line appeared on the shimmering quartz, outlining the pattern he had traced.

Kester nodded to Tithian, who closed his eyes and swept his hand across the pit. A plank of psychic energy appeared where he had gestured, anchored directly into the base of two massive crystals. The platform was about as broad as the king was tall, constantly changing from one translucent color to another.

Fylo eyed the platform cautiously, then advanced one foot onto its surface. The plank sagged beneath his weight, crackling and hissing blue sparks beneath his heel. The giant retreated to the crystals to which he had been cleaving.

"More solid!" he ordered.

Tithian opened one eye and glared at the giant. "I will—but you must be fast. I can't support your bloated carcass for long." The king returned his concentration to the platform, which settled on an opaque, granite red color and ceased to shimmer.

At the same time, the circle Agis had traced above his head began to fill in, darkening to jet black. Wisps of cold fog trailed beneath it, writhing about like street dancers in the Elven Market.

"Now, Fylo!" Agis gasped, already growing pale from the effort of holding his circle's form against the tides of mystic force flowing through the crystal cover.

Casting a wary eye at Tithian's face, the giant stepped onto the platform and squatted down with his hand next to his hip. There was a great rush of air as he filled his lungs, then he fixed his eye on the black circle Agis had created. Inside that circle, there would be none of the magic that flowed through the rest of the crystal lid and made it impossible to break.

Fylo gave a mighty shout and drove his knuckles straight to the heart of the circle. A terrific boom echoed through the pit, and the half-breed's hand bounced away from the cover. The platform beneath his feet did not waver even slightly, nor did the lid break.

"You coward!" Tithian yelled, opening his eyes. "Is that as hard as you can hit it?"

Fylo scowled and started to say something, but Kester cut him off. "Pay him no attention," she said, noting that Agis's body was starting to tremble from the effort of keeping his circle open. "Try again, Fylo. This time ye know the plank won't sink, so ye can hit even harder."

The giant looked away from Tithian, then closed his other fist. "Fylo break lid!" he promised.

The half-breed's knuckles crashed into the crystal. Sharp pops and cracks echoed off the shaft walls, followed by a victorious bellow from the giant. Shards of crystal rained down on Fylo's head and shoulders, then tumbled toward Kester and Tithian. The tarek covered her head and felt several fragments bounce off her forearms, opening a series of sharp cuts in her leathery hide. A moment later, the pit was filled with a lyrical chime as the jagged pieces bounced into the darkness below.

Kester felt a cool breeze descending over her body and looked up. She saw a star-shaped fracture centered in the black circle above the noble's head, easily wide enough for a man—or a female tarek—to slip through. Ragged shafts of predawn light streamed into the pit, illuminating Agis's weary face in a sickly green glow. To her distress, Kester could also see a few yellow tendrils of morning sunlight streaming across the sky.

Castoffs began to leave their perches on the yellowed skulls. They streamed out of the crack in a wild flock, chortling and screaming loudly in mad delight as they escaped into the open air. Even through the crystalline lid, the morbid and spiteful tone of their muffled voices made Kester's hide prickle.

"Once more, Fylo!" she urged, climbing toward the exit. "That's wide enough for us, but not for you."

The giant glanced down at Tithian, who now had a steady trickle of sweat dripping from the tail of his long auburn hair. The king gave the half-breed a reassuring nod and returned his eyes, bulging with strain, to the platform. Fylo drew his hand back for another blow.

A pair of familiar voices spoke from the area beneath his feet. "You're not leaving without us!" declared Wyan.

"You should know better than to play games with us, Tithian," added Wyan. "We taught you everything!"

The sallow faces of Sacha and Wyan rose from beneath the platform. They drifted up past Fylo's fist and hovered near his head, causing him to hold his blow.

"Get out of the way," Tithian said. "We weren't going to leave without you."

"Don't lie to us!" Sacha hissed.

The head clamped his teeth down on one of Fylo's dangling earlobes and began to pull, drawing a pained howl from the giant. Wyan bit the other one, also tugging on it. To avoid having his ears ripped away, the half-breed was forced to turn in a circle.

"What do you think you're doing?" Tithian demanded.

"Stop at once!" Agis commanded.

The only answer the heads offered was to pull harder. Blood began to stream down the sides of Fylo's head, and he had to spin on his heels to keep up with his attackers. The giant slapped at the pair madly, but succeeded only in battering his own head more than theirs.

Although Kester did not understand the reason for their vicious attack, she did not let that deter her from responding. She pulled a dagger from her chest harness and flung it at the bloated head. The blade hit its target in the temple, sinking clear to the hilt. Sacha cursed through his clenched teeth, but did not fall dead, nor did he release the giant.

Kester looked to Tithian, stunned that her dagger had not dropped the head. "They're your heads. Do something!"

"Like what?" the king replied. "Let the platform fail?"

She lifted her eyes to Agis and found the noble balanced precariously on the end of a crystal. He was trying to reach out to snatch one of the heads away from Fylo's ears, which were at about the same level as he was. Above him, the black circle that he had created earlier was slowly turning gray. Worse, the magic of the crystal lid was flowing across the cracks that Fylo had opened, and the star-shaped breach was slowly beginning to seal itself.

"Agis, no!" Kester cried, pointing at the black circle overhead.

The noble glanced at the graying circle. Then, without a second's hesitation, he returned his attention to the giant. He barely missed as he snatched at Wyan's topknot.

The two heads whipped their chins harshly to one side, giving Fylo's ears a terrific yank. The half-breed spun around quickly, and one foot slipped off the platform. For several moments, he tottered precariously on the edge of falling. Kester reached for another dagger.

Sacha and Wyan gave their chins another sharp jerk, and Fylo stepped off the narrow platform completely. He fell with his back down, his confused cry echoing through the pit. The two heads finally released his ears and darted for the exit.

Kester threw her dagger, and it sliced through Wyan's cheek. Other than knocking him temporarily off course, it had no effect. Agis nearly fell from his perch trying to grab them, but they dodged his perilous lunges and slipped through the exit, along with a small stream of Castoff stragglers.

"Don't let it close, Agis!" Kester yelled, pointing at the crack.

The noble stared after Fylo for an instant, then pulled himself upright and reached up to touch the graying circle. When it began to darken and the crack stopped filling, Kester breathed a sigh of relief. Only then did she look toward the bottom of the abyss to see what had become of the giant.

Fylo lay in the narrow place where he had gotten lodged before, the bloody tip of a sharp crystal poking through his shoulder. His eyes were glassy and vacant, though it was obvious that he had survived by the rise and fall of his rib cage as he breathed.

Kester had a sinking feeling in her twin stomachs. If she knew Agis, the giant's condition was sure to interfere with what little chance they had of opening the gates in time to save the *Shadow Viper*.

Tithian's voice broke the uneasy silence. "I should have had Borys throw them into the firepits of Urik!" he shouted, climbing past the crystal where Sona's glowing visage still clung to a yellowed skull. "I should have had Fylo stand on their faces until their bones crumbled into dust!"

As the king reached her level, Kester asked, "Why did your heads do this? It makes no sense."

"They're treacherous ingrates!" Tithian snarled, hardly pausing as he continued his climb.

From the top of the pit, Sacha sneered, "Flattery won't help you now."

He was peering down through the crack. Kester could see that her dagger was gone from his temple, leaving a bloodless, gray-edged wound in its place.

"True," added Wyan, who still had a knife lodged in his cheek. "We've already decided who we're going to let out—and who we're not."

The tarek was up and climbing instantly, her powerful arms pulling her from one crystal to another with ease. When she reached Agis's side, she did not pause even long enough to lean out and grab the edges of the hole. Instead, she simply leaped from the highest crystal, thrusting her gangling arms up through the breach and slapping her hands down on the freezing stone outside.

The tarek drew herself into the breach, barely able to force her broad shoulders into the small opening. The sharp edges scratched and scraped at her hide, but she was more aware of the crushing pain in her chest as she tried to squeeze through. Nevertheless, through a determined combination of squirming and pulling, her massive torso soon emerged on the top side of the cover.

Sacha and Wyan had already retreated out of sight. Kester found it much easier to pull her hips through, and soon found herself standing atop the crystalline cover. There was no magic running through the lid inside the area protected by Agis's black circle, so the footing there was as solid as granite. The edge of the pit lay just a short leap away, and a few feet beyond that lay the dagger that had pierced Sacha's temple.

Kester slowly turned around, searching for the heads. The sky now glowed with the full radiance of early dawn, casting a harsh yellow light over the ground. The tarek found Sacha and Wyan hovering beneath Sa'ram's Bridge, where even her long arms could not reach them unless she first crossed a wide expanse of shimmering crystal. The rest of the enclosure was deserted. Even the Castoffs had already gone, though their maniacal chortles were drifting back over the crystal walls. There were no sounds to suggest that the Joorsh attack had begun, and the tarek dared to hope that Mag'r would not sink her ship before they could get the gates open.

"I'm sending Tithian up next," called Agis, his voice rising through the narrow crack beneath her feet. "Keep a close watch on him and kill him if he tries anything."

The king's gaunt hands reached through the narrow opening and began searching for a hold on the cold stone. Kester grabbed his wrists and pulled. As he rose out of the narrow crevice, the sharp edges of the pit marked him with a trail of red abrasions.

"I don't have the hide of a baazrag!" Tithian hissed, clutching his satchel to his chest so it wouldn't be scraped free. "Be careful."

"No time to be careful." Kester deposited the king roughly at her side and motioned toward Sacha and Wyan. "Keep an eye on yer two heads. After what they did to Fylo, I don't trust 'em much."

Taking Agis's advice and keeping one eye on Tithian, she knelt beside the crack and reached through for the noble. Although her action appeared to put her in a vulnerable position, the tarek was not worried. Between herself and the king, there was not much space left on the black circle of solid ground. If Tithian made any sudden moves, it would be an easy thing to knock him onto the shimmering crystal with a shoulder or leg. Besides, she did not really expect him to attack her. Not only would he need her to command the *Shadow Viper*'s crew if he wished to leave the island, but he had seemed more willing to cooperate with others since his dream of becoming a sorcerer-king had been shattered.

When she did not feel Agis take her hand, Kester demanded, "What're ye waiting for down there?"

"He won't leave," Tithian answered. He reached into his satchel and withdrew a coil of giant-hair rope, surprisingly large for the sack from which it had come. "He wants to save the giant."

Kester sighed in frustration, then peered down the hole. "We'll be lucky enough to save ourselves, let alone your giant," she said, addressing Agis's shadowy form.

"We can't leave him like that." The noble gestured toward the bottom of the pit. Although Kester could not see the giant from her position, the image of the bloody crystal protruding through his shoulder remained vivid in her mind. "Now pass me the end of the rope. I'll go down and see if I can get that spike out of his shoulder, then tie him off."

"What then?" she asked. "We'll never get him out through this little hole."

"At least he might not die while we're looking for a way to remove the cover," Agis replied.

"It's already past dawn!" objected Kester. "How long do ye think Mag'r'll wait for the gates to open before he sinks the *Shadow Viper*?"

"He'll wait," Agis replied. "If he sinks your ship, we have no reason to open the gates—and he's smart enough to know that."

"Ye can't know for sure!"

"I agree with you," Tithian whispered. He knelt at Kester's side, holding one end of the rope out to her. "Perhaps we should open the gate for Mag'r—now."

Kester bit her lip, neither meeting the king's gaze nor taking the rope from his hand. "What about Agis?" she asked.

"He can look after Fylo," the king suggested, being careful not to look into the pit. "We can come back for him later."

Kester fell silent and motionless. Like Tithian, she avoided the noble's eyes, though it seemed to her that she could feel them watching her from the shadows, like the black gaze of an owl.

"I can imagine what Tithian's whispering to you," said Agis, his voice rising through the crevice clear and steady. "Don't listen to him. We have many things to do this morning: make sure that we *all* escape the pit, find the Dark Lens, save your ship. But if we panic and start jumping from one unfinished step to another, we're doomed."

Kester remained silent, wondering how the noble could think that everything on his list was still possible at this late hour.

"Weren't you the one who said we had to work together to escape?" Agis pressed. "Did you mean it—or were you voicing the lies of a pirate?"

"Damn ye, and damn yer giant," Kester growled.

"A wise decision," Tithian said, starting to rise.

Kester grabbed his arm and pulled him back to her side. "Ye stay here," she said, taking the rope from his hands and pushing one end down to the noble.

"Thanks for staying," Agis said. "You won't regret it."

"No—but you might," Kester growled. "If Mag'r sinks my ship, ye'll buy me another—and a good crew to man it!"

"I'll give you two ships," the noble replied, smiling. "But you'll have to man them yourself—with *hired* crews."

Kester stood and looked at Tithian. "Ye stay here to keep the hole open—and don't think about leaving. If I see ye step one foot off this circle, I'll kill ye," she said, fingering the two throwing knives left in her chest harness. "I'll go tie off our end of the rope."

With that, she leaped over to solid ground and walked toward the bridge footings, uncoiling the rope as she went.

Tithian watched the tarek leave, silently cursing her for a fool. Nevertheless, he did as she asked, summoning the spiritual energy to take over Agis's duties. "Go ahead," he said, glaring down through the crack. "But remember, you're wasting precious minutes."

"Minutes that are not as precious as my life," the noble's muffled voice replied. "I'll wait until Kester returns."

"As you wish," Tithian said.

As the king spoke, the last of the Castoffs, Sona, drifted into view. She stopped at the noble's side, casting a faint glow over his weary face, and began to thank him for freeing her and the others. Tithian, even less interested in her gratitude than in saving Fylo, stepped away to prepare his escape.

The king found Sacha and Wyan waiting for him, hovering at the edge of the black circle. He snatched them by their topknots and slammed their faces into the crystal lid.

"Why'd you do that?" demanded Sacha.

"Because I want to!" Tithian replied. He plucked the throwing dagger from Wyan's cheek, then shook it at the two heads. "Just be thankful I'm not using this to pluck your eyes out!"

"This is not the way to treat your saviors," objected Wyan, spitting out the broken nub of a gray tooth.

"Saviors!" Tithian roared. "By attacking Fylo you almost got me stuck down there."

"A small risk to take," said Sacha, speaking in a voice quiet enough that no one beyond Tithian's earshot could hear it. "You can't have Agis or anyone else around when you recover the Dark Lens."

Tithian held the heads up and frowned suspiciously. "Why not?" he asked. "After the way the Dragon lied to me, I'd just as soon let Agis kill Borys."

"That would be acceptable," replied Sacha. "Except that I'm sure Agis would want to keep the lens afterward—and you don't want that."

"Why not?"

"The lens is a tool," explained Wyan, also speaking in a soft voice. "Like any tool, it's only as powerful as the person using it. In Borys's hands, it could never make you a sorcerer-king. But in the hands of someone else, someone even more powerful, it could."

"No one's more powerful than the Dragon," Tithian scoffed.

"Wrong," said Sacha. "There is one who could give you what you want: Rajaat."

"Stop wasting my time with your stories," the king hissed. "Rajaat's dead."

"Gone, but not dead," Wyan replied. "What do you think Borys does with his slave levy?"

"He uses their life energy to keep the Shadow People imprisoned in the Black—at least that's what Agis and Sadira think, according to my spies in the Asticles household," replied the king. He cast a nervous glance down at the crack where Agis waited, but saw no sign that the noble could hear or see any of what was happening on top of the lid.

"What makes you think a fool noble and his slaves know what they're talking about?" asked Sacha.

In a fawning voice, Wyan added, "Rajaat is not dead; he's locked away—and Borys uses his levy to maintain the spells that keep him imprisoned."

Tithian accepted the news with little emotion, for he had not yet confirmed its significance to him. "If I take the Dark Lens to him, Rajaat will make me a sorcerer-king?"

"It's not our place to promise that," Wyan said. "We're only his spies in the city of Tyr."

"But, through the Shadow People, we've told Rajaat of your ambitions," said Sacha. "And we've received word back that if you aid him, you'll be pleased with your reward."

Tithian smiled and released his grip on the pair's topknots. "What do I have to do?"

Before the heads could answer, Kester came rushing back from the bridge. She stopped at the edge of the pit, about two yards from the blade that had pierced Sacha's temple. In her hands, the tarek held the last pair of throwing knives from her harness. Her eyes were fixed on the dagger in Tithian's hand.

Inside his mind, Tithian heard Wyan's voice. *Get rid of her. She's sided with Agis.*

"What's going on here?" Kester demanded.

"Not what you think, apparently," Tithian replied, slowly extending the handle of his dagger to Kester. "I thought you might want this back." When the tarek made no move to accept the weapon, the king shrugged and laid it on the ground. "I see Agis's paranoia is catching."

Kester seemed to relax, but did not sheath her own weapons. "What about them?"

"We came to apologize," said Wyan.

"Sometimes our jokes get carried away," added Sacha.

"That was no joke," the tarek said, fangs half-bared.

"It certainly wasn't. Fylo was hurt badly," agreed Tithian. With scornful look, he waved the heads back from the circle, then returned his attention to Kester. "You should come back over here. Agis doesn't trust me to keep the crack open, and he won't take the rope down to Fylo until he sees you."

"What?" the tarek shrieked, sheathing her daggers. "He's wasting time waiting for me?"

"He hasn't moved," Tithian said with a smirk. He

leaned down and plucked the slack rope. "See? No weight."

Kester leaped onto the black circle. She collected the dagger that Tithian had laid down a few moments before and knelt beside the crack. She started to put her face down to speak to Agis, then abruptly drew back as Sona's glowing visage rose from the hole. Once the Castoff had drifted away, she leaned down and said, "I've had enough waiting, Agis!"

Despite her anger, Tithian noticed that she was keeping one eye fixed on him. Smiling, the king stepped over to where she could see him more easily, clasping his hands behind his back. He turned his gaze on the dagger lying at the edge of the pit, the one with which Kester had attacked Sacha, and opened a pathway to his spiritual nexus. Being careful not to alarm the tarek by moving even slightly, Tithian visualized the knife resting in his hand. A prickle of energy rose from deep within himself, then he felt the cold weight of the weapon's hilt in his palm.

"Now that you're here," Tithian asked, "is our friend going after Fylo?"

The king leaned forward as if to look over the tarek's shoulder. Instead of peering down at Agis, however, he began counting down the prominent row of vertebrae showing between Kester's muscular shoulders. This had to be done exactly right, Tithian knew, for he had seen enough gladiatorial contests to realize that tareks often fought for many seconds after death. If his strike did not paralyze as well as kill, Kester could easily take him with her.

"He's climbing down now," Kester said, frowning at the king's proximity.

Tithian's arm flashed, plunging the dagger deep

into Kester's back. The tip entered exactly where he intended, low and between the shoulder blades, so that the blade severed the spinal cord on its way to the heart. The tarek's astonished cry died in her throat, and her body went limp without so much as a reflexive twitch.

"We should have left when I wanted to," Tithian said.

The king shoved Kester's shoulders into the narrow crack, then jumped on her back to force her farther down. If he could jam her body in the crevice securely enough, Agis would not be able to free it before growing too exhausted to keep the lid's magic from sealing itself.

Once he felt convinced that it would be impossible to dislodge the body within the necessary time, Tithian leaped off the dark circle. His feet had barely touched solid ground before Agis's muffled voice sounded from beneath Kester's body. "Tithian!"

The king turned around. He could see Kester's back jerking as Agis tried to pull her free.

Yes, Agis? he asked, using the Way so his words would not be muffled by the pit cover. *You haven't changed your mind about my offer of immortality, have you?*

Don't flatter yourself, the noble replied.

You could have tried lying, you know, Tithian said. *There's a chance that I might have wanted to believe you enough to fall for it.*

Sacha and Wyan floated over to his side and started to urge him to leave, but the king raised a hand to keep them silent.

Whatever else you are, you're not stupid, Agis observed. *Besides, I'm not the liar around here.*

True, but look what your honesty's earned you, the king

said. *You're too noble for your own good*. There was a note of genuine remorse in the statement.

When Agis did not respond, Tithian kept a watchful eye on Kester's body, knowing that his old friend was trying to stall him until the passage could be cleared.

Agis took a moment before answering. *I'm not as virtuous as you think*, said the noble. *If I was, your talk of the Dark Lens would never have diverted me from my original purpose.*

The lens is real enough! Tithian objected.

I know—but so is my promise to return you to Tyr, Agis said. *By putting that off, I've stained my honor and broken my word, in principle if not in deed.*

I wouldn't know about such distinctions, replied the king. *Perhaps that's the reason you're doomed to fail, while I'm destined to become a sorcerer-king.*

I thought that wasn't possible? Agis inquired, the tone of his question betraying both distress and suspicion.

Come now, do you think I'd betray you for anything less? Tithian asked. He started toward the exit, motioning for Sacha and Wyan to follow along. *I'm sorry I can't stay longer, my friend, but I have an Oracle to find.*

Don't think you've won, Tithian! This isn't over!

The king paused and studied Kester's body for a moment. The tarek's body was still jerking as Agis tried to clear the exit, but Tithian saw no sign that his friend was close to dislodging the corpse.

The king smiled. *Of course it's not over*, he allowed. *I still have plans for you.*

TWELVE

The First Giants

A jagged boulder sailed over the wall, smashing the chitinous plate between the sparkling, many-faceted eyes of a mantis-headed warrior. The giant bellowed and raised his hands to the wound, stumbling backward until he tumbled off the ramparts and crashed headfirst atop a rock pile. The Saram's neck snapped with a loud crack, then his enormous body rolled onto a pair of boys who had been passing stones up to their elders.

The death went almost unnoticed amidst the chaos of the battle. All along the wall, Saram tribesmen stood silhouetted against the yellow sky of dawn, hurling stones and insults at the enemies surrounding Castle Feral. The Joorsh were responding with a barrage of their own. From every corner echoed the sound of boulders shattering against the ramparts, a steady cadence of resonant booms that rumbled through the citadel like an exploding volcano.

Along with Sacha and Wyan, Tithian watched the fighting from the relative safety of the citadel floor, where they were moving across a small stretch of open ground in the company of a dozen terrified goats. Although far from giant-sized, the beasts were huge for their species, and the king needed to stoop just a little so that his head would not protrude above their shoulders. Hundreds of such creatures—sheep, goats, even erdlus and kanks—had broken free of their pens with the thunder of the first Joorsh volley. For the last quarter hour, they had been charging around the castle floor in panicked herds, turning the whole granite plain into a maelstrom of hoofed mayhem.

The domestic animals were not the only source of confusion. The Castoffs had spread throughout the castle and were flitting from one beasthead to another, searching for the bodies to which their heads had once been attached. Whenever they paused for more than a moment near a Saram, the warrior turned away and fled, crying for Bawan Nal, who was nowhere in sight, to save them.

A few spirits had apparently located the correct bodies. Their ethereal visages adhered to the Sarams' beastly faces like masks, causing the victims unbearable pain. In one place, a stone-hurler had forsaken his duties to bang his reptilian head against the wall. Another warrior stood over a cart of spilled boulders screaming in agony as she plucked the feathers from her ternlike face.

As the bird-headed woman tore at her avian features, a small boulder came soaring high overhead. It did not drop until it was well inside the citadel walls, falling just a short distance ahead of Tithian's herd. The projectile shattered instantly, filling the air with mordant-smelling rock dust and blasting the herd with pieces of rock. Bleating madly, the goats reversed direction and fled, nearly bowling Tithian over in their terror. When they were gone, the king and his disembodied companions found themselves alone, a hundred yards of open granite between them and the silvery enclosure they had been trying to reach.

Two dozen burly, vicious-looking Saram came rushing from the compound's gate. All had the heads of fanged and venomous beasts: vipers, spiders, and centipedes of all kinds. One of the giants even had the bony skull of a death's head bat, while the distinctive fangs of a needle-toothed shrew protruded from the narrow snout of another. In their hands, the warriors carried steel-tipped lances as tall as trees, while their bodies were covered by plates of mekillot-shell armor.

The king turned and sprinted after the goats.

* * * * *

"Are you ready, Fylo?" Agis asked, peering down the sparkling shaft.

The giant still lay with the crystal jutting up through his shoulder, blood oozing from the wound and dripping steadily into the abyss. Although his eyes were only half-open, they were attentive and turned in the noble's direction. In his good hand, he held the end of a rope stretched taut between himself and Kester.

Agis had used a dagger from the tarek's chest harness to cut the length of cord off the rope Kester had draped through the crack before dying. Given the effort it had required to saw through the sturdy giant-hair fibers, he felt certain that the giant could pull as hard as he wanted without breaking the line.

"Fylo ready," the giant reported, his voice a strained croak.

"Then pull!"

The giant gave the line a hard tug. Kester's body remained stuck for a moment, then abruptly popped out of the crack and dropped limply into the abyss. After a long fall, it landed in the half-breed's lap, causing his body to jerk from the impact. Even at the top of the shaft, Agis heard the eerie sound of shoulder bone grinding against quartz crystal, and a deep groan of agony rumbled from between the giant's clenched teeth.

The sound had not even died away before Fylo pointed at the pit cover. "Go. Catch traitor Tithian."

Agis nodded, knowing that without help, he could not pull the heavy giant free of the crystal. "I'll be back when I find some way to get you out," Agis said, climbing into the star-shaped crack. "I won't leave you here."

The giant nodded. "Fylo know."

"You're a brave friend," Agis said. He pulled himself up into the yellow light of dawn.

The noble's chest had barely risen out of the cracked lid before he felt himself being pinched between an immense thumb and forefinger. He was plucked out of the hole, then lifted high into the air.

"How fortunate we were to arrive just as you were leaving," hissed a sibilant voice.

Agis's captor turned him around, and the noble found himself staring at the face of a Saram giant. The warrior had enormous fur-covered ears, wrinkled nostrils, and huge scarlet eyes set into the gnarled, fleshless skull of a death's head bat.

"Take me to Bawan Nal," Agis said, noticing that another two dozen beastheads stood behind his captor. Most seemed to have the heads of serpents, spiders, and insects. "It's important that I speak to him at once!"

This drew a malevolent chuckle from the entire company.

"Bawan Nal also thinks it important to speak with you," the warrior replied. "It's not often that he calls the Poison Pack away from its duties in the Mica Yard."

* * * * *

The tip of the forked wand glowed yellow and bowed downward ever so slightly, pointing toward the center of the enclosure, where a single Saram giant guarded the entrance to a subterranean passage. Armed with a bone battle-axe as tall as a faro tree, the sentry had a hairless head more or less conical in shape, with beady eyes and small, peaked ears. His pointed muzzle ended in a pair of flaring nostrils, with a pair of venom-dripping tusks hanging from beneath his upper lips. He hardly seemed able to contain himself as he bustled to and fro, swinging his axe in great, exuberant arcs and testing the cool breeze for the scent of intruders.

Tithian allowed himself to peer at the giant for only an instant, then backed away from the corner, fearing the guard would be alerted to his presence by the awful stench of goat offal clinging to his clothes. The king moved a short distance down the enclosure wall, a huge sheet of silvery mica that sprang directly out of the bedrock, then returned his divining wand to his shoulder satchel.

"The lens is in there—and they left only one sentry to guard it," he announced, pulling a tiny crossbow and a quiver of a dozen dartlike quarrels from his pouch. "This is going to be too easy. I had expected ten times that number."

"You're overconfident," said Sacha, hovering close to his ear. "So far, you've inspired me with nothing but doubt."

"Only a fool could have believed that pack of giants was chasing us," agreed Wyan. "You jumped into a dung-filled pothole for nothing."

"If I'm such a fool, how come you two were hiding there when I arrived?" Tithian countered, fitting a tiny quarrel into its slot on the crossbow.

That done, the king turned his free palm toward the ground, preparing to cast a magical spell. The energy came to him slowly, and all from the direction of the citadel's gate, for he had to draw it all from the isle of Lybdos itself. If any plants had ever grown on the peninsula's barren granite, they had long since been devoured by the domestic flocks of the Saram. Finally, Tithian had enough energy to use his magic. He started toward the enclosure entrance, hunched over and moving slowly.

He had taken no more than three steps when the muffled clatter of a ballista echoed over the walls on the far side of the castle. A pained roar followed, and Tithian looked toward the gate. He saw a lion-headed giant fall from the wall, clutching at a long harpoon piercing his chest. The king smiled, for the sight suggested Mag'r had not yet sunk the *Shadow Viper*, and that could simplify matters greatly when the time came to escape.

Returning his attention to the task at hand, Tithian shuffled forward and stepped around the jagged corner of the mica wall. He held his hands in front of his stomach, folded over each other and with the crossbow concealed beneath them.

The sentry's nostrils sniffed at the breeze, and he

squinted in the king's direction. "You're a funny-looking goat," he said. He started forward, adding, "Don't run. It'll only make me mad."

"Don't worry," Tithian snickered. "The last thing I have in mind is running."

Gnashing his tusks together, the sentry hefted his axe and charged. Tithian waited a moment for the guard to build momentum, then raised his crossbow and fingered the trigger, speaking his incantation at the same time. The bowstring clicked softly, launching the tiny bolt at the giant. As soon as the needle cleared the groove, it began to sputter and hiss, spewing blue sparks from its tail.

As the needle streaked away, the giant came into range for his own attack, leveling his axe at the king's head. Tithian threw himself down, and the blade clattered against the granite bedrock at the king's side, so close that the impact sprayed his face with hot shards of chipped blade. In the same instant, the tiny quarrel pierced its target's chest.

The sentry slapped at the puncture as though stung by an insect. Then, absentmindedly scratching at the wound, he sneered at the king's prone form. "It'll take more than a blue flash to kill Mal."

A wisp of grayish smoke shot from the tiny wound, then Mal's rib cage gave a great heave. A muted discharge sounded inside his chest. His beady eyes bulged in surprise, and a horrid gurgle, half-growl and half-groan, rasped from his throat. The axe slipped from his grasp, his knees already buckling.

Tithian rolled. He heard the crash of the bone axe handle striking the granite floor, then saw the dark shadow of an axe head spreading outward around his body. The flat of the blade fell squarely on him, sounding a sharp crack inside his skull. An instant later, the sentry's lifeless corpse fell on top of the axe, and the king's body erupted into agony.

The ground began to spin, and a terrible ache throbbed from his skull clear down to his legs. It hurt to breathe, and he felt his mind drifting off into the gray arena of nothingness. With a start, the king realized he was falling unconscious, allowing his mind to retreat from the fiery pain flaring inside his head. He could not allow that, for to sleep now would be to die. Worse, it would be to fail, with the Oracle all but in his grasp.

"Stand, you miserable cur!" yelled Sacha.

"Die now, and the Shadow People shall have your spirit as their slave—until Rajaat is free!" threatened Wyan.

Tithian seized on their angry words, visualizing his fingers closing around a burning rope. He began pulling hand over hand, hauling himself out of the darkness, into the blinding light and searing agony that was his body. Within moments, he was once again fully possessed by his pain.

For a moment, Tithian tried to accept his physical anguish, to let it wash over his body like a searing wind, uncomfortable, but sufferable for short periods of time. It was no use. He had never been good at enduring pain, and he was no better at it now. If he was to survive this, he would have to rely on an old trick, one that he had found useful since his adolescence.

Marshaling his spiritual energy, the king used the Way to form an image of his friend Agis. His own pain he viewed as a bottomless vial of syrupy brown poison, and this he tipped toward the noble's open mouth. Tithian felt better immediately. He could still feel the agony of the giant's crushing weight, but it went straight into the brown vial, and from there down Agis's throat. The king's ribs still ached, and his head still throbbed, but no longer was the pain overwhelming.

Slowly, the king dragged himself from beneath the axe blade's crushing weight, then rose and stood at the dead giant's side.

"You're looking better," observed Sacha. "More fit to be one of Rajaat's servants."

"What happened?" inquired Wyan.

"Agis is bearing my pain for me," Tithian replied. "Remind me to reward him when we return from freeing Rajaat."

"He'll never survive that long," replied Sacha. "Our task will take months."

"Agis will find a way," the king said absently, studying the interior of the enclosure.

It was roughly rectangular in shape, surrounded by ragged slabs of mica that rose from the granite bedrock like a tall, silvery hedge. In the center of the enclosure, a pearly film shimmered over the entrance to a dark tunnel, just large enough for a Saram giant —or a small Joorsh—to crawl through. The passage tilted to one side, so that anyone passing down it would be forced to lean sharply to the right.

Tithian started toward the tunnel, saying, "Besides, it hardly matters if Agis isn't alive when we return. If he's not, I'll just raise him from the dead." When neither of the heads said anything in reply, Tithian asked, "Rajaat will grant me such powers, won't he?"

"Rajaat can bestow you with magic," replied Wyan. "What you learn to do with it is not for him to determine."

Tithian reached the passage and stopped. The tunnel entrance was covered by a single flake of mica, as thin as paper and as clear as glass. Behind it, the hole descended into the bedrock at a steep slope, lined on both sides by smooth walls of the mineral. The floor and ceiling looked like the torn edges of a book, showing the ends of hundreds of closely-pressed mica sheets.

"What are you waiting for?" snapped Sacha. "Go get it!"

The king opened his satchel and removed a black belt, so wide it was almost a girdle. The buckle was hidden by a starburst of red flames, with the skull of a fierce half-man in the center. As Tithian laid the belt over his arm, the stiff leather crackled like breaking fingers.

"That's the dwarven Belt of Rank!" gasped Wyan.

Tithian nodded. "A little token for the ghosts of Sa'ram and Jo'orsh," he replied. "You remember those slavers Agis is so mad about?"

"The ones that mistakenly raided Kled," confirmed Wyan.

"Yes, except it was no mistake—and they weren't after slaves," said the king, smiling.

With that, he pressed his fingers against the shimmering mica. He felt a brief burning sensation as they sank through, then he was looking at his hand through the silvery sheet. The membrane reminded him of the lid that covered the pit where he had left Agis. Remembering how difficult it had been to get out of there, he hesitated before stepping through.

"You two wait here," Tithian said to the heads. "I may need you to help me get back through this."

"I'll come with you," said Wyan. "Sacha can wait here."

Tithian considered this for a moment, then shook his head. "Have you forgotten that I found the lens by locating the undead spirits of Jo'orsh and Sa'ram?" Tithian asked. "I'm more certain of finding them down there than the Dark Lens. It wouldn't do to have them recognize you from the days of Rajaat."

"As you wish," replied Wyan. "But if you fail—"

"You won't do anything to me that will be worse than what Sa'ram and Jo'orsh do," Tithian replied.

The king stepped through the mica, then looked back toward Sacha and Wyan. The two heads continued to hover outside the entrance, watching him with suspicious frowns.

"Hide yourselves!" Tithian ordered. "I don't want you here when I send Jo'orsh and Sa'ram out!"

The pair narrowed their eyes and began to drift away. "We'll be watching!" warned Sacha.

The king shuffled down the slanted tunnel. Each time he touched the mica's slick surface, a feverish tingle buzzed through his fingers. The air felt sweltering and still, heavy with the stale smell of dankness. There was no sound, save for the whisper of Tithian's breath hissing past his lips, and the soft crunch of his boots on the floor. As he advanced down the corridor, the color of the walls changed from silver to lavender, then to green, brown, and finally, when he had gone so deep that the entrance was only a point of light far behind, the tunnel became jet black.

Soon it grew too dark to see what lay ahead, and Tithian stopped to prepare a light spell. When he opened his palm to summon the energy he needed, his whole arm began to tingle with the same burning sensation that he felt whenever he touched his fingers to the walls. Before he could close his fist to cut off the flow, the strange force rushed into his body of its own accord, as if it were being driven into him by some external pressure.

Hissing in pain, Tithian opened his palm and tried to expel the searing energy. Nothing happened, save that the smell of his own scorched flesh rose to his nostrils. Fearing he would burst into flames, the king fished a wad of glowing moss from his satchel and cast his spell.

A blinding flash filled the passage. The fiery tingle inside Tithian's body faded as his spell consumed the energy that had pervaded his form. The rancid stench of burning flesh did not fade, however, nor did the scalding feeling inside his body. The king found himself sucking his breath through clenched teeth, and the vial inside his mind was overflowing with the brown syrup of pain.

To his dismay, the spell did not work quite as he had planned, either. Instead of the soft crimson glow he had expected, the corridor was filled with hundreds of globes of scarlet light, erupting into existence one moment, then, an instant later, expiring in a maroon burst.

It took Tithian's eyes a few moments to adjust to the strange illumination. When they did, he almost wished that he were still blind.

Crawling up the corridor were two skeletal lumps, about the size of Saram giants and warped into shapes scarcely recognizable as manlike. Their legs were gnarled masses, with knotted balls for feet, while the thighs, knees, and calves were all curled together in a single coil. Long, twisted shards of bone jutted out from their shoulders, lacking any sign of elbows, wrists, or hands. One figure had fused ribs and a hunched back, with a slope-browed skull sitting on his squat neck. The other's torso was more normal, except that his neck ended in a knobby stump with no head at all.

Regardless of whether or not they had skulls, a pair of orange embers burned where their eyes should have been. Where the chins had once been, coarse masses of gray beard dangled in the air, unattached to any form of flesh or bone.

Tithian took an involuntary step backward. His research had revealed to him how to find Jo'orsh and Sa'ram, what he needed to make them listen to him, even how to force them to forsake the lens—but it had not prepared the king for the horrors he saw before him.

Nevertheless, he gulped down his fear, then demanded, "Are you Jo'orsh and Sa'ram, the last knights of Kemalok?"

Tithian asked not because he doubted their names, but because he wanted to remind the spirits of who they had once been. The king had learned that after dying, a dwarf who violated his life's focus slowly forgot his identity, over the centuries becoming an unthinking monster. Such oblivion, it seemed, was the only way for him to escape the terrible pain of betraying the very essence of his own being. For Tithian's plan to work, Jo'orsh and Sa'ram could not be allowed that small comfort. They had to be reminded of who they were.

The spirits showed no sign of recognizing their names. Instead, they continued to shuffle forward, stopping less than two paces away. They remained motionless for a moment, then voiced two deafening wails that sent pangs of fire shooting through Tithian's head. A scorching gale blasted over his face, searing away the top layer of his skin and leaving what had been underneath cracked and wrinkled. He opened his mouth to scream, and a fiery draught filled his lungs. The inferno of pain quickly spread through the rest of his body, charring his bones and searing his flesh, until even his joints erupted into unbearable anguish, burning away the few vestiges of youth that remained to the king. He focused his thoughts on the vial inside his mind, trying to enlarge it so that he could pass more of this new pain on to Agis.

The vial shattered, spilling its contents back into Tithian's body. His mind was filled with a churning torrent of misery. Agis's face disappeared in the flood, leaving the king feeling feverish, weak, and scorched.

Tithian dropped to his knees and brought his satchel around in front of him. The hand he thrust into the pouch was that of an old man, gaunt and flecked with liver spots, flesh hanging off the wrist in pallid folds and the joints swollen with infirmity. The king gasped, and though he could not hear it above the keening of the spirits, the voice that rattled in his throat felt coarse and feeble.

Still, the gruesome pair did not end their wails, and Tithian sensed that he was growing older by the instant. He pulled an owl's feather from his satchel, then turned his palm toward the ground. Again, the energy that rushed into his body caused him great pain. He could feel it literally broiling his flesh from the inside out, but that hardly seemed noticeable compared to the agony being inflicted on him by the two spirits.

Tithian tossed the feather into the air and croaked his incantation, using his tongue to feel his way through the syllables. Again, the spell did not work quite as he had expected. Instead of imposing an absolute silence over the area, it muffled the keening, so that the terrible sound seemed to echo from the far end of a long canyon.

The searing agony slowly faded, leaving a thousand minor pains in its place. Every joint throbbed with a feverish ache, his stomach churned as though he had eaten a meal of brimstone, and his ears rang with a terrible chime that would not die away. Nevertheless, Tithian knew that he had, for now, survived the ill effects of the keening.

The king pushed himself to his feet and stood before the two spirits, his head swimming from the effort. Doing his best not to tremble and not to cower when he met their fiery gazes, he demanded, "Again, are you the last dwarven knights, Jo'orsh and Sa'ram?"

To the king's surprise, this time the spirits answered—and they seemed anything but unthinking. "We are not dwarves, human!" thundered the figure with the head. "We are Jo'orsh and Sa'ram, the first giants! We have felt your magic searching for our Oracle, and you shall not have it, thief!"

Tiny red flames sprouted from the stumps of the spirits' arms. They began to crawl forward, slowly bringing their twisted limbs around to point at his face. Tithian backed away, stumbling and nearly falling when his old man's legs did not respond as he had expected. He started to reach into his satchel for the components to another spell, then, remembering how the last two spells had seared his flesh, he elected to try something different.

Tithian closed his eyes and visualized himself as a statue, carved from a solid block of granite. As he summoned the spiritual energy to use the Way, the statue's features changed with no input from him. The gaunt features became haggard and almost skeletal, deep circles appeared beneath his eyes, and his hawkish nose protruded so far that his thin-lipped mouth seemed little more than a shadow. His shoulders hunched over, and his long hair stuck out at all angles.

Although repulsed by the image, Tithian did not bother to change it. The flesh had become stony and resistant to fire, which was what mattered most at the moment. He forced himself to stop retreating, then stood up straight as his two attackers approached.

The bony creatures stopped less than a pace away, pointing their arms straight at Tithian's chest. The flames at the end of their stumps shot out, washing over the king's body as had their scorching breaths earlier. The fire had little effect, swirling harmlessly over his breast.

"You may have fathered giants, but you were born dwarves," Tithian said. He focused his eyes on the embers floating above the necks of the headless spirits, then quoted the first line from the dwarves' sacred text, the *Book of the Kemalok Kings*: "'Born of liquid fire and seasoned in bleak darkness, we dwarves are the sturdy people, the people of the rock. . . .'"

While he spoke, the king formed the ludicrous image of a bearded, hairy dwarf, as he understood that the ancient dwarves were portrayed in their portraits. He used the Way to project this construct toward the burning embers of the headless bone creature. He was not making a mental attack so much as simply hoping to contact whatever passed for the thing's mind.

He continued to recite: "'It is into our bones that the mountains sink their roots. It is from our hearts that the clear waters pour. It is out of our mouths that the cool winds blow. We were made to buttress the world, to support the cities of the green races, to carry the weight of the verdant fields upon our shoulders.'"

Tithian's dwarf construct passed into what remained of the spirit's intellect, and the king was suddenly blinded by a brilliant crimson glow. The ground vanished from beneath his feet, sending him tumbling head over heels into the red radiance.

The king visualized a pair of wings sprouting from the dwarf's back, trying to bring the descent under control. He had a queasy feeling in his stomach as a surge of energy rose from deep within his aged body, and the appendages appeared on the back of his mental construct. Wisps of smoke began to rise from the wings almost instantly, then they burst into flame.

Hoping to reach the spirit's memory before his construct went the way of his wings, Tithian had it repeat the opening lines from the *Book of the Kemalok Kings*: "'Born of liquid fire and seasoned in bleak darkness, we dwarves are the sturdy people, the people of the rock. It is into our bones that the mountains sink their roots. It is from our hearts that the clear waters pour. . . .'"

The dark circle of a cave's mouth appeared in the crimson glow, directly in front of Tithian's construct. As the imaginary dwarf continued to fall, the black disk grew larger and larger. Soon, it replaced the crimson fire altogether, and the king's construct was lost in the darkness. Somewhere in the blackness, a stream of water trickled into a still pond, and Tithian smelled a sweet odor of dampness. On his skin he felt a cool breeze, carrying on its breath the promise of shelter and safety.

It was then that Tithian noticed that the spirits had stopped attacking his physical body. They now stood to each side of him, their mangled arms lowered and no longer spouting flame. The orange embers had been replaced by the glowing effigy of true eyes, with

bushy eyebrows, long gray lashes, and a calm seren-
ity that bespoke of ancient wisdom and integrity of
character.

Inside the mind of the headless spirit, a pair of
flickering brands appeared in front of Tithian's construct, lighting the darkness for him. To the king's
surprise, he discovered that his dwarf was not standing in a simple cave passage, but in a vast subterranean courtyard. Directly ahead lay the arched
entrance to a magnificent tower, flanked on each side
by a sconce holding one of the torches that lit the
area. The keep rose high overhead, its roof joining
directly into the ceiling of the cavernous chamber in
which it had been built.

Tithian took his construct past the bronze-gilded
doors and entered the keep. He found himself standing in a dimly lit foyer. To one side of the entrance sat
a low stone bench, sized for the short legs of dwarves.
On the other side was a higher bench, appropriate to
the longer legs of humans. Another door opened on
the opposite side, and above this arch hung a pair of
crossed battle-axes, ready to fall on the neck of anyone who passed through that portal without permission.

A pair of dwarves stepped through the inner door.
Both were dressed in gleaming suits of steel plate,
embossed with simple geometric patterns and trimmed
in gold. One of the figures carried his helmet beneath
his arm. Still, all that could be seen of his visage were
a pair of steady brown eyes and his proud hooked
nose, for his long hair and bushy beard formed a
mane that hid everything else from view. The second
dwarf wore his helmet with the visor down, leaving
nothing but a pair of green eyes and the tufts of his
long beard exposed to view.

"Why have you called us back to the caves of our ancestors?" demanded the helmeted figure. "Why have you come to us speaking of the roots of mountains, of clear waters and cool winds—of the people of fire and darkness?"

"The time has come for you to rejoin your king, Sa'ram," Tithian replied, reasoning that the dwarf who refused to show his head would be the ancestor of the beasthead giants.

The dwarf showed no reaction to the mention of his name, but said, "That is not possible. We have a duty to perform to our descendants."

"You have a duty to perform to your king!" Tithian said sharply. "Rkard has summoned you, and you must obey."

"Rkard is dead," replied Sa'ram, angry orange embers beginning to glow behind his visor. "He has been dead these many centuries."

"Rkard has been reborn, and I have come to summon you back to his service," the king said. If the spirits discovered his lie, Tithian had no doubt that he would suffer a terrible and lingering death. But he had no intention of letting them find him out. He had come prepared to corroborate his story, or he would never have made such an outrageous claim. "My body holds in its hands the symbols to prove that I speak the truth."

Tithian found his construct ejected from the spirit's mind. Once again, he was standing in the sweltering mica tunnel, flanked on either side by a giant-sized lump of fused bone that had once been a dwarf.

These symbols—show them to us, ordered Sa'ram. Lacking a mouth, or even a head to put it in, he used the Way to send his message.

Tithian held out the Belt of Rank, draping it over

Sa'ram's fleshless arm.

"That is the Goblin's Head," objected Jo'orsh. His eyes also began to glow orange. "It is the crest of the dwarven general, not the king."

"Were they not one and the same when Kemalok fell?" Tithian countered. Judging by the orange color returning to their eyes, his plan was not working quite as well as he had hoped. He plunged his hand into his shoulder satchel, then said, "Nevertheless, I feared that one symbol would not be enough. That's why I brought this as well."

Tithian pulled a jewel-studded crown of white metal from his satchel, then slipped it over the stump of Jo'orsh's arm.

"Rkard's crown," confirmed the spirit. He sounded strangely disappointed, and the orange glow faded from both his eyes and those of Sa'ram. "What does he wish of us?"

"Return to Kemalok," Tithian replied, breathing a secret sigh of relief. "There, you'll find a young dwarf-human crossbreed with crimson eyes. He is the vessel in which Rkard has chosen to reincarnate himself. You must guard this child from harm, for it is his destiny to unite the armies of men and dwarves under the Tower of Buryn's banner."

Despite what he said, Tithian had no knowledge that Rkard had been reincarnated in any child. Instead, the king had fashioned the lie after several painstaking months researching archaic dwarven legends and interrogating his disembodied tutors. He had based his final story on the ancient dwarven belief that the kings of Kemalok would always rise to answer their city's call for protection. Since he knew that Rkard had, in fact, recently risen to protect the city, Tithian felt confident that Sa'ram and Jo'orsh would not have too much trouble accepting his fabrication.

For several moments, the two spirits stared silently at each other. Finally, Jo'orsh shook his head. "We cannot answer our king's call," he said. "Our duty to guard the Oracle—"

"Is not as great as your duty to your king," Tithian said, watching the pair carefully. After judging that the spirits had accepted him as a true messenger of Rkard, he added, "Nor is it as great as your duty to uphold the oath you swore to kill Borys."

Sa'ram's eyes flashed. *We cannot keep that oath.*

"Not directly, but the time will soon be at hand— when Rkard is old enough to assemble the armies of men and dwarves," Tithian said. "The weapons he needs are within his grasp: the Scourge of Rkard, a sorceress with the magic of the Pristine Tower, and, here on Lybdos, the Dark Lens. All you must do is guard the child until he's old enough to slay the Dragon. I'll stay with the lens until you return for it."

"No. We have learned that there are worse evils than Borys," objected Jo'orsh. "Otherwise, we would not have forsaken our pledge to kill him, nor condemned ourselves to this." He ran the gnarled stump of an arm down his skeletal body.

If the Dragon dies, Rajaat will be freed, Sa'ram added. *He'll resume his wars on the green races and won't stop until all of them have perished. We cannot condemn all the races of Athas to death to avenge the dwarves on Borys, or even to spare ourselves an eternity of suffering.*

"That's why we must all do as the king commands. Rkard has returned to defend not only the dwarves of Kemalok, but all the races of Athas as well," Tithian argued, bringing all his persuasive talents to bear— even though he cared little for the causes he espoused so eloquently. "The Dragon and his champions have turned the land into a wasteland. If we don't kill Borys, there'll be nothing left for the dwarves or any other race to inhabit."

"And what of Rajaat?" demanded Jo'orsh. "It will do no good to kill Borys if Rajaat destroys the world."

"We'll find a better way to take care of Rajaat. But even if we cannot, what difference will keeping him locked away make if Borys destroys the world?" Tithian asked. "For too long, we've tried to trade one evil for the other. We must eliminate them both, or Athas will perish as surely as if we had let them both roam free."

His words have the ring of wisdom, Jo'orsh, observed Sa'ram.

"He has never fought Rajaat," countered Jo'orsh. "He did not see the massacres of the Green Age."

"But your king did. He's the one who sent me to take over for you here," Tithian countered. When the two spirits still seemed unconvinced, he added, "On the way to Kemalok, you'll see what has become of Athas. After your journey, you won't think the world is a better place with Borys free."

"And if we do?" asked Jo'orsh.

"Then all you have to do to save the Dragon is kill one child and return to the Oracle. But I'm sure you'll see that your king is right, or I would never suggest such a thing to you," Tithian said. In truth, it did not matter to him whether the spirits protected Neeva's child or killed the young mul, so long as they left Tithian alone with the Dark Lens. "Now go! You have no choice, for your king has summoned you. You must keep the pledges you made when you were alive!"

He's right, Jo'orsh, said Sa'ram. *We must see what has*

become of the world. It may be that we've done more harm than good.

"And it may be that we're about to," Jo'orsh responded. "But we shall see."

The two spirits started up toward the surface, Sa'ram carrying the belt and Jo'orsh the crown. Tithian watched them for a short time, then started down the tunnel. With the two spirits gone, all that separated him from the lens were a few yards of darkness.

THIRTEEN

The Battle of Titans

"Forget Mag'r! You're going to lose the Oracle to Tithian!" said Agis.

"The Oracle can take care of itself," grunted Nal, paying little heed to his prisoner.

Agis sat in the crook of the bawan's elbow, where he had been trapped since being delivered by the Poison Pack. The noble and his beasthead captor were peering out from behind a jagged merlon, watching Joorsh warriors wade back and forth through the Bay of Woe. The giants were filling the sails of Balican schooners with boulders from Lybdos's rocky shores, then slinging the makeshift sacks over their shoulders and returning to their battle posts in the silt to hurl the stones at the Saram castle.

As Agis and Nal watched, a group of Joorsh launched a flurry of boulders in their direction. A half-dozen smashed into the ramparts with thunderous booms, shaking the castle to its foundations and dislodging jagged chunks of wall. One missile knocked a hanging turret from its buttress, plunging the screaming beasthead inside to his death. Two more struck Saram warriors in the heads, drawing geysers of hot blood and stunned death cries. Another stone shattered the merlon behind which Nal stood, sending a painful crash through Agis's ears and gashing his face with jagged shards of stone.

"It seems the battle is going against your tribe," Agis observed, using his sleeve to wipe the blood from his face.

"I didn't have you removed from the crystal pit because I value your observations," replied the bawan.

Nal moved past several of his own stone-hurlers to find a new position on the wall. He stopped behind a free merlon and peered out over the isthmus connecting Castle Feral's peninsula to the forests of Lybdos. At the far end of the causeway, Sachem Mag'r stood on the island's shore, as tall as the thorny trees behind him and twice as round. He was flanked by thirty of his largest warriors, all with kank-shell bucklers strapped to their forearms and spiked, schooner-mast war clubs resting over their shoulders. In front of this company stood twelve more warriors, six to each side of the causeway and waist-deep in dust. Between them, the two lines held a massive battering ram, capped with a wedge-shaped head of granite. To deflect boulders dropped on them from the castle walls, these giants wore crude, mekillot-bone armor over their shoulders and heads.

To one side of the isthmus sat the *Shadow Viper*, half-submerged in the silt bay and turned so that its bow ballistae and the port catapults could fire at the castle. Behind the ship stood a pair of Joorsh warriors, using mekillot shells to shield the decks from Saram boulders and shouting commands at the weapon crews.

The catapults and ballistae clattered, launching two massive spears and a volley of stones. Nal ducked as the boulders sailed over the walls, but the crow-headed warrior at the next merlon was not so quick. The barbed tip of a harpoon came shooting out of his neck, scattering blood-soaked feathers in all directions. A garbled cackle rattling from his beak, he fell at his bawan's side.

Nal put a foot on the warrior's chest to hold him still. Cradling Agis in one arm, the bawan grabbed the base of the spear with his free hand.

"As bad as this looks, the Joorsh are the least of your worries," Agis said, cringing as the bawan snapped the shaft off. "You've got to do something about Tithian, or neither you or Mag'r will have the Oracle when the battle is over."

"Even if the Oracle did not have its own defenses, it is protected," the bawan said. He rolled the wounded warrior over, grabbing the spear just behind its barbed head. "A Poison Pack sentry remains with it."

"One sentry!" Agis objected, realizing that Nal had just inadvertently revealed the location of the lens. When the noble had been plucked from the crystal pit, the bat-headed Saram who had been sent to fetch him had spoken of being summoned from the Mica Yard. "A single guard won't stop Tithian."

"A member of the Poison Pack is no ordinary guard," Nal responded, slowly pulling the shaft through the crow-head's throat.

"Tithian is no ordinary man," Agis replied. "If you won't kill him yourself, let me do it for you."

"What kind of fool do you take me for?" scoffed the bawan. The broken end of the harpoon emerged from the wound. "Do you expect me to believe you'd kill your companion on my behalf?"

"Not on your behalf," replied Agis. "On my own. Tithian betrayed me."

"You're wasting your breath," said Nal. "I won't fall for your ruse."

"It's no ruse," Agis insisted. "Tithian and I were never partners. We each wanted the Oracle for our own reasons."

"And I suppose you no longer want it?" mocked Nal. He tossed aside the broken spear. "You've suddenly decided that killing Tithian is more important than the Dark Lens?"

"You were inside Tithian's head!" Agis objected, avoiding a direct answer to the question. "You know what he'll do if he gets the Oracle!"

The bawan nodded. "That's true. I also know what he intends for you." He ripped the crow-head's breech-cloth off the warrior's loins, then stuffed the filthy rag into the gaping wound to stanch the bleeding. "If you know as well, you could be telling the truth."

"Let me go after him," Agis pressed.

Before replying, Nal rose back to his feet, pulling the wounded warrior along with him. "Back to your post!"

The crow-head obeyed, looking dizzy and weak. His feathery ears twitching in irritation, Nal turned his full attention to Agis. "No. However much you despise Tithian, you still want the Oracle for yourself," he said. "Besides, you must repay me for all the trouble you caused by freeing the Castoffs."

"How?" Agis asked.

Nal pointed across the causeway to where Mag'r stood with his bodyguards.

"Surely, you don't think I can kill the sachem single-handedly?" Agis asked.

"No, but if Mag'r has not yet assaulted the gate, it's because he still hopes you'll open it. I want you to oblige him," said the bawan. "The Poison Pack will take care of the rest."

The bawan pointed toward the gate area. The company of fanged warriors that had fetched Agis from the crystal pit now stood waiting on the cliff overlooking the entry yard. In addition to their steeltipped lances, each member of the pack had an entire cartload of boulders sitting nearby.

"It seems a risky plan," Agis observed. "Once the gates are open—"

"I'll kill Mag'r, and that will end the battle—if not the war," Nal interrupted. "The Joorsh chiefs will fall to bickering over the next sachem. By the time they sort the matter out, my reinforcements will arrive from the outer islands to replace our losses against the Balican fleet—and I will have returned the Castoffs to their pit."

After he spoke these last words, he snapped his beak closed with an angry clack and lowered his head toward Agis. For a moment, the noble feared that Nal would attack him, then the bawan said, "It's the least you can do to repay me for what you have done."

"You brought this upon yourself when you refused to give the Oracle to the Joorsh," Agis replied. "And I don't see that you need me to open the gates."

"Mag'r is no fool," the bawan replied. "If he doesn't see you, he'll smell a trap and stay away."

Agis sighed. "If I do this, will you at least send a detail of your own warriors to guard the lens? Perhaps they'll even be lucky enough to kill Tithian."

"And where am I supposed to get these warriors?" Nal demanded, waving his hand around the citadel.

"The Castoffs that you unleashed have left me with nothing to defend the walls. The Joorsh could break through in a dozen places."

What the bawan said was true. There were several gaps along the walls, with unconscious Saram slumped down behind the merlons, draped over rock carts, and even sprawled on the staircases. More than a dozen of the warriors who remained standing had been beset by Castoffs, and were tearing the hide from their own faces or banging their heads into the walls.

"If I didn't need you to lure Mag'r into my trap, I would kill you now for the trouble you have caused," said Nal, one golden eye fixed on a flock of nearby Castoffs.

"What you've done to them is wrong," said Agis. "I'm glad they're free."

"Don't be too glad," said Nal. "One of the bawan's duties is to protect his tribe from the Castoffs. Once this battle is over and I have time to gather them up, I'll make their return to the pit as unpleasant for them as the Castoffs are making my warrior's lives right now."

With that, the bawan climbed down from the wall. He took Agis to the path leading down into the gate-yard, stopping beside the huge stone ball at the top of the path. "After you open the gates, make sure that the Joorsh see you," said Nal.

Agis eyed the scene below. The path had been carved into the cliff with a high lip on its outer side, so that it formed a deep channel down which the stone ball would roll. At the bottom of the steep slope, this gutter curved gently to the right and opened into the entry yard, directly across from the gates themselves.

Between the trench-path and the gates sat the small courtyard where most of the killing would take place. It was surrounded on all sides by the high walls of the outer curtain, the two gate towers, and the cliff upon which the noble and Bawan Nal now stood. A dozen ordinary Saram warriors crouched atop the gate towers, boulders heaped at their sides. The Poison Patrol manned the clifftop, ready to charge down the path as soon as they threw their cartloads of boulders down into the yard. Only the walls of the outer curtain were lightly manned, for any warriors there would be visible on the shores of Lybdos, and might cause Mag'r to grow suspicious of a trap.

In the courtyard itself, Nal had laid a pair of dead beastheads near the exit, where they would be seen by anyone entering the castle. Their purpose, Agis assumed, was to reassure the Joorsh that the gates had not been opened without a fight. The noble was about to comment on the bawan's preparations when he noticed that the stonework around the gate was not up to the quality of the rest of the castle. The blocks were much smaller and fitted together less tightly, as if it had been necessary to rebuild the entryway and the task had been done in a hurry.

"You intend to capture Mag'r in the yard?" Agis asked.

"How perceptive," Nal replied sarcastically.

"Then there's a flaw in your plan," the noble said, eyeing the huge stone at his side. "That ball will never stop when it hits the gateway. It'll crash through the front wall like paper."

"Probably," replied the bawan. "But what makes you think I intend to loose the ball?"

"How else can you seal the gate after I open it?"

Nal put the noble down and gestured for him to

descend the path. "You shall see soon enough," he said. "Now go."

Agis started down the trench path at a run, keeping his eyes fixed on the broken ground beneath his feet. When he had guided the dead bear up the lane, the surface had not seemed quite so uneven, perhaps because of the great size of the beast's paws. To Agis's feet, however, the loose rocks and enormous potholes were sizable obstacles, and he had to pick his footing carefully. As he ran, Joorsh boulders continued to pound the gate area, filling the pit with deafening booms and rumbles.

Whenever the path was smooth enough that Agis could lift his eyes without running the risk of breaking a leg, he searched the courtyard below for a place to hide. Once the Saram sprang their ambush, he knew, stones and lances would rain down into the pit with unimaginable ferocity. If he had not concealed himself in a safe place by then, it would hardly matter that he now knew where to look for the Oracle.

To his dismay, there were no doorways or arrow loops into which he could duck, no alcoves where the sentries had once gone to escape the blazing sun, not even any man-sized nooks or crannies in the stone blocks. The only place he could see that would be sheltered from the rain of boulders and lances was beneath the gate arch itself—which hardly seemed like a wise place to stand, given that it would be the Joorsh's only escape route once the battle began.

The best chance of survival appeared to lie outside the citadel. After opening the gates, Agis would use the crossbar to prop them open, then wait on the other side of the walls. Once the ambush ended, picking his way back through the ranks of wounded Joorsh might be difficult—but not nearly as difficult as surviving a torrent of Saram boulders.

Upon reaching the bottom of the pit, the noble saw that Nal had thoughtfully left a spiked club propped against one wall. The weapon was just long enough for him to reach the gates' crossbar, which hung several feet over his head. The noble picked up the cudgel and went to one end of the beam.

That was when he saw Brita, the chameleon-headed sentry who had challenged Fylo when they sneaked into the castle. She stood a few feet to one side of the gate, her skin exactly matching the color and texture of the red granite blocks from which the walls had been built. Only her body's shadow, the fact that her breechcloth had not changed color with her skin, and the huge bone sword in her hand alerted him to her presence.

"What are you doing here?" he asked.

"Punishment, for letting a dead bear walk into Castle Feral," she replied. The flange behind her wedge-shaped head flared in anger, then she added, "Now open the gate—and be sure to show yourself."

Agis pushed the club up to the crossbar, groaning with effort as he lifted the heavy timber. The beam tilted toward the other side of the arch, finally sliding off its hooks and crashing to the ground. The noble tossed the war club aside and braced his hands against the gate. Slowly, he began to push.

The gate was about a quarter of the way open when a tremendous boom and a terrific shock ran through Agis's body, knocking him away from the gate. He landed halfway across the yard, flat on his back and trembling in shock.

"Get up, coward!" hissed Brita. She had directed one of her conical eyes toward him and the other toward the gate. "You're not hurt."

Although he was not sure his aching bones agreed, Agis pushed himself back to his feet. The gate had been pushed shut again, and the head of a *Shadow Viper* harpoon was sticking through it. The weapon could only have come from the Joorsh ranks.

Agis closed his eyes, picturing Mag'r's face and summoning the energy to use the Way. It was not an easy task, for he was still tired from his efforts in the crystal pit. In the short time since, he had recovered part of his strength, but far from all of it.

Once he had Mag'r's puffy eyes and bloated cheeks securely in mind, Agis sent a thought message to him: *What's wrong? I thought you wanted us to open the gate for you.*

My little spies? came the reply.

It's Agis, the noble replied. *Don't let anything happen to our ship, or I'll bar the gates again.*

In the next instant, Mag'r's voice came booming over the causeway. "Let the gates open!" he ordered. "Charge, Beast Eaters!"

A great roar rose from the Joorsh ranks, then the ground began to tremble beneath Agis's feet as Mag'r's warriors rushed across the isthmus. Boulder after boulder crashed into the walls of Castle Feral, filling the gateyard with a clamorous din such as the noble had never before heard. The Saram on the front wall responded with halfhearted battle howls of their own and hurled boulders down at the causeway.

Agis glanced upward, expecting to see the faces of the Poison Pack peering down from the lofty walls overhead. Instead, he saw nothing but yellow Athasian sky. Taking no chances that the ambush would fail, Nal had apparently withdrawn his troops from sight.

"What are you waiting for?" demanded Brita,

using her sword to wave Agis ahead. "Open the gates!"

The noble rushed forward and placed one hand on each gate. Pumping his legs furiously, he slowly managed to get the heavy panels moving outward. When the gap between them grew too great for his arms to span, he concentrated all of his efforts on the one that had not been pierced by the harpoon. For a moment, it seemed to stick. Then it broke free and swung outward of its own volition. Giving it one last shove, the noble wrapped his arms around a bone slat and jumped on. His intention was not to hide, but merely to get out of harm's way as soon as possible.

As Agis swung outward with the gate, he saw that the Joorsh warriors with the battering ram had cast their weapon aside. They were wading back to the shore to climb out of the silt. At the same time, Mag'r's Beast Eaters were charging across the causeway, shaking their spiked clubs in the air and screaming threats against their Saram brethren.

Overhead, boulders flew in both directions as the Joorsh charged, and so much rubble rained down around Agis that he felt as though he had gotten caught in a landslide. As the Beast Eaters reached the end of the causeway and stepped onto the small deck before the gate, the Joorsh stone-hurlers turned their aim elsewhere. The lull lasted only a moment, for the Saram quickly began to drop boulders down on the heads of the Beast Eaters. The invaders responded by raising their kank-shell bucklers to deflect the deadly rain.

Their efforts met with little success. Aided by the incredible height of the walls over the gate, the boulders came crashing down with a force unmatched by the long-distance hurling that had taken place so far.

The Saram stones smashed through the bucklers as though they were glass, spraying shards of kank shell in every direction, snapping Joorsh arms, and shattering Joorsh skulls with resounding cracks. Within moments of stepping off the causeway, a quarter of the Beast Eater company lay sprawled before the gate, either moaning and writhing in agony, or silent and still, like the rocks that had killed them.

The survivors rushed into the courtyard. A few muffled clatters sounded from inside, but it was nothing like the incredible din Agis expected to hear when the Poison Pack made their attack. The yard remained relatively quiet for a moment, until a triumphant Beast Eater cheer blasted out of the gate.

At the other end of the isthmus, Mag'r answered with a deep-throated war cry and signaled the second wave to charge. This time, he led the charge himself, waving a huge obsidian sword over his head and lumbering forward in great, swaying strides. Behind him came the giants who had been holding the battering ram, armed with a motley assortment of clubs and lances. Clearly, any of them could have outrun their king, for they were forced to trot at half-speed behind his waddling form. Nevertheless, none of them attempted to pass, though Agis did not know whether their reluctance was out of respect for their leader, or merely because Mag'r's immense bulk so completely filled the causeway that they would have had to jump into the dust harbor to get past.

Again, Saram boulders began to drop outside the castle, but the rain was not nearly as thick as before. The small contingent of beasthead warriors were splitting their attacks between the courtyard and the isthmus, with the result that they did not have much effect in either place.

Mag'r, charging through the sparse hail with a jubilant grin on his fleshy lips, hardly seemed to notice the stones that did fall near him. Knowing what would happen once the giant passed through the gateway, Agis could hardly bear to watch as the sachem waddled to his death.

As Mag'r reached the opening, he fixed his gray eyes on Agis's form, which was still clinging to the gate. "Good!" He stretched a chubby arm down to pluck Agis off the gate. "Come, you'll fight at my side!"

The noble's heart jumped into his throat. He released his hold and dropped off the gate, allowing the sachem's pudgy fingers to close on thin air. Mag'r frowned and looked as though he would stop to pluck the noble off the ground, but was carried into the courtyard by the momentum of the second wave's charge.

Agis threw himself beneath the gate, then watched from his shelter as the rest of the company rushed into the courtyard. By the time the last giant had passed through the gates, the apron had become, quite literally, a mountain of dead flesh and stony rubble. Only a small space directly in front of the gates remained relatively clear, for it appeared that the Saram had deliberately avoided dropping any boulders in this area. Agis found this puzzling, since the Saram ambush would work better if their enemy's only escape was blocked by bodies and stones.

Mag'r's deep voice began issuing orders inside the courtyard, and Agis crawled from his hiding place. To both sides of the isthmus, he saw Joorsh warriors wading toward the castle entrance from the Bay of Woe. At the same time, the clatter of boulders dropping into the courtyard increased in frequency, fixing the attention of Mag'r and his warriors on the walls above their heads.

Agis saw Brita's camouflaged form slip out of the courtyard. She grabbed the gate with the harpoon in it and began to quietly pull it closed. Nal's plan, the noble realized, was even more ingenious than it had appeared. Once Brita closed the gates, the true slaughter would begin—leaving him locked outside the castle, while Tithian remained inside with the Dark Lens.

Agis rushed over to the body of the nearest Joorsh and pulled the warrior's bone dagger from its sheath. The weapon was taller than the noble, and he had to hold it like a two-handed sword, but he suspected he could wield the blade well enough for his purposes.

By the time Agis turned back around, Brita was reaching for the second gate. Hefting the borrowed blade over his head, the noble rushed forward. The chameleon-head turned one eye on him and one on Mag'r, her club-ended tongue flickering in anger. Paying her gesture no heed, Agis swung his blade with all his might. The beasthead deftly pulled her leg out of the way, narrowly avoiding a gash across her knee, and kicked.

The giant's toe caught Agis square in the stomach, wracking his body with pain and causing him to drop his weapon. The noble went tumbling across the rocky apron, not stopping until he hit a pile of Joorsh corpses.

Agis was still trying to shake the dizziness from his head when he saw that his brief skirmish with Brita had been noticed. Ignoring the steady clatter of boulders in the courtyard, Sachem Mag'r stepped up behind the Saram spy and sent her reptilian head flying with one hack of his obsidian blade. Agis barely had time to roll out of the way before her body crashed down on the same pile of corpses into which he had tumbled.

Mag'r scowled and pointed his sword at Brita's body. "What was she doing here?" he demanded.

As the sachem spoke, the first Joorsh reinforcements began to arrive from the Bay of Woe.

"She was hiding, I guess," Agis replied.

The noble cast a nervous glance around the apron. To all sides, Joorsh were slowly hauling themselves onto the barren rock, silt pouring off their bodies in long gray streamers.

The king frowned and stepped toward the noble. Before he could ask another question, a deafening thunder erupted inside the courtyard. Even from his side of the gate, Agis could see tons of boulders pouring down into the courtyard. The Joorsh warriors cried out in a single shocked voice. A cloud of rock chips and dust came roiling out of the gateway to engulf Mag'r.

"It's a trap!" the sachem yelled.

Agis ran for cover, sprinting at an angle for the cliffs that flanked Castle Feral's gateworks. He narrowly avoided the outthrust hands of several Joorsh who were just climbing onto the apron, and dove into a hollow at the base of the bluff. He crawled to the back of this hole, hoping that it was small enough to keep the giants' thick fingers from plucking him out.

The noble need not have worried. No sooner had he found his hiding place than a soft, low-pitched rumble issued from the gates, growing louder and more resonant with each passing moment. The dust haze settled enough for him to see Mag'r looking back through the gate, and the rumble developed into a roar. Castle Feral began to shake so badly that Agis could see centuries of encrusted dirt and loosened building stones dropping onto the apron outside his hole.

Mag'r spun and threw himself away from the gate. Half his reinforcements did likewise, but the other half were still standing on the apron when a cataclysmic bang shook its barren stones. A massive granite ball came blasting from the gateyard. The gateworks erupted into a shower of jagged masonry, cutting down every living thing that stood before the blast and raising a thousand plumes of dust as the shattered stones splattered into the Bay of Woe.

The ball continued on, plowing into the mountain of rubble that covered the apron, flinging dead giants and huge boulders high into the air, then arcing out over the silt bay to vanish from sight beneath a long plume of dust.

Like Mag'r and the Joorsh warriors who had survived the explosion, Agis could only stare in openmouthed wonder as the debris stirred up by the stone came drizzling back to the ground.

Finally, the shower stopped. Mag'r appeared from the far side of the gate, a mountainous silhouette lumbering through the dust haze. Behind him came a dozen more Joorsh forms, long spears or heavy clubs clutched in their hands, too dazed to speak and stumbling over the rubble like the survivors of an inferno that had destroyed an entire city.

"Come out, spy!" yelled Mag'r, pulling an enormous dagger from its sheath. "Don't make me search for you, or your death will be twice as painful!"

Agis remained motionless and silent in his little alcove, content to take his chances. It would not be long, he suspected, before the Poison Pack charged to his rescue.

Sure enough, the noble soon heard the clatter of stumbling giants coming from the rubble-strewn gateyard of Castle Feral. The sound was followed by the raucous battle cry of the Poison Pack, an angry wail so full of hissing and chirping that it sounded almost ghostly.

Forgetting about Agis, Mag'r raised his sword and charged into the courtyard. The rest of the Joorsh followed, but the Poison Pack began to pour out of the castle onto the apron. Peals of thunder rolled over the peninsula as the two groups of warriors met, their weapons clashing like bolts of lightning. Angry yells and savage snarls filled the air. Dripping fangs sank into unprotected flesh, while bare hands smashed arachnid skulls and snapped serpentine necks. Soon giants from both tribes were crashing to the ground, their blood running in dark rivers and gathering in steaming lakes.

For a few awestruck moments, Agis watched the battle without moving. Then, once he judged that the giants were too preoccupied with each other to bother with him, he slipped from his hiding place and crept along the wall. Just a few feet away danced the legs of fighting giants, their blows echoing off each other like clashing mountains. Once, Agis was nearly crushed when a Saram toppled over in front of him, and another time he was bowled over when a Joorsh tooth, still slick with the giant's saliva, crashed down on his shoulder.

Eventually, the noble reached the hole where the castle gate had once stood. The place was even more littered with bodies and rubble, if that were possible, than the rest of the apron. The gateyard was an impassable jumble, except that a valley of crushed stone and flesh marked where the granite ball had rolled through.

In the center of this valley, Agis saw Bawan Nal and Sachem Mag'r, the only living beings in the gate-yard, battling furiously. Nal fought with his back to the trench-path, thrusting first with a lance he carried in one hand, then slashing madly with the crude bone sword he held in the other. His owlish eyes blazed with a murderous light, and his hooked beak hung half-open, ready to clamp down on any appendage that came too near it.

Although Mag'r faced away from Agis, the noble did not doubt that the look on the Joorsh's face was every bit as angry and determined. The sachem was making good use of his single sword, turning each parry into a counterattack, thrusting first at the bawan's throat and slicing next at his abdomen.

Both giants fought with a grace and skill that the noble found surprising, but the advantage clearly belonged to the larger Joorsh. Mag'r towered a full ten feet over his foe and was making good use of his size to force the Saram back. From all appearances, it would take him only a few more passes to drive Nal clear to the trench-path—cutting off any hope Agis still had of catching Tithian before the king captured the Dark Lens.

The noble slipped into the gateyard and picked his way along the edge of the valley of crushed stone. Filled as it was with death and unwashed giant flesh, the place smelled incredibly foul. Agis tried to breathe through his mouth and put the stench out of his mind, but the farther into the courtyard he went, the worse the odor became.

The noble was just trying to slip past one side of the battle when Mag'r let out a mighty bellow and pressed forward with a vicious series of slashes. At first, Nal gave ground rapidly, and it appeared he would be driven back to the trench-path before Agis could gain it. Then the bawan stopped and ducked a high attack, countering with an abdomen slice that the noble feared would bring an end to the battle.

Mag'r saved himself only by jumping to one side, almost crushing Agis as the giant landed at the edge of the valley of crushed rock. The ground trembled, and the rubble shifted beneath the noble's feet, then he found himself struggling to regain his balance as the giants' combat raged over his head.

Agis looked up and caught Nal's golden eyes flitting away, fixing on Mag'r's black sword as it flashed down from the sky. The bawan lifted his own blade to parry. The two weapons met high overhead, filling the canyonlike space between the giants with a tremendous clap that rattled the noble's ears.

The sound had not even died away before Nal's lance darted forward, a gray bolt of lightning streaking past just yards above Agis's head. The Joorsh twisted away with surprisingly agility for his rotund figure, but still took a shallow gash across the abdomen. Several gallons of warm blood spilled from the wound, nearly knocking the noble from his feet as they splashed over his head.

Screaming in rage, Mag'r countered the successful attack by smashing a bare fist down on the lance, snapping the shaft in two. The head of the broken weapon landed a short distance away. Keeping a close eye on the huge feet dancing all around him, Agis scrambled across the rubble and picked it up.

As the noble retrieved the weapon, he heard a tremendous crack far above. He looked up to see the pommel of Mag'r's sword arcing away from Nal's face, taking the top mandible of the Saram's beak with it. The bawan roared in pain and stumbled back, raising his free hand to cover the gruesome wound.

Mag'r moved forward to press the attack, and once more Agis found himself many steps behind the battle. He could see the Joorsh striking repeatedly at the beasthead, rapidly beating down the weaker giant's guard. Raising the head of Nal's broken lance, the noble rushed forward. As he came up behind Mag'r, he took a deep breath and, holding the lance in both hands, drove it into the king's fleshy calf.

Roaring in pain, Mag'r stopped his attack in midswing and looked down. Agis saw the giant's puffy cheeks grow red with fury, then the noble glimpsed Nal's white sword arcing toward the Joorsh's shoulder. The bone blade bit deep into Mag'r's stout arm. Mag'r stumbled back.

Agis, diving between the Joorsh's legs, narrowly avoided being crushed. He rolled once, then came to a rest in the no-man's-land between the two giants. Nal's blade passed low overhead on its way toward Mag'r's knees, but the sachem blocked. Shards of obsidian and bone showered down on the noble's head.

Nal raised his foot to step forward, lowering it toward Agis. The noble tried to scramble away, but gasped in agony as the giant's heel came down on his left arm. He tried to pull free and heard a bone snap.

The giants' swords crashed together over Agis's head once, twice, three times. Beads of foul-smelling sweat fell all around. Mag'r and Nal rocked back and forth, grunting and cursing, smashing each other with their elbows and fists. Agis could do nothing but lie on the ground and scream in pain.

At last, Nal raised his leg to smash a knee into his foe's thigh. Letting his arm dangle at his side, Agis staggered away. Keeping a watchful eye on the battle, he saw Mag'r smash an elbow into Nal's face. The Saram grunted, stumbled back two steps, and crashed to the ground a dozen yards away.

Agis reached the path leading up to the castle, and stopped to remove his belt. As he tied his injured arm to his side, he watched Mag'r lumber forward and kick the sword out of Nal's hand. The Joorsh touched the tip of his weapon to the Saram's throat. He did not even pause before pushing the blade in.

Agis turned and staggered up the trench-path, keeping his head low so that Mag'r would not see him.

FOURTEEN

The Obsidian Oracle

Tithian stared into the utter blackness of the Dark Lens, trying to comprehend what he saw—or rather, didn't see. Shaped like an egg and about the size of a small kank, the Oracle's surface glimmered with the sheen of polished obsidian. Through this glassy skin swam languorous streaks of scarlet, often vanishing from one place and, in the same instant, reappearing another. But beneath these torpid lights, the king saw nothing—unless inviolable gloom could be called something.

The king had looked into obsidian depths many times before, and always he had found some hint of light: a gray-streaked flaw, tiny bubbles with a pale gleam trapped inside, an impurity that gave the whole stone a colored tint. Not so here. The blackness of the Oracle was more absolute than at the bottom of Tyr's deepest iron mines, or even inside the cryptic dungeons of the Golden Palace. More than the absence of light, the lens held within it the embodiment of darkness.

265

Tithian smiled. Had he been born a dwarf instead of a human, his life's focus would surely have been to find this lens.

The king shuffled forward, stepping out of the mica tunnel and into the small chamber with the Dark Lens. The room was lit by a curtain of crimson rays spilling down from above. When Tithian looked up to find their source, he was astonished to see the sun's fiery orb shining down through a wide fissure that ran the entire length of the ceiling. The crack was just a little wider than a man, and, like the room itself, lined with glistening sheets of mica.

As Tithian tottered forward on his old man's legs, the uneven floor crackled with each step, the ends of mica sheets bending and popping beneath his weight. He felt a sweltering heat rising from the Oracle. The closer he approached, the more flushed and tender his skin felt. Beneath his robes, sweat began to roll down his body in runnels, and soon wisps of steam were rising from the finely woven hemp of his garments.

At last Tithian reached out and touched the glassy surface of the lens. A soft sizzle rose from beneath his fingertips and searing pain shot through his hands.

Without removing his hands from the hot glass, Tithian worked his way around the lens, his heart pounding with anticipation as he ran his fingers over every inch of its searing surface. He did not stop until he felt blisters rising on his wrinkled flesh.

"By Ral, not a flaw anywhere!" Tithian cried, his voice trembling not with agony, but exhilaration. "Nothing but the Dark Lens could be so perfect!"

Continuing to whisper the word "perfect" over and over, the king went to the narrowest end of the lens and placed his satchel on the ground. Putting one foot just inside the mouth, he grabbed the other side and pulled. Slowly the orifice began to widen, the sack's magical cloth stretching to many times its original size. As the aperture grew large enough to walk into, Tithian felt a cool breeze and saw a whirling gray murk inside.

When the king had stretched the sack as far as his arms would allow, he placed the satchel's mouth over the narrow end of the lens and pulled. As the Oracle slowly passed inside, the opening expanded almost to the point of tearing, but the body of the satchel did not bulge or swell at all. To all appearances, it looked and felt as empty as it ever had.

Eventually, Tithian pulled the sack up to the point where the lens touched the floor. Stretching his arms wide, he reached around the back of the Oracle and grabbed both sides of the bag. He pressed his chest and face against the glass and rocked the huge stone, each time pulling the satchel a little farther along. Soon, only the end remained outside.

His chest heaving from his exertions and his face burning where it had been in contact with the hot glass, Tithian sat down on the floor and braced his feet against the lens. With a feeble groan, he pushed against the stone, at the same time pulling on his magic sack. Aching knots of pain formed in his thighs and forearms, but the lens did not move. His newly aged muscles were not up to the task.

Cursing his weakness, Tithian closed his eyes and opened a pathway to his spiritual nexus, preparing to use the Way. To his surprise, he did not feel the familiar surge of energy rising from deep within himself. Instead, his feet seemed to meld with the lens, and the heat of its surface ceased to burn his soles. A torrent of energy rushed from the Oracle up through his legs. The stream flowed into his abdomen, where he had expected to feel the warm tingle of his own energies, and formed a smoldering knot that seemed ready to burst into flames.

The king felt more excited than afraid. That the energy had come to him through the obsidian sphere only confirmed what he had guessed earlier: it had to be the Dark Lens.

Putting his growing delight out of his mind, Tithian pictured the most powerful gladiator he had ever owned. An image of Rikus slowly emerged inside his mind: a rugged face, pointed ears set close to a bald pate, and a hairless body that seemed nothing but knotted sinew and thick bone.

Once he had the picture securely locked in his thoughts, the king substituted his own face for Rikus's. The expressive black eyes were replaced by beady brown ones, the heavy-boned features became thin and haggard, and a long tail of graying hair dangled from what had once been a bald head. The resulting image, an old man's gaunt face sitting upon a mul's powerful shoulders, seemed ludicrous even to the king.

Tithian opened himself to the fire in his stomach, calling on it to empower the image he had created. The energy rushed into his sinews, charging them with new life and vitality. In his bones and joints he felt a suppleness that he had not experienced in decades. The king flexed his muscles, rejoicing in his body's newfound vigor—then screamed.

A burst of agony shot through Tithian's arms. The muscles began to swell, taking on the dimensions and shape of those he had pictured on Rikus's body. The change did not occur solely inside his head, nor was it illusory, as he would normally expect from using the Way. The power of the lens was actually transforming him.

Tithian watched in astonishment as the rest of his body changed into that of a mul. After his arms came his shoulders and neck, then his chest, back, and stomach. Each transformation brought a fresh surge of pain, but it barely registered on his stunned mind. The king was too busy contemplating the significance of what was happening to dwell on his discomfort.

During her travels, Tithian knew, Sadira had learned that the horrid monsters called New Beasts were created by the untamed magic flowing from the Pristine Tower. If so, it seemed likely that the Dark Lens was the tool Rajaat had used to control that magic. The king reasoned that the ancient sorcerer had relied on the Way to shape the tower's mystic energies, then used the power of the lens to give them a physical reality. The process was not so different than that by which Tithian had bestowed Rikus's body on himself.

As the last pains of his change faded away, the king looked down and saw a pair of bulging thighs where his scrawny legs had been a moment before. Noting that they were even covered by the thick coppery skin of a mul, Tithian straightened his knees, thrusting the Dark Lens completely into the bag.

No sooner had the Oracle disappeared than the satchel mouth returned to its normal size, tightening around Tithian's new legs. Silently congratulating himself for a job well done, he tried to push the sack down over his knees so he could withdraw his feet.

The king suddenly found his buttocks scraping across the floor. Before he realized what was happening, the satchel slipped over his hips and started up his chest. A numbing cold spread over him from breastbone down, save his feet still burned where they touched the lens. He cried out in astonishment and scratched at the floor, cutting his fingertips on the sharp edges of mica sheets.

Despite the strength of his new body, Tithian could barely stop himself. The Dark Lens seemed to be falling, dragging him into the satchel after it. The king tried to kick away from the hot glass, but to little avail. His feet remained fused to its surface.

Great clumps of floor tore away in Tithian's hands, and he slipped farther into the satchel. The mouth of the bag came up past his armpits and over his head, engulfing him in a cold, formless world. The king lashed out and caught the edges of the satchel. It began to turn in on itself.

Fighting against the tide of panic rising inside him, Tithian tried to break contact with the lens by visualizing himself standing on a granite floor. For an instant, his soles were filled with pain, and he smelled the acrid stench of charred flesh. The Oracle separated from his feet.

Tithian instantly began to change back into the scrawny, sickly-looking ruin of a man he had been before bestowing himself with the traits of a mul's body. Waves of pain rolled through his limbs and torso as each group of muscles shriveled back to normal size. This time, he felt every instant of the agony acutely.

Despite the pain, Tithian retained his grip on the satchel and endured the transformation while floating just inside the sack's mouth. He did not feel the burden of his own weight, and no longer did he experience any sensation of up or down, sideways or forward, or even of past and present. He simply existed, connected to the outside world only by the tenuous grip of his aching fingers.

With each passing moment, the Dark Lens appeared to grow smaller and smaller. Tithian assumed that the change in size meant it was falling away from him, but he could not be sure. In the formless gray world inside the satchel, there was nothing by which he could gauge movement or direction. The lens simply seemed to be shrinking, until it now appeared no larger than his own head.

Even through the pain of his ongoing transformation, Tithian realized that it was not normal for an item to fall away so rapidly. Usually, he just opened his hand, and the object drifted away as if buoyed on a cloud. The king stretched out one of his hands and pictured it resting on the lens, attempting to summon the artifact in the same way he would summon any other.

Nothing happened, save that the lens continued to fall away. A cold lump of fear formed in the pit of Tithian's stomach. "Come to me!" he screamed.

The lens did not stop falling. Tithian closed his eyes and visualized it resting in the palm of his hand. As he summoned the spiritual energy to use the Way, he felt himself being drawn toward it. Again, the sack began to turn in on itself, and he knew he could not continue to hold it while trying to recover the lens. He had to make a choice: release his grasp on the mouth of the satchel, or lose the Dark Lens.

Tithian opened his hand and released the satchel.

There was no sensation of movement, nothing drifting past in the horrible grayness to mark the passage of distance. The king knew that he moved only because the satchel opening was growing smaller and the lens was growing larger. He could not feel the air brushing his face as he slipped through it, or even

whether the temperature was hot or cold. Tithian
simply felt numb.

Some time later, the king caught the Oracle. It
might have been a few moments or a day that had
passed, Tithian could not tell. He had no more sensation of time than he did of distance. All he knew for
sure was that he struck the lens with a terrible jolt.
Again, he felt a surge of fiery energy rise through his
body without causing him pain, then he sat down on
the lens, held fast by the mystical energy he was
drawing from its depths.

After he had re-established contact with the Oracle,
the sensation of falling returned to Tithian's stomach,
and he felt a cold breeze brushing past his face. The
king slowly turned, looking in all directions, trying to
find some means of further orienting himself. He saw
nothing but the opening from which he had come,
glowing red with the sun's light and rapidly vanishing.

Hoping to stop the lens's fall before the opening
disappeared entirely, Tithian visualized himself as a
wyvern. In his mind's eye, he saw the long, barbed
tail wrapped around the lens below, his huge leathery
wings beating the air furiously in an attempt to raise
himself and his cargo up to the opening.

Energy sizzled from the lens into his body, and his
back and shoulder blades burned with fierce, blistering pain. In the next moment, the stumps of a tail
and two wings sprouted from his body. As the appendages steadily grew longer and larger, their roots
sent long tendrils of anguish burrowing through his
body. He began to shudder uncontrollably, though as
much from fear that he would lose the Dark Lens—
or be lost with it—as from his pain.

Gulping down his misery and shock, Tithian waited

until the agonizing transition was complete and the unbearable pain subsided. Then, making sure his tail was securely wrapped around the lens, he flapped his new wings as hard as he could. The air throbbed with each stroke, and the gray mists swirled around him like smoke on a windy day.

The king and his lens continued to fall. He looked up and saw nothing but a crimson dot where he had hoped to see the satchel opening.

Forgetting about his wings, Tithian leaned over the side of the Oracle and peered into the grayness below. He opened himself to the power of the lens once more and used the Way to visualize the satchel opening directly beneath himself. Again, he felt his body erupt with fiery energy. An instant later, the crimson dot appeared below the Oracle.

"By Rajaat, yes!" Tithian cried. "If we can't fly up to the exit, we'll fall out of it!"

No sooner had he spoken than the king suddenly felt as though he were beneath the Oracle instead of on top of it, and he knew he was once again falling away from his goal. As Tithian watched, the satchel opening faded from a dot to a point, then blinked out of sight altogether. He could not tell why he had failed. The lens might have changed the direction of its movement, or simply turned over so that he was looking at the exit from its bottom instead of the top. In either case, all he knew for sure was that he had been traveling toward the dot one moment, and away from it the next.

Tithian folded his wings in despair and settled down to consider his situation, keeping his wyvern's tail securely wrapped around the lens. The king felt ready to burst from the dozen conflicting emotions welling up inside him. An angry rush filled his ears, and never in his life had he wanted so desperately to kill someone—but who could he blame for his current troubles?

At the same time, in his lower abdomen, an icy ball of horror grew steadily larger. After Borys had returned Sacha and Wyan to him, he had decided to store them in this satchel precisely because it seemed a difficult place from which to escape. Did the fact that they had never escaped mean that escape was impossible?

What Tithian felt most, though, was the tangled knot of frustration snarled in his chest. He had planned every step of his journey, prepared for every contingency, and overcome every obstacle—from Agis's pursuit to escaping the crystal pit—for what? So he could fall into his satchel and die? He could not accept that possibility, but neither did he seem able to escape it.

The king took a long series of deep breaths, trying to calm himself, and attempted to focus his thoughts on solutions to his problem. Clearly, something about the nature of the Dark Lens made it behave differently inside the sack. Perhaps it had something to do with the nature of obsidian, the king decided. It seemed reasonable to assume the same properties that made the glassy mineral so useful to sorcerer-kings and other powerful mages might interfere with the satchel's mystic nature.

Tithian held out his hand and thought of one of the obsidian balls he had placed into the satchel before leaving Tyr. A black dot appeared in the grayness below, then streaked up to land in his palm in the same instant. There was nothing strange about the way it came to him.

"It's not the obsidian," Tithian muttered, tossing

the ball aside.

The globe hovered in the air, lingering behind the plummeting lens and fading out of sight as quickly as it had appeared. Next, thinking the magical nature of the lens might be the problem, the king opened his hand and thought of the forked wand he had used to lead him to the Oracle in the first place. Again, it appeared instantly, then simply drifted away when he tossed it aside.

That left only the strange red glow swimming through the surface of the lens. Perhaps the artifact's strange energy interfered with the satchel's magic. The king thought briefly about trying to drain it of power, hoping it would behave like an ordinary piece of obsidian, but thought better of that idea. He had no idea how long that might take, or if it could be recharged once he had done it.

Tithian removed his black cassock, slitting the tattered shift in the back so he could pull it over his cumbersome wings. When he had finally succeeded, he spread the garment over the top of the Oracle. Holding it securely in place with his wyvern's tail, the king reached through a sleeve to touch the hot surface of the lens itself.

He visualized his cloak growing larger and darker, spreading over the entire Oracle to form a taut shroud, as impervious to energy—mystic or otherwise—as it was black. A fiery surge rose through Tithian's hand, then passed through his body and into the tattered cassock.

Before the king's eyes, the many rips and tears in the cloth drew together, sealing themselves so tightly that no sign remained of them. The robe stretched at all corners, creeping over the surface of the lens until it had sealed every inch beneath a seamless cover.

Even where Tithian's tail passed through the cover, the cloth melted into his leathery hide without any visible joint.

Tithian removed his hand from what had been the sleeve of his cassock. Once he tied it off, he lost all sensation of movement. His body began to drift, and, had it not been for his wyvern's tail still wrapped securely around it, he would have become separated from the lens.

Although he was relieved, the king stopped short of crying out in celebration. He had grown familiar enough with this strange place to realize that just because he had no sensation of falling did not mean he had stopped moving. He opened his fingers and thought of the extra dagger he had placed in the satchel. A beautiful bone dirk, intricately carved with the figure of a two-headed serpent, appeared in his palm. Tithian released the weapon, allowing it to drift away from his hand.

The dagger sailed away as though he had thrown it.

For a moment, Tithian could not quite believe what he saw. His senses told him that he was stationary, and his logic told him that after sealing the Oracle's energy within his cloak, it should behave as did everything else in this strange place. Things weren't happening at all as he had expected.

The king pressed his palms to his temples and closed his eyes. Fighting back the wave of panic rising in his chest, Tithian tried to think of where he had gone wrong, to identify the crucial detail that would help him understand what was happening to the Oracle.

The only thing that came to him was a growing awareness his own frustration.

Tithian switched his thoughts to his satchel. He knew even less about it than he did about the lens. He had found it in Kalak's treasury soon after becoming the King of Tyr, along with a hundred other magic objects. He had quickly learned how to use it, then forgotten about it until he began to prepare for this trip and realized he would need a way to carry the Dark Lens. He could remember nothing about the sack that would help him escape.

The king raised his hand and thought of the book in which he stored his spells. An instant later he was holding a well-worn volume with a leather-bound cover and parchment pages. Trying to remember all the spells that might help him make sense of his current situation, Tithian opened the book, uttering his angriest curse. This would take time, and time was one thing that he did not have. Sooner or later, the giants would realize that their Oracle was missing. Even more dangerous, Agis might escape the crystal pit and come looking for him.

Tithian fixed his eyes on the mystic runes in his book, impressing his memory with their magical shapes, silently mouthing the strange syllables of the incantation, and rehearsing the awkward gestures his fingers would have to perform to shape the mystic energy when he released it.

It was not until he had memorized his first spell that it occurred to him that there were no living plants inside his satchel. Quite possibly, he would not be able to summon the mystic energy he needed to cast a spell. On other hand, his experiences in the mica tunnel suggested to him that he might be able to use the energy of the lens to cast his spells—albeit with unpredictable results. Tithian put the book aside and reached for the sleeve that he had knotted to seal off the Dark Lens.

The king stopped short of untying it. All around him, above and below as well as to every side, strange eddies had formed in the grayness. They were about as tall as a man, oval in shape, and from the center of each one peered two heavy-lidded eyes. Some eyes were blue, others were brown, green, or black, but no matter what the color, all were equally lifeless and glazed, and all were fixed on Tithian's face.

"We didn't expect you so soon, Tithian, but welcome all the same."

The voice, issuing from beneath a pair of brown eyes, had a bitter, nasal quality that seemed vaguely familiar to the king.

"Where am I?" Tithian demanded, desperately trying to link the voice with a face.

"Nowhere," chorused a hundred monotonous voices.

The king scowled. "I'm in no mood for jokes," he warned.

"We never joke," replied the voice.

"Then answer my question," Tithian snapped.

"We have."

Echoes of the same voice began to well up from Tithian's memory. He had heard it a thousand times, but the lethargic tone seemed sorely out of place, making it difficult for the king to place firmly.

"Who are you?" he asked.

"No one," came the reply, again from a hundred voices.

"Don't play games with me!" the king yelled. "I won't stand for it!"

This brought a chorus of dreary and humorless chuckles.

Tithian untied the sleeve of what had been his cassock, then thrust his hand down to touch the hot surface of the Dark Lens. A surge of energy rushed up his arm, but, much to his surprise, the sensation of movement did not return. Apparently, the lens had reached the end of its journey.

"Tell me who you are," the king threatened. "Or I'll use the power of the Dark Lens against you."

"You've already done all the harm to us that you can, my brother."

This time, Tithian recognized the voice. "Bevus?" he gasped.

"I was Bevus once," said the figure.

As the voice spoke, the brown-eyed eddy began to coalesce into the form of the king's long-dead younger brother: a youth of about seventeen years, with the beady brown eyes and hawkish nose so typical of the Mericles line. There the resemblance to Tithian ended, however. Where the king's features had always been gaunt and sharp, with a hard, bitter edge to them, Bevus's were well-proportioned and warm, with a tender quality that bespoke his sheltered upbringing.

In spite of the fiery energy flooding through him, Tithian suddenly felt so cold he began to shiver. "Then I'm dead?" he gasped.

This brought another chorus of funereal chuckles. "Worse," answered Bevus, curling his gray lips into a hateful snarl. "You're alive, and we want to keep you that way!"

He drifted toward the king, and all of the other gray eddies also began to close in.

"Stay back!" Tithian warned.

Bevus's face flopped down onto his chest, exposing a bloody, jagged wound in the back of his neck. The slit ran from the base of his skull clear through the spine, stopping just short of the adam's apple. Barely enough skin remained intact to keep the head from falling off his shoulders. It was, as Tithian remembered, the condition in which the young man's dead body had been discovered.

The king raised a hand to shield his face and looked away, unable to bear the sight. "In the name of our ancestors!" he cursed. "Think of how you look!"

"You shouldn't have done it," came the reply.

Tithian returned his gaze to his brother. Bevus and the others had stopped advancing. "You think I did that?" the king gasped, gesturing at the gruesome wound.

"You deny it?" asked Bevus. His words were muffled and difficult to understand, for he had left his head dangling on his chest.

"Yes, I deny it!" Tithian yelled. As he spoke, he felt a terrible, icy lump where his heart should have been. "I'm not the one who did that to you!"

In truth, the king's recollections of that time were a fog. He had been a young templar in the Royal Bureau of the Arena when he had learned of his parents' untimely deaths at the hands of a marauding slave tribe. Two of his compatriots had taken him out to console him with drink, and the conversation had turned to his inheritance. He had angrily berated his brother, accusing Bevus of convincing their parents to disinherit his older sibling in his favor.

Tithian and his friends had drunk some more. Barely able to stand, they had filled their waterskins with wine, hired some kanks, and ridden off toward the Mericles estate. That was all king had ever remembered of that night.

The next dawn, Tithian had awakened in the desert not far from his family lands. At first, he had thought that his friends had led him into the desert and let him vent his wrath until he passed out from drink and exhaustion—then he had discovered that the robes of all three were soaked with blood. The king remembered being seized by a terrible sense of disgust and hatred. He had killed his two sleeping companions and gone to the irrigation pond at the Asticles estate. There, he had washed both himself and his robes. Once everything had dried, he had hiked down to the house and passed the day weeping in the company of Agis and Lord Asticles, who had assumed he was distraught over the death of his parents and warmly offered their condolences.

It had not been until three days later, after he had returned to his duties in the Bureau of the Arena, that he had heard how someone had brutally murdered his brother. Of course, there had been those who whispered that Tithian had murdered his younger brother to recover the Mericles fortune, but Agis and his father had steadfastly maintained that Tithian could not have been responsible, as he had been at their estate, mourning. No more questions had been asked, since the Asticles name was well-known for honesty—and since King Kalak had seen good advantage in having a wealthy noble serve in the ranks of his templars.

Bevus said, "A man always knows who his murderer is—even if the coward hides behind another's face!"

"It couldn't have been me. I passed that night at the Asticles mansion," he said, falling back on his customary alibi.

"You're choking on your own lies," Bevus scoffed. "You killed me."

"Never!"

"An' I suppose ye never killed me?" growled a tarek's lifeless voice.

Voice after voice asked the same question. There were nobles who had speculated too openly that Tithian might have been responsible for not only the death of his brother, but of his parents as well. Several voices belonged to templars who had stood in his way as he climbed the ranks of the king's bureaucracy, and others to slaves who had tried to escape his service. There were even the voices of a few noble ladies and templar priestesses, heartless women who had laughed at a young man's awkward advances.

Tithian recognized all of the voices, and he remembered killing each and every one of them—not by issuing an order or passing a coin over some bard's palm, but murdering them himself. Sometimes, if they were weaker than he was, he had strangled them with his own hands. If they were stronger, he had planted a dagger in their backs at unsuspecting moments. For the cautious ones, there had been poison. For the slaves who had thought dying to be easier than serving their master, always some slow and hideous death to prove them wrong.

The king remembered the details of each and every murder right down to what he had been wearing, what the victim had said as he or she fell, even the foul odors that had come from their bodies as they expired. The only exception was the murder of Bevus, which, with the same certainty that he remembered committing all the other murders, he knew he could not have done.

"Do you remember now?" Bevus asked, starting to advance again.

"Stop!" Tithian yelled, opening his body to the fiery energy of the lens. "I didn't kill you then—but I will now."

Bevus stopped at Tithian's side and laid a hand on the king's wing. "You fool—you can't kill a dead man. Do you think we would have brought you into the Gray if you could hurt us now?"

"*You* lured me down here?" Tithian roared.

"We called the lens," confirmed Kester's voice. "Ye followed it."

"Yes, Kester knew you would," Bevus confirmed. "She said it would be the one thing you valued more than your life."

A chill finger scraped down Tithian's leathery wing, drawing a howl of agony. It felt as though Bevus were ripping away a strip of hide, but when the king looked over his shoulder, he saw that was not the case. His brother's incorporeal finger had penetrated his flesh without tearing it, causing a painful welt that seemed to be the sole injury caused by the digit's passage.

"And do you know what the best part is? I can keep doing this forever, and you'll never die!"

Tithian screamed and flailed at his brother's face. His hands sank right through Bevus's chin. As spirits, it seemed his captors could not be harmed bodily. But, as the king knew better than anyone, the worst pain was seldom physical—and after the trouble they had caused him by bringing him into the Gray, he had every intention of making them suffer now more than they had in life.

Tithian looked at the nearest set of eyes. Recognizing the voice as that of Grakidi, a young slave he had once used as an example to keep Rikus from trying to escape, the king visualized himself laying a purple caterpillar on a slave boy's upper lip.

Grakidi's terrified face appeared in the center of the

eddy, and the caterpillar instantly crawled up his nose. An instant later, blood began to stream from both nostrils, and the slave screamed in terror as the eddy faded from sight.

Tithian forced a smile across his lips, feebly trying to ignore the pain of his terrible wounds. "You see? You *can* kill a dead man—over and over," he sneered, glancing over his shoulder at the third welt that his brother was raising on his wing. "What are a few scratches compared to the joy of murdering you all—again?"

As he spoke, he fixed his gaze on a set of lavender eyes. They belonged to Deva, a young noblewoman who had been fond of Bevus, and who had lacked the good sense not to voice her suspicions in public. She had been one of his less imaginative murders. Still, when he visualized an obsidian blade pressing against her throat, the woman screamed and vanished before the tip could pierce her skin.

More than half of the other spirits also succumbed to the terror tactics, fading silently into the Gray. The others were not so easy to chase off. Assuming forms that resembled the bodies they had occupied in life, they crowded around, gouging at Tithian's face with talonlike fingers and ripping at his flesh with keen-edged teeth. As with Bevus, each attack sent an icy bolt of pain shooting through his flesh, and ugly welts began to rise over his entire body.

Shrieking with pain, Tithian fought back in the only way he could, by identifying each of his attackers and recreating their deaths. Using the power of the Dark Lens, he fashioned a dozen different kinds of murderous utensils: the dagger he had used to kill the templars who had accompanied him into the desert, the looped wires with which he had choked unsuspecting rivals, the lingering poisons he had so graciously poured for women who spurned him, the rare venomous beetles he had sent scurrying under the door of a hated superior, even the crude axe he had once used to vent his wrath on an undeserving servant. With each attack, another spirit screamed and vanished, leaving one less set of claws to rake at him. Had it not been for his own agony, the king might well have enjoyed his encounter with the spirits.

At last, after Tithian had recreated the dagger that he had plunged into Kester's back just a few hours earlier, only two spirits remained: Bevus and one other that he did not recognize. Although his brother continued to torment him, slowly running a claw down his spine, the second spirit remained motionless. It had neither spoken nor laughed the whole time, and its beady black eyes did nothing to help the king identify who it had been. Tithian racked his brain, trying to remember all of the people he had murdered and match them with someone that he had chased off, but he could not think of who this last spirit could be.

"You have an excellent memory for murder," snickered Bevus.

The king hardly heard, so awash was he in pain. From head to foot, his body seemed nothing but a single, aching welt. Even his wings were so red and abused that they looked like the twin dorsal crests of some deformed lizard. He felt dizzy and sick from the pain, perilously close to falling unconscious.

"It's too bad you can't remember how you killed me," Bevus continued. "Perhaps it's because you were in such a drunken stupor."

Fighting through his pain, Tithian visualized a large steel-bladed axe that had been in the Mericles family for years. It had been found in the desert several weeks after the murder and was commonly assumed to be the murder weapon.

Bevus merely laughed. "It wasn't the axe, dear brother," he said, flopping his half-severed neck around. "Your friends didn't do this to me until after I was dead."

Tithian closed his eyes, trying again to remember what had happened that night. He and the two templars had dragged the liveryman out of bed, claiming they were on official business so they would not have to pay for his kanks. They had galloped the beasts through the dark streets, trampling a half-dozen derelicts too drunk to leap out of the way. At the night gate, they had merrily bragged to the guards that when they returned they would be wealthy men, and they had ridden into the desert. After that . . .

It was no use. Tithian could remember no more.

The king looked toward the last spirit. "Were you there that night?" he asked. "Perhaps you were one of my brother's guards?"

"Weak fool!"

Tithian's jaw dropped as he realized the identity of the last eddy. "King Kalak!" he gasped. "I didn't kill you!"

"Of course not. The honor belongs to that jackal, Agis, and his friends," hissed Kalak, coalescing into solid form. Although he had been well on his way to becoming a dragon when Tithian had last seen him, he now assumed the shape of a skinny old man with a bald, scaly pate and a face buried beneath wrinkles. "You merely betrayed me to them."

"Then what are you doing here?" Tithian asked.

"I came to see if I should help you," said Kalak. "I thought you might avenge my death—but I see that's unlikely. You're as big a coward as ever. If you can't face your brother's murder, you'll never murder Agis."

"I didn't kill Bevus!" Tithian protested, his pained voice a mere croak. "Everyone else—but not him."

"I know what happened," snorted Kalak. "You called on my magic—"

"King Kalak, no!" protested Bevus, reaching out to quiet the old man.

Kalak slapped the hand away, then continued to address Tithian. "When I saw how you killed your brother, Tithian, I ranked you a true murderer—as fine as any since Rajaat," Kalak said. He paused a moment, then shook his ancient head in disgust and reached up to take the battered circlet from Tithian's welt-covered head. "But I was wrong. You don't deserve this."

Kalak flung the crown into the grayness, then looked back to Bevus. "If you really want to torture your brother, I suggest you let him go."

"Why should I help him?" demanded the spirit.

"You wouldn't be helping, fool. Tithian can't remember murdering you, and he balks every time he has the chance to kill Agis," the sorcerer-king sneered. "If a coward like him uses the Dark Lens against Borys, nothing you can think of will compare to what the Dragon does to him."

As Kalak faded away, Bevus turned to consider his brother's tormented form. "I think Kalak is underestimating me," he said, reaching for Tithian's eyes. "Don't you?"

The king turned his head away, fighting through his pain to keep his mind clear. Bevus began to harass him, tracing agonizing circles around the king's eye sockets, moving just slowly enough so that Tithian could always look away in time to save his eyes.

As he was tormented, the king focused his thoughts on saving himself. He did not try to remember what had happened the night of Bevus's death, but concentrated only on accepting that the first person he had ever murdered had been his younger brother.

A sickening pall of self-loathing settled over Tithian, and for a moment he was more conscious of it than of the physical pain tormenting his body. He felt a foul darkness welling up inside himself, coming from a recess so deep and hidden that he had not even known it existed. As the guilty secret rose into the light, he recognized it for the hideous beast it was—but instead of recoiling from the terrible knowledge, he embraced it as a part of himself.

All at once, a placid sense of relief descended over Tithian. He understood what had happened on that brutal night, and why everything since had come so easily for him: his rise through the templar ranks, his consolidation of the family fortune, even the fortuitous alliance that had made a king of him. And he also understood why, when all else had failed and no amount of treachery or bribery would win him what he wanted, he had always relished the final option—insisting, whenever practical, that he perform the deed with his own hands.

Now that he thought about it, Bevus's death had been his starting point, the moment when he had discovered what he really enjoyed in life, and when his destiny had become clear to him.

The king raised his arms to embrace his brother, saying, "Come to me." As he spoke, he used the Way to change his body into the ghostly semblance of a matronly woman. She had graying hair and sparkling brown eyes, with a slender nose, high cheekbones, and a stern, yet pleasant smile. "Yes, my son," Tithian said, speaking in the soothing voice of his mother. "Give me one last embrace before we say goodbye."

As Tithian's arms closed around his brother's shoulders, Bevus looked up with horror-stricken eyes. "No!" he screamed.

"Yes," Tithian replied, pressing his lips to the young man's cheek. At the same time, the king raised his hand and summoned his bone stiletto. When the weapon appeared in his hand, he brought the blade down between his brother's shoulder blades. "Goodbye, Bevus."

FIFTEEN

Fylo's Return

Agis threw the satchel down, then reached out and grabbed Sacha by the topknot, plucking him from midair. "Where are Tithian and the lens?" demanded the noble.

"He never left this tunnel," answered the head. "The spineless wretch betrayed us all."

Agis smashed his prisoner into a gleaming wall of black mica. "Liar!"

"Would I be down here if I knew where Tithian was—or the lens?" countered the head. "I came to search for them, the same as you."

Gripping Sacha's hair with one hand, the noble slowly surveyed the mica-sheathed room, searching every corner and nook for some sign of what had happened to the king. He did not bother to light the shattered harpoon he had brought as a makeshift torch. The crimson sunlight that spilled through the fissure in the roof illuminated the chamber in bright scarlet colors.

"You're wasting our time," said Sacha. "Tithian's

not here. I looked."

"I'll look myself," Agis said, systematically moving along every wall and peering into every dark corner. When he did not find the king, he returned his attention to Sacha. "If you're telling me the truth, then explain how Tithian disappeared from this room with the lens."

Sacha rolled his eyes toward the crevice in the roof. The crimson orb of the sun hung about a quarter of the way from the eastern end. "Maybe he climbed," suggested the head.

Squinting against the glare, Agis studied the crack more carefully. Tilted at a steep, almost vertical angle and covered on both sides with slick sheets of mica, the rift would be a difficult, though not impossible, climb. It was just wide enough for a man to scale by pressing his back against one side and his feet against the other—or, in Tithian's case, to ascend through levitation.

"You'll have to think of a better lie than that, Sacha," Agis said. "From what Sadira has told me, the lens would never fit through that crack."

"It would if it was in the satchel," suggested the head.

Agis eyed the satchel. He was tempted to say that the Dark Lens would never fit inside, but he had seen Tithian draw enough objects out of the bag to know that there was something magical about it. "If the Dark Lens was in there, Tithian wouldn't be gone," said Agis, casting an eye at the crumpled sack. "He'd never leave it behind."

In spite of his words, the noble laid Sacha on the ground next to the satchel, placing a foot on the disembodied head to hold him place. "Still, there's no harm in checking. How does this thing work?"

"Put your hand inside and picture the lens," the head said. "If it's in there, it will come to your hand."

"What does the lens look like?" the noble asked.

"How should I know?" Sacha snarled.

"Rajaat used it to imbue you with the powers of one of his Champions," Agis replied, pressing his foot down on the head.

"It's big, obsidian, and round," came the strained reply. "That's all I remember—I was in pain, and the tower was full of flashing light."

Agis gripped the satchel beneath the elbow of his broken arm, preparing to thrust his good hand inside. Before he did so, he looked down at the head and said, "If this is a trick, I'll tie you to a rock and drop you in the Bay of Woe."

"I want to locate the Oracle as much as you do," snarled Sacha. "And to find out what happened to Tithian."

Agis put his hand inside the sack and pictured a large obsidian sphere, similar to the ones that they had found in Kalak's treasury when they killed him. An instant later, he felt the cool, glassy surface of obsidian in his hand. The noble pulled his hand out of the satchel and saw that it contained an obsidian ball about the size of his own head.

"Too small," hissed Sacha. "Try again."

Agis tossed the sphere aside and returned his hand to the satchel. This time, however, as he pictured what he imagined the Oracle to look like, he also concentrated on the cool, smooth feel of the glassy stone, hoping the added detail would compensate for never having seen the lens.

When nothing came to his hand, the noble shrugged. "Nothing."

Sacha looked back toward the ceiling. "Then he

had to have taken it out through the crevice," said the head.

Keeping the satchel tucked under his broken arm, Agis picked Sacha up again. "What about magic, or the Way?" he asked. "Could Tithian have used his powers to take the lens out of here without going through either exit?"

"Anything's possible with the lens," said Sacha. "Which is all the more reason we should leave now."

Agis frowned. "Why are you so anxious to get me out of here?"

"Because that traitor Tithian has a good lead on us," sneered Sacha. "Let's go."

Agis shook his head. "I think not," he said. "It strikes me that you're trying to hide something. Tithian's still down here, isn't he?"

"Don't be ridiculous!" hissed Sacha. "You can see for yourself we're the only ones here."

"And what about Wyan?" asked the noble. "I suppose you're going to tell me you don't know where he is?"

Sacha's gray eyes widened. "He was supposed to be watching the entrance to the tunnel," he said. "Didn't you see him there?"

"No, I didn't," Agis growled, stuffing Sacha into the satchel. "And I'm tired of your lies."

The noble closed the sack and folded the top over to form a tight seal, then, using his knees to help hold it, he bunched it together in a ruffled wad. Next, he tore a strip off his cape and used it to bind the sack closed, using the surest knot he knew. Once that was done, he dropped it near the exit, where he would not forget to pick it up on his way out of the chamber.

The noble began searching the chamber again, this

time more carefully. Several times, he used his broken harpoon to scratch away at crannies and niches that seemed suspiciously deep or straight, hoping to find a secret door or hidden passage lurking behind them. Twice, he even resorted to peeling sheets of mica off the walls when the light played tricks on his eyes and he thought he had spied a torch flickering behind them.

Agis discovered nothing but more mica. Whatever had become of Tithian, it seemed that he was not here—and the noble doubted that the king had any intention of returning. He looked around the room one last time, then turned to leave.

That was when he heard a giant's heavy breath puffing down the tunnel.

* * * * *

With his wyvern's tail wrapped around the Oracle, Tithian continued to fly through the Gray, traveling in what he hoped was the direction from which the red flash had appeared a few moments earlier—or had it been longer? The king had no way of telling. All he could do was flap his leathery wings, keep his nose pointed straight ahead, and hope that he was flying on the correct course.

After driving away his brother and the other murder victims, Tithian had rested for a time—he did not know how long. His welts had slowly faded, and with them his pain. By that time, he had regained his strength and was ready to continue his search for the exit.

The task had been more difficult than he expected. At first, he had called on the Oracle's power to visualize the opening to his satchel. The effort had failed miserably. Although he had created more than a dozen red circles resembling the exit, after passing through them he always found himself back in the Gray.

Next Tithian had tried magic, and the results had been even more devastating. Because there were no living plants in the Gray, he had turned to the Oracle for his power. But when he had summoned the energy into his body, its intensity had burned the flesh from his hand. From that, the king had deduced an important lesson: as a mindbender, he was experienced enough to channel the power of the lens through his body without injury. But as a sorcerer, he could not control the savage energies.

Next, Tithian had tried to use the Way to make a compass out of his bone-handled dagger. When he balanced the blade on his finger, the tip had always pointed slightly to the left. It had taken him only a short time to realize that by following it, he would do nothing but fly in circles.

The king had just decided to stop and try to think of something new when he had glimpsed a faint red flash. Casting aside his useless dagger, he had turned toward the light and flown as fast as he could, pulling the Oracle along with him. Tithian had seen no more red lights, flashes or otherwise, since.

Cold fingers of despair were just beginning to creep into the king's heart when he spied a small point of darkness in the Gray ahead. He redoubled his efforts and flew toward it as fast as his wings would carry him. He did not even allow himself to blink. It was the first substantial form that he had seen since chasing his brother away, and the thought that it might disappear before he reached it terrified Tithian.

To his relief, it did not. As he approached, the dark point became a dot, then a circle, and finally he identified it as the back of a head—a disembodied head with a long topknot of hair.

"What are you doing here?" Tithian demanded.

The head slowly turned around, and the king saw by the broad cheekbones and yellowed teeth that it was Sacha. His gray eyes darting to the lens, Sacha said, "I see you've found the Oracle—though I don't know what you think you're going to do with it in here."

"Aren't you supposed to be watching the entrance to the tunnel?" the king bristled, resisting the impulse to leap too quickly to the question foremost in his mind—how to escape.

"I did what I was supposed to," Sacha snarled. "That's why I'm in here with you."

"What do you mean?" Tithian asked.

"Somehow Agis freed himself and located the Oracle chamber," the head explained. "When we saw him enter the compound, I came down to warn you. All I found was the satchel—with no sign of you or the lens. Agis showed up a little later and stuffed me in here."

"Does he know where I am—or the lens?"

"No, he thinks you used magic or the Way to disappear," replied Sacha.

"Good—then I'll be able to take him by surprise," snickered the king. "Now, tell me how we get out of here."

"When you put Wyan and me in here, there's only one way we ever found," Sacha replied, laughing bitterly.

Tithian scowled. "And what's that?"

"We wait—until someone takes us out."

* * * * *

Agis looked up the tunnel and saw the blocky silhouette of a small Joorsh crawling toward him. Although the figure was not large enough to be an adult, it filled the corridor completely. The noble could see that, even had the giant been willing to let him pass, there was no room to squeeze between the lumpy body and the passage's slick walls—much less to do so without alerting the warrior to his presence.

The Joorsh stopped crawling, and Agis feared that the giant had glimpsed him peeking around the corner. Although his heart began to pound like a Gulgian war drum, the noble forced himself to remain motionless. If the Joorsh was not sure of what he had seen, the last thing Agis wanted to do was draw attention to himself by making a careless move.

To the noble's immense relief, the giant peered back over his shoulder. "I see the Oracle, Sachem Mag'r!" he called. His voice was that of a boy, but it was so loud that it shook the narrow tunnel. "A red glow, just like you said! It's real bright!"

"What?" Mag'r's coarse reply thundered down the passage with a deafening rumble. "You see a *bright* glow, Beort?"

Beort nodded. "Very bright," he said. His tone was not as enthusiastic as it had been a moment before.

"Something's wrong!" the king growled.

Before the youth could look down the tunnel in Agis's direction, the noble backed away from the corner. He picked up Tithian's satchel and slung it over his uninjured shoulder, then he crossed the tiny chamber to where the crevice in the ceiling met the far wall. He paused there to pull his injured arm from its makeshift sling.

The limb was in no shape for a climb. From the elbow down it was grossly swollen and discolored, with a huge purple lump directly over the break itself. The noble tried to lift it and discovered that the muscles would not obey his will. The injured arm had become a dead weight.

A quick glance at the wall's sheer surface confirmed Agis's suspicion that it could not be climbed with a single functioning arm. The noble closed his eyes and visualized a healthy, fully functioning limb in its place. He opened his spiritual nexus and felt a surge of power rise through his body, then he guided this energy into his injured arm.

A pang of agony shot from the point of the break back through his arm and even into his chest. Agis concentrated on the image of an oasis pond, keeping his muscles and mind relaxed, allowing his suffering to flow through him like the wind. The edge quickly faded from his pain, and soon the anguish tapered to a dull ache.

Agis opened his eyes again and tried to lift his arm. A surge of spiritual energy flowed into the limb, bringing with it a fresh wave of agony, but his hand slowly rose into the air. He flexed his fingers, curled them into a fist, and opened them again. Then, convinced that his arm would serve in spite of his injury, he stepped over to the wall. Using thick sheaves of mica for handholds, he climbed.

Agis had not healed his arm; he had merely used the Way to animate it, much as he had animated the dead bear when they entered the castle. To move the limb he had to summon energy from deep within himself, then consciously direct it to do what he wished. Each time he did so it sent a fresh wave of pain rushing through him, but the noble hardly noticed. He was accustomed to pain. Besides, he felt certain that letting the giant catch him would result in agony much more severe than what he was suffering now.

Just a short distance from the ceiling, as Beort's knees were scraping along the floor outside the chamber, the noble heard a soft hiss from one of his handholds. The mica peeled away from the wall, and Agis felt himself beginning to fall. The satchel slipped off his shoulder, landing on the floor below. He paid it no attention and thrust his good arm up into the crevice, his fingers madly grasping for another grip. He found the edge of another sheet, clutched at it, and pulled.

His fingertips scraped along the surface of the crevice, finding purchase in a rough-edged hollow. Agis quickly transferred his weight to this arm and pulled himself up into the crevice, bracing his back against one wall of the fissure and his feet against the other.

As soon as he felt secure in his new perch, the noble looked down at the satchel he had dropped. Although he didn't know what Tithian had stored inside, it seemed too valuable an item to leave behind. He closed his eyes, preparing to retrieve it with the Way.

In the same moment, a rush of hot breath filled the room, and Beort crawled inside. Agis opened his eyes again and found himself looking down on a mass of greasy braids, as large as a kes'trekel's nest and just as tangled. The Joorsh boy's shoulders were so broad that he had to turn them sideways to fit through the chamber entrance, and his arms were as long as a normal man was tall.

"There's nothing here!" Beort yelled. His gaze fell on the satchel, and he reached across the room to grasp it. "What's this?"

The noble began to climb, leaving the sack to the young giant. Although he tried to move as quietly as possible, he was more concerned with speed. Even if the Joorsh heard him, Beort would have to turn over on his back before he could thrust one of his long arms up into the rift. The noble ascended quickly and quietly, pushing his back up the fissure a short distance, then bringing his feet up. By the time the young giant had pulled Agis's binding off the satchel and peered inside, the noble was already halfway up the crevice.

Stuffing Tithian's satchel into his belt, Beort craned his neck and peered up into the crevice. Although safely out the youth's reach, Agis climbed even faster. The youth squinted in the noble's direction, trying to shield his eyes against the sunlight with a massive hand. "What's that?" he asked, rolling onto his back. "Come down, you!"

His heart pounding from the hard climb and the exhilaration of escape, Agis returned his attention to his ascent. He had neared the top of the shaft, where the silvery mica reflected the sun's crimson rays with such intensity that even the air seemed to glow blood-red. Just a few more moments, he told himself, and I'll be safe.

The ruddy light was suddenly replaced by a shadow. Agis looked up and saw one of Mag'r's brown, puffy eyes peering down into the rift.

"What's wrong, Beort?" he demanded. "Where's the Oracle?"

"Ask the man," came the reply.

The youth pointed toward the corner of the rift, where Agis had halted his climb, his legs trembling as much from fear as from the strain of keeping his back pressed against the wall of the crevice. His broken arm, no longer needed for the climb up the narrow fissure, hung limply at his side.

The sachem's eye shifted to the noble, then his fleshy lips curled into a fiendish smile. The giant thrust his pudgy hand into the crack. He pinched Agis between his thumb and forefinger, plucking the noble from the crevice. Mag'r was a mess, with dried blood caked around the wound where Nal had gored him. The gash across his huge stomach had been sewn shut with what looked like sail rope.

When he looked past the giant, Agis saw that they were in the southern end of the compound, where the mica walls formed a cul-de-sac around the rift from which he had just been plucked. Although the rift ran east-west, directly beneath the sun's path, the silvery sheets of mica surrounding it were all angled so that they would reflect any stray rays down into the cleft.

"Where's the Oracle?" Mag'r demanded, drawing Agis's attention back to his bloated face.

"It's not down there," the noble replied, keeping his voice, and himself, calm through an act of will. To escape the giant, he would have to keep a clear head.

"I know where the Oracle is not!" the giant bellowed, his breath a hot, rancid wind. He closed his fist around the noble's body and squeezed. "I want to know where it is!"

Gritting his teeth against the pain in his broken arm, Agis said, "I didn't get here much before you, and all I found was an empty satchel." He gestured toward the cleft below. "Beort has it now."

Mag'r scowled, then knelt on the ground. "Give me the sack, Beort." The sachem thrust his long arm into the rift, then returned to his feet with the satchel in his hand. He opened it up and peered inside, then started to toss the satchel away. "It's empty."

"Empty?" Agis echoed, hoping the young giant had not let Sacha escape. The disembodied head inside the sack remained Agis's best hope of tracking down Tithian and the lens. "Let me keep it anyway."

The giant shrugged, then handed it to Agis. "What good is an empty sack?"

"Not much," the noble admitted, "but I found it down in the tunnel where the Oracle should have been. There might be a connection."

Scowling, Mag'r reached to take the satchel back. "What connection?"

Agis pulled the sack away from the giant's fingers, tucking it under his arm. "I'll tell you after you take me to the quartz enclosure," he said.

"Speak now, if you want to live."

Agis shook his head. "You're going to kill me anyway," he said. "But Nal has thrown a giant into the crystal pit who doesn't deserve to die. I'll tell you what I know after you rescue him. You might even want to make him a member of your tribe—he's clearly an enemy of the Saram."

Mag'r scowled and shook his head. "After what you did at the gate, I can't trust you."

"What happened at the gate was Nal's doing, not mine," Agis replied. "Besides, an empty sack and a dead body will do you no good. If you want my help in finding the Oracle, you'll have to do as I ask."

The sachem pondered this for a few moments, then reluctantly nodded. "I'll help the giant out of the pit," he said, "but I won't take him into my tribe. I see no reason to trust him just because my enemies did not."

Limping badly from the lance wound that the noble had inflicted on him earlier, the giant exited the mica compound, leaving Beort in the Oracle chamber.

As they crossed the barren granite grounds of Castle Feral, Agis was astonished. He had expected to see lakes of Saram blood and mountains of beasthead bodies, with Joorsh warriors chasing down and slaughtering their captives.

But Mag'r's victorious army had gathered the defeated giants at the far end of the citadel, where Nal's body rested atop a huge funeral pyre. While the Saram knelt in a circle around their dead bawan, the gray-haired Chief Nuta walked back and forth in front of the burning body, sternly lecturing them on the folly of trying to keep the Oracle for themselves.

The chief's efforts were hampered by a cloud of Castoffs swirling overhead. They occupied the attention of the nervous Saram far more raptly than either Nal's body or Nuta's lecture, despite the two Joorsh shamans dancing in the prisoners' midst to keep the spirits at bay.

"It looks as though you intend to let the Saram live," Agis said.

"That's right," Mag'r replied. "Jo'orsh would be angry if we killed all our brothers—especially after winning the war."

"Still, it's very generous of you to forgive them."

Mag'r fixed a brown eye on the noble. "Don't expect the same mercy," he warned. "You're no giant. Jo'orsh doesn't care what happens to you."

With that, the sachem stepped into the enclosure. The giant-hair rope that Kester had tied to the footings of Sa'ram's Bridge still ran over to the edge of the pit, but the line now lay slack and loose. After Agis had been taken from the pit, the crack in the crystal cover had sealed itself, cutting the cord in the process.

As Mag'r lumbered forward, the noble's heart

sank, and he was overcome by a sick feeling of disappointment. The crystal pit's cover had grown milky and opaque, suggesting that Tithian had already taken the Dark Lens far from Lybdos.

"I never should have listened to him!" Agis hissed, his anger with himself growing by the moment. "This is what comes of breaking promises!"

"What promises?" asked Mag'r, frowning.

Agis started to tell the giant of his suspicions, swearing that though he might not survive to hunt Tithian down himself, Mag'r and his giants would do it for him. Then, remembering another promise that he had made, he thought better of it and stopped.

"I'll tell you in a minute," the noble said. "First, you rescue Fylo."

Mag'r knelt at the edge of the pit and studied the lid for several moments. Finally, he shrugged and said, "No handle."

Before Agis could object, the king reached out and smashed his fist through the center of the cover. It shattered into dozens of fragments that fell into the pit, leaving only a few jagged bits sticking out from the sides. The noble cringed, trying not to think of what the falling pieces might do to Fylo.

Mag'r peered down into the hole, then said, "I see him."

Agis looked over the edge. For a moment all he could see were beads of sweat dripping off his brow and plummeting into the darkness, then his eyes grew accustomed to the lack of light and he saw Fylo, still lying impaled on the crystal. The half-breed's free arm and his legs were dangling down into the pit, while his eyes were closed and his chin lay slumped onto his chest. Although he had suffered several gashes from falling shards of crystal, none of the cuts were bleeding very badly.

"You'll have to go down and pull him out," said Agis.

Mag'r frowned at this idea, then shouted, "Hey, you!"

Several yellowed skulls fell from their perches and bounced off Fylo's torso, and the half-breed opened his eyes. He looked toward the top of the pit, his gaze cloudy and unfocused. "Agis?" he called.

"The Sachem of the Joorsh is coming down to get you," the noble replied. When Mag'r frowned at him, Agis added, "Go on—can't you see that he needs help?"

Grumbling angrily, the Joorsh king dropped his captive. When Agis hit the ground his knees buckled, and he tumbled end over end, landing next to one of the jagged shards of crystal still protruding from the edge of the pit. Tithian's satchel fell at his side.

In front of the satchel's mouth, a tiny area of the broken lid began to clear, shimmering with a strange, mystic power. For a moment, the noble simply watched the limpid area expand and grow more translucent. Then he realized what was happening. The magic of the Dark Lens was flowing into the crystal shard, and it could only be coming from one place: the satchel.

As Mag'r started to climb down into the pit, Agis grabbed the sack and pulled it back. He folded the top over and crawled away from the edge of the hole. The motion attracted the sachem's attention, and the giant promptly climbed back out.

"What's wrong?" Agis asked, rising and moving away from the shard into which the magic of the lens had spilled.

"I'm no fool," the giant replied, grabbing the noble. He went over to the footing of Sa'ram's Bridge and

pointed to the rope which Kester had left tied there.
"Tie your feet together," he ordered, glancing at the
highest point of the bridge. "And make the knot
strong, or you'll be sorry."

"You don't have to do this," Agis objected. As he
spoke, he carefully tucked the satchel into his sling,
knowing that even Mag'r was not a big enough fool
to let a prisoner roam free. "I promise—"

"Tie!" Mag'r growled.

Agis did as he was ordered, once again using the
Way to animate his broken arm, testing the knot several times to make sure it was secure. When he was
finished, a fair length of rope remained.

Mag'r used some of the extra line to bind the
noble's arms to his sides. Once the king was satisfied
that his prisoner could not easily slip his bonds, he
carried Agis over to the bridge and tied the other end
of the rope to the railing, leaving the noble suspended over the pit.

"Now I can watch you while I rescue your friend,"
the sachem said, chuckling at his cleverness.

With that, Mag'r returned to the edge of the pit and
began his descent, knocking more than one skull off
the sharp crystals lining the pit. As Agis waited, his
broken arm began to throb, and the ache caused him
to sweat more profusely. Every few seconds a few
beads of perspiration would roll off his brow and
vanish into the abyss below. The noble did not mind,
considering a little pain and a few ounces of body
water a small price to pay for having discovered the
location of the Dark Lens—and probably of Tithian,
as well.

When the sachem reached his destination, he
grabbed the half-breed's arm and pulled him roughly
off the crystal. Fylo cried out in pain and glanced up

at Agis. A thankful smile creased his lips, then he closed his eyes and slumped into Mag'r's arms.

"Stupid giant!" the sachem cursed.

With that, the sachem laboriously ascended the pit again, dragging Fylo's unconscious body up behind him. The sharp crystals scraped over the half-breed's gravelly hide, opening tiny scratches that did nothing to rouse him. Once Mag'r reached the top, he pulled the half-breed out of the hole and laid him aside.

"Where's the Oracle?" he asked, looking up at Agis.

Agis briefly considered trying to talk the giant into letting him borrow the lens for the purpose of killing Borys, but he quickly rejected the idea. Even if Mag'r were disposed to make such an agreement, which seemed doubtful in the first place, the sachem had shown no inclination that he would be willing to trust the noble.

Mag'r rose. "If you break your word, I'll—"

"I have no intention of breaking my word," Agis interrupted. "But I didn't say I knew the Oracle's location. I promised to tell you what I knew about its connection to the satchel that Beort found," Agis finished, being careful to remind Mag'r of exactly what he had said. "You'll have to figure the rest out for yourself."

Mag'r scowled, then nudged Fylo toward the pit. "Tell me what you know—now!"

"The satchel belongs to my companion, Tithian," said the noble. "Because of where we found it, we can assume he found the Oracle."

"Where'd he go?" the giant demanded.

"As I said, you'll have to figure that out for yourself," Agis replied. He did not feel honor-bound to give a more direct answer, since he had not known the information when Mag'r had plucked him from the fissure—and certainly would not have agreed to reveal it if he had.

The sachem started to nudge Fylo toward the pit again. "Tell me!"

"Don't hurt him!" Agis said. "I'm not certain, but I suspect you've been closer to the Oracle than you think."

"Down there?" Mag'r asked, pointing at the pit.

When the noble did not answer, Mag'r knelt at the edge of the pit. "Perhaps Nal had nothing to do with your friend's injury," the giant suggested. "Perhaps your friend was trying to hide something when he fell?"

The sachem peered into the darkness for several moments, and at first Agis could not think of what he expected to see in the murk. Then he remembered how, as Beort had come crawling down the mica tunnel, the youthful giant had called out that he could see a red glow coming from the chamber.

Agis waited until a few drops of perspiration had gathered on his brow, then closed his eyes and visualized the beads slowly beginning to glow with a red light. He felt the tingle of spiritual energy rising from deep within himself—and remembered something else about the exchange between Beort and Mag'r. The moment the youthful giant had described the glow as bright, the sachem had realized that something was wrong.

After softening the red glow in his mind, Agis shook his head to release the beads of sweat on his brow. They plunged into the pit, and as they passed into its black depths, they began to flicker with a scarlet light so faint it was almost imperceptible.

Without a word, Mag'r clambered into the pit and

began to climb down. Agis waited until the sachem had descended past the narrow neck where Fylo had been impaled, then began twisting his good arm back and forth within its rope bonds. He managed to open up enough space to twist his hand around and grab Tithian's satchel.

Pausing just long enough to make sure he had a secure grip, Agis pointed the mouth of the sack at one of the crystal shards still protruding from the side of the pit. A faint stream of glimmering energy poured out of the sack. As soon as it touched its target, the milky color faded from the crystal. The shard slowly expanded along the rim of the pit, its limpid edges reaching out to connect with the adjacent pieces.

As the shards connected with each other, the lid seemed to draw more energy from the satchel, and the crystal restored itself at an ever-increasing pace. Still, the process seemed to take forever, and Agis began to worry that Mag'r would discover his error before the pit sealed itself.

At last, the final sections of the lid connected to each other and formed a complete ring around the edge of the pit. About the same time, a muffled roar of rage rumbled out of the hole, and Agis knew that the sachem had reached the bottom. A distant rattle began to echo up from the pit, presumably as Mag'r angrily searched through the ancient bones covering the floor. It was followed a moment later by the vicious shrieks and roars of wild animals, and the giant's pained howls began to echo up from the depths of the abyss.

Mag'r's voice began to grow louder, and the noble knew that his captor was climbing up from the depths. Agis watched helplessly as the crystal ring expanded inward, closing the pit's entrance at the pace of a stone-worm. Soon, the sachem's curses became intelligible as he swore at the animal spirits pursuing him. The opening to the pit remained large enough for an angry Joorsh to push through, and there seemed no possibility that it would close in time to save Agis.

"You'll die slow, you little trickster!"

Through the opening below, Agis could see the giant's plump head weaving its way up through a tangle of crystals just a few yards below the lid. The sachem's eyes were burning with hatred, and a pale swarm of bones was swirling around his ankles. Mag'r thrust one, then two hands through the opening and tried to pull himself out.

His hands began to pass back through the crystal, much as Agis and his companions had sunk through it earlier. Mag'r cried out in alarm, trying to move his hands so he could renew his grip on a more solid surface. His efforts were in vain, for his fingers were already caught deep inside the crystal.

"Brace your feet, or you'll fall and end up like Fylo!" Agis called. "Then be patient. One of your warriors is bound to find you sooner or later."

Mag'r did not take the noble's advice, choosing to glare up at him instead. "You'll never leave the island!" he hissed. "My warriors—"

The giant's hands passed through the bottom side of the cover, bringing an abrupt end to the threat. Mag'r plummeted into the darkness, his screams ringing off the walls of the abyss. A moment later, his voice fell abruptly silent as the crystal lid sealed the opening through which he had tried to climb.

The sound had barely died away when a familiar, antagonistic voice sounded from Fylo's direction. "Well done. I didn't think you were that smart," said Wyan, rising into view from behind the unconscious half-breed. He began to drift toward Agis, his eyes fixed on the stream of shimmering energy pouring from the mouth of Tithian's satchel. "Am I to take it that it was the Oracle's power that sealed the pit?"

The *Shadow Viper* Sails

To Agis, the gnawing sounded like a faro-rat clawing at the stones of a thorn silo—though he stood to
lose something far more valuable than a few bushels
of needles. Each time Wyan's teeth closed on the
rope, the resulting vibration grew increasingly sharp.
It would not be long before the line snapped, plunging the noble headfirst onto the crystal pit's pellucid
cover.

"Letting me drop will do you no good," Agis
warned.

The noble struggled to hold back the black curtain
of unconsciousness. Even without the burden of a
broken arm, he had been hanging upside-down,
sweating in the sun, for too long. His dehydrated
body was near the limit of its endurance. No matter
how accustomed he was to pain, the time would soon
come when he simply fainted.

Wyan stopped chewing, then drifted down to look
into the noble's eyes. "If you don't want to drop, give
me Tithian and the Oracle."

"What makes you so sure I have them?"

"I'm no fool," replied Wyan. "I saw what happened when you opened the satchel. The magic of the Dark Lens spilled out to repair the crystal lid. And if the Oracle's in there, Tithian must be, too. He wouldn't let himself be separated from it."

"That may be," said Agis. "But I'm taking him and the Oracle back to Tyr."

"You'll find that difficult with a broken neck," countered Wyan. He started to drift upward.

"Wait!"

The head opened his mouth in the parody of a smile. "Change your mind?"

"No," Agis said, locking gazes with Wyan's colorless eyes. "But I'm sure you'll change yours."

As he spoke, the noble created a mental image of a carrion-eating kes'trekel, and a surge of energy rose from deep within his body. He sent the gray-feathered raptor sailing toward his tormentor. Agis felt a slight tingle as the probe left him, then he saw its ragged wings flash against the gray irises of Wyan's eyes. In the next instant, it disappeared into the darkness beyond, carrying with it a part of its creator's intellect.

Agis was astounded by what he found. The interior of Wyan's mind was the most desolate thing he had ever seen, a vast plain littered from one end to the other with the corpses of tiny men and women. They were about half the size of halflings, with silver, mothlike wings growing from their backs. They all had slender, sharp-featured faces, pointed ears, and pale, lifeless eyes.

There was nothing else inside Wyan's intellect; in all the sweeping expanse beneath the kes'trekel, the noble could not see a single animate thought. Agis dropped his kes'trekel down to the corpses. As befitted its nature, the raptor dug into the grisly feast, swallowing the little bodies almost whole.

When there was no response, the noble began to feel confused. The dead flesh was the substance of Wyan's mind, and to have it devoured should have caused him such unbearable pain that he could not help but counterattack. Yet the disembodied head seemed quite content to let the kes'trekel gobble down all he wished.

After allowing the bird to gorge itself, Agis pictured the kes'trekel changing into Fylo's animal-brother. He felt a surge of energy deep within himself, then the raptor's narrow back broadened into that of the bear, and its feathers changed to bony armor. The beast began pawing at the little corpses, throwing them aside and digging a great, deep pit.

The bear had dug down more than a dozen yards, and still Agis could see nothing but more dead, winged bodies. By this time, the noble had burned up so much spiritual strength that he doubted he could win a battle even if he did find an animate thought. He cut off the flow of energy, withdrawing his probe.

"Satisfied?" Wyan asked, his gray eyes twinkling with amusement.

Agis took several slow, deep breaths. "Why couldn't I force you to come out?"

In a smug voice, the disembodied head replied, "My mind is at rest. I fulfilled my life's desire long ago—when I killed the last pixie." Wyan drifted closer to the satchel in the noble's hand, asking, "Now, will you give me the sack?"

"No," Agis replied, clutching it more tightly.

As he did so, the noble made sure to keep the mouth of the satchel open and pointed toward the cover below, so that the Oracle's energy continued to flow into the crystal. Until he was free, he intended to keep the lid intact, on the chance that Mag'r had survived his fall.

Wyan sighed in mock disappointment, then gnashed his teeth together and began to rise again. "You leave me no choice," he said. "Tithian will be disappointed though. I think he intended to kill you himself."

"He'll never have the chance," Agis replied. "If I hit that lid, both my body and this satchel will melt through before you can get to us."

To illustrate his point, Agis put the hand of his broken arm into the satchel. Next, he pictured something he was sure Tithian would have stored inside: a silver coin. An instant later, his palm was full of them. The noble withdrew his hand and let the coins slip from between his fingers. They hit the lid with a glassy chime, then melted through and dropped into the pit.

"After the rope breaks, do you really think you can streak down to the lid and tear this satchel from my death grasp before I slip through?" Agis asked.

"No," the head admitted. "But I won't release you until I have the satchel."

"Then it seems we're at a standoff," the noble suggested.

"I think not," said Wyan, looking toward Fylo's unconscious form. "I think it's time for a snack."

With that, he streaked down to the giant's neck.

"Don't!" Agis yelled. "I swear—"

"You'll do nothing—as long as you're hanging up there," Wyan said, settling down on Fylo's gullet.

The head's long tongue slipped from between his teeth and felt along the side of the giant's neck. After a moment, it stopped probing, and Wyan drifted over to where it touched.

"A nice strong pulse," the head called. "I'd say this is definitely his jugular."

With that, the disembodied head sank his teeth into the giant's skin, ripping away a mouthful of bloody flesh. A dull moan escaped Fylo's lips. He rolled his head toward Agis, but stirred no farther.

"Stop!" Agis demanded.

Wyan looked toward the noble. "Certainly not. A few more bites, and I'll have my biggest feast in centuries—unless, of course, you give me the satchel," he said.

The noble shook his head. "You'll never finish your meal," Agis threatened. "Without you here to harass me, it won't take me very long to get free of these bindings."

"I realize that," said Wyan. "But by then, this compound will be awash in a lake of your precious giant's blood. It's a pity Sacha won't be here to share it with me."

With that, he buried his teeth in Fylo's neck and ripped away another mouthful of flesh. Again, the giant groaned, and this time his eyes flickered. Still, Agis doubted that Fylo would wake in time to save himself.

In his own mind, the noble pictured himself as an arrow in a flexed bow, summoning what remained of his spiritual energy to animate the image. Once it was ready, he looked toward Fylo, waiting for Wyan's next bite and hoping it wouldn't be the one that sent the giant's blood shooting into the air like a geyser.

Wyan spit out the flesh, then started to lap at the wound with his tongue. "Tasty," he called. "I'll enjoy this."

Agis loosed the arrow, shooting his probe straight into the dark pupil of the giant's eye. Inside, the noble found himself adrift in a black fog, illuminated only by distant, flickering flames of pain. "Fylo!" Agis screamed. "You must wake up—you're in terrible danger!"

The giant's head, taking the form of the morning sun, poked up from the eastern horizon. "Go 'way," he said, his voice rumbling across the darkness like an earthquake. "Fylo hurt."

The sun sank below the horizon, plunging the giant's mind back into complete darkness. Agis felt himself crash into something hard and rocky, then he tumbled down a stony slope and finally came to rest on the broken ground of a narrow ledge.

"Fylo, come back!" Agis yelled, using the Way to make his own voice as loud as the giant's. "This is your friend, Agis."

A halo of red light suddenly appeared above the horizon, and the noble dared to think he had roused the slumbering giant. His hope was short-lived. The glow faded a moment later, without so much as the crown of Fylo's head appearing this time.

"Fylo, I need your help!" Agis yelled. "You must wake up and help me."

This time the halo appeared more gradually, followed by the glowing disk of Fylo's head, and soon even his eyes showed above the dark horizon. Finally, an entire glowing face rose into the sky. It illuminated an archipelago of craggy thought-islands jutting out of the dark, whirling sea of the giant's anguish.

"What Agis need?" Fylo asked, peering down at the mountainous island into which the noble had crashed.

The giant's voice whistled through the archipelago

like a windstorm, stirring up shadowy spouts of dust and raising a dark haze that obscured his beaming face.

"I need you to wake up," the noble replied. "Wyan is trying to bite your neck open, and I'm hanging from a trestle over the crystal pit. If you don't open your eyes, we'll both die—"

The noble was cut off in midsentence as the stone vanished from beneath his feet. A blinding light burst over the archipelago, and his probe turned to ash in a flash of pain. Agis found himself completely outside Fylo's mind. At first, he feared the giant's death had caused his ejection.

Then the noble heard Fylo's angry voice booming off the enclosure walls and knew that wasn't the case. At the edge of the crystal pit, the half-breed suddenly sat up and plucked Wyan off his throat. The head's teeth were clamped on the gray wall of a thick vein, and Agis feared that in pulling his attacker off, the giant would tear open his own vein.

Before that happened, Fylo stopped pulling and squeezed. Wyan opened his mouth, and the giant flung his attacker away. The disembodied head struck a distant wall with an impact that would have cracked the skull of a normal man. Wyan simply bounced off and bobbed through the air, wobbly but uninjured.

Fylo shook his head clear, then raised his hand to the ghastly wound where his shoulder had been impaled. As his fingers explored the cavernous hole, he winced in pain and gazed up at the noble with a dazed expression.

Agis cast an anxious eye toward Wyan and saw that the head was already recovering his equilibrium. "Fylo, get me down from here!"

Squinting at the noble's form, the giant pushed himself to his hands and knees. He crawled over to the bridge footings and, with a loud groan, used his uninjured arm to pull himself to his feet. He reached for the noble, then abruptly drew his hand back and braced himself against the bridge. His eyes closed. He began to sway, and Agis thought he would fall.

Wyan drifted toward the pit along a weaving, bobbing path.

"Fylo, hurry!" Agis called.

The giant opened his eyes, then thrust out a shaky hand and grabbed the noble's rope off the trestle. When he tried to pull the noble to him, however, the rope went taut against its anchor, almost unbalancing him. With an angry growl, Fylo threw himself away from the pit, giving the line in his hand an angry jerk. Agis heard the clatter of stone, then the railing to which the rope was tied broke away. Fylo tumbled back and flailed his arms wildly in an attempt to keep his balance.

The rope slipped from the giant's grasp, and Agis sailed away. He crashed to the enclosure's granite floor a short distance away, rolled more times than he could count, and came to a stop against a crystal wall. Despite the sharp pangs throbbing through his broken arm, Tithian's satchel remained clutched firmly in his good hand. Somehow, he had even managed to keep the mouth pointed in the general direction of the crystal pit.

Wyan came streaking down on Agis. The disembodied head clamped his teeth firmly onto the edge of the satchel mouth, then began trying to tear the sack free.

* * * * *

"Wyan!" gasped Sacha.

"I can see who it is," Tithian snarled. "Tell him not to move!"

Like Sacha, the king was staring at the sallow-skinned head that had just emerged from the gray mists ahead. It was visible only from the upper lip to the brow, as if it were peering at them through a narrow opening. More importantly, at least to Tithian's way of thinking, it had appeared straight ahead —which suggested he was still flying in the right direction.

Sometime earlier, a stream of mystic energy had begun to pour from the Dark Lens. Tithian had started to fly in the same direction as the flow, hoping it would lead him to the exit. As hard as he had flapped his wings, however, he never seemed to reach the end of the glimmering beam. He had almost stopped following it, fearing that the effort was as pointless as every other attempt he had made to escape this place.

Then the beam had flickered several times, and now here was Wyan, peering in at them. It could only mean they were approaching the exit. Tithian beat his wings harder, dragging the lens and Sacha through the Gray as fast as he could.

"Wyan, can you see us?" Tithian asked.

Who? the head replied. Instead of speaking, he used the Way to ask his question.

"Tithian and Sacha, you fool!" Sacha snapped. "We're in the sack."

I thought so, he answered. *Come out.*

"We're trying!" Tithian yelled.

In spite of the king's best efforts, he and Sacha appeared to be no closer to Wyan than they had a few moments earlier.

Hurry! I can't fight him much longer, the head replied.

"Who are you fighting?" Tithian demanded. "What's happening?"

Agis has the bag, Wyan reported. *I've got a bite on it, and I'm trying to pull it away, but he has a tight grip. And Fylo will be coming over to help him soon.*

"Then get us out of here," Tithian ordered.

How? demanded Wyan. *The way this fight is going, I'll be joining you.*

"No!" Tithian and Sacha screamed the word at the same time.

"Whatever happens, don't let him push you in here. We'll all be stuck," the king added.

What do you want me to do? the head demanded.

The king thought for a moment, then said, "Before I got trapped in here, I heard the *Shadow Viper's* catapults. Is it still dustworthy, and is the crew still alive?"

Probably, replied Wyan. *Mag'r's been very busy since the battle ended. I don't think sinking the ship would have been a priority for him.*

Tithian smiled, then ran his liver-spotted fingers over the serpent-headed dagger in his belt. "Good," he said. "Make sure Agis sees them before he leaves, Wyan."

And?

"That's all," answered the king. "Agis will do the rest for us."

* * * * *

Wyan suddenly released his hold on the satchel. "You win," he said, backing away. "We've got to get out of here."

"What?" Agis demanded. "You're giving up?"

"For now," the head acknowledged. "After the way Fylo screamed when I bit his throat, we don't have long before the Joorsh arrive. Now be still, and I'll bite you free." Wyan floated over to Agis's side and began gnawing on the rope.

When the line slackened, the noble began to untwine himself. "That's enough," he said.

Wyan drifted away, waiting patiently while the noble untied his legs and stood.

"Don't come too close," Agis said. "I don't trust your change of heart."

"Of course not. You know me better than that," sneered the head. "But it will be easier to take the satchel from you than from the giants."

"Don't be too sure of that," Agis replied.

Fylo came over to join them. The giant looked only a little better than he had a short time ago, though he had apparently recovered enough of his balance to stand on his own. "What now, friend?" he asked.

"We leave," Agis answered, glaring at Wyan suspiciously.

"I'm the least of your troubles," sneered the head, looking away.

Agis followed the head's gaze and saw that Mag'r's young assistant, Beort, had finally tracked down his master. The youth stood in the gateway, staring at Agis and the others.

"Where's Sachem Mag'r?" he demanded.

"Not here." Fylo shrugged and looked around the compound.

The boy pointed at Agis. "He must be here. That's his prisoner."

Fylo seemed at a loss to answer, so Agis spoke up. "The sachem told him to watch me."

The youth scowled at Fylo, then asked, "Who are

you, ugly?"

"Me Fylo," the half-breed answered, his tone sharp.

"I've never heard of any Fylo. . . ."

The youth let his sentence trail off and backed out the gate, his eyes going wide. Fylo tore a crystal from the wall and started to hurl it after him.

"No! He's just a child," Agis yelled. "Besides, attacking him outside the compound would raise the alarm anyway. Just pick me up, and let's get out of here."

The giant did as asked and limped out the gate. Once they were outside, the noble saw Beort scrambling toward the far end of the compound, where Chief Nuta continued to expound on the evils of keeping the Oracle past the proper time. The young giant was screaming for help, and Joorsh warriors were already turning to see what was wrong.

"Where go?" Fylo asked, his eyes searching the citadel for a likely escape route.

"In your condition, there's only one way out of here," said Wyan. "You'll have to go through the gate."

Fylo's eyes went wide. "Sachem Mag'r smart," he objected. "Put guards there."

"Wyan's right," Agis said. "Neither one of us is in any condition to be climbing over walls or down cliffs. I'll tell you how to get past the guards on our way."

By the time they reached the path descending into the courtyard, Chief Nuta was leading a dozen giants after them. The pursuers were still near the back of the citadel, but their angry shouts echoed throughout Castle Feral. In every corner of the fortress, exhausted Joorsh warriors were rousing themselves from their campsites and looking toward the source of the disturbance.

Fylo remained calm, as the noble had instructed, and brushed his hand over his beard. Agis grabbed onto a greasy braid of hair and clung there, with Wyan hovering close by. Then, without looking back toward his pursuers, the giant picked up a large boulder and lumbered down into the rubble-strewn gateyard.

On the other side, two weary sentries guarded the great breach where the gates had once hung. They seemed more puzzled than concerned by the commotion above. Although they had risen from the stone blocks on which they had been sitting, their heavy clubs still leaned against the shattered remains of the wall. One of them was not even watching Fylo, but instead kept his attention fixed on something outside the castle, in the Bay of Woe.

As Fylo approached with his burden, the sentry watching him raised a puzzled brow. The half-breed ignored him, keeping his eyes on the ground and attempting to trudge out the gate without having to give an explanation.

The sentry, a thick-waisted giant with the tattoo of a goat on his forehead, held out a hand to stop Fylo. "What's going on up in the castle?" he asked.

"Beastheads," Fylo answered.

The second guard, who was almost gaunt by comparison to the first, looked away from the Bay of Woe. "We know they're beastheads," he said in a sarcastic voice. "What are they doing?"

Fylo met his gaze, as if to answer, and swung the hand holding the boulder. The blow caught the guard completely by surprise, connecting beneath the ear, exactly where Agis had instructed Fylo to aim. The giant's eyes rolled back in his head, and his knees buckled.

As the unconscious sentry collapsed, his partner reached for his club with one hand and clamped his other on Fylo's shoulder, spinning him around. "What are you—"

The half-breed hurled his boulder at the sentry's foot, and the question erupted into a pained howl. Fylo ran for the causeway, following the path the granite ball had cleared earlier as it blasted across the debris-covered apron. Although he was not a fast runner, his clumsy gait was more than adequate to escape the sentry hopping after him.

As Fylo lumbered across the narrow isthmus, Agis poked his head from behind the giant's beard. "Well done!"

That was when the noble saw what the gaunt sentry had been watching in the Bay of Woe. The battered *Shadow Viper* lay a short distance from the causeway. Without a shipfloater, it rested up to its gunnels in silt. Otherwise, the ship sat on an even keel and looked reasonably dustworthy, despite its pock-marked decks and snapped masts. Dozens of slaves stood along the rail, watching Fylo's escape with envious eyes. Now that there was no longer a sentry watching them from the gate, a few were probing along the side of the ship with their plunging poles, looking for a place shallow enough that they could wade ashore.

"Take me to the ship, Fylo," Agis ordered.

The giant stopped and turned to face the derelict, but made no move to go out to it. "You say run to other side of Lybdos!" he objected.

"I know, but I can't abandon those slaves," Agis said.

"Can't carry them," Fylo said. "Too many!"

"You're not going to carry them," the noble replied. He glanced toward the gate and saw that they were in no danger of being caught by the thick-waisted sentry. The giant was still trying to hop across the wreckage, using his club as a cane. Agis returned his attention to the ship. "The *Shadow Viper* can escape by itself. All it needs is a shipfloater."

"You?" scoffed Wyan. "From what I've heard of your talents, the ship won't make it out of the bay before you collapse."

"I'll get us started," Agis replied. "After that, Tithian will have to take over."

"Tithian!" Fylo blurted. "Him not here!"

"He's in my satchel," Agis replied. As an afterthought, he added, "At least I hope he is."

"He is," Wyan reported. "I saw him while you and I were scuffling over the bag. He'll be thrilled to help, I'm sure." He smiled, a strange twinkle in his eye. "I'll go tell the slaves to ready their plunging poles."

With that, Wyan floated ahead to prepare the crew. Fylo stepped into the silt, shaking his head as he waded after the disembodied head. "This too dangerous," he said. "Head-thing only help slaves so you let Tithian out of sack."

"Yes, I know," Agis replied. "But it makes no difference."

"Does too!" Fylo countered. "Can't trust Tithian."

"I know that better than anyone," Agis replied, clutching the satchel. "But I can't abandon those slaves just because I'm nervous about letting Tithian out. It's the same as murdering them."

"No. Joorsh kill them, not Agis," the giant insisted.

Agis shook his head. "Those slaves wouldn't be here if I hadn't hired Kester to carry me to Lybdos. That makes me responsible for their safety."

Fylo considered this, then said, "Maybe. But Tithian not care about slaves," the giant said. "Maybe him not want to help."

"He won't want to, but he'll have no other choice," said Agis. "Once he's on that ship, he'll keep it afloat—or sink and suffocate with the rest of us."

A boulder sailed over Fylo's shoulder, bringing the conversation to an end. The stone hit a short distance ahead, sending a silvery plume of dust high into the sky. The giant twisted around to look back toward shore. Agis saw the thick-waisted sentry grabbing another boulder off the bank of the isthmus, apparently thinking it wiser not to wade into the silt with only one good foot. The guard hurled the rock at them, nearly falling over as he tried to brace himself on his injured foot, and the stone fell wide.

"Let's go," Agis said. "I don't think he has much of a chance to hit us."

As Fylo complied, an angry roar erupted from the entrance to Castle Feral, and Nuta led his warriors out the citadel gate. They began picking their way across the rubble-strewn apron, the chief shouting, "Stop, sachem-killers! Oracle stealers!"

Fylo ignored the orders and started toward the *Shadow Viper* with renewed vigor. As they approached, Agis saw that the battle had taken a heavier toll on the ship than had at first been apparent. A massive crack ran the length of the ship's keel, which had been raised so the ship could rest on the bottom of the bay without tipping. Half of the catapults sat in splintered ruins, as did both of the stern ballistae. The ripped sails lay draped over the capstans and hold covers, with tangled mounds of useless rigging heaped on top of them. Even the hull, more or less protected by its immersion in the silt, had not escaped the fighting completely undamaged. Through the craters in the deck, Agis could see at least two places where the slaves had fastened makeshift patches to the interior wall.

Despite the ship's condition, no bodies lay in sight. At first, Agis took this to mean that the slaves had escaped relatively unharmed, but when he saw barely twenty crewmen standing at the gunnels, he realized that was not the case. They had probably thrown the dead overboard, for in the heat of the crimson sun corpses would quickly begin to stink.

They reached the ship, and Fylo set Agis on the rear deck. As the noble climbed over a crumpled sail to slip into the floater's pit, he found Wyan waiting at the helm, along with a yellow-haired half-elf crewman. The slave's ankle was swollen and purple, and he managed to stand only by supporting himself on the ship's wheel.

"You're a brave man for coming to our aid, sir," said the half-elf. "Most others wouldn't have done the same, and the crew is thankful—whether we make it or not."

"We'll make it," Agis assured him, slipping into the floater's seat. "But we'd better move fast."

"Aye, captain," replied the half-elf. He looked forward, then commanded, "Ready your plunging poles!"

Agis used his good hand to lay his broken arm across the dome, gasping at the pain it caused. He focused his thoughts on the obsidian beneath his hands. A moment later, he smelled the briny aroma of salt water and felt himself rocking back and forth to the gentle sway of lapping waves. He visualized the battered *Shadow Viper* floating on the surface of the sparkling sea, then groaned as a heavy weight settled upon his spirit. The caravel rose out of the dust. The crew raised a haggard cheer and plunged their poles into the silt.

As the slaves pushed off, a series of sonorous grunts sounded from the isthmus shore. An instant later, the bay erupted into a gray haze, boulders dropping all around the *Shadow Viper*. A loud crash sounded behind Agis, then the helmsman's broken body flew past the noble amidst a torrent of shattered planks and beams.

A shard of broken wheel struck Agis squarely between the shoulder blades. The fragment did not pierce his flesh, but the impact drove him face-first into the floater's dome. His broken arm exploded in pain, and his concentration lapsed, allowing the *Shadow Viper* to settle back into the bay.

"Agis!" screamed Fylo's deep voice. The giant's fingers closed around the noble's shoulders, pulling him upright. "You hurt?"

"I'll be fine," Agis gasped.

Keeping his broken arm on the floater's dome, he looked over his shoulder. In place of the helm, a broken-edged hole opened below deck, a gray boulder resting in a pile of rubble that had once been Kester's stateroom. Farther away, Nuta and his party of warriors were wading out from the isthmus, each giant holding another boulder to hurl at the *Shadow Viper*.

Fylo pointed toward the mouth of the bay, where the cove opened up into a broad expanse of featureless dust. "Take ship to deep silt. Joorsh can't follow," he said, taking a huge harpoon off the rear deck's rack. "Fylo slow them down."

"No!" Agis yelled. "We have catapults. You run."

"Where to?" the giant asked, puzzled. "Agis only friend. Not let Joorsh hurt him." With that, the half-breed turned and waded back to meet the pursuing warriors.

Wyan floated up from Kester's stateroom. "What are you waiting for? It was your idea to save this worthless bunch of slaves."

Grimacing with the pain of his broken arm, Agis pulled the satchel off his shoulder. "Can you get Tithian out of there?" he asked.

"Of course."

The noble laid the satchel on the edge of the floater's pit. "Then do it," he said. "I don't know how long I'll last. Besides, when the next boulder hits, it would be better to have an extra shipfloater."

As the disembodied head drifted over to the satchel's mouth, Agis returned his attention to the floater's dome and raised the *Shadow Viper*. The effort added to his agony, and he began to feel sick. The slaves leaned against their plunging poles. The caravel's response was sluggish, for it rode dangerously low in the silt.

Agis focused on the smell and the sound of the sea inside his mind, trying to raise the ship higher. The pain of his broken arm intruded on his thoughts, making the waves choppy and unpredictable. In addition to moving slowly, the ship began to lurch and roll. The noble stopped trying to concentrate so hard, and the sea calmed again. If Tithian did not take over soon, Agis knew they would sink.

A pair of thunderous battle cries sounded behind the ship. Now that the *Shadow Viper* was under way, Agis allowed himself to look back. He saw Fylo charging straight at Nuta, who was raising his boulder to throw. Behind the chief, the other Joorsh warriors were rushing forward to support their leader.

Nuta hurled his boulder, and Fylo ducked. The

stone glanced off the half-breed's injured shoulder. He screamed in pain and dropped to one knee, burying himself up to his chest in silt. For a moment, Agis thought the giant would pitch forward and vanish beneath the surface of the bay. Then, as the chief started to pass him by, the half-breed seemed to gather his strength. With an angry bellow, he rose and thrust his harpoon deep into Nuta's ribs.

The chief screamed and fell. As the grizzled giant disappeared into the silt, Fylo jerked the bloody harpoon free and, screaming a war cry, turned to charge the rest of the company. His astonished enemies stopped and launched their boulders at him. The half-breed countered by flinging his harpoon at the next warrior in line, then disappeared beneath a hail of gray stones.

A curtain of pearly dust rose where Fylo had fallen. For a long time, Agis could do nothing but stare into it, amazed at the giant's actions. By attacking so fiercely, he had forced the Joorsh to use their boulders against him, buying precious time for the *Shadow Viper* to escape. In his death, the lonely half-breed, who had struggled all his life to find a single friend, had committed the ultimate act of fellowship. Now, though he might never know it, he would have a whole shipload of comrades.

"Goodbye," Agis whispered sadly. "In all the cities of Athas, the bards shall sing of your great friendship."

The surviving Joorsh warriors began to emerge from the dust curtain. With their hands now empty, they were free to use their arms for balance. They were wading through the silt with a strange, twisting gait that seemed half running and half dancing, plowing great plumes of silt into the air. Although they no longer had anything to throw at the *Shadow Viper*, they appeared confident that they would catch the caravel, for it continued to ride low and make sluggish progress.

Returning his attention to the ship, Agis found Tithian—at least he thought it was Tithian—crawling from the satchel. The king's auburn hair had become coarse and gray, and the ever-present diadem no longer sat upon his head. His skin had paled with age, growing flaky and wrinkled, while dark, angry-looking circles sagged beneath his eyes. Only the darting brown eyes and sharply hooked nose remained the same as the noble remembered.

"Tithian?" the noble gasped. "What happened to you?"

"Do you really want me to explain now?" the king replied sharply.

As Tithian continued to pull himself out, a huge pair of leathery, batlike wings slipped free of the satchel. For a moment, Agis didn't know what to make of them. Then, as they slowly stretched across the deck, he realized they were attached to the king's back.

"In the name of Ral!" the noble gasped.

"More like Rajaat," Tithian replied, glancing at the appendages with pride. He gave them a tentative flap, then looked down at Wyan, who was hovering at his side. "Shall we go?"

"That's not why I brought you out of the satchel," Agis snapped. "Look behind us."

"I saw what became of Fylo," the king replied. "I always knew your principles would be the end of you. Now it seems they're also getting your friends killed. I have no intention of being one of those friends."

"If you take over here, the whole ship can escape!" Agis said. Even as he spoke the words, he was visualizing the image of a griffin, a huge eagle with the body and claws of a lion.

"I see no reason to take that chance," Tithian replied, lifting himself into the air with a single beat of his mighty wings. "I can escape with the Dark Lens alone."

"That remains to be seen," Agis replied, locking eyes with the king. Keeping just enough of his mind focused on his duties as a floater to keep the *Shadow Viper* from sinking, the noble launched his griffin into Tithian's mind.

The noble found himself flying through a cavern of inviolable gloom. Nowhere in the blackness could he find even the hint of a light, much less anything that might be called illumination. The place seemed the very embodiment of darkness, more so than any of the times in the past when Agis had contacted the king's mind.

Through his griffin's mouth, Agis yelled, "You can't escape by hiding. I'll find you, and when I do you'll save this ship!" His words vanished into the murk without echo.

"I've no intention of hiding," replied the king.

A crimson wyvern flashed into existence above Agis's griffin. The winged lizard had appeared in mid-dive, its talons extended and its venom-dripping tail barb arcing toward the griffin's heart. Flapping his construct's powerful wings, the noble rose to meet the attack. As the two beasts came together, he used one of his massive claws to slap aside the poisonous tail, then opened his sharp beak in anticipation of closing it around the wyvern's serpentine neck.

The beasts hit with a thunderous boom. As Agis tried to close his beak on the wyvern's neck, he sensed a searing heat coming from the lizard's body, and the smell of singed feathers filled his nostrils. Then, to the noble's astonishment, the lizard began to flap its wings, driving the griffin back with such awesome strength that Agis could not resist.

The wyvern carried them out of Tithian's mind. In the next instant, they emerged over the vast blue sea in the mind of the amazed noble. As Agis was still trying to comprehend the raw force behind the counterattack, the king's construct suddenly separated from the combat and dove away. At first the noble was confused, but then he saw the object of the wyvern's assault: a caravel, pitching and reeling in the stormy waters below. The wyvern was descending on it with tucked wings and extended claws.

Outside the noble's mind, the *Shadow Viper* suddenly lurched to a standstill, and Agis heard the ship slaves screaming in panic. He looked up from the floater's dome to see the crew standing frozen along the gunnels, bracing their plunging poles against the deck to defend against a huge crimson wyvern diving out of the olive-tinged sky.

"This can't be!" Agis gasped.

"It is," replied Tithian, also looking skyward. "That's the power of the Dark Lens."

"All the more reason to take it from you!" Agis said, turning his attention inward once more.

Agis sent his griffin after the wyvern, at the same time attacking from below. The rattle of a dozen ballistae sounded from the caravel, then a flight of spar-sized harpoons streaked up from the decks to pierce the wyvern's breast. The lizard's wings went slack, and it crashed onto the *Shadow Viper*'s bow, shaking the entire ship both inside and outside the noble's mind.

Agis descended on the injured beast and pinned it to the deck. The wyvern arced its tail up to impale him, but the griffin dodged aside, then used his rear claws to rip the appendage off at the root. The lizard tried to beat him off with its wings, and the noble's harbinger tore them to ribbons. It rolled onto its back and raked its filthy talons across its attacker's breast. The griffin retaliated by catching the wyvern's serpentine neck in its beak and biting down hard. The fanged head came off, and the wyvern fell motionless to the deck.

Agis had his griffin step back. During the battle, the wyvern's heat had scorched the feathers from the beast's head and blackened its leathery body in a dozen places. Nevertheless, the griffin was the one that remained standing, and that was the important thing.

To the noble's surprise, the wyvern did not fade away, as a construct normally did after being destroyed. Instead, it simply lay on the deck, wisps of gray smoke rising from beneath its body.

Without allowing his griffin to vanish, Agis stopped attacking and turned his attention outward. The noble found himself slumped over the floater's dome, so drained of energy that he could hardly breathe. He could feel the obsidian drawing the last of his strength from his body, leaving him with a sick, hollow feeling in place of his spiritual nexus.

As he pushed himself to a sitting position, Agis smelled smoke coming from the bow. There, he saw that several crewmen had abandoned their posts along the gunnel to rush forward and pour bucketfuls of silt over the fires started by the wyvern's

searing remains. He looked over his shoulder and
saw that the mountainous forms of the Joorsh warriors had closed much of the distance between themselves and the fleeing ship.

Agis turned to Tithian. Although the king's aged
face showed the strain of having his wyvern destroyed, he did not look nearly as tired as the noble.

"Take your place at the floater's dome," Agis
ordered.

Tithian shook his head. "I think not," he said.

"Don't make me send my griffin in to take control
of your mind," the noble threatened.

"I'll admit that you put up a valiant fight, Agis,"
Tithian allowed, a condescending sneer on his cracked
lips. "But do you really think you're powerful enough
to overcome the Oracle?"

A series of terrified shrieks erupted from the bow,
then Agis saw one of the slaves who had gone to fight
the fire rise into the air, impaled on the wyvern's severed tail. The noble turned his attention inward,
bringing his griffin to its feet.

Exhausted by the fight and his efforts to keep the
Shadow Viper afloat, the noble was too slow. The
wyvern's tail arced across the deck and pierced deep
into the griffin's breast. The stinging poison flooded
through his chest in an instant, filling it with a scalding vapor that turned everything it touched to ash.
Agis felt as though his heart were bursting into flame.
He heard himself howling—not in pain, but in out-
rage—and everything went dark.

Tithian withdrew from the noble's still mind and
found himself on a sinking ship. Without Agis to
keep it afloat, the *Shadow Viper* was going down fast.
Already, the main deck had disappeared beneath the
bay, and dust was pouring over the gunnels of the

quarterdeck in billowing waves. The closest Joorsh was just three steps away from grabbing the caravel's stern, and panicked slaves were calling for mercy from the giants.

Tithian went to Agis's side. The noble lay slumped over the floater's stone, blood seeping from his ears and nostrils, his glazed eyes focused on nothing. A red froth poured from his mouth. No breath—shallow or otherwise—passed his dead lips.

"Don't try to save him!" objected Wyan, hovering at Tithian's side. "There isn't time!"

"I'm over that folly," said Tithian, taking the noble's hand. "But I need something of Agis's."

The king slipped the Asticles signet off the noble's finger, then the whole ship jerked. He looked back to see that a Joorsh had grabbed the stern rail and was preventing the caravel from sinking any farther into the silt.

Tithian let the noble's hand drop, grabbed the satchel, and launched himself into the air, barely escaping the giant's clumsy attempt to swat him down. With the warrior's angry voice roaring in his ears, he flapped his wings hard and quickly rose into the olive sky. Once the king was safely out of reach, he began to circle slowly so that Wyan could catch up to him.

While he waited, he watched in amusement as the frustrated Joorsh plucked crewmen from the *Shadow Viper*'s deck and hurled them at him. The tenth slave was just arcing down toward the silt when Wyan finally arrived.

"You fool!" snarled the disembodied head. "You nearly lost the Oracle—and for what? A souvenir?"

"This is no souvenir," Tithian replied, holding the ring out to him. "Open your mouth."

Frowning in puzzlement, Wyan obeyed. Tithian placed Agis's ring on the head's gray tongue.

"Take this to Rikus and Sadira," the king ordered. "Tell them that they're to meet Agis in the village of Samarah. The time has come to kill the Dragon."

EPILOGUE

Cursing the long, echoing halls of the Asticles mansion, Neeva rounded the corner at a dead run. At last she saw the nursery at the end of the corridor. Its ivory door, engraved with a grinning jackal's face, was closed tight. She drew both her swords without missing a step.

"Rkard!" she yelled. "What's wrong?"

No answer. For her son, that was even more unusual than the terrified wail that had alarmed her in the first place. Neeva did not even stop at the closed portal, simply kicking it off its leather hinges on her way through.

A pair of huge, hideous monsters stood on the opposite side of the room, peering through the large window where Rkard usually waited to greet the dawn sun. They were hardly more than skeletal lumps, with twisted shards of bone sticking out of their shoulders in the place of arms. One figure had a hunched back and a slope-browed skull, while the other had a squat neck and no head at all. Regardless of whether they had heads or not, pairs of orange embers burned where their eyes should have been. Where the chins had hung, coarse masses of gray dangled in the air, unattached to bone or flesh of any kind.

As Neeva charged across the room, they backed out of sight. She thrust her swords out the window, then leaned through, ready to attack with a vicious series of slashes and thrusts.

They were gone. The only thing she saw outside the second story window were acres and acres of Asticles faro trees.

From inside the room, Rkard's small voice said, "Don't kill them, Mother. They didn't mean to scare me."

Neeva turned around and found her son hiding in the corner, his red eyes bulging from their sockets as he stared at his lap.

"What did they . . ."

Noticing what her son was staring at, Neeva let the question trail off. Across his tiny lap lay the Belt of Rank, and on his head, cocked at a steep angle to keep it from falling off, was King Rkard's bejeweled crown.

Neeva sheathed her swords and knelt in front of her son. "Rkard—where did you get these?"

The young mul fixed his red eyes on her, and she saw something in them that she had never before seen: tears, ready to spill down his chiseled cheeks. Rkard clamped his jaw closed to keep it from quivering.

Finally, he seemed to gather his strength. "Jo'orsh and Sa'ram brought them to me," he answered. "They said I'm going to kill Borys."

The Dark Elf Trilogy
By <u>R. A. Salvatore</u>
The *New York Times* best-selling author

Featuring Drizzt Do'Urden, hero of *The Legacy* and *The Icewind Dale Trilogy*

Homeland   Book One
Journey to Menzoberranzan, the subterranean metropolis of the drow. Possessing a sense of honor beyond the scope of his kinsmen, young Drizzt must decide – can he continue to tolerate an unscrupulous society?
ISBN 0-88038-905-2

Exile   Book Two
The tunnel-mazes of the Underdark challenge all who tread there. Exiled from Menzoberranzan, Drizzt battles for a new home. Meanwhile, he must watch for signs of pursuit – the drow are not a forgiving race!
ISBN 0-88038-920-6

Sojourn   Book Three
Drizzt emerges in the harsh light of Toril's surface. The drow begins a sojourn through a world entirely unlike his own and learns that acceptance among the surface-dwellers does not come easily.
ISBN 1-56076-047-8

Look for Drizzt's return in
Starless Night
Book One of R. A. Salvatore's new fantasy trilogy in hardcover goes on sale in October 1993!

On Sale Now
Each $4.95/CAN $5.95/U.K. £3.99

FANTASY ADVENTURE